ASHLEY HALL

ASHLEY HALL

by

Marie Murphy Duess

Ashley Hall

For more information, visit www.MarieDuess.com
Cover photo ©iStockphoto.com/magnez2
Additional photos
©iStockphoto.com/MikePanic
©iStockphoto.com/ffranny
©iStockphoto.com/JayLazarin

Printing History: First Printing 2014

PRINTED IN THE UNITED STATES OF AMERICA
10 9 8 7 6 5 4 3 2 1

For

"Sister"

also known as Joy Hillmann

my beautiful big sister…my guide…my dearest.

ACKNOWLEDGMENTS

I would be nothing without my husband Ed.

Here's a story about him: From the time we were married, I would tell him that *someday* I was going to write a book...*someday* I was going to be the writer that I had always longed to be. One Saturday I left him home with our two children who were still quite young. When I returned, the kids were very excited, took me by the hands and led me upstairs to a small alcove in our bedroom. There on top of a desk was a brand new Brother Word Processor (that's how long ago it was) wrapped in a huge blue bow.

On top of it was a note that read "It's *someday*."

Without Ed, all my characters would still be calling to me in the night; they would never have been set free. Thank you, darling, for believing in me even when I don't.

~

Mai-Ann and Buddy, my delight, my reason for smiling even on bad days. I don't *just* love you, I *like* you, too. I would want you to be my friends if you weren't my children. Some parents would not be able to say that, but I am, and I say it proudly. Thank you for the honor of being your mother.

I love my son-in-law, Gerry, too—now how great is that?

~

I thank my sister, Joy, for reading the original manuscript and telling me to "go for it." Your strength amazes me, Sister. You've always been my hero, and I love you.

~

And to my other sisters, Kathleen and Patricia, and my brother Dennis. You've been so faithful to me and have loved me like a "little" sister even though I came late into your lives. Please know how much I love you.

~

I have an extraordinary editor, Ann LaFarge, who again was right on the mark with suggestions, comments, and edits. Your encouragement means more to me than I can say. Thank you, Ann. I am so lucky to have found you and that you were willing to help me make my work better. You are invaluable to me.

~

Every writer needs a good copy editor for the final proof, and mine is the best. Sincerest thanks to Emily Dibala for taking out every comma that wasn't necessary, putting in every period that was, and for getting rid of the ellipses that I'm fond of sprinkling in every paragraph. You're the best.

QUEENS, NEW YORK

1960–1963

Guardian of Secrets and Broken Hearts

ASTORIA, NEW YORK

Summer 1960

35–18…35–16…34–20

Bridget Riordan looked up at every apartment building doorway to find the correct address the listing agent had given her.

"It's between 34ᵗʰ and 35ᵗʰ avenues on 28ᵗʰ Street," the woman had told her. "Just look at the numbers…it'll be clear as day." Clear as day it might be, but Bridget was terrified that she'd get lost in Queens and never find her way back to the subway. She kept looking back, over her shoulder, to memorize the way she had come. *I walked straight when I got to the bottom of the steps, one block, turned left, walked one block, turned right. I don't know…do I really want to live here? Maybe the Bronx? Brooklyn maybe? There was a boy from back home who moved to Brooklyn…maybe that would be better? Who in Ireland ever heard of Queens? But isn't it nice here…the gardens in front of the brownstone homes? Is Brooklyn like this?*

The air was getting hotter. Drops of perspiration trailed down her spine beneath her pale blue suit. She looked up toward the sky but the sun wasn't visible any longer, it was lower in the sky, hiding behind the buildings. She knew it was there because it gleamed against the windows of the buildings on one side of the street—the east side—turning them sparkling ochre.

Golden windows, she thought. *Well, America's streets may not be paved in gold as they say, but the windows are gold this time of day.*

Her gaze rested on one of the buildings ahead of her, on a name painted in elegant letters in cream against the red brick side of the building: Ashley Hall.

She hadn't noticed names on any of the other buildings she'd passed.

Ashley Hall…Bridget played with the name as she walked toward it. It sounded regal, familiar. She knew by the addresses she was passing that Ashley Hall couldn't be the building she was looking for. It was too far down the street, yet she was drawn to it. She stopped looking at addresses and walked toward the building. When she stood in front of it, she looked at the number on the door. It was *not* the address the listing agent had given her.

The door was set back at the end of a courtyard that was flanked by two wings of the building. Bridget felt that the wings were bidding her to enter, like arms reaching out for her. She stepped slowly into the courtyard of Ashley Hall.

She touched the carefully trimmed boxwoods on the other side of a black wrought iron fence; the south wing of the building stood beyond the hedges. Her father had planted boxwoods around the cottage to please her mother, but it hadn't pleased her as he had hoped. Oh, but didn't they all get a good laugh out of his wanting to make up for plowing over her garden when he came home from the pub too late that one night. And didn't they laugh when her mother grudgingly agreed that the boxwoods could stay, but he'd still have to replant the garden anyway. To make the point, she placed the shovel in one of his hands and the hoe in the other.

Bridget looked down at the red and yellow impatiens that had been planted along the fence on the raised brick garden bed. The flowers made her smile. She hadn't seen planted flowers since coming to New York until today in the tiny gardens in front of the private homes. There was an abundance of colorful cut flowers at the markets on every corner in Manhattan—roses, orchids, hydrangea—but none that were actually growing out of the earth…at least not where her hotel was located.

"You want something?" A woman's voice asked her.

Bridget looked up to see an older woman with a watering can just getting ready to sprinkle water onto the impatiens planted on the other side of the courtyard. She wondered where the woman had come from since no one was in the courtyard when she entered it.

"No…I don't think so…I was just lookin' for an apartment that's for rent on this block and saw this garden…"

"Good, they told me they'd be sending someone to see the apartment…come on then." The short, round woman put the watering can down and turned to go into the building. "You're early…wasn't expecting you until six tonight."

Bridget was about to say that the woman misunderstood, that she wasn't there to see the apartment in this building; but then she stopped. *Ashley Hall*…she turned the name over in her mind. She looked back at the boxwoods and the impatiens. *Maybe not the Bronx…not Brooklyn.*

Bridget followed the woman into the building.

♦ ♦ ♦ ♦

"It's small, but what does a single woman who works all day really need with a large apartment?" the superintendent asked Bridget Riordan. "It's a nice quiet neighborhood—primarily *Italians* in the private homes on the block, don't you know, and we only have one child in this entire building. Lives on this floor, but she's a quiet little girl. No apartment has more than one bedroom, so it's not favorable to having children live here. And they're only living here because of a favor, I'm told. The landlord is friends with an Italian who took pity on the family. They were homeless. Living in their car. That's what I heard. Had a business…some money, I guess…but lost everything. Anyway, the child isn't anything to worry about. She's a little mouse; afraid of her own shadow, don't you know. Mostly couples without kids and widows live in the building…a few bachelors…*older* men."

Bridget looked around the room, half listening to the tiny, gray-haired woman who wore a faded navy blue dress, covered by a lighter blue floral print cobbler apron, and laced black shoes. It wasn't much of a flat. She walked into a tiny alcove and opened the large closet, then looked into a bathroom that was directly across from the closet. There was a kitchenette hidden behind French doors. The doors had been painted so many times one could see a myriad of colors of the previous paints in the corners of the glass panes. *Must have been lovely once,* she thought, noticing that the cabinet doors were also all glass panes. *Elegant, even…in the beginning when it was first built, before the war.*

Two good sized windows shed light in the room; one had a fire escape beyond it. Looking down, she realized the apartment was above an alley. The other window overlooked the tiny back yard of a small brownstone. And from both windows she could see the elevated train tracks in the distance. The four o'clock sun shone through a smaller window into the kitchenette, splaying rectangles of rainbow light on the row of white cabinets and the stove.

Ashley Hall, Bridget thought again, standing in the center of the empty studio apartment, *guardian of secrets and broken hearts. Or at least it will be if I move in.*

"Well?" asked the superintendent.

Bridget sighed. It wasn't what she had dreamed she'd live in when she came to New York from London, but the reality was that it was all she could afford on her salary. Manhattan was too expensive, unless you lived in the slums, and someone in the hotel where she was staying told her Queens was a good place for the most part. This building was rent controlled, and in a nice residential neighborhood.

I don't want to live here, she thought, looking out through the grimy window panes and down at the neighbor's grassless backyard. *I want to live home, in Ireland. I want to be in County Galway where I belong, and have always belonged, and will always belong. Where buildings are named and not numbered.*

3

But this one was named…Ashley Hall.

"I'll take it then," she said to the woman, whose frizzy gray curls were as wiry as any Bridget had ever seen. She saw the woman smirk a little, and Bridget wondered if it was because of her brogue. She'd found that her Irish accent either elicited a pleasant smile from the people she met in New York or provoked a smirk of distaste like the one she was seeing on the superintendent's lips now.

"Thirty-five dollars a month," said the superintendent, "and I need the first month's rent and one month's security. Come down to my apartment and sign the papers if you have the money."

"I have cash," Bridget said, placing her hand on the straw pocketbook that hung from the crook of her arm.

"Cash is good, I'll write out a receipt for you. Let's go down."

They left the apartment. The door was at the landing just where a wide staircase divided by a wrought iron banister led up or down.

"This is the sixth floor, don't you know," the superintendent said, pointing at the staircase, "and these will just bring you up to a door that lets out onto the roof. Must be 95 degrees up there now. Too hot today. We don't allow anyone to hang their laundry up there—landlord thinks that's not very classy, don't you know. There's a laundry room in the basement with a washer and dryer—you'll need quarters to run a load—and there's a room with lines for hanging clothes down there, too. Of course, you should know that the apartments up here on the top floor get hot in the summer, what with the sun beating down on the tar roof. But a good fan in the window will cool you off in the night. It's six stories high, so I don't expect you'll be walking up from the lobby, but if there's anything wrong with the elevator, or there's a fire in the building, these stairs will bring you down."

Bridget didn't answer. The super pushed the black *down* button at the elevator. "The day you move in, my husband will put up cushioned pads on the walls of the elevator. Don't want them getting scratched, don't you know. I polish the brass in this elevator every week, and I don't appreciate fingerprints on the bars across the walls so try not to hold on to them. 'Course I tell all the tenants that, but I still find fingerprints all over the brass. It's a nice building, Miss, and we try to keep it nice."

The elevator arrived and the inside door slid open. The super pulled on the outer door and held it for Bridget. "I don't know if you noticed our lobby, but it's a beauty, and we keep it that way. Nice and clean and elegant."

"I did notice," Bridget said quietly, "and it is indeed lovely."

"That leather furniture, the two couches and the high back wings on each side of the fireplace, are forty years old, if they're a day, but in perfect condition. I soap them with conditioner three times a year. We don't allow tenants to just sit in them whenever they feel like it, with the oils from their

4

hands and hair staining them, but you can tell any gentlemen callers to sit there and wait for you. No need to have them go up to your apartment. No room in there and all…it's more like a bedroom and you don't want to entertain in your bedroom, now, do you?" Bridget knew the question was intended as a statement.

The superintendent looked at Bridget pointedly. "We're a decent building, don't you know. Good people live here for the most part. Hard working, middle class, but decent. No 'shenanigans' as you Irish put it. There's other Irish Americans in the building, of course. Mostly quiet and polite, but a few I wouldn't spit on. There's a few Jews, and some Polish. Our landlord is Irish-American, but he's a decent sort. My husband and me come from German immigrant families ourselves."

"There won't be any gentlemen callers, Mrs…I'm sorry," Bridget fumbled, feeling her cheeks burning in embarrassment, "I've forgotten your name."

"Biermann," the woman answered tartly, "with *two* n's. German, not Jewish, don't you know."

"Of course…Mrs. Biermann…"

The elevator stopped, and Mrs. Biermann indicated that Bridget could push open the outer door. They walked to the left, and through a door that looked like every other on the floor, except for a sign that stated: SUPERINTENDENT.

Mrs. Biermann led Bridget down a narrow hallway to a rather spacious living room. As in the apartment Bridget was taking, all the walls were decorated with picture molding painted the same color as the walls, in this case a rose-tinted beige. There was a walnut desk against one wall. Mrs. Biermann sat at the desk chair and opened a large ledger. She asked, "Now, how do I spell your last name again?"

"R…i…o…r…d…a…n," Bridget spelled out. "Only one n."

Their eyes met for a moment, and Bridget saw the old woman's eyes narrow. She wasn't certain that Bridget was making fun of her. Bridget looked away to hide a smile.

"You can move in the first of the month," Mrs. Biermann said.

"That's two weeks away. The flat is empty."

Mrs. Biermann looked up at her. "Yes, but we rent from the first of the month."

"If I pay for half the month, may I have it now? I'm living in a hotel in Manhattan and I'd like to get settled right away. I start work next Monday."

"I'll have to ask the landlord, Mr. O'Darry. I'm not sure if…"

"It's all right," said a man from another room. "Go ahead and let her have it."

"I have to ask O'Darry," said Mrs. Biermann, annoyed.

An older man, thinner than any Bridget had ever seen in her life and at least a head shorter than she, appeared at the living room doorway. "I said to do it."

He smiled at Bridget, and she was astonished that there wasn't a single tooth in his mouth. Shiny pink gums gleamed at her. He wore blue overalls with just a sleeveless undershirt beneath, and at least two day's whiskers protruded from his cheeks and chin.

"My husband," Mrs. Biermann said with a frown. "He does all the maintenance in the building."

Bridget held out her hand to him. She tried not to grimace when her white cotton summer glove met his oil-stained hand.

"Eighty-four units, four boilers, and every machine and appliance in the building, that's what I take care of. Which apartment are you taking?" he asked.

His wife answered, "6A."

He nodded and studied Bridget. "Where you from?"

"Ireland...or I've just moved from London, really...but originally from County Galway."

"You're legal, right?" he asked.

She was aghast that he would even think differently. "I am, sir. I have a work visa, and I'll be applyin' for me green card within the month. I plan to become a citizen. I'm stayin' in America for the rest of me...*my*...life."

"I don't care about that," he said, moving deeper into the living room. "I just wanted to make sure you're on the up and up. Where you working?"

"Ace Labor Life Insurance Company," she answered, touching her pillbox hat to make sure it was on straight. "It's a company that insures unions, I'm told."

"Unions will be the end of this country...and so will insurance companies," Biermann said, sitting down in a chair and picking up a newspaper. "Communists—every one of them union leaders are Commies."

"Perhaps...I don't know about that. I needed a job and they hired me." Bridget turned to Mrs. Biermann, "Well, what will it be? Will I move in now or have to wait?"

Mrs. Biermann looked at her husband. He nodded. "All right, you can take possession tomorrow, then, if you have the half-month's rent. When will the moving company be in?"

"I don't have any furniture yet. I'll have to buy some. For now, I have an army cot and a trunk and two suitcases. I'll come by taxi in the mornin'. No need for the padded walls in the elevator, Mrs. Beirmann."

Bridget handed over the cash to the wire-haired woman, who wrote out a receipt and placed it in Bridget's white gloved hand. "You'll get furniture, though, won't you? This isn't a *flop* house, don't you know."

"No, it's *Ashley Hall*," Bridget said with a smile.

"What?" Mrs. Biermann asked.

"Ashley Hall…this building…the name is on the side…up at the top, near the roof."

"It has a name?" Mrs. Biermann asked, looking at her husband, who just shrugged.

"Yes," Bridget said, "it has a name. An elegant name…"

Mrs. Biermann shook her head as she handed Bridget one key to 6A and one key for the front lobby door. "I didn't know that it had a name, but it doesn't matter. It's just a building in the middle of Astoria, and I don't know how special it is, but it's clean, because I make sure it's clean, but it's no more elegant than any other building, whether it has a name or not."

6A

RIORDAN

Bridget asked the cab driver to lift her trunk out of the back of his cab, which he agreed to do reluctantly. "But I'm not carrying it in for you," he made very clear.

"That's fine, then, just leave it on the curb," she said, already on the sidewalk, looking up at the front of Ashley Hall. It was a two winged building, with a courtyard that led to stately front doors made of glass and black mullions that formed diamond shapes below arched tops. She looked up to the top of the building, and counted six stories. Rows of windows shone in the rising summer sun in the very middle of the building, and she searched to see if there were any faces in those windows, but she could find none.

It was a warm morning, promising to be another scorching day. She sighed and looked down at her two suitcases and the brown leather trimmed trunk that the cab driver had placed on the sidewalk beside her. There were wheels on one end of the trunk and she decided to carry the suitcases to the doors first and then pull the trunk closer.

The first set of glass doors led into a small vestibule where locked oak doors barred the way for strangers who didn't belong inside. There were brass plates on each side of the vestibule that contained names, apartment numbers and little "call" buttons beside the names.

Yesterday, the Superintendent had let her in. Today, Bridget had a key to let herself in. It took two tries, but on the second, the key turned and the door pushed open. Now Bridget had to figure out how to keep the door open while she carried the suitcases in and pulled the trunk behind her.

She looked around the lobby. The floor was made of polished travertine tiles in shades of brown and beige, covered by a silk red and brown patterned oriental rug, and the walls were of caramel colored tile decorated with tiny relief figures. A black marble mantelpiece that surrounded a fake fireplace graced the center of the opposite wall, and at each side of the lobby three travertine steps led to another level. The second levels were set apart with black wrought iron balustrades topped with brass handrails. Except for two leather couches beneath large windows on each side of the front doors and a high-backed red leather chair on each side of the fireplace, there was no other furniture.

Bridget put her straw purse down and used it to hold the oak door ajar. She walked back to the doorstep, lifted her suitcases, and leaned her back against the inside door to push it open. She put the suitcases on the floor and went back to the curb for her trunk. She struggled to get it over the step into the vestibule, while holding the heavy glass door with her backside. Then she leaned against the inside door again to push it open. Just as she did so, the door gave, and she fell backward. Someone tried to grab her, but she landed on the floor.

"I'm sorry," a little girl said, her blue eyes wide, her curly blond hair forming a messy halo around her face. "I didn't mean to make you fall. I thought I'd help."

Bridget stared up at her.

"Why don't you use the door stop?" the child asked, leaning down and securing a long brass hook that was attached to the back of the door into an eye on the door stop secured to the marble floor. "It's easier that way."

Bridget watched as the little girl secured the door open, smiled at Bridget, and then walked over to help her stand up. Once Bridget was upright, the child reached down and picked up the straw purse and handed it to her.

"Thank you," Bridget said.

"Are you moving in?" the child asked.

"Aye, to the sixth floor on this side," Bridget answered, indicating the right side of the building.

The little girl pulled her bottom lip in with her teeth and just looked up at Bridget for a long moment. Finally, she said, almost in a whisper, "I can help you, if you want me to."

"Well, if you could just help me get the trunk up those steps and to the elevator, I should be all right the rest of the way."

"Okay."

Together they lifted the trunk, which was really much too heavy for the child, and they struggled with it until it was on the next level and near the elevator. Then the little girl ran back and grabbed one of the suitcases and waddled toward the stairs.

"Oh, let me do it," Bridget said, "that's too heavy for you."

She noticed for the first time that the girl wore a yellow cotton dress, white socks and Mary Jane shoes with one buckle done and the other strap left open. "You could trip on that strap, darlin'," Bridget said, taking the suitcase from the child.

"I can't get it fastened," the little girl said, lifting her foot to look at the shoe. "I got the other one done, but not this one. It's okay. I won't fall."

"Did you ask your mother for help?"

"She's working," the little girl said, taking the smaller suitcase, using both hands to carry it up the three steps behind Bridget.

"You're all alone? But you can't be more than ten years old!"

"I'm eight. My sister is upstairs sleeping. She's a teenager. She sleeps a lot. I'm not allowed to go outside until she wakes up and comes down with me. I can come down to the lobby if I want, but I'm never allowed to go into the basement alone, and I'm not allowed to go into any other person's apartment or talk to strangers, not *ever*. I get kind of bored watching TV all morning. Mommy knows that, but she's afraid for me to go outside. There are girls who live across the street, but I'm not allowed to cross by myself. Mommy's afraid I'll get hit by a car. My mother worries a lot when she's at work."

Bridget remembered the superintendent telling her about there being only one child in the building. "Do you live on the sixth floor?"

The child nodded very solemnly, and looked away, as though afraid that she'd told a stranger more than that stranger should know.

"Well, that's fine then! We're neighbors, darlin'. I'm moving into 6A today."

The child was all smiles again. She reached up with a small, white finger and pushed the elevator button saying, "Its name is Otis."

Bridget was confused.

"The elevator. Its name is Otis…the name is on the floor as you step in. I'll help you get to your apartment. You're over near the stairs, aren't you? You have the one room. You'll like it here. I promise not to bother you. I'm a very good girl. If I'm not, Mommy says they'll throw us out and we'll be homeless again. So I'm really, really good. I'll never bother you."

"I'm sure you are, darlin'," Bridget said opening the door of the elevator when it arrived. The child pointed down, and sure enough, the name *OTIS* was visible in brass at the entrance of the elevator. Bridget laughed. "Just hold the door and I'll pull the suitcases and trunk into it."

They rode halfway up to the sixth floor in silence. Bridget saw the child's blue eyes studying her. "What's your name?" she asked the little girl.

"Audra."

"That's a grand name."

When the elevator stopped, Audra jumped over one of the suitcases to open the outside door and hold it open for Bridget. They could hear someone on another floor ringing for the elevator, but Audra moved her body in front of the automatic door, standing straight in imitation of a soldier, so that it could not close. Once everything was off the elevator, Audra pushed the suitcases over to the door of 6A while Bridget pulled the trunk.

"Audra!" They both jumped when they heard another woman's voice.

The little girl spun around and said, "I'm right here…I'm right here, Paige."

"Were you going up to that roof again?"

Bridget peeked around a wall to see who was speaking. A girl around sixteen years old stood in the doorway of another apartment. Her dark curly hair was at all angles, there was a line on her soft cheek from where a wrinkle on a pillowcase had left an impression, and she was wearing blue baby doll pajamas.

Audra took several steps toward her sister. "No, I wasn't. I promise. I was helping this lady."

Bridget stepped into view of the other girl then. "She was, and I don't know what I would have done without her. I'm moving in and Audra here helped me up the elevator with my bags."

The older girl studied Bridget for a long minute, then realizing she wasn't dressed, moved her body behind the door and blushed. "Oh," she said.

"Can I help her, Paige?" Audra asked her sister.

"No, leave her alone. Come back inside. Don't be a pest."

"Oh, no, she's no pest. She's a sweetheart," Bridget started, but the older girl reached out and took Audra's arm and gently pulled her into the apartment.

"Welcome to the building," the older girl said. "If you need anything, please just ring the doorbell. I'll be home all day. My mother will be home around six-thirty, but if you have something heavy you need help with, my step-father will be home around four."

Bridget was touched by the girl's offer of help. "Thank you very much," she said.

"But Paige, she needs my help *now* and I…" Audra was saying when the door closed leaving Bridget alone in the hallway. She heard the lock turn in the girls' apartment door and the older girl say on the other side, "Audra, how many times do we have to tell you not to talk to strangers and not to wander around this building?" Then the voices moved away, deeper into the apartment.

Bridget turned and went back to her own door. The air in the tiny apartment was stale and very warm from the late June heat. She opened the windows and noted that the lock on the window against the fire escape was so thick with paint that it was literally painted open. There would be no way to lock it. It concerned her and she decided that the first chore in the room would be to get the little screw driver she had in the trunk and try to fix the lock herself. If she couldn't, she'd have to ask the superintendent, a thought that didn't please her. She had hoped to avoid both the male and female superintendents. Yet, it would be too easy for someone to come down from the roof and open the window and kill her in her bed...or *worse*. She laughed at herself. "Worse than death?" she asked out loud.

Suddenly, very sober again, she thought, *Yes, there are worse things than death and don't I know it.*

6B

SOMMER

Germaine Sommer quietly lowered the peep-hole cover on her apartment door. Her little white and brown fox terrier stood at the end of the hallway, wagging his tail, excited that something was going on.

"There's a new tenant next door, Corky," she said to the dog. He barked once and spun around on his hind legs. His tongue wagged as quickly as his tail. "A woman," Germaine confirmed for him.

She walked slowly back down the hallway on stiff legs and turned left into the kitchen. The kettle was just starting to sing with the boiling water for her breakfast tea. She took a biscuit from the red and white checked breadbox and sliced it in half, spread butter over both sides and a little strawberry jam, and placed the biscuit on a china dish. She put the dish on a linen placemat at the table near the window that looked out over 28th street.

She noticed that it was quiet on the street. All the grownups had gone to work and it was too hot, even that early in the day, for the children to be outside playing. The quiet made her melancholy. She preferred hearing the voices of the children drifting up through her windows. It reminded her of her own childhood in the Bronx and when she was a newlywed living in Brooklyn with Ernest. It had been such a long time since there were children in her life…

Germaine poured the boiling water over tea leaves that she had spooned into the teapot when she first woke up and before she took the dog for his early morning walk, and replaced the cover to let the tea steep until it was almost as black as coffee. She liked her tea strong.

"Well, Corky," she said, not looking at him. "I guess you'll want your breakfast first, won't you? I have the Alpo right here." Germaine took the half can of dog food from the small refrigerator and spooned the contents into a ceramic dish. She held on to the edge of the counter as she placed the dish on the floor for the dog, and groaned when she pulled herself up. Her old bones and tired muscles were complaining a lot lately. Corky looked up at her as if to make sure she was all right. Germaine laughed, "Oh, go on…eat your breakfast. I'm fine, little fella."

She lowered herself onto a chrome chair cushioned with red plastic, and sighed as she settled herself more comfortably. She blessed herself and said grace silently. She looked across the table through the window. All she could see from this high in the building were the rooftops of the row houses across the street, but she liked seeing the birds sitting on the chimneys and on the wires that were strung along the street. These were her friends now. Her Corky and the birds outside.

Oh, sure, she said hello to the other tenants when she saw them on the elevator or on her way to the incinerator closet, but there weren't any of the old neighbors left except the Jewish couple on this same floor, but they kept to themselves. Germaine had been here long before them. She moved into the building just after the war. The building was twenty years old by then. People came and went in the building…or died of old age.

Many of the originals died right in their beds in this building, more and more within the last five years—just like poor old Grace next door. It wasn't even three weeks, and they already rented the place out. The body wasn't even in the ambulance before the painters were laying down their drop cloths and changing the walls from that soft pink that Grace so liked to white. Plain old white walls. How did these new people stand the boredom of that color? She looked around at her cream colored kitchen walls and the bright red café curtains at the windows. Soft and warm colors, not like that stark white they always painted the apartment walls between tenants.

She smiled at the idea of them trying to cover her living room walls after she went. White over burgundy would take at least four coats. Oh, wouldn't she like to be a fly on the wall to hear old Biermann cursing her for it! Well, he had his security deposit. He can use that to cover the walls.

Germaine expected that she would die in her bed, too. It worried her that no one would know that she was lying there dead in her bedroom. She worried about Corky. He could die of starvation if no one knew she was gone and he was left alone. Of course, she spoke with Gertrude once or twice a month, but that sister of hers was always so busy, what with all her grandchildren and volunteering at the hospital twice a week. She was so far away in New Jersey. Germaine couldn't remember the last time they drove to Astoria to see her. She always had to take the bus to Emerson to see them, an hour and a half it would take—two subway trains to the bus station first and then the ride on the bus to Emerson's five corners, as they called that stop. But it was a short walk to Gertzy's house from the bus stop, and it was a lovely neighborhood to walk in.

She supposed she understood why they didn't come to Astoria. It was so much nicer at Gertzy and George's house. They had two whole acres of green lawns and tall trees, and a pool, and George's workshop where he made birdhouses and mailboxes. He was always such a talented carpenter. She understood why they didn't like to come to the city. And George didn't like to drive on these busy streets now that he was older. But that trip was hard on Germaine with her knees so painful. She made the mistake of suggesting once that one of her nephews come to get her, but Gertzy's answer was chilly and brought on a barrage of how busy her boys were. Germaine wasn't invited for a full four months after that. She'd never make that mistake again.

She had wanted to move out to Emerson when she retired from Steinway's. She thought maybe she could live with Gertzy and George, now that all their children were married and they were alone in the house with five empty bedrooms. But Gertzy said they were never really empty as all the grandchildren stayed there on weekends. It wouldn't be convenient. And there were no apartments in Bergen County that Germaine could afford to rent. "It's a very ritzy area, you know," Gertzy had told her. "I can't see how you could possibly afford to live out here."

So Germaine stayed at Ashley Hall. It was a good place, really. Close to the shops and bakeries on Broadway, and not that long a walk to Steinway Street and the movie theaters there. It was only a short subway ride to Manhattan, and Times Square, where she could see a stage show if she wanted. She always wanted to, but never did. The tickets were expensive, even the balcony. And she had no one to go with.

They couldn't raise her rent where she was, as if she would even pay more than $15 a month. Her pension couldn't allow anything more than that, and the $50,000 she had in the bank couldn't be touched. Her lawyer took care of that money. He was investing it, he told her. He kept saying that she should use it to go on a vacation or buy something nice, but she wouldn't think of it. She might need that for her old age. Of course, she knew that she could actually buy a house in Emerson with that money—half that amount, really—that's what her lawyer told her—and maybe even a bigger house than Gertzy's, but her husband had always told her not to touch their accounts. It was for a rainy day or for their old age in case they needed nursing care. Or maybe the baby would need it someday for her education. He was such a good sensible man; she would never go against his advice. It was in 1926 when he told her that, just before he dropped dead on the street of a heart attack, and him only thirty years old. She was left with a young girl to raise and $50,000 in the bank that she wouldn't touch—just in case.

The thought of her daughter brought quick tears to her eyes, just as it always did. *Don't think of it. Think of other things.*

"Corky, my little fella, come here," she called to the dog. He ran to her side and jumped up onto her lap; he smothered her face with sloppy, adoring kisses. "I could swear that you are smiling, little guy," she said to him, which brought on more kisses. She shared the last bite of her buttermilk biscuit with him. First he licked the strawberry jam, then licked the butter off the bread before he took the piece in his mouth and swallowed it whole.

Eamon Williams changed the sheets on his bed and straightened up the apartment with great care. Not that it needed much work. He was by nature a very neat man. He opened the closet to hang up his peacock blue smoking jacket, and stood back to survey the closet—one of three—that held his casual jackets and shirts. Neat as a pin, all the same colors hung side by side from beige to brown to blue to black. He took the one empty hanger and hung up the silk smoking jacket, certain to make sure it was facing in the same direction as all the other jackets.

He glanced down at his shoes, noticing that one pair needed a shine, then closed the closet door and went into the bathroom. Green tile walls, trimmed with black, and a mosaic tile floor shone brightly. He had cleaned the bathroom the night before…and the night before that. The tiny white porcelain sink had nary a hair in it, and the ceramic soap dish that protruded from the tile wall was immaculate, just as the toothbrush holder was. He opened the medicine chest, took a toothbrush from the top glass shelf, and placed it beside his in the holder. He smiled.

Looking at himself in the mirror then, his smile faded. He was showing signs of age. Lines creased his face on each side of his nose to his chin, and it reminded him of a marionette. He hated it, but what was he to do? He was 40 years old, and aging gracefully wasn't in his genes. His mother was dreadful lately—lines all over her face, a double chin, and her pores huge. He moved closer to the mirror to check the pores on his nose and chin. Not too large yet. Just the lines at his mouth.

He shouldn't have smiled so much in his life; maybe that's what caused the lines. Everyone always told him his smile was brilliant, so he used it at his every opportunity. Smile Eamon, he'd tell himself, they'll forgive you anything if you smile brightly.

Eamon turned on the water faucets—hot on the left and cold on the right—and filled the sink with warm water. He covered his face in shaving cream and used his straight edge to remove every whisker that had the audacity to show itself on his skin and neck. When he wiped his face with a warm, wet towel, he examined himself in the mirror and, assured that he was hairless, let the water out of the sink and fastidiously wiped the sink down with the towel until it was shiny again. He threw the towel into the built-in metal hamper on the wall behind him. He stripped down and showered, then donned a pristine white undershirt and tight boxer shorts. His underclothing was always white. If anything started to turn gray or yellow, he threw them out.

He looked into the mirror again, and although it was small, he was tall enough that he could see that his chest was still powerful looking beneath the white cotton shirt. He maintained a good figure for a man his age. No paunch, no flab hanging over his belt. Playing tennis twice a week was a help keeping him fit. He was slim, wide on top, with just the right musculature across his chest and shoulders. His shirts fit beautifully and his suits were tailored to enhance his wide shoulders and narrow waist.

"A fine specimen of a man," his mother has always told him—even when he was only sixteen. "You're a fine looking man, Eamon. Women will swoon over you, my boy."

She was right. Women did swoon over him. Women would say to him that they couldn't understand why no one had swept him right up long ago. Of course, there was something alluring about a confirmed bachelor…a well-dressed, handsome, smiling bachelor who always had time to listen to their woes, enjoy stories about their children, listen sympathetically to their complaints about their husbands, and laugh at their jokes and foibles with affection and no judgment. He knew that the fact that he drank "dirty" martinis helped his reputation—women loved it when he ordered them. He drank no more than two. He had never been drunk in his life. Smoking was his only real vice, and he smoked moderately.

He looked down at the toothbrush he had just placed beside his in the ceramic holder and a thrill coursed through him.

It would be used in the morning by the one and only love of his life. They'd have relaxing drinks at the St. Regis, then a leisurely dinner in the restaurant, and finally they'd get a cab back here, arriving long after the other tenants were tucked in, and share coffee and bagels in the morning before going off to Forest Hills to play tennis.

Eamon dressed in his navy pin-striped suit over a white shirt, tied his pale blue tie—which he knew enhanced the color of his eyes—and finally donned his dove-gray fedora. He'd taken the day off, the first of summer. He rarely took an entire week off as most of his associates at the bank did. He just needed days here and there around weekends, with a few saved for the holidays when he would visit his brother and his family and then go skiing in February. Today he'd visit the museum, walk in Central Park, shop at Bloomingdales…maybe Saks…and then dinner.

He was just about to leave his apartment when he heard a commotion in the hallway. He stepped away from the door. Eamon had no intention of getting into the middle of a banal conversation with the other tenants on the floor. He recognized the voice of the little girl across the hall and then her sister's. There was a third—a woman—but not the girls' mother. He liked the girls, but he didn't want to get involved today.

The noise stopped, all voices had left the hallway, and so he opened his apartment door and then locked it behind him. He noticed a suitcase in the hall near the studio apartment and the door to the apartment was ajar, so he stepped as quietly as he could to the elevator, hoping to avoid a conversation with the new tenant, whoever he or she was.

The elevator was waiting for him. The sign of a good day.

The apartment was dark all the time. It was impossible for the sun to shine through the windows since they faced the courtyard, and the rest of the wing of the building blocked the light. It was one of several things Vera hated about the apartment, but she never said it to Danny.

Vera stretched out on the bed under the bright pink sheet, lifting her arms above her head and letting her long legs reach all the way to the bottom of the mattress. She yawned and then relaxed her body. She turned on her side and looked at the window, at the closed blinds.

One day they would own a house, probably on Long Island, but maybe in Connecticut, and it would have four bedrooms, and a full dining room, a modern kitchen, and lots of pretty curtains and drapes… oh, and furniture, of course. Nice furniture…not the junk they had in their living room here. And wall to wall carpeting—in every room. None of this hardwood floor stuff that his mother so admired. Thick wall to wall carpeting in every room…white carpeting…well, maybe blue in the bedroom.

One day. But now, until Danny could make ends meet without his father's money, they would live here and she'd keep her mouth shut about it. He was stressed enough.

Vera turned onto her side and stared at the closed venetian blinds. His parents would come to love her—or at least accept her—eventually. She would do anything to make that happen. Anything at all. But not for the money. They could keep their stinking money. She didn't want their money, and all the strings that were attached to it.

She wasn't a bimbo just because her family had no money. She wasn't trash. She worked her tail off to make enough money to put herself through Katherine Gibbs Secretarial School and support herself at the same time. Okay, so she didn't go to Harvard or Yale or Vassar. But Gibbs had a great reputation. She worked all day in the office, went to classes at Hunter

College every night, and then worked a second job on the weekends in the bakery; and because she had to do it all on her own, that meant she was trash? She was low class because of it? "Not one of *us*," she whispered aloud, rolling her eyes in exasperation.

Darn tootin' she wasn't one of them.

Vera dropped her legs over the side of the bed and sat for a long moment before getting up. Danny had left for work two hours earlier, and she noticed that he had left his clothes from the day before thrown on the chair in the corner, strewn over the threadbare seat cushion. He just didn't get it that there wasn't a servant around to hang his clothes up for him. Was she supposed to be the valet? She replayed in her mind the same argument that they had every week when he realized that his suit pants were creased or—gasp—his suit jacket was wrinkled!

"Hang up your suit when you take it off," she'd say, not angry, just practical.

"Can't you just do it when you see it on the chair?"

"I'm not the maid, my love. I'm the wife."

"Right, and wives do those sorts of things," he would tell her, trying to sound reasonable.

"Wives who don't work two jobs maybe."

Vera was tired of it. She was getting worn down by it. She stood up, went into the bathroom to use the toilet, washed her hands, and then returned to the bedroom to hang up Danny's suit and put the white shirt in the dry cleaner bag—it was still crisp and clean, but he'd worn it once, so of course, it had to be brought to the cleaners to be washed and starched and folded just so. He had taken his clothing to six dry cleaners until he found the one that folded his shirts exactly the way he wanted them folded…exactly the way his parents' dry cleaners folded them. Of course, that dry cleaner was all the way up on Steinway Street, which meant they had to take a bus or walk eleven blocks to get to it, when there was a perfectly good dry cleaner one block away on 34th Avenue.

"Stop!" she said aloud, placing her forehead on the arm of his suit. She breathed in the scent that clung to it…his smoky aftershave…the scent of Danny. Vera smiled and closed her eyes, rubbing her cheek against the fabric. She loved Danny so much it hurt her inside. Sometimes she wished she'd never met him, but why bother wishing it, because she had, and they fell in love, and they married…without family or friends around them to ruin that intimate and romantic day. No church…because they wouldn't have been able to please her Catholic parents or his Lutheran family.

Of course, now they were all mad at Vera and Dan, but Vera believed that they would get over it eventually. Her mother had already called her at work twice, after saying she'd never talk to her again for as long as she lived. Vera had not believed it when her mother had said it, and she almost laughed when she answered her phone at the office and heard her mother's icy voice on the other side.

"Your grandmother's birthday is next Saturday, and I don't want you to forget to call her. This doesn't mean that I'll ever speak with you again, but I won't have you breaking your grandmother's heart any more than you already have."

"Will she speak with me if I call, do you think, Mommy?" Vera asked.

"I haven't the foggiest idea. You wouldn't deserve it if she did, but it would be horrible if you don't at least try."

"Mommy…"

"I'm hanging up now, Vera. There's nothing you can ever say to me to make me forgive you. Good bye, Vera. Have a nice life."

Her mother hung up and left Vera holding the phone to her ear. Her mother was cold, but she had called. It was only a matter of time when she'd call again. Vera pretended to say goodbye to her mother so that the other secretaries around her wouldn't know her mother had hung up on her. "Okay, Mommy, I'll see you over the weekend. Bye now," she said into the heavy black receiver, wishing that it was true.

The other girls at work didn't know that Danny's and Vera's parents were angry. They knew that there was a civil ceremony on a bright sunny Friday in May, but not that there had been no family or friends in attendance. They didn't know that Danny's father told him that as long as he remained married to "that horrid little beggar" he could not work at the family's consulting firm, that he was fired, and that there wouldn't be a single dollar coming his way now or ever. They didn't know that Danny's mother stripped the bed in his bedroom, emptied his dresser drawers and his closet, took everything out of his bathroom, and threw everything in boxes and told Philip, their "man", to take it to Goodwill.

Good old Philip took out two suits, four shirts, some jeans and sweaters, and a pair of dress shoes, and hid them in his own room until he could sneak the contraband to Danny. They didn't know that his mother also went to the family's antique bible in the library and crossed Danny's name off the list of family members so many times that the pen went through the page.

None of Vera's coworkers knew any of this. They didn't know that her father, his work cap in his hands, his heavy work boots still on his feet, went to the parish priest asking if it was true that his daughter would go straight to hell if she were in an accident or became sick while married outside the Church. She heard from her sister that her father had sobbed in the priest's arms when the priest told him that she was indeed living in sin.

That hurt Vera more than anything. The thought of her sweet, strong, gentle Daddy crying over her in the priest's arms, terrified that his daughter would go to hell. Thinking of it made her heart constrict.

"But I'll go to confession," she told that same priest when she went to beg him to tell her father that she wasn't going to hell.

Father Gallagher was very gentle—not the least bit mad or mean as she had expected him to be—when he said to her, "It doesn't work that way, Vera. You can't go to confession, and then go home and live with your husband as man and wife. You have to be repentant, and mean it. You have to heal the wound, not just put a band aid over it. Come here to me and I'll convalidate your marriage. I can do it quietly, without any fanfare. Then your father can be at peace with it, and you will be reunited with Christ."

Vera wanted to. She really wanted to. But Danny would never do it.

"You know, Vera, that you can't receive the sacraments before you are married in the eyes of our Lord and the Church," Father Gallagher said very quietly.

"You're excommunicating me?" she asked.

"No, Vera. You've excommunicated yourself. You and the Church are no longer in 'communion'. You're choosing to do it your way, not God's way. Not the Church's way."

She became angry, "Well if the Church doesn't want me, then I don't want the Church."

Father Gallagher smiled so gently it almost broke her heart; it certainly defused her anger. "The Church wants you, Vera, and always will...always and forever, as does our Lord. The Church wants you united to it through the laws of God. And, Vera, no matter what you say or how ignorant you act about what you've done, you knew the very moment you entered City Hall that you were going against all that you had been taught in this very same Catholic school."

No, the secretaries sitting in the secretarial pool around her—the older ones and the younger ones, the wise ones and the foolish ones—knew nothing about the circumstances of Vera's marriage and the fact that neither she nor Danny had family supporting them emotionally or any other way.

{ 6E }

KRAMER

Joseph Kramer knew that a new tenant was moving into the studio at the foot of the stairs. Biermann had told him last night when they met in the basement. Joseph was getting the laundry off the line for Martha, and Biermann came in to check to see if there was any clothing left in the washing machine. That was one of the rules: no clothes could be left unattended in the washing machine after 10 p.m.

"Where's the wife?" Biermann had asked.

"She's just a little under the weather tonight. I thought I'd help."

Biermann and Joseph did not like each other. There was an unspoken animosity between them, but Joseph could not remember when it had started. Maybe it started when Biermann realized Joseph was Jewish. Joseph suspected that was the case.

Biermann was of German descent, sure, so what? They were all Americans, no? But maybe, just maybe somewhere in his own subconscious, he too felt *something* about Germans—American or not. He didn't think so, but maybe he did. It wouldn't be unusual. So many of his family were lost in the camps...uncles, aunts, cousins...his poor old grandfather.

Yes, there were feelings. But Biermann had them, too. Anti-Semitism...why did it always surprise him whenever he came across it? It was everywhere. So, Biermann is from Germans...I'm from German Jews...so we can't like each other? Ach...it's stupid.

Sure, he and Martha could live in a predominantly Jewish neighborhood, but this had been closer to work. The factory was within walking distance...a long walk, yes, but still, close enough. He wasn't going to move because of stupidity. People minded their own business in the building. All the years they've been here, and he and Martha knew maybe five people in the whole building. It was like that in New York. You could be anonymous. They liked it. Even the next door neighbors, the Walshes—with the little girl and her beautiful, sad-eyed sister—two years they've lived next door and I barely know them.

"New woman moving into the studio tomorrow," Biermann said. "An Irisher, right off the boat."

"Oh," Joseph had said. "Well, that's nice." He pulled a sheet from the line and folded it before putting it in the basket.

"Hasn't got no furniture yet, that's how new she is to the country," Biermann added.

"So, she's a new immigrant…I'll tell Martha. Maybe she'll bake her a cake to welcome her." Joseph pulled a towel into his hands to fold. He knew she wouldn't bake a cake, but he said it anyway.

"Yeah, that would be nice. She seems like a nice woman…for a foreigner." Biermann disappeared into the furnace room without saying goodnight. Joseph shrugged.

He told Martha over breakfast, before she left for the market. She didn't seem interested, so he let it drop. If she wanted to bake a cake, she knew what to buy. She kissed his cheek and left him alone without mentioning the new tenant.

Joseph sighed in the silence of the apartment. He picked up the newspaper and read it from cover to cover. When he was finished, he stared out the window, wondering what to do.

He didn't work on Fridays now that he was semi-retired, and he always offered to go with Martha to the market, but she always said no. He suspected that it annoyed her that he was home with her more now. He used to work ten…sometimes twelve…hours a day, Monday to Friday and two Saturdays a month, and now he only went in three days a week, for no more than five hours, just to check the books and prepare the payroll. Soon, maybe next year, he'd make Broadhurst hire a full-time accountant, a Chief Financial Officer, maybe. That's what Joseph was, but he never had the title or the salary that went along with it. No title…no fancy salary…yet, they couldn't let him fully retire because no one knew how to keep the books or do the payroll the way he did. All these years, his whole working lifetime, he never trained anyone to take over his job, and Broadhurst never insisted he should. But he should have. It's his own fault he's still going in at all…this isn't retirement. This is waiting. Waiting for retirement while being retired. What's that? Stupid, that's what it is.

What does Martha want him to do? Is she mad because he didn't retire completely and then they could move to Florida like her sister did? Is she mad because he retired *just a little bit* and is home in her way now? She acts like he's a pest. She doesn't want him to help her do anything, not even clean a little, or cook a little, or run to the market a little. Oh, but the laundry he could get off the line...*that* she lets him do. Why? Because it gets him out of the apartment and she gets time alone while he's down there.

Maybe he should tell Broadhurst he'll come back full time. Get rid of the little schmuck he hired to learn Joseph's system. You'd think that fancy school he graduated from would have taught him how to do payroll.

Or maybe he'll retire completely and stick it to Broadhurst. Let the little schmuck learn how to do payroll on his own. Sink or swim.

"I'm tired," Joseph said to no one. "It's time for me to go...move to Florida with Martha."

He hadn't heard her come in.

"I don't want to move to Florida...what are you saying? Florida? Who are you talking to anyway? Yourself? You got money in the bank?" She pulled the bags out of the metal cart she always used to transport the groceries from the store and placed them on the table.

"Yes, I got money in the bank. A little...for us...for our retirement." Joseph pulled two more bags out of the cart and then folded it, and slid it into the hall closet near the apartment door.

"You're retired?" she asked, waving her hand. She was being sarcastic.

"Martha, stop picking on me," Joseph said, moving behind her, putting his arms around her waist and pulling her closer to him. "You love me, right?"

"Huh!" she said, but she didn't pull away. "I love you, sure. Now get out of my way. I have to put these groceries away."

"I'll help," Joseph offered. "Then we'll go for a walk. Perhaps to Manhattan? A museum? How about a show?"

"I have no time for that. I have an appointment to get my hair done at three and then Helena and I are going to dinner on Steinway Street. I told you that already. Go find something to do with yourself."

She turned, still in his arms. He looked into her face, thinking it was still a pretty face. She was a little wrinkly, but what woman her age wasn't? She had a nice figure, a little softer, a little saggier, but still she kept herself nice. Her chestnut colored hair was gray at the temples and there was one white streak from left of center. She hated it, but he loved it. He wouldn't let her dye it. He said it was very attractive; sexy even. But that always annoyed her. Sex wasn't part of the bargain anymore. She acted like he was a sex maniac even when he used the word sexy. That part of the marriage was behind her, even if it wasn't behind him. They were only in their sixties. Not ancient. She gave in, once or twice a month, just because she had to. He got it over with quickly.

But he loved her. She was his wife. She was beautiful. She had given him a son. The only child. Their son. Their beautiful boy. His Joey. His war hero Joey. Gone six years now...for a war—a *conflict*—that no one really understood. She never got over it. He never got over it.

Martha pushed at him now, "Go…go do something. Do a crossword puzzle. You're such a noodge."

Joseph let her go, but not before placing a quick kiss on her lips. He walked into the living room. His broad shoulders sagged under his crisp green shirt. He looked around the room, again trying to decide what to do.

For the first time since he "retired" he realized that he was lonely.

In fact, he was a very lonely man.

6G

LaCorte

Frances LaCorte was eager to get into her apartment and take off her stockings, garter belt and tight linen dress. It was unbearably hot in the subway and walking from the station in the late afternoon heat didn't help. It felt like the heat was radiating from the sidewalk. She knew that the apartment wouldn't be much cooler—warmer, if anything—but at least she could get undressed, put on a loose shift and sit in front of the fan with a Coke.

She pulled her light blue chiffon scarf from her neck and wiped the perspiration on her chest with it as she watched the elevator move from floor to floor, hoping against hope that no one else on a lower floor had rung for the elevator. When the bell rang to announce she was on the sixth floor, she rushed at the door and pushed it open without looking through the little round window to see if anyone was on the other side, and slammed it into Joseph Kramer. The edge of the door hit him squarely in the nose, and he jumped back, grabbing his face. Blood began to stream between his fingers.

"Oh my God, Mr. Kramer," she said. "I'm so sorry. Oh God, please, come into my apartment and let me help you."

"No, no," he mumbled. "I'll just go back…"

"Please, don't let your wife see you bleeding like this. She'll pass out," Frances said, putting her arm up over his shoulders to lead him toward her apartment door, which was directly across from his. "Let's get the bleeding under control before you scare the hell out of poor Mrs. Kramer."

"She isn't here…she's at…" he began to say, but now the blood was dripping down his wrist and onto the marble floor. Kramer's face went white, and he looked as though he was going to fall. He stretched out his arm and leaned against the wall.

"Holy God," Frances said, "it must be broken. Come inside," she insisted, her key already turning in the lock as she pulled him into the hot, stuffy apartment.

"The blood will…" Joseph started to say, indicating that it would drip on the throw rug in her hallway. She pushed the pale blue chiffon scarf up against his face, dragging him along with her the entire time.

They went into her kitchen and she led him to a chair. "Here sit," she said. Then she turned on the faucet and ran cold water in the sink. She drenched a dish towel that hung beside the sink and wrung it out. "Put this on your nose while I get ice," she instructed him.

She opened the Frigidaire, then the tiny metal door of the freezer, and pulled out the ice tray. She had overfilled the tray and the handle that was supposed to release the cubes was frozen down against the ice. Panicky now, she ran hot water over the tray and released the cubes after three pulls on the handle. She dumped them into another towel and replaced this one with the one that had already become scarlet from Mr. Kramer's nosebleed. He still held her scarf in his other hand.

She took both the scarf and the bloodied towel from him as he positioned his head back and put the ice-filled towel against his face.

"I can't believe I did this," she said throwing the towel and scarf into the sink now. "I was rushing, Mr. Kramer. I couldn't wait to get into the apartment and I never looked to see if…"

Joseph Kramer held up his hand to silence her. "It's all right, Mrs. LaCorte. It's just a bloody nose, not a gun shot. I'll survive. It's slowing already."

She took a deep breath and shook her head. "Still…I feel awful."

Frances's apartment door was wide open and they heard a child's voice shriek. "There's blood everywhere, Daddy. Look at the floor. Someone got shot…someone is bleeding to death."

Then they heard a knock on the door and a man's baritone voice asked, "Is everyone all right in there?"

Frances grimaced at Joseph and chuckled a little. She rushed out of the kitchen to the end of the hallway. "Yes, Mr. Walsh, everyone's fine. I accidentally hit Mr. Kramer with the elevator door and he has a bloody nose. Did we scare you?"

The six-foot-four man was so large he filled up the doorway. He must have been washing up when he heard his daughter's shrieks since he was dressed in work pants, dirt and grass stains on his knees, and just a sleeveless undershirt. Tufts of red curly hair, like that on his head, stuck out at the neck and sides of the shirt. She couldn't help but look at his chest and arms, at the muscles that pushed against his skin. "He's an architect," his wife had told Frances once when they were chatting in the elevator, but Frances always thought he looked like someone who could build buildings than the one who drew up the plans for them.

"Does he need to go to the hospital?" Walsh asked.

Frances shrugged and motioned that he should come inside. She walked into the kitchen where her bleeding neighbor still sat with the ice against his nose.

"Hey, you need to go to the hospital, Kramer?" Walsh asked from the doorway of the kitchen.

Kramer took the towel from his face and looked down at it. "No, I don't think so. It's stopping…almost stopped, really."

"Broken?" Walsh asked.

Frances' hands were shaking now and her stomach was queasy. She looked at Mr. Walsh and noticed that Audra was standing just behind her father, peeking around his hip, her eyes wide with fear.

"Hey, sweetie," Frances said to her. "I'm sorry you got scared. Come in…it's okay."

But Audra just shook her head and placed her small fingers into her father's hand. He looked down at her and squeezed her fingers gently. "It'll take more than blood to scare my kid," he said, smiling reassuringly at her, knowing that what he said was anything but true.

"Ah, little Audra, poor little girl," Mr. Kramer said, smiling, but wincing when he did. "Mrs. LaCorte is just showing me that she's the better boxer, that's all. She bobbed and weaved better than I did."

Mr. Walsh laughed, but Frances said, "Don't tell her that! She's scared stiff as it is."

But little Audra laughed, too, and moved a little closer into the room. "My father was a boxer when he was in the Navy," she said in a tiny voice.

"He was?" Frances asked.

Audra nodded. "They called him Kid Candle," she reported seriously.

Both Frances and Mr. Kramer looked at Audra's father. He shrugged with a crooked smile. "One blow and I'm out," he said. The adults laughed, but Frances could see that the little girl didn't understand why. The child really believed the whole cockamamie story, and it made Frances smile all the more.

Walsh tugged a little at Audra's hand. "Well, I guess our services aren't needed here, baby. Let's go home. I'm beat." He looked at Frances and Mr. Kramer. "It's a hot one today."

"Brutal," Frances agreed. "Were you working in this heat?"

"Worked without any shade today. I'm burned to a crisp." He pointed to his shoulders and back. "By the way, sorry about not having a shirt on. Don't tell my wife I was walking around like this. She'll blow a gasket. She doesn't care how hot it is, we have to keep up appearances…and gentlemen don't go around shirtless, you know." He winked.

Frances just smiled. Mrs. Walsh certainly kept up appearances…or rather pretenses … like a real pro. It didn't matter how much shouting went on in that apartment until all hours of the night—nor how many bruises

Mrs. Walsh had on her arms the next day—she always dressed impeccably and held her head up in the elevator as though no one on the sixth floor had heard a thing or knew what went on the night before. And she made him dress like a model when he wasn't in his work clothes. Frances wondered where they got the money for some of his suits and shoes. Frances knew that Eleanor Walsh wasn't exactly honest when she told her that he was an architect—at least he wasn't one presently. Frances had heard that he was working for a landscape company in New Jersey somewhere.

Mr. Kramer stood up and said, "Me, too. I better go home and change this shirt and try to get the blood out before it sets."

"Let me do it for you," Frances said.

"No, no," he said, but when he stood, he felt a little dizzy and grabbed the edge of the table. Walsh didn't notice because he was already moving toward the door.

Frances pushed Mr. Kramer back down into the chair and followed Mr. Walsh and his little girl to the door, thanked them, and then closed the door behind them. When she returned to the kitchen, she sat down opposite the injured man. "Where's your wife?"

"She's getting her hair done and then meeting her friend for dinner. I was just going out to get a sandwich at the deli."

"Don't go into your apartment alone. I'll worry myself sick. You look so pale. Can't you stay here until we know you're all right? How about a nice cold Coke? Or a cup of tea? I'll make you a sandwich here."

He agreed to the tea only.

Frances put water in the kettle and placed it on the gas flame. "I'll just go and wipe up the blood in the hallway, and then change into something cooler while this boils. I'm dying in this heat."

She pulled an oscillating fan from her living room, aimed it right at him and turned it on. "This will help a little," she said smiling at him. "Take off your shirt so I can soak it."

He agreed reluctantly, unbuttoned his shirt and handed it to her.

"I'll be right back."

She brought a wet towel from the bathroom and wiped up the puddles of Mr. Kramer's blood from the marble floor. She threw it into the bathtub when she returned, ran cold water in the sink, submerged the shirt, then began to undress. She had to peel the stockings off her legs, and her garter belt was glued to her skin when she pulled it off. It was such a relief to be free of it. Even the warm air in the bedroom felt cool against her back and belly. She chose her favorite pink cotton shift from her closet and pulled it over her head. She brushed out her damp red hair and fingered some of the strands to help them spring back into waves. She checked her image in the mirror. She wasn't glamorous right now, but she was comfortable.

31

Why would she care that she didn't look fashionable? It was only old Kramer from across the hall. But she dotted some lipstick on her lips before leaving the bedroom.

Back in the kitchen, Kramer was pouring boiling water into two ceramic mugs. The water was already turning a dark garnet. "You found the tea?" Frances asked, smiling brightly at him.

"The box was right here on the table."

Frances took the sugar bowl from a cabinet and a container of milk from the refrigerator.

"No milk," Kramer said, waving it away when she offered it.

She noticed he put two spoonsful of sugar in his tea. She placed a teaspoon next to his mug. "You like it sweet, I see," she said.

"Hot and sweet…never iced. You know, Mrs. LaCorte, that drinking hot tea on a warm day cools you off faster than iced tea."

"No, I didn't know that."

"It's true." They looked at each other over the rims of their mugs. He smiled at her, and he didn't wince this time. His nose was red and slightly swollen, but there were no bumps. It wasn't crooked, so it probably wasn't broken. Frances was relieved.

She studied the rest of his face. Frances had never really looked at him before. Oh, they had seen each other often in the hallway and on the elevator, but just a word or two, a little chat once in a while on their way in or out of the building, but she'd never really looked at him. He was a nice looking man, she decided. He had a strong chin, with just the hint of a dimple in it, and high cheek bones. It surprised her that she'd never noticed the color of his eyes before now. They were a most unusual shade of yellow-green. Like a cat's. Beautiful. She wanted to keep looking at them now that she had discovered them.

His dark hair was graying at the temples. She guessed that he was in his sixties; in fact, she was sure of it because she remembered his wife saying that he was about to retire…that was months ago. He was tall. He was sitting sideways at the table, casual, his elbow on the edge of it.

"How long have you lived in the building?" he asked her.

"Oh, let's see," she thought out loud, "I was divorced six years ago in May…so, I've lived here six years this month."

"Six years," he pondered, relaxing back in the kitchen chair and crossing his legs. "Six years you've lived here," he said again. He played with the handle of his mug. "All those years, and we've barely spoken a word to each other."

Frances laughed, "I was just thinking the same thing, Mr. Kramer. We're all in a hurry all the time around here, aren't we…too busy to stop and chat…rushing around."

"Oh, some of us rush faster than others," he said, fingering his nose in a teasing way.

She laughed again. She decided that old Kramer from across the hall, as she always thought of him, was very charming…and not quite as old as she thought. She was almost fifty herself, although everyone at work told her she looked like she was in her thirties.

"You know, I don't even know your first name," he said.

"Frances," she told him, adding, "Francesca, really."

"Italian?"

"Yes. My father was from Taormina…in Sicily…and my mother's parents were from Rome."

"Where did the red hair come from?"

"A bottle," she answered him, blushing a little, but laughing.

"Well, your heritage certainly explains your big dark eyes."

They fell silent. He stirred his tea.

"I don't know yours either," she said.

He raised one eyebrow not sure what she meant.

"Your name; your first name."

"Joseph. Not Joe, but Joseph. No one has ever called me Joe in my entire life. I don't know why that is, I never said not to call me Joe to anyone, but no one ever did."

"Maybe because you have a very regal stature. You don't look like a Joe. You look and act like a Joseph."

"I had a son who was named for me, but from the moment he was born, we called him Joey. He looked like a Joey, all smiles and friendliness. Everyone who knew him liked him. We lived in Rego Park when he was growing up, and everyone knew our Joey. We couldn't walk down the street that the merchants didn't call out from their stores, 'Hey, Joey, how are you today?' It didn't matter who they were or what nationality—Italian, Irish, Polish—they knew our Joey and they liked him."

"Where is he now?" Frances asked after draining her mug.

Joseph looked up at her and she saw that his eyes were watery. He shook his head. Frances knew what he was telling her without his saying a word. His hand rested on the table and she placed hers on top of his. "I'm sorry, Mr. Kramer…Joseph."

"Korea," is all he said in answer.

She sighed. "Korea. My husband was never the same when he came back from the South Pacific." Frances leaned on her elbows and ran her fingers through her hair. She felt depressed suddenly. "He was just a kid when he left in '42. We were engaged. We were in love…really in love…or so I believed. He got all shot up and they sent him home. I knew his heart wasn't into getting married after he got home—he was different…morose—but I loved him. I thought I could change him once we were married, but his drinking got worse until he was drunk more during the day than he was sober."

"And love became hate?" Joseph asked.

Frances thought it over. "No. Not hate. Just apathy...and apathy is worse than hate."

"Is it? Apathy?" Joseph thought it over.

"I stopped wanting to try, you know? I was completely indifferent to him. Drink...don't drink...sleep...don't sleep...work...don't work. I was supporting both of us, and then I decided why should I? The truth is he just didn't love me. I'm sorry he went to war, I'm sorry he got shot, I'm sorry it screwed up his brain, but after fifteen years of living in apathy, I wanted a life without it. I don't care how lonely a life it is."

"Was he a mean drunk?" Joseph wanted to know.

"No, he wasn't a mean drunk. He was...I don't know...what?...absent? Yeah, he was absent. Drunk or not drunk, he was absent; I didn't know when he was or wasn't drunk at the end. When I told him I was leaving, he just looked at me and asked if he could keep the apartment, just as though I was telling him I was heading for the grocery store. 'I'll stay here, okay with you?' he said." She sighed, "It was the last thing he ever said to me."

Frances sat staring into space, remembering that moment, her husband looking small and vulnerable, far away, staring at the television while she was telling him their life together was ended. Where had the man she loved gone?

Suddenly and inexplicably, Frances was overcome with tears. She swallowed hard, but she just couldn't control a sob. It burst out of her, surprising her as much as it surprised Joseph. It had been years since she had cried over her failed marriage.

She was mortified, but the man sitting across from her didn't look uncomfortable at all. He just looked concerned, his yellow-green eyes filled with tears again—only this time the tears were for her—and that made her cry all the more.

"I'm sorry, Francesca," Joseph Kramer said in a whisper. "You should be loved. You deserve to be loved. We humans need it more than we like to admit. Why is it that when bad things happen, instead of turning to each other, we turn away? What sense does it make to turn away? We need arms to hold us."

He looked away from her, down into his cup, as though he were saying it to himself as much as to her. Frances stood and rushed into the bathroom, unable to answer him. She washed her face and buried it in a wash cloth to muffle her sobs.

When she was calmer, she opened the bathroom door, and he was standing there. Blood stained his white tee shirt. It was already drying and turning brown. His nose was more swollen than it had been and the skin around his eyes was starting to darken and bruise. But his yellow-green eyes searched her face as though she was the only person that mattered at that moment, and she fell forward against his chest. He put his arms around her and held her.

"I was concerned," he said, explaining why he was standing there waiting for her. She could feel his breath on her temple when he spoke. He moved his hands over her back, very gently, consoling her.

She had nothing on under her shift, and she wondered if he realized that. It embarrassed her. It also excited her. It stirred her deep inside. A very old but familiar warmth spread from her belly to down between her legs.

Frances knew that she was about to make one of the biggest mistakes of her life, so she was hoping that he was going to be repulsed by her next move and run from her apartment. She dropped her head back and looked into his eyes, those eyes that in the last hour she had come to like so much. She touched the gray hair at his temples, and then brushed her finger over his full mouth and down to the dimple in his chin. He allowed her to do it. He didn't pull away...just continued to look into her eyes.

She reached around his waist and pulled his hips against hers. She wanted him to know that she was naked under her shift. She felt him harden as she pressed even closer.

She was a willing participant if he was.

He was.

6A

RIORDAN

Bridget tossed and turned on the army cot. The fan didn't give her much relief. It just pulled in the night air that was almost as warm as the day had been. She pushed the sheet away and lie in her long nightgown, which was slick with perspiration against her skin. It was only June. Is this what she had to look forward to for the entire summer?

She was nervous about that window near the fire escape. She couldn't fix it. There were too many hardened coats of paint on it. Before going to bed she lined glass coke bottles on the windowsill so that if someone tried to get in, they'd knock them over and alert her. She placed the cot near the door so that if she had to bolt, it would not be far to get out. She positioned it between the door and the potential intruder to give her time to unlock the door and start screaming.

Would anyone respond if she screamed? She heard that in New York people could scream and no one paid any mind. No one wanted to get involved...that's what she was told in Ireland...and in London.

Bridget glanced around the apartment. There were little spider web type cracks in the plaster ceiling. She'd have to keep an eye on them. She remembered that the ceiling in her granny's house had crashed down around their ears one day, and it started with just a few tiny cracks that everyone had ignored. As soon as those cracks got larger, she'd be callin' Biermann, and that was for sure. She was a woman, she was single, but by God, she wouldn't be pushed around. Not anymore. Not by anyone, especially that toothless hobbit and his wire-haired wife.

Bridget heard the rumble of the elevated train in the distance. It was only a few blocks away, and on this floor of the building, she could not only see it, but there was nothing blocking the sound. It didn't bother her, though. She liked the sound of it. It almost lulled her into a light sleep, but then a car horn on the street blew and she heard people arguing, and she was wide awake again. It's true that New York never sleeps, she decided.

She stood up and reached for her purse. She took out the wad of money in it and counted it again. She still had $8,235. She decided to buy some furniture tomorrow and then put the rest of the money in a bank account; if nothing else she'd buy a daybed and a table and chair. She needed some place to eat. Maybe a bed would help her to sleep. And she'd buy a new lock for the window at the fire escape...maybe two locks.

She relaxed again, and let herself lie back on the cot.

"I'll be all right," she said out loud. "I'll be all right. I can do this. America isn't so bad."

She didn't really believe that. Oh, sure, America was all right, but it wasn't home. It wasn't Ireland. It wasn't Mam and Da's house. There were no sheep, no horses, no long haired setters running free in the fields. It was hot and humid here; it was noisy and hard edged. It wasn't home.

She'd never go home again. Not ever. She'd never face them. Not with The Lie and The Secret hanging over her.

She fell asleep holding her square, straw handbag against her chest.

Late Summer 1960

6B

SOMMER

Germaine was surprised by the doorbell. She rarely had company. As she moved from her chair at the window of her living room to the front door, she tried guessing who it could be.

Her sister? No, they never drove to Astoria, and it was a Saturday, so they'd have the family over to swim in the pool. Her nephews, her niece? They usually didn't have the time, especially on the weekend. Mr. Biermann, maybe. There wasn't any reason for the superintendent to come to her apartment as far as she knew.

Corky ran ahead of her, then back again, then back to the door, tail wagging, his muscular little body quivering with excitement. "Oh, Corky boy, I'm moving as fast as my legs will allow. Have a little patience."

When she reached the door, she pushed up the peephole cover. It was her neighbor, Mrs. Walsh. Well, now that's a surprise. Germaine turned the deadlock, pushed aside the chain, and unlocked the bolt in the doorknob.

Mrs. Walsh was dressed for work even though it was Saturday. Germaine always admired the way the woman dressed, very chic and always in good taste. Today she wore a peach colored dress and her high heels matched the color of her dress exactly, as did her leather purse. She wore a little white pillbox hat on her dark hair. So cheery, Germaine thought, before she said, "Why, Mrs. Walsh, it's so nice to see you."

Corky barked twice and backed up, dying to jump on the visitor but knowing that that was absolutely not allowed. Instead, he spun on his back legs twice, in a happy dance.

Mrs. Walsh laughed and reached down to pat the dog's head. "I love fox terriers. We had one when I was growing up. They're such loyal little dogs, but full of energy, aren't they?"

"Well, he's calmed down now that he's five years old, but as a puppy, he kept me hopping, I'll agree. I almost gave him away, but now I'm happy I didn't. What would I do without him?"

Mrs. Walsh stood up straight then and said, "May I speak with you for just a few minutes, Mrs. Sommer?"

Germaine opened the door wider and welcomed her neighbor inside. "Shall I put a cup of tea on?" she asked.

"Oh, no, thank you. I need to get to work."

"But it's Saturday."

"We're working on a special project this week, and I have to be there. I can only stay a moment."

Germaine led the woman into the living room. "You look so pretty today."

Mrs. Walsh frowned a little, "I always worry when I wear bright colors being the size I am. Larger women should wear dark clothes, they say, but I do love color and sometimes you just need to brighten your day with a pretty dress, don't you think so?"

Germaine smiled and nodded.

"I have a favor to ask of you, or rather an offer. I think I may be able to offer an answer to a problem you have and one that I have."

"I'll do you a favor if I can," Germaine said, but she worried. What could this stranger want from her?

"Mrs. Biermann told me that it's getting difficult for you to walk Corky lately because of your arthritis. My older daughter, Paige, has gotten a summer job and she won't be able to take care of Audra all day starting next week. I thought that you might be able to watch Audra from about ten in the morning—that's when Paige leaves for work—until my husband comes home at three-thirty. Of course, we would pay you, and Audra would walk Corky for you as long as you watch her from your window. She's wonderful with pets, she'd love to have her own, but we just can't manage it right now."

Germaine sat back in her chair now. A child to take care of, at my age?

"Mrs. Sommer, my Audra is a good little girl. She won't be any trouble. She loves to read and watch television. She likes to play cards, too, and we have board games for her. She won't bother you, I promise. She's a quiet child, and she makes no demands about going outside. She knows I don't allow it when we're not home. It's too dangerous for her to cross the street, and she doesn't argue. I can't possibly leave her alone in the apartment, she's much too young. What if there was a fire? An emergency? But I have to work; I can't quit my job, Mrs. Sommer. I've worked very hard to get the position I have, and I don't want to leave it. I find I'm a better mother when I'm working—when I feel fulfilled intellectually—than when I'm not." She looked down at her hands when she added, "The extra income is important, too."

When Mrs. Walsh finished speaking she was almost out of breath. Germaine could hear the urgency in her voice. They were both silent for a long minute. Then, more slowly, Mrs. Walsh explained, "My Paige surprised me with the news that she had gotten a job. She never told me she wanted to work. I guess she wants to save for college. Of course, I'd pay for her education; I want her to go to college. I went to college for two years and I know how important it is to get a degree in this day and age, but…well…money is a little tight…and my husband doesn't agree that she needs an education. I wouldn't ask if I had any other…"

"I'll do it!" Germaine said, sitting forward again, reaching over to touch Mrs. Walsh's hand. "I'm a little lonely, and this might be just the ticket for me to fill up my days."

"I'll pay you $10 for the week every Friday. I get paid on Thursday, so when Audra comes over on Friday morning she'll bring the…"

"That's fine, let's just see how this works out. I do know your little girl, and she is a sweetie pie. But let's give it a trial, just to see if she's not too bored with an old lady like me."

"And she'll be wonderful with Corky. You'll see, Mrs. Sommer, she loves dogs and she's so gentle."

"Corky will love having someone to play with. I suspect little Corky gets bored. We'll try it out. When do we start?"

Mrs. Walsh was so relieved that tears sprang to her eyes and for a moment she couldn't speak. She tried to smile her tears away. After a moment, she said, "Monday morning at ten?"

"Okay, Mrs. Walsh. Monday morning at ten."

Fall 1960

Eamon Williams took one more deep breath before entering the building. The air was crisp and promised a beautiful autumn. He loved New York in the autumn, and after this past hot summer, the cool October air was a welcome relief. It put a spring in his step, as his mother always used to say, and a twinkle in his eye.

He walked into the vestibule of the building, unlocked the heavy oak doors, and entered the lobby. Mrs. Walsh and her older daughter were already waiting at the elevator door. They each carried bags of groceries. Mrs. Walsh was still dressed for work, so he assumed Paige had met her mother at the train station and they picked up some groceries for dinner. The refrigerators in these apartments were too small to hold much food, and he had noticed that Mrs. Walsh shopped almost every night on her way home from the station.

"Ladies," he said, doffing his fedora.

"Good evening, Mr. Williams. It's a beautiful evening, isn't it?" Mrs. Walsh said.

"Ah, that it is," he agreed, opening the outer door of the elevator when it arrived to allow them to enter it first. He started to recite a poem to them.

"O suns and skies and clouds of June,
And flowers of June together,
Ye cannot rival for one hour
October's bright blue weather."

Before he went on, Paige continued for him,

"When springs run low, and on the brooks,
In idle golden freighting,
Bright leaves sink noiseless in the hush
Of woods, for winter waiting;"

Her dark eyes were sparkling and he was pleased that she knew

41

the poem. Together they finished:

> *"When comrades seek sweet country haunts,*
> *By two and two together,*
> *And count like misers, hour by hour,*
> *October's bright blue weather."*

The three of them laughed. "You like poetry, Miss Walsh?" he asked her.

She blushed and said, "Please call me Paige."

"I can't remember who wrote that poem," Eamon said.

"It was Helen Hunt Jackson," Mrs. Walsh said. "It's one of our favorite poems."

He was surprised, and he hoped that he hid that fact. He just hadn't imagined that the Walshes were cultured. But of course, how would he know that? The extent of their exchanges was "good morning" and "good evening" on the elevator.

"That's right," he said quickly. "Helen Hunt Jackson...I remember now."

"My favorite poet is Joyce," Paige said wistfully.

"Ah," said Eamon, smiling brightly at the young woman.

> *"Bid adieu, adieu, adieu, Bid adieu to girlish days,*
> *Happy Love is come to woo thee and woo thy girlish ways,*
> *The zone that doth become thee fair,*
> *The snood upon thy yellow hair."*

The elevator stopped, but for a long second none of them moved to leave. They stood in silence, thinking of the poetry he had just recited, and he wondered, did Paige realize that he had chosen that poem especially for her...because she was on the brink of leaving her girlish days behind her?

"Well," Mrs. Walsh said, sighing, interrupting their musings, "that was one of the nicest elevator rides I've had since we moved into the building." She laughed as she went to the door and pushed it open with her shoulder.

Eamon moved to assist her, and held the door for Paige. She smiled shyly at him over her bag of groceries.

"We'll have to share our love of poetry again someday," Eamon said to her.

She nodded but said nothing. Just then Mrs. Sommer's apartment door opened and the little Walsh girl burst out. "Mommy, Mommy, guess what I did today?"

The little blond head rushed past Eamon's elbow. She threw her arms around her sister's waist and looked up into Paige's face. "Paige, Corky and I went to the park with Mrs. Sommer today, and I made a new friend. And then we..."

"Audra," her mother said sternly. "What do you say to Mr. Williams?"

She looked confused. Her blue eyes turned up to him.

"I went to the park…"

"No, Audra, he doesn't want to know that. You're to say hello…or good evening. You don't just run past an adult like a ruffian without addressing him."

The child's enthusiasm and excitement faded. She was embarrassed that her mother had scolded her. Paige flung an annoyed glance at her mother.

The little girl said, "Hello, Mr. Williams."

Eamon smiled and ran his finger over the child's cheek. "Good evening, young Miss Walsh. And how are you this beautiful day? Did you do anything special with Mrs. Sommer today?" He would give her the opportunity to tell her story even if her mother wouldn't.

Her enthusiasm returned a little and her eyes brightened. "I went to the playground over at the projects, and we had such a good time. I made a new friend."

"No school?" he asked.

"After school," she answered, "when I got home from school. Daddy wasn't home yet, so Mrs. Sommer took me and Corky to the park."

Mrs. Walsh's voice brought Eamon's eyes up and away from the little girl. What did he hear in it? Anger? No, more like alarm.

"Daddy isn't home?" Her face had gone pale. "It's only Tuesday."

He noticed that Paige closed her eyes and took a deep breath. Her face grew pale and solemn. She hoisted the bag of groceries higher in her arms.

"Let's go, girls…good night, Mr. Williams," the woman said quickly and ushered her daughters into the apartment.

Eamon heard Mrs. Walsh ask her little girl, "Did he call Mrs. Sommer to tell her?" before the door closed behind them. "Did he sound all right?"

He stood looking at the closed door. The happy mood he'd been in when he entered the building was gone.

As he turned toward his apartment he noticed that Mrs. Sommer was still standing in her apartment doorway. Their eyes met, but they didn't speak. They barely knew each other but Eamon could tell by the look in her eyes that they were thinking the same thing. She smiled sadly and nodded to him before she closed her door and locked it.

He let himself into his apartment and hung his suit jacket over the back of his desk chair in the living room. The apartment was stuffy in spite of the cool air outside, and he lifted the lower half of the two windows in the living room, then went into the kitchen to open that window. He rolled up the sleeves of his white shirt and loosened his tie.

Eamon prepared a salad for himself and threw a steak under the broiler. He sat at the kitchen table and opened The New York Times while he waited for the steak to cook. He laughed aloud when he read that Nikita Khrushchev banged his shoe on the table to get attention at a United Nations meeting. Maniac, he thought, a dangerous maniac. When he came across a story about a young mother named Madelyn Murray who withdrew her son from school because she was so anti-religious she refused to allow him to endure reading the bible every day, he shook his head and sighed. The story disturbed him more than the story about Krushchev.

He wasn't sure why. It seemed wrong on the surface that this woman was so adamant about her son not reading the bible, yet was it so wrong? This was America after all. The kid had rights. But to sue the Baltimore Public School system over it…well that didn't seem quite right either. What about the kids who wanted to read the bible? These issues always confounded Eamon. What was right? What was wrong? For his mother, right and wrong were always clear…there was no gray area. But he knew that wasn't always the case.

He'd have to discuss the article with John. John had a way of seeing all the facets to a story. Their political conversations were some of the best Eamon had ever enjoyed—smart, clear, reasonable, even when they disagreed, and they disagreed a lot what with Eamon being a Democrat and John a die-hard Republican.

Now Honora…well she'd have another opinion altogether. She was a Democrat, like him, but much more progressive. He suspected she was a socialist. He avoided political conversations with Honora.

Eamon smiled when he turned the page. John would certainly have something to say about Khrushchev's shoe pounding, and they'd have a good laugh over it together.

After dinner, Eamon went to his bookshelves to look for the book of poetry by James Joyce. It was a thinly bound book with a red cover, and contained just a few of Joyce's published poems. He found it and thumbed through each page. It wasn't all that valuable to him; he'd read it several times. He decided to give it to Paige Walsh.

Eamon left the apartment and crossed the hall. He rang the Walsh's bell and a moment later he heard the peep hole cover slide open and then close. The door opened and Mrs. Walsh stood there. Her eyes were red and watery.

"Mrs. Walsh, I'm sorry to bother you. I just thought Paige might like to have this." He held out the book of poetry.

Eleanor Walsh looked down at it and took it in her hand. Worry—a different sort of worry—touched her face now. "This is very kind, Mr. Williams…but…you know Paige is only seventeen…"

"Oh, that shouldn't be a problem…she already knows Joyce's writings. She'll certainly understand it, she's an extremely bright girl even though she's only a teenager, and I have already read it many times. I thought she'd enjoy…" Then it hit him…what Mrs. Walsh was suggesting. He was mortified. He wished he'd never thought of giving the book to the girl.

"I'm sorry," she said immediately. "I'm not myself right now. Of course

…you didn't mean… It's just that Paige is so mature, many people think she's older than she is, and I always feel the need to protect her."

He reached out to touch her hand. She was correct. The girl is mature…she has the eyes of an old soul.

"Not at all, Mrs. Walsh, I do understand. You just can't be too careful…there are creeps everywhere."

She smiled gratefully. "I'll give this to Paige right away. She'll love having it. When she's finished reading it, she'll return it to you."

"No," he said "I intended to give it to her as a gift. I want her to keep it." He bent his head forward in an informal bow, and walked away, back toward his door. They didn't say goodbye.

When he reentered his apartment, he looked at his watch and saw that it was seven-fifteen. John would be home from work. He could use a good conversation with John. He sat at his desk, lit a cigarette, and dialed the number.

When he heard his friend's voice, his spirits were immediately lifted. "Hey, it's me," he said.

6G

LaCorte

Joseph Kramer held Frances LaCorte in his arms while she slept. Four months he had held her this way, and four months he agonized over it, detested himself for it, swore he'd never go to her again, and then found himself back in her bed, or in a New York City hotel room, more and more frequently, taking more risks, feeling even more guilty.

They would be caught. It was only a matter of time. Someone would find him sneaking into her apartment, or see them together in New York, walking close together, their shoulders touching, though never their hands. Someone would see and suspect. Someone would tell Martha. Someone would...one of these days. He had to end it. He had to stop this addiction.

He looked down at her face, her cheek was pressed against his chest, her tight red waves against the white of his skin looking almost like dried blood.

He *was* bleeding, every time he left Frances, he bled. Every time he sat across the dinner table from Martha he bled. Every time he looked in the mirror he bled. He held his razor to his throat just that morning, thinking that he should bleed in real time. Get this pain over with; he didn't think he could handle it another minute.

He didn't do it. He couldn't end his life. He needed more of Francesca.

He needed to feel her hands on his face, on his chest, over his thighs. He longed to feel her breasts beneath the palms of his hands, and her lips—open and accepting—searching with the same passion he felt as her hips moved up to match the rhythm of his hips. He needed to feel himself inside her, to feel her spasm and quiver in relief—if for just one more time—and then to feel her leg thrown over his and her cheek on his chest when she was spent and sated.

It disgusted him to think that he was throbbing with desire like a boy in his teens every time he thought of this woman. He couldn't bear more than one day without her in his arms, or even just to hear her husky voice, especially when she was whispering in his ear...words of longing...words of desire for him.

Joseph moaned now with the agony of his situation, and he pushed the naked sleeping woman onto her back, and placed *his* face on *her* chest now, burying it beneath her cream-colored breasts and on her soft abdomen. Her breasts were still so firm and round, not deflated with age, and he turned his head and pressed his lips to the pink areola, then whispered her name in Italian.

He felt her hand touch the back of his head. "Darling," she said, moving her legs apart, thinking that he wanted more of her...more *from* her...and willing to give it even in her sleep.

What would he do without her...when he had to give her up? How would he live?

"Francesca," he murmured against her breast again. "Francesca..."

Her hand stroked his hair three times before she asked, "Why are you hurting so? Let it go; please just let it go. She won't find out."

Joseph moved off her, and fell on his back again. He covered his eyes with his arm. "I'm just tired."

Frances rolled onto her side away from him and then sat on the edge of the bed. She stared at the darkness beyond her bedroom window. "She's not allowed in my bed, Joseph. I have so little of you, I won't share you with her in this bed. I'm selfish in this room...under these sheets. I want you to myself, so leave her across the hall, I beg you."

"She's with me wherever I go. We are bound together by marriage, by years of history, by a son who is dead."

"I have so little of you," she repeated in whisper.

He sat up now and said, "No, you have more of me than I've ever given to her or anyone else. It is she who has so little of me...not you...I breathe for you, I get up in the morning for you, I shower and shave and dress for *you...you*, not her."

Frances sighed. "But it is she you are bound to, as you just said, and that means I have none of you, Joseph. I have your hands all over my body, I have your tongue in my mouth, I have your penis inside me, and, yes, I have some of your time. But I have nothing else of you, Joseph."

"You have my love," he offered sadly, running his finger down her spine to the curve of her hip.

She turned to look at him, but there was no smile on her lips, no brightness in her eyes. "I have your long subdued passion...passion isn't love."

Joseph pulled his naked body from the bed with effort. They had had this argument before. "I love you, and I long for you as I've never longed for anything in my life, but I can never leave her."

"I haven't asked you to. I've asked you to just keep her out of my bed when you are with me."

Four months, and always the same argument.

Fall 1961

6E

KRAMER

He was staying much too late at the club these nights. Martha had been so relieved when he told her that he'd joined the club, just to have somewhere to go to get out of her hair. But she thought he'd be there in the daytime, not at night, too.

Then there was the Astoria Center of Israel—so much going on there, he told Martha. They were never religious. They observed Passover, sure, and Rosh Hashanah...sometimes Hanukkah...but they never even belonged to a temple before. On top of all of that was the chess in the park. Yes, he liked chess, he was good at it. But hours upon hours?

She heard the elevator. One could always hear when the elevator reached the floor, and the door squeaked just the tiniest sound when it opened. Martha was relieved. He was home finally. But then there was no key in the door. Instead, there was noise at the next door. She heard the fumbling, the key drop to the floor, the curse, and then the banging and the belligerent mumbling. "Let me in." Bang, bang, bang. "I shaid let me in."

Martha put her head back against the arm of the sofa and closed her eyes. *Not tonight.*

The door next to her apartment opened, and the noise in the hall stopped. There was a long silence. She knew the routine. Always silence before the banging and the shouting and the crying.

Her bedroom was farther from the Walsh's apartment walls, and so she pushed the crocheted afghan off her legs and dropped her feet to the floor. She walked slowly into the bedroom.

Martha was hoping to be in the living room when Joseph came home. She had brushed her hair until it shone, powdered her nose and put on some lipstick. She was wearing her prettiest nightgown and her pink quilted robe that he liked so much. Martha had wanted to be reading her book, lounging on the sofa, when he walked into the apartment.

Now that was spoiled.

She had heard the older girl screaming at her mother earlier that evening. It was so loud she could make out some of the words. "I can't do this anymore, Momma...we need some peace...I'm going to leave, I swear to God, I'll go live with Aunt Maggie." So unlike the girl who was usually so quiet.

Joseph had called Mr. O'Darry about a month after the Walsh family moved in. He explained that the noise was disturbing Martha. O'Darry said he'd look into it.

"Don't use our name," Joseph had said into the phone. "It's not too bad, just one or two nights a week, but we thought we'd call to see if anyone else had complained."

When she asked Joseph why he wasn't more aggressive about it with O'Darry, he just shrugged and said, "Have you seen the size of that man? And when he's been drinking, there's no telling what he'd do. And isn't he a nice guy when he isn't drinking? He'd do anything for a person who needs him. You've seen that."

Martha had seen it. The previous winter, when she slipped on the ice on her way home from the hairdresser, he was coming home from work and saw her go down. Her ankle was broken, and Walsh picked her up in his arms and carried her all the way into the lobby and put her on the couch there, then went to the superintendent's apartment and called the ambulance. He went all the way to the hospital with her, cracking jokes and holding her hand until Joseph got to the emergency room. Mr. Walsh never left her side until he knew Joseph was with her.

And there was the time that the dog from across the street ran in front of a car and was hit, and the dog was yelping in pain. Mr. Walsh picked it up and held it to his chest and ran to the veterinarian's office two blocks away. The dog lived. It lost a leg, but it lived because of Mr. Walsh. The Italian man who owns the dog still gives Mr. Walsh a bottle of his homemade wine every Christmas with a basket of breads and cookies. He thinks Mr. Walsh is a saint.

There was good in the man. Martha knew that. But there was darkness, too.

A loud bang from next door made Martha jump. The silence phase is over.

She heard Joseph's key in the door a few minutes later, and breathed a sigh of relief. She remembered how she wanted to look when he arrived home, and she ran her fingers through her hair and straightened her quilted robe. She picked up the book and pretended to be reading it. So, she wasn't in the living room, but the bedroom was as good...maybe better.

Joseph poked his head into the room. "You're still awake? Are the neighbors keeping you from sleep?"

"It just started...I was awake." She didn't like the way Joseph was looking lately. His eyes had dark circles beneath them and he rarely smiled.

He took off his coat and hung it in the closet, then sat on the slipper chair in the corner of their bedroom to take off his shoes.

"Did you eat, Joseph?" she asked, knowing that he would tell her that he did.

"Yes, I grabbed a little bite at the club."

"Are you tired?" she asked him now. "I've been waiting for you."

When Joseph looked up at her from the armless chair, she smiled at him to be certain he understood that she was inviting him to make love. They hadn't done so in more than two months, and he had not asked in all that time. It worried her. She didn't like doing it anymore, but it was what married people did...no? So she was a good wife; she'd invite when he didn't ask, let him know that she knew her duty.

Joseph looked surprised and then looked down at the floor. "I am tired. It was a long day."

"A long day? Playing games? Talking with your friends?"

"Sure...I'm not a young man anymore. You know that," he told her, going into the bathroom.

Martha knew how old he was. She knew also that he was still virile...still always hard and eager when he asked her to be with him in that way...sometimes joking, sometimes pleading. He was never too tired for her before. There had been a time when he didn't have to plead with her, but lately...after Joey...maybe that's why he doesn't ask now.

He was still handsome, and she still loved his smile and the touch of his hand in the small of her back whenever they were entering a room or when he was leading her to their table in a restaurant. She missed him...missed his asking.

A wave of disappointment coursed through her as she lay on her bed in her pretty nightgown and quilted robe. For what did I dress like this?

Martha heard him showering and wondered why in the world he would shower this late at night when he was just coming to bed to sleep. He was a morning showerer. Always the same, shave and shower, every morning. Now he showers at night? Since when?

The raised voices from next door distracted her. Normally she couldn't hear them in this room. They were louder tonight than usual. The shower turned off and in a few minutes, Joseph came out in his pajamas. He wound his watch, took off his wedding ring, and placed both on his bureau.

"Will we go to Manhattan tomorrow?" she asked as he lowered himself under the sheet and the blanket.

"Why?" Joseph wanted to know, punching at his pillow, just as he had every night for thirty-eight years. It comforted her. It was all the same.

She was being silly. There was happiness in the same routine. There was peace in it. Okay, so he showered at night, but he still punched his pillow.

"We could go to a museum if you want…or maybe a matinee? You wanted to see 'Milk and Honey,' no? Molly Picon does a somersault on stage. You laughed when you read it in the papers."

Joseph rolled over to his back then and stared at the ceiling.

"This is the land of…milk and honey…this is the land of…" Martha sang to him.

He smiled, but he was quiet a long time before he answered, "Sure, why not, Martha. We'll go to Manhattan if you want. We'll go see Molly Picon do a somersault on stage."

Martha reached over and placed her hand on top of his. "Joseph?"

He didn't look at her. His fingers didn't twist around hers as they always had whenever she touched his hand. He continued to stare at the ceiling.

"Joseph?"

"I'm tired, Martha." He yawned and closed his eyes.

"I was just going to suggest that you see Dr. Haber. You don't seem yourself lately. Maybe you should see the doctor, maybe tell him you're tired all the time…"

"Good night, Martha," he said, turning on his side, away from her.

Martha was surprised. Surprised by Joseph; surprised by his staying at the club so late, by the fact that he had showered at night when he always showered in the morning; surprised by his aloofness; surprised that in all the years they'd been married he never went to bed without kissing her goodnight, if only on her forehead, but in the last few weeks…no it was months…he rarely remembered to do so.

She was surprised more by the fact that she wanted to cry.

She hadn't cried since Joey's death; not since the day those soldiers showed up at their door in Rego Park and asked to speak with her; not since the day the coffin came off the plane and later was lowered into the family plot at Mount Hebron in Flushing. Not since they tried to give her the flag, but she wouldn't take it, and so they handed it to Joseph, who took it without even looking up at them—or at her. Not since she buried her only child…her Joey.

During those days she cried morning, noon and night. Since then, she would tell people that during those days she cried out all the tears God had put into her when He made her. There would be no more tears for her for the rest of her life. They were gone; she was washed out of tears. The last one fell when they covered her precious son with the first shovel of earth…like a faucet that was turned off.

Yet, here she was, all these years later, verklempt over Joseph not kissing her goodnight…fighting back the tears…for what?

She wondered: does fear come naturally with age? Because she was afraid…of what, she didn't know. But she was afraid.

6D

ALLCOCK

"Danny, I want to have Thanksgiving Dinner here."

Vera waited for her husband to respond, but he said nothing, so she continued, "My parents and sisters and your parents."

Still Danny said nothing. He just continued to move the forkful of dinner she had prepared for him into his mouth, never moving his eyes from his plate. She knew though that he was having trouble swallowing the food because he took a slug of Rheingold to wash it down. By the time he placed the glass back on the table, half of the amber beer was gone. He continued to stare at his plate, then put his fork down.

"Danny, I want to have Thanks..."

"I heard you the first time," he said.

"It will be all right," she said very calmly.

"They don't even talk to us, Vera, let alone to one another, and you want to have them all over for Thanksgiving...in this tiny, squalid little box of an apartment."

Vera held her temper, but she had trouble keeping sarcasm from her tone when she said, "It isn't squalid, Dan. It's small, maybe it's in Astoria, but it's immaculate. I keep it immaculate. The whole building is immaculate, and it's what we can afford on both our salaries. I know you're worried that your parents will find it beneath them...and you, of course...but it's really a very nice apartment building, in a rather nice neighborhood—albeit a working class neighborhood—which, by the way is what we are, working class—and it's our first home so I want..."

Danny rubbed his hands over his face and then over the top of his ash blond hair. "Vera, stop. Okay? Please stop."

"We have to break the ice..."

"We don't have an ice pick strong enough," he told her, pushing his half-full plate away from him. "I don't want to break the ice, anyway. I hate them for how they treat you, Vera, I hate yours and mine, and I have no desire to put you through that. For Christ's sake, you don't even have a full kitchen, how the hell will you cook a turkey big enough for all of us? Please, just let it go, Vera."

Vera glanced at the kitchenette, trying to picture not just a turkey in the tiny oven, but all the vegetables in pots on the top of the stove. Where would she put the serving dishes? She almost grimaced at the thought of the pandemonium. Yet, she just didn't want to give up on the idea.

"Please, Danny," she said, calmer now, no sarcasm, "I want this to stop between us and our families." She waited for him to say something, and when he didn't, she said, "I miss my parents...I know you miss yours."

For a split second, Danny looked as though he was going to cry. The fair skin around his eyes turned red, and he bit his lip, but he got up and walked away from the table to look out the window of their living room— or rather the living/dining/kitchen room

"I've spoken to my parents, Danny," Vera told him.

He was surprised and turned to look at her, "You called them?"

"No, my mother called me first...during the first summer we were married. She called me a few times since then. My sister, Meagan, called then, and before I knew it, we were talking every week, sometimes more. My father got on the phone a couple of times, but I could tell that it was hard for him, his voice would crack as though he wanted to cry, and then my Mom would get back on the phone."

"But you haven't seen them?"

"No, Dan. Not once. I told them I wouldn't see them until you were also welcome and until they would accept you and our marriage."

Danny smirked. "Well, I see that hasn't happened since we haven't been invited over."

"It's not you, Dan. It's the fact that we're not married in the Church. They're Polish, they grew up believing that when a Catholic doesn't marry in the Church, that person is living in sin...excommunicated or something...and it's killing them. You've got to understand that..."

"No, Vera," he said slowly and deliberately, still looking out the window, "I don't have to understand. I'm not Catholic and that has nothing to do with me. It's wrong, just as wrong as my parents wanting us to marry in the Lutheran Church."

Now Vera smirked. Annoyed, she picked up the dirty dishes and put them into the sink with more force than necessary. "It hasn't got a goddamned thing to do with what church we're married in when it comes to your parents. If you married an Episcopalian...or a Presbyterian...or a Quaker, it would have been acceptable. Let's see, what did your father say again? Oh, that's right. He said, 'I'd rather see you marry a Negro than a white-trash, dumb Polack.' Wasn't that it?"

Danny didn't answer her.

"It's not quite that personal with my parents, so don't go comparing," Vera said.

She squeezed the dishwashing detergent into the sink and while it filled with hot water, she put on her Playtex gloves. She washed and rinsed the dishes, placed them on the side of the sink in a drainer, and then scrubbed the pots. It felt good to scrub; it helped to curb her rage. Every time she thought of what his father had said about her, she wanted to scream. How dare he...how dare he talk that way about me without even knowing me. How dare he look down on my family...and for that matter, to look down on anyone. Who the hell does he think he is?

Vera felt Danny's arms embrace her from behind, and she leaned back into him. No matter how angry she was, his touch could melt her, his embrace could render her weak.

"I love you," he whispered into her ear. "What he said has nothing to do with us, darling."

Vera turned within the circle of his arms to face him. "Danny, I have to ask you this. What do you think about my family? Do you wonder if your father is right...that the Polish are drunks and mean and beat their wives? That we're stupid? Do you ever think to yourself that your father has it right?"

"Vera," Danny said, burying his face in her neck. "Vera, please..."

"I need to know if you think that, Dan. Because if you do, you're so wrong. My father is an angel. Sure, he has a couple of beers with his buddies sometimes, and yes, he's a blue collar worker, but never—not once in my entire life—has he ever raised a hand against my mother or me and my sisters. I need to know that you understand that."

Danny leaned forward and captured her against the sink. "Of course I do, Vera. And I need to know that you understand that my father isn't the stereotypical rich business man who goes to the county club and drinks martinis and takes his friends' wives to bed with him, or that my mother is an alcoholic socialite who is bored with her life and lounges by the pool all afternoon ordering servants around. Don't you see, honey, there are these pigeon-holes for every class."

"They pigeon-holed me," she said, sadness replacing her anger. "Your parents pigeon-holed my parents."

Danny let her go. "If you continue to blame me for that, it will destroy our marriage."

"I just want them to get to know me. I want them to get to know my parents and sisters. I want them to see that we're good, honorable people Danny. They never will until they have a chance to know us."

She followed him when he walked away into the bedroom. "They miss you as much as my parents missed me, Dan. We need to give them an opportunity to get back into your life...and to see that we're happy and I'm not poor white trash. Thanksgiving is that opportunity."

"No."

She was incredulous. "Why? Why, Danny?"

He looked miserable when he looked at her. "They'll never accept you. They'll never accept..." he looked around the bedroom, at the threadbare chair, at the scarred and beaten bureau, and the dark and scuffed hardwood floors, "this place. It will just confirm for them what..." he obviously didn't know how to put it any other way, "they already think of you. No one they know would live like this...dress like..."

Vera felt cheap and dirty and low class suddenly. She had never worn a strand of matched pearls around her neck. She didn't wear dresses by Dior or suits by Chanel. She wore what she could afford and what looked nice.

She looked over his head at the mirror above their dresser. She saw herself dressed in the plain blue dress she had put on that morning, in her faded apron and yellow rubber gloves, which were still dripping suds.

He was telling her that his parents—maybe Danny, himself—would be embarrassed by her. And now Vera understood that he'd never buy her a home in Connecticut, because she would never fit in there...she was this apartment...tiny and squalid.

Vera ran from the apartment, letting the door slam behind her. She bolted up the stairs to the roof, pushed open the heavy metal door, and ran out into the autumn dusk. She pulled off the wet gloves and hurled them over the side of the building. How tempting it was to throw herself over the side of the building, too. It would free Danny. He could go back with his tail tucked between his legs, and his parents and the country club set would welcome him back...poor wayward boy who needed a fling with the "other kind." She was a nothing...to them she'd never be anything but a Polack...a dumb Polack. She wanted to throw her head back and scream with anger and frustration.

A noise startled her and she spun around to see Mrs. Walsh standing behind her, looking alarmed, a bed sheet half folded over one arm and pinched at the corner between her thumb and forefinger. She wore a red sweater over a black dress. She looked frozen to the spot.

"Mrs. Allcock? Are you all right?" Mrs. Walsh's voice was very calm, but her green eyes were very large.

Vera crumbled. That's the only way she would be able to describe it later when she thought of it. She literally crumbled to the tar roof. Mrs. Walsh dropped the sheet and knelt down beside Vera.

"Hey there, what's the matter? Aw, honey, don't cry. What's wrong?"

Vera was so overcome by the gentle, motherly way Mrs. Walsh spoke to her, that she fell against the older woman and sobbed into the red sweater, "He thinks I'm white trash."

Mrs. Walsh's arms folded around Vera. "Oh, honey, sh, don't cry."

"I can't bear it. I can't bear him looking down on me like his parents do." Vera had no handkerchief, no tissue, and tears and snot poured from her, but Mrs. Walsh just continued to hold her and allow her to weep against her sweater. "I don't deserve it...I *don't*," Vera cried, pulling the red sweater into her fist.

When Vera calmed down a little, Mrs. Walsh pulled a wad of clean but wrinkled tissues from her sweater pocket and held them against Vera's nose. Vera took them and blew, then wiped her face, but tears continued to course down her cheeks.

"Listen, honey, the first year of marriage is always tough, but when you have family issues, it's ten times worse. It gets easier if you just..."

"It's not that, Mrs. Walsh. His family thinks I'm trash—low class trash—and I think my husband is starting to think so, too. I can tolerate them thinking it, but not him. Oh, God, not of me," Vera wailed, completely unglued again. "I'm not trash," she said looking up at the older woman. "I'm not, Mrs. Walsh."

"No, of course, you aren't, dear; not at all." Mrs. Walsh took both of Vera's shoulders in her hands and made Vera look at her. "Class hasn't got anything to do with where you come from or how rich or how poor you are. Only people who don't have class think that. People with real class know the difference. I've known dirt poor people who could mix in with royalty and make the royalty look like commoners. And I've known people with lots of money and huge houses who cheat and carouse and are so vile that I wouldn't allow my daughters to associate with them."

Vera buried her head in her hands, but Mrs. Walsh shook her shoulders to make Vera look at her again. The woman's face was round, framed by soft waves of graying hair, with just the hint of a double chin, and sadness in her eyes that made Vera want to wince.

"I want you to listen to me, Mrs. Allcock. You may not believe me right now or understand what I'm saying, but you'll mark my words one day. You have a great deal of class, honey. It hasn't got anything to do with education, or money, or breeding...it has everything to do with character. And I see character in your face. I'll bet your parents have character, too. Where they live or the kind of work they do doesn't matter."

Vera leaned back against the five foot brick wall that separated the roof from the air. "I don't know what you mean by character."

"Well, it's an individual's nature—a person's morals and ethics...courage...and integrity. It's how a person handles adversity and how honest that person is in dealing with others...and with herself...and how a person stands up for what she believes. It can't be purchased. It comes from your soul and your heart."

Vera thought it over, still unsure if she really did have the kind of character Mrs. Walsh was talking about.

"You've got to show your husband that you have it," Mrs. Walsh continued. "You've got to be steadfast in not allowing him or anyone else make you feel less than you are because of where you live or how much money you have—your socioeconomic status—do you like that expression? It's something I'm hearing a lot lately...socioeconomic..." She laughed gently at herself and cupped Vera's cheek in her hand. "Anyway, you have to make sure your husband digs down deep into his own soul to find his character and stands up to his parents for what he believes in. What he has to believe in is you, in your love for each other, and in the fact that he chose you and you chose him. He won't if you don't."

Vera wiped her face with the wad of tissues again while Mrs. Walsh moved back against the wall next to her. They sat shoulder to shoulder now. The older woman still wore her high heels from work. They were red, like the sweater, with a round toe, and Vera detected a bunion on the woman's left foot because it pushed against the edge of the shoe. She wondered if it was painful, but that's not what she asked the other woman. What she did ask was completely unexpected...by both of them.

"Why do you stay with him?"

Mrs. Walsh was taken aback, looked as though she was going to pretend she had no idea what Vera meant, and then her face relaxed as though it was too much work to pretend not to know. "Because I've had one failed marriage and I won't have another one. Because my family told me this marriage wouldn't work out, but I wouldn't listen, and now I don't want them to gloat. But mostly because he's had a tough life. I know he takes it out on me and my daughter—generally when he drinks, but he only goes to the bar to be with his friends...friends he used to work with when he was an architect. You see, he's allergic to the alcohol. It turns him into someone else. And being with them just makes him angry because he lost his business...*we* lost the business...and he can't do what he used to do."

She played with the pocket of her sweater. "We met in that bar...it's a nice place in Manhattan—on Seventh Avenue. Every Wednesday night he and his coworkers went there for a drink, and I happened to go in with some of my friends one night, and...well, we met and hit it off. It wasn't a mad passionate love. He was lonely...he was a widower...and I was lonely. I was newly divorced and felt pretty low. He made me feel like a woman again."

She shrugged and added, "Even now when I walk into a room—an overweight, middle aged mother of two children—he tells me I'm a beautiful woman...of course, he says all this when he's sober. I fall for it every time." She looked down at her hands. "It's another story when he's not."

Mrs. Walsh straightened her sweater and stretched her legs out in front of her. Vera saw that she had loosened her stockings from their garters and rolled them down and knotted them just above the knees. It was something her own mother did…and her grandmother…when they weren't wearing their girdles.

"After being married to a so-called high class serial adulterer, who had been my childhood sweetheart, but who left me with a baby for another woman he'd impregnated, hearing that I'm beautiful and I'm loved from my present husband is a heady experience. He may be mean and abusive when he's drunk, but he makes me feel loved when he's not. He's pretty much sober five days out of the week. He can be moody and dark, especially since losing his business, but he's a gentle and considerate lover and a man who thinks I'm…well, that I'm beautiful."

Eleanor Walsh sighed and closed her eyes. "He came from nothing, but after the war he went to school for architecture and got a job in a firm in New York. He was a big, handsome red-headed Irishman—rough around the edges, and always trying to prove himself…but he always thought he fell short. I talked him into starting his own architectural firm—I felt he could do better on his own, we could make more money. I told him I'd manage the business while he did the designs and drawings. He didn't want to. He said I had more faith in him than he had ability, but I pushed. We set up shop, and in the beginning we were doing good. Too good, maybe. The money was coming in, we had a beautiful apartment in Manhattan, Paige was taking equestrian lessons and going to a private school. We had nice clothes, went to fancy restaurants—never even thought to save for rainy days. Then I got pregnant with Audra, and I wasn't paying as much attention to the business as I should have. We hired a nanny, and then some employees for the firm, neither of which we could afford. We started to get deeper into debt, but I always thought that it would be fine; that's what businesses do—borrow from the banks in order to grow."

She stopped talking. Vera touched her arm. "What happened?"

"One of his buildings collapsed…almost killed a woman and her child. I'm not sure why—in the end, they decided that it was the builder who screwed up—but during the investigation, they found that Brendan's license had expired, that we didn't have all the credentials we were supposed to have for the business during the time he was working on the plans for the building."

Mrs. Walsh let out a bitter laugh. "As the business manager, I was supposed to get everything we needed. He asked me a few times, but I just kept telling him not to worry, I took care of everything. I thought I *had* but…long story short, we lost everything. We're still paying off our debts. We'll be paying them until the day we die, I think. We lost our apartment, one of our cars…everything."

"Why didn't he get a job in an architectural firm after that?"

"The truth is no one would hire him. Even though it wasn't his fault, his reputation as an architect was questionable now. He started drinking. There was a landscape architect in New Jersey that my husband used to work with when we had the firm. He found out we were living in our car, and he looked for us and offered Brendan a job. It was because of Brendan that this man had a company—Brendan always recommended him to our clients…a really good man…Italian with a big loving family. Now Brendan works for *him*—digging holes and planting bushes. He's as strong as an ox, my husband, and a hard worker. But even though he hates what he's doing and misses his drawing table, pencils and protractors, he'll never go back to architecture. He tortures himself by still meeting up with his friends in that business…asking them what their projects are and listening to them talk about work. They must think he's insane…sometimes *I* think he's insane…he suffers and broods, tries to ease the pain with booze, and then takes it out on us."

"How awful…for both of you," Vera said.

Mrs. Walsh smiled sadly. "If the truth were known, he sort of likes being the victim. It's part of his personality…things haven't been easy for him. His father died when he was a baby, his big brother died when he was a kid, and his first wife and little girl were killed in an automobile accident while he was serving in the Navy during the war. He couldn't even get home for their funeral. He never got over that…he never will. He feels like the world is against him. Everything and everyone except the bottle. But when the booze wears off, he's different. He can be so kind. He's a paradox."

The two of them sat for a long time in silence. Mrs. Walsh let her head drop back against the bricks. "You asked why I don't leave him. I want to—he can be really mean to me and to my older daughter when he drinks. I don't know, maybe I deserve it, but Paige doesn't. I just can't leave. I stay and take it…make her stay and take it. I tell her he's really a good person— she's safe with him in other ways—he's as moral as the day is long." She shook her head and laughed at herself. It wasn't a joyful laugh, but rather a heartbreaking one. "And that's more than I've told a soul since I married Brendan. You'd make a good psychiatrist, Mrs. Allcock. I can't believe I've said all this to you."

Vera couldn't help ask, "And your older daughter? Does she like him despite…"

Mrs. Walsh shook her head no. "It's complicated. I wanted a father for her—his child was dead and I thought Paige could replace the one he was missing—I think that may be why I married him in the first place, but with all that had gone on in his life, he just…well, you can't replace a child with another child. He adores Audra, but he never really accepted Paige. Sometimes he's meaner to her than he is to me, but I know he'd take a bullet for her. He'd kill anyone else who hurt her."

Vera closed her eyes and said, "What a strange world we live in."

Mrs. Walsh agreed. "We human beings are peculiar. And some of us don't have much character...like me. That's why I admire it so much in others...like you." She smiled and put her hand on top of Vera's.

Vera sat up then. "If you had a previous marriage, then you and Mr. Walsh are not married in the church, right?"

A shadow passed over the older woman's eyes. "Yes, that's correct. But no one around here knows that. As far as Saint Patrick's is concerned, that's where Audra goes to school, Paige is my present husband's daughter, just like Audra is, and I don't go around broadcasting that I'm a remarried Catholic. We've had enough scandal in our lives. So, keep my secret, okay?"

"We're not married in the Church, either," Vera told her. "Dan's a Lutheran. We eloped."

Mrs. Walsh moaned. "Not a good thing."

"My parents are heartbroken," Vera told her.

"I'm sure they are...I'd be heartbroken if Paige or Audra weren't married in the Church. And I'd never forgive them if they left the Church."

"Even though you..." Vera started to ask, but Mrs. Walsh sat up straight and looked into Vera's eyes.

"I chose...let me repeat that for you, Mrs. Allcock...I and I alone chose to remarry after a divorce. I did it knowing full well that it wasn't sanctioned by the Church, or by God for that matter, but I did it anyway. I'll never blame the Church for my not being able to receive the sacraments. The law is the law. We have to learn to accept the consequences of our choices and not blame others who make the rules. It's as simple as that. That's what I try to instill in my girls."

They sat on the tar roof, side by side, for a long time, each in her own thoughts. A breeze lifted the sheet that Mrs. Walsh had dropped.

Vera reached over and picked up the corner of the sheet and held it up with a smile. Mrs. Walsh laughed. "You caught me. I come up here to hang the bed sheets and towels so that they smell fresh and clean." She pointed to a portable wooden dryer rack. "I hate the way clothes smell when they're out of a dryer. Nothing like line dried laundry, you know. I try to make sure I do it when Biermann isn't going to be up on the roof...which is most of the time. So far, no one has turned me in."

Vera laughed, too. "Your secret is safe with me...all of your secrets."

They helped each other stand up. It was easier for Vera than for Mrs. Walsh, and Vera gave her a hand. Together they finished folding the sheet and the towels. The older woman kissed Vera's cheek then and said, "Go back down to him, Mrs. Allcock. You're both so young, and there may be problems, but I think you love each other. I've seen you together in the elevator. I know the real thing when I see it... so make this work. Don't look for insults that aren't there, either. That's death to a marriage. Go make it work out, honey."

Vera nodded, not certain she knew that Mrs. Walsh was correct, but she didn't have another choice. She loved Danny too much to leave him.

"And never, and I mean never, think of ending your life again, even for a split second." Mrs. Walsh's face was very serious and stern. "There is no sin greater than that…and besides, there isn't a man on the face of the earth worth killing yourself over…believe me, I know that personally…I've stood on that ledge plenty of times, but I always come to the same conclusion."

"You knew? You knew what I was thinking?"

Mrs. Walsh closed her eyes when she nodded.

"I wouldn't have done it. I was just being dramatic."

Vera took a few steps away, then she turned and looked at the woman— a woman scarred in so many ways, wise in so many ways, vulnerable in just as many ways—and she ran back and kissed Eleanor Walsh's soft cheek, wanting to impart the same sort of comfort to Mrs. Walsh that the woman had given to her minutes before. The woman accepted the affection with a sad smile.

When Vera descended the stairs, Danny was just coming up. "Jesus, Vera, were you up there all this time? I've been all over the neighborhood looking for you. I was frantic. You scared the hell out of me."

"We don't have to have Thanksgiving this year, Danny," Vera told him, "I'll wait until you're ready, but when you are, I want you to know that I will look your parents right in the eye and make sure they realize that I have character…maybe even more character than they do…and I will never allow them to make me feel ashamed or inferior. No one, Dan, will ever make me feel that way again. I want you to know that."

He smiled up at her from the first step. She was shaking and had to grab the banister so that he wouldn't see that her hand was trembling.

"As long as I'm alive, no one will ever even try to," Danny said, holding his hand out to her. She noticed that his hand was trembling, too. She glanced up at the roof door before going down to him. Mrs. Walsh was standing in the open door. Vera could tell that Mrs. Walsh had heard what she'd just said. The older woman was nodding her head and smiling.

Christmas 1961

Germaine Sommer finished wrapping her last gift and put it under the tree. It was only a tabletop tree, but it looked nice and festive. She hadn't put up a tree in years. What for? There was just herself and Corky to enjoy it. Not worth the time. And of course back then she had to buy a real tree, and drag it up from the Avenue herself.

When she told Mr. Walsh that she wished she could have a tree in her apartment now that little Audra was with her before and after school, he showed up the next afternoon with a box. It was a silver aluminum tree. She'd never seen anything like it...and he had another box, a bigger one, with another silver tree in it for his apartment. He wouldn't take a dime for it, either. Told her it was her Christmas gift.

Germaine was as excited as Audra was. Mr. Walsh took the artificial tree from the box and read the directions, and then the three of them put it together. Each branch fit into a hole in the middle pole. Then there were short pieces of the wired foil that they turned around the center pole to hide it. When it was ready, they stood back and studied it and thought it was the prettiest thing they'd ever seen.

"Don't put lights on it, though," Mr. Walsh warned her. "The foil will melt." He brought in another box that contained a small spotlight and attached a color wheel to it. He plugged it into a socket in the wall beneath the tree and the color wheel began to turn, changing the color of the silver tree from a pinkish-red tint, to a green tint, then a blue and finally gold. It was breathtaking. Not the sort of tree from her childhood, but brilliant nonetheless. And little Audra's face was as bright and happy as the tree.

That same afternoon, after Audra went home with her father, Germaine went down into her storage unit in the basement of the building and brought up a cardboard box that contained all the ornaments she had collected with Ernest. There weren't very many, just enough for the small tree. Some were from her childhood that her parents had given them when they married, and some from his family's collection, others they had bought together when they were newlyweds. All were from Germany, mostly globes in various colors with hand-painted designs on them. Some were shaped like candy canes, some were teardrop shaped, and others shaped like stars. One had the Nativity scene inside it and was decorated with glittery dust. That was her favorite one.

There were eight garlands of tiny colored balls, strung on delicate white cord that she hung in swags from the ends of the branches. And then Germaine found two ornaments, one was a sweet pink paper ornament and the other was the Christkindl—the child Jesus forged in bronze. The paper ornament had an old family photo glued onto it. Ernest held the baby, while Germaine stood behind the chair looking down at her sweet little one. How old was the baby in the photograph? Two? Three? All those shiny blond curls and two pink round cheeks. So pretty...so soft...her baby was.

Germaine put the Christkindl on the tree, but stuffed the pink ornament back into the box. She didn't want Audra to see it and ask all sorts of questions. She avoided questions about her past when the little girl asked. It would be too hard to explain.

She had come to love Audra. She loved doing homework with her and reading to her. They watched the Three Stooges every day together, even though Mrs. Walsh didn't want Audra watching that show. They were too rough, Mrs. Walsh would say. "I don't want her thinking it's all right to be violent and hit people and poke at their eyes...those stooges are nothing but ruffians."

But Germaine would let the little girl watch them anyway because she loved to hear Audra scream with laughter at Moe, Larry and Curly's antics. And then there was Abbott and Costello, now they were funny, too, and not as violent. Poor Lou, always in trouble, and that silly Stinky...a grown man all dressed up as Little Lord Fauntleroy. It was all senseless and ridiculous, but Audra loved to watch them. Germaine had never watched any of these shows before Audra came into her life. There were so many things she hadn't done until Audra came into her life.

Germaine placed the last gift under the tree and stood back. There were fifteen gifts. Some were for her sister and brother-in-law and their children and grandchildren. A bottle of brandy for the Beirmanns. There were two gifts for Paige Walsh, such a nice young girl. Germaine bought her a barrette for her hair and crocheted her a soft white sweater. There was one for the Walshes—a fruit cake she'd made—a squeaky toy for her little

Corky, and the rest, six in all, were for Audra. There was a sweater she had crocheted, and a hat and gloves, some coloring books. Audra loved to color. She'd assign one side of the page to Germaine and take the other side and they would sit side by side at the kitchen table. Finally, and most importantly, there was a doll...a talking doll, a Chatty Cathy. Audra had seen the commercials on television about the doll, and all she ever said was, "I hope Santa Claus brings me Chatty Cathy. That's all I want, Mrs. Sommer. Do you think he will? Have I been a good girl? Good enough? Will I get Chatty Cathy?"

Germaine made sure of it, but not before asking Mrs. Walsh if it was all right. Mrs. Walsh was a little annoyed, Germaine could tell, because she said she had no idea what else to get the child from Santa since it was all she had asked for. In the end she said it was all right. Germaine would give it to Audra first thing Christmas morning, but she would tell the truth, that *she* had bought it for her. She didn't want the child thinking that Santa brought it. Germaine wanted Audra to know how much she'd come to love her...and she wanted the little girl to love her back. Santa could go to the Walsh's apartment with different gifts.

Germaine made sure she got the blond doll so it would match Audra's hair, and it wore a blue dress because that was Audra's favorite color. Germaine crocheted a little sweater to match the one she made for Audra. She would sew more matching outfits for the doll and the little girl in the coming months.

The doorbell rang and Germaine peeked out. It was that lovely woman from next door, the Irish girl. She opened the door and said, "Merry Christmas!"

"And Happy Christmas to you, Mrs. Sommer. Are ye sittin' and waitin' for Father Christmas then?"

Bridget Riordan was wearing a red velvet dress with a black collar and a white silk bow at her throat. "I have a little something for ye, for under your tree," she said while holding out a beautifully wrapped box.

"I have something for you, too," Germaine said. She always made extra apple and currant stollen and wrapped it in aluminum foil and put a bow on it. She baked and wrapped one every year, but until this year, she had never had to give it to anyone and would end up eating it herself. She had never had an unexpected guest on Christmas Eve before. She went into the kitchen to get it while Miss Riordan put a wrapped box on the table near the tree.

"Now that's the shiniest tree I've ever had the pleasure to lay my eyes upon," the Irishwoman said. "Imagine that! A silver tree!"

Germaine came into the living room and handed Miss Riordan the stollen. "I know...it's something else, isn't it? Mr. Walsh bought it for me."

Miss Riordan sat in the chair. "Really? Mr. Walsh did? Well, it's lovely.

It's unusual, but it's very nice."

"Miss Riordan, can I get you a cup of tea? Or maybe some eggnog? I bought a quart today to share with Audra. She loves the store bought kind, and there's plenty left over."

"Please call me Bridget. We've been neighbors for six months now, you know." Corky jumped up on Bridget's lap and looked into her face. "You can call me Bridget, too," she told the dog, laughing. Then she said, "Well, I suppose a glass of eggnog would be lovely."

Mrs. Sommer snapped her fingers with pleasure. "Then we'll have eggnog and we'll toast to a Merry Christmas." Leaning over conspiratorially, she asked, "Will I put a little brandy in it for you?"

The Irish woman laughed, "What's eggnog without a bit of spirit in it on a cold Christmas Eve? Of course, put the brandy in it!"

When the glasses were half empty, Germaine asked, "Will you be alone tomorrow, Bridget?"

Bridget nodded. "Aye, I'm afraid so. And you?"

"The Walshes invited me over, but I'd already told my sister I'd come for the day. Her family will be there."

"Isn't she in New Jersey? How will you get there?"

"Oh, I take the bus...first a couple of trains to Penn Station, and then the bus to Emerson. It only takes about an hour and a half...maybe two hours if it snows."

"It's supposed to snow tonight, Mrs. Sommer."

Germaine looked out the window toward the street light. Nothing was coming down yet. "Well, maybe it will hold off."

"You never had children?"

Germaine never liked to answer that question, but she did now. "A daughter...Eunice."

"Oh, that's nice. Will she be at your sister's tomorrow?"

"No."

The younger woman seemed to wait for more information. Germaine looked out at the street lamp again, then said, "My daughter died ten years ago. Cancer. Leukemia. She had two children, a boy and a girl. They live in Arizona."

Bridget put her glass on the coffee table and leaned forward. "I'm so sorry...I hope my asking didn't upset..."

"No, it didn't. Well, just talking about it upsets me, but not the question. It's normal to be asked."

"Do you see your grandchildren often?"

Germaine shook her head no. "I was there to take care of them when she was sick. I lived with them for three months, but right before she died, I got a cough and her husband brought me to his doctor. He said it wasn't a cold. He told me that the climate wasn't good for me there, that I should go back east as soon as possible. I didn't want to. I wanted to stay, but my son-in-law insisted that everything would be fine there, that they didn't need me. He had hired a nurse, you see, to take care of my daughter who couldn't even get out of bed anymore, and he said the nurse would take care of the children, too. He said I was risking my own life by staying in that climate. When we got home from the doctor, my suitcase was already packed by the nurse, and my son-in-law had the airplane ticket for me. It took a long time for me to realize it had all been planned. I didn't want to fly; I had never flown in a plane before. But he said it would be an adventure. He had arranged to have my brother-in-law meet me when I landed at Idlewild."

Bridget sat back against the chair again; her face was dark and her body stiff. "Did they at least have the decency to let you say goodbye to your daughter?"

"Yes, I said goodbye, but she was sleeping and I didn't want to wake her. She only lived two more days after I left. I got to kiss her goodbye." The pain in Germaine's heart made her take a deep breath twice. Then she said, "But not the children. They were at a friend's house, you see, and it was a long ride to the airport in Arizona, so we had to leave before the children came home. I couldn't kiss them goodbye. I couldn't tell them I loved them. There wasn't enough time."

Bridget said nothing, so Germaine said, "They wrote to me and I to them."

"Wrote?" Bridget asked.

"The first year they wrote a lot, but they were just little children then. They stopped writing altogether a few years ago. They used to send me Christmas and birthday gifts, but that stopped. And about six years ago, my son-in-law wrote to ask me not to send them gifts anymore. They were too old and I should save my money. He told me it always confused them, anyway. It would get them asking painful questions. I didn't want to make trouble for them, so I stopped. I get a Christmas card every year, though, with a photo. I'll show you." Germaine went into her bedroom and took a card from her bedside table and brought it back to Bridget. "They're growing up so much. They're teenagers now."

Bridget looked at the photo while Germaine stood beside the chair and looked at it too. "My granddaughter, Alice, looks just like my Eunice. Isn't she a beauty? But the boy, Donald, is the spitting image of my husband. Neither one of them looks like their father. That must bother him."

"Too bad about him," Bridget said under her breath. She looked at the signature on the card and read, "Bob, Ginger, Alice and Donald. Who's Ginger?"

Germaine took the card and photo from Bridget's hand and said, as she walked back into her bedroom, "The nurse."

Bridget finished her eggnog and carried the glass into the kitchen.

She was rinsing it out just as Germaine walked in. "Oh, don't bother yourself with that. I have nothing else to do."

The Irishwoman turned from the sink and hugged Germaine tightly. "I'm so happy I stopped by to see ye and say Happy Christmas," she said.

Germaine patted her back. "I am, too. It was nice to have you here."

Bridget pulled back and said, "Are ye lonely, Mrs. Sommer?"

Germaine thought it over a moment and then said, "I was…very lonely, though I really didn't know it. Then Mrs. Walsh asked me to babysit for Audra and that changed things. From the first day, when that little blond head came into the apartment with a shopping bag filled with games in one hand and a little ball for my Corky in the other, I haven't been lonely since. And I've changed her life, too. Before then, the poor little thing wasn't allowed outside all day long while her mother worked. She wasn't allowed to cross the street where all the little girls in the neighborhood lived. I take her down every day now, and cross her, and I sit in a chair and crochet and let her play with her little friends. She's a different girl because of it. And now that she's in school, I walk up to Saint Patrick's every afternoon to get her, and we go to the park when it's not too cold, and I push her on the swings. She's shy, and it's hard for her to make friends. I don't understand why, but the other children at school don't bother much with her. They tease her something awful. But there's a little girl from down the block that she's gotten very close to…a little Jewish girl."

"A Jewish girl? She doesn't go the same school with Audra, then?"

"No, I don't know what school she's in, but she is nice and polite. She's a beauty—as dark haired and dark eyed and Audra is fair. She's a giggler, too, and I love to hear them playing with their dolls."

"Do the Walshes know?" Bridget asked.

Germaine nodded, "They do. They even allowed Audra to stay and eat with the family on one of the Hanukkah nights. Audra was all abuzz about it…how they lit candles, and the mother put a black lace veil over her head first, and how they played with a funny looking top, and how Hannah's father gave them chocolate that looked like gold coins. Hannah has two older brothers."

Bridget smiled then. "How interesting…I've never been in a Jewish home meself."

"And then Hannah came over to the Walsh apartment to decorate their Christmas tree with Audra. My goodness, Mr. Walsh makes a big affair of it all…he must have dozens of boxes of ornaments and tinsel. And Mrs. Walsh made eggnog and cookies and they sang carols. A night later, Hannah's father came over with one of his sons and they asked if Mr. Walsh would help them pick out a Christmas tree and some trimmings because Hannah was begging her parents for one and they had no idea what to pick."

Bridget was astounded. "Not really?"

"So, off goes the two little girls with their fathers, and Paige and the brother—who looked to me like he couldn't take his eyes off Paige—and they all go down to the supermarket and pick out a live tree and some lights and ornaments, and Mr. Walsh and Paige helped them put the tree up."

Bridget laughed when Germaine added, "Mr. Walsh kept calling it their Hanukkah bush!"

They sat quietly for a few minutes, each in her own thoughts, until Bridget said, "Well, I'd better go back to my apartment and let you get to bed. You'll have a long day tomorrow. I wish I had a car. I'd drive you to your sister's house. I hate that you have so far alone."

Germaine and Corky walked Bridget to the door, "Mr. Walsh offered to drive me, but I don't want to take him away from Audra on Christmas morning. And I've been doing it for years…every Christmas since my husband died."

Bridget picked Corky up, kissed the top of his head, and let him lick her chin in return. "Does this one go, too?"

"No, the Walshes will take care of him. He'll be with his Audra; he won't even know I'm gone. Mr. Walsh loves to play with him, and Mrs. Walsh feeds him treats he probably shouldn't have. Paige is an animal lover of the highest sort. He'll be in good hands."

Bridget nodded and bid goodnight to Germaine again. "Have a good holiday, Mrs. Sommer. Have a grand holiday."

Germaine closed the door behind her neighbor and listened until she heard the door next to hers close and lock. *Poor girl*, she thought, *so far from home and all alone*. She'd have to have her for Sunday dinner soon. And to think she brought me a present. A present…*for me*…from someone who doesn't have to give me a present.

Now fancy that.

6E

KRAMER

"We'll be leaving for Florida the day after New Year's Day if it doesn't snow. Ach, the traffic will be terrible of course, and it takes us three days to drive down there...sometimes four. We'll send you a crate of oranges and grapefruits, Martha, as usual."

Joseph pulled a playing card from his hand and put it on the card table. His friend, Hy, dealt him another one. "The traffic is heavier every year," Hy said. "All of us snow birds heading down to Boca at the same time. I don't know why we can't leave a week later...even a month later. No, she has to get down there in January."

Martha laid down three cards. "I understand why Shelly wants to go so soon. Life becomes so dull after the holidays. The days are long and cold and dark. I dread it myself."

Joseph glanced up at his wife. She'd been dropping hints like this for more than a month. All through December, on Hanukah especially, she was wistful and quiet, talking about how she dreaded the winter months.

"You and Joseph should come down and stay with us for a week. Maybe you could find a place near us and be snow birds, too," Shelly said, laughing and placing her many-ringed fingers on Martha's arm. "Just think what fun we would have."

"Who would you send oranges to if we moved down there, too?" Joseph asked, smiling, studying his cards.

"My children, my sister, why I have so many people to send oranges to that I...oh, you're just teasing me, Joseph Kramer."

Joseph leaned over and kissed Shelly's cheek. "I am...it's too easy and too much fun to tease you."

"Well, I say you *should* do it," Hy said, playing his cards. "It would do you good. Once I retired, I knew I'd go crazy staying in New York all winter. I was getting bored stiff. And the cold bothers my knees now. Down there I golf all winter and my knees don't hurt a bit."

"Joseph is anything but bored," Martha said without taking her eyes from her cards. "He's busy all week, and even on the weekends sometimes."

"Doing what, I'd like to know?" Shelly asked, looking surprised.

"I'd like to know, too," Hy agreed.

Joseph stiffened. He'd told Martha he was with Hy at the club just a few nights earlier. Would she say it...would Hy deny it?

"I keep myself busy at the library," he said quickly.

Martha looked up from her cards. "The library?"

"And at the club and the ACI, of course...there, too. But I'm doing research at the library." He wondered if the blush creeping up his neck would give him away. Would they suspect he was lying?

"Research?" Hy asked, very interested now. "Research for what, I'd like to know."

"I'm...researching...I'm thinking of writing a book." Joseph's stomach turned and burned. "I'm out," he said, throwing his cards on the table.

"What are you doing?" Hy said, indicating the cards with his fingers. "You have two pair and you're out?"

Joseph hadn't even noticed the pair of fours and eights. "I'm kidding," he said, trying to smile and knowing that the smile must look tight and phony.

"Some kidding...are you sick?"

"I've been begging him to go to Dr. Haber," Martha said then. "He's not himself lately."

"Now stop...I just don't feel like playing any longer. We've been at it for hours."

When the three of them looked at him with curious frowns, he said, "Besides, Santa Claus will be here soon. We should go to bed or we'll find coal in our stockings."

"We're Jewish, Joseph," Shelly said. "The only stockings I have are nylon and my feet smell so bad that Santa wouldn't want to come near them with coal let alone anything else...maybe air freshener...I don't know."

Joseph and Hy laughed out loud and Joseph kissed his friend's cheek again. "You make me laugh, Shelly. You always have." He poured red wine into her almost empty glass.

"What's the book about?" Martha wanted to know. She was holding the fan of cards against her red dress just under her throat. There was no mirth in her eyes. They were dark and probing.

Joseph realized that she wasn't going to let it go. "Being Jewish in a Christian country at Christmas," he told her. His eyes held hers.

He wouldn't look away. If he did, it would be over...she would know he was lying.

"I like it," Hy said, pondering it. "I think it has possibilities." The stout and balding Hy leaned back against the folding chair and put his left arm over the back, thinking the topic over carefully. "You've got something there, I think."

"It's not easy," Shelly agreed. "You could interview Jews about it...about how hard it is to be in school and have to sing Christmas carols—especially religious ones—and know your father, the *Rabbi*, is sitting in the audience."

"And the Christmas trees...two years my father agreed to have a tree...but both years, they fell down. What do you want from a Jewish man and his sons...what do we know of putting up a tree in our parlor? Ach, it was not a pretty sight, I tell you that." Hy shook his head remembering the fiasco. "After the second year, my mother said no more. We'd celebrate Hanukah, and go to the Jewish Catskills for Christmas. Where is it written that we have to have shrubs in the house? Not even in the Christian Gospels does it say it."

Martha continued to stare at Joseph, and he continued to hold the stare. Then he smiled gently, winked at her, and she looked away. She put the cards on the table and stood up. "More coffee, Shelly? Hy?"

Shelly waved her hand. "I've had enough...I won't sleep as it is. I'll just finish my wine and we'll go. Get our coats, Hy."

"Where'd I park the car?" Hy asked. "Was it on this street or the next?"

"Ach, you are such an *alter kocker*," Shelly said, shaking her head. "You can't remember your name sometimes. It's on *this* street—on the other side—don't you remember? It's in front of the other apartment building." She picked up her glass and the small china plate that her cake had been on and walked into the Kramers' kitchen, saying as she went, "He's driving me crazy lately."

Martha patted Hy's shoulder. "I'll get your coats," she said gently and went into the bedroom.

Joseph carried his and his friend's empty glasses into the kitchen. Shelly turned to him when he entered, took his arm and whispered, "Bring her down to Florida, Joseph. She's sad lately. I don't know what's wrong with her, but maybe she needs a change of scenery. We have plenty of room. Maybe it will do you good, too. We have libraries in Florida."

Joseph had to chuckle at her last sentence. She was so serious. "We'll see...we'll see," he told her. "I don't like driving so far, but we'll talk."

There was a flurry of putting on coats and gloves and hats...kisses and hugs...and wishes of a happy new year, a safe trip...more invitations...and several goodbyes. As Shelly passed the hall table, she noticed a hand-made card and picked it up in her beige kid-glove. "What's this?"

Martha smiled and said, "The little girl next door made us a Hanukkah card. She wanted to send us a Christmas card, but her mother explained that we celebrate Hanukkah and not Christmas, so she made that for us. It's sweet, isn't it?"

It was made of blue and white construction paper, and it had a gold Star of David on the front. Inside a child's hand had printed, "Merry Hanukkah, Mr. and Mrs. Kramer from Audra Walsh."

"Think of that," was all Shelly said.

"Her older sister helped her with it. She's a teenager."

"Well, well, who'd have thought? It *is* sweet."

There were more goodbyes and kisses, and Joseph walked to the elevator with his friends. "I'll go down in the elevator with them," he said to Martha. "I'll make sure Hy finds his car."

She waited until they were all on the elevator before she closed the door.

She finished bringing the dishes to the kitchen then took the white embroidered tablecloth off the card table and put it on the chair. It was clean; it just needed a good shaking out of the window.

Martha turned the folding card table onto its side and pinched the lock on one of the legs to close it. She took her time doing the other legs, then carried it into the bedroom and slid it behind her chest of drawers. When that was finished, she folded the four matching chairs and put them in the hall closet, wondering why they never just used her dining table to play cards. It seemed ridiculous, but Joseph said that it was easier to play cards on a card table. The dining table was too big to reach in the middle.

Martha glanced at the elaborately scrolled walnut wall clock that hung in the living room. Ten-forty…it was late and she was tired. She flirted with leaving the dishes until the morning. She and Shelly had rinsed the dinner dishes and she'd do the same with the dessert plates. They could wait until she got up tomorrow. But then she changed her mind. She'd rather get up to a clean kitchen. How long would a few dishes and pots take?

She filled the sink and washed the crystal stemware first, then the dishes, rinsed all of them in hot water, and put them on the rubber drainer. She took a clean dish towel out of the cabinet and wiped the china dry, then stacked each plate on the kitchen table. Joseph would help her carry them to the living room to put away in the china closet.

The pots took longer, especially the roaster that she had used for the chicken. She poured detergent and baking soda into the black enamel vessel and ran hot water into it. She'd leave it soaking for the night.

She straightened the kitchen, wiped down the stove until it shone, swept the floor, and hung the dishtowel on the side of the sink to dry.

When she returned to the living room, the clock read ten after eleven. Where in the world was Joseph all this time? That Hyram, he must be keeping Joseph talking in the lobby. Shelly wasn't much help, she was such a yenta. Joseph should have known better than go down with them.

Martha saw the tablecloth on the chair and picked it up. She went over to open the living room window. The two windows were at the front of the building, overlooking the courtyard and out toward the street. She was surprised to see that there was a blanket of snow on the ground...just a little, but it was snowing steadily. The cold air was a shock to her lungs.

She took the tablecloth in both hands and shook it out...cake and cookie crumbs joined together with the heavy snowflakes. She could see them in the ambient light from the other apartments on the lower floors as they floated down with the snow. She loved the snow. She'd miss it if they moved to Florida. She leaned on the window sill for a long moment, breathing in the cold, fresh air.

Martha hoped that Joseph wasn't out in this weather helping Hy look for the car...he had no coat on.

She started to pull the tablecloth inside and the light caught the diamonds on the bracelet at her wrist, a Hanukkah gift from Joseph just the week before. It sparkled when she turned her wrist this way and that.

"A diamond bracelet?" she had said when she opened the black velvet box. "Joseph...so expensive...what are you doing? Can we afford this?"

Joseph had taken the box from her hands and pulled the bracelet out. He placed it around her wrist and fastened it. He took her hand and turned it up, then he kissed the underside of her wrist where the bracelet lay against her skin. His lips had lingered there. She could feel her pulse quicken beneath his mouth...her stomach tightened a little as it had long ago when she was aroused.

He said nothing else. He didn't smile. He didn't ask her to sleep with him, which she half expected and didn't mind the thought of at that moment. When she tried to say thank you, he raised his hand to stop her. He simply kissed her wrist again and then left the room.

Her Joseph was sick. She knew it the moment he kissed her wrist. He was dying...of what she had no idea. Cancer? Something else? A disease whose name she'd never be able to pronounce? He was waiting until the holidays were over to tell her. Four times during that week she was going to ask him. Four times she was going to say, "Tell me, Joseph. I can handle it. What are you dying from?"

But she didn't. She was afraid to hear it. She *knew*...but still, until it was said in words, she didn't have to face it. And he probably felt the same way. If he told her, it would be real and they'd *have* to deal with it.

He wasn't at the club all day long. She had suspected as much. He must be going for medical tests. All alone, with no one to hold his hand. And now she knew he was going to the library, too. He said it tonight. But he wasn't doing research for a book. He was doing research about this unnamed disease that would take him away from her. A disease that would destroy their quiet life together…destroy Martha because there was no life without him.

Her Joseph was sick …her dear, gentle Joseph…was dying.

 OTIS

Frances knew he hadn't intended it. It was as much a surprise for him as it was for her that he was in the courtyard just as she was coming home. It took all the strength she had not to run into his arms.

His hand was raised, he was waving to people who were walking away from the building—most likely the friends he had told her were having dinner with him and his wife that evening—and his hand froze in mid-air when he saw her turn into the courtyard. If the people looked back... if they were present there just outside the courtyard...she didn't know, because all she could see was Joseph.

All day, throughout the entire Christmas Day at her parents' home in Elmhurst, she thought of him. What was he doing now...and what about now...and now? Was he laughing? Was he miserable? She had watched the clock, wondering at every hour if he was thinking of her, too. They had agreed that they wouldn't see each other that week, especially not on Hanukkah or Christmas Eve and Christmas Day, not under any circumstances. It was too risky.

And then there he was, standing in his gray suit and white shirt, no overcoat, no hat, no tie...just Joseph in the light of the lamps on each side of the building doors.

The first flakes of snow had started to fall, and some glistened on his dark hair and shoulders. She stopped walking for a moment, just to look at him as long as she could, then approached him slowly. Joseph opened the door for her without speaking and put his key into the inside lock. He was trembling. He pushed the door open and she moved past him, breathing in his aftershave.

Side by side, but not touching, they walked to the elevator, and Joseph pushed the button. It came quickly. Joseph pushed the number "6" on the brass panel, and the doors closed. The elevator started to lift.

Without either of them saying a word, he reached over and took her waist in his hands and pulled her to him. Frances reached out and pushed the "stop" button. They were caught between the second and third floors, but they didn't look to see where they were, because they buried themselves in each other's arms.

Hungry...*starving*...for him, she opened her mouth and accepted his lips, his probing, insistent tongue. She unbuttoned her wool coat and his hands found her breast over the thin silk dress she wore. She knew he could feel her nipples harden under his touch. He lowered his head to graze on her neck and shoulder, claiming whatever skin he could with his mouth, pushing the coat farther down her arms, until she was restricted and couldn't move them, completely his captive. He pushed her against the wall of the elevator and pressed his hips closer, as hungry for her as she was for him.

Frances's head fell back and Joseph's lips found her throat beneath her chin. She wanted to hold him, but she was still imprisoned by her coat and his hips. He was in control and she could do nothing but accept. She felt dizzy and the longing for him grew so intense that she whimpered and her knees buckled.

He held her up and kissed her lips again, more gently, more longingly than he ever had before.

"Joseph, please...I need you so much. I feel faint with it."

He was almost in a frenzy after she said that. She had never seen him like this, pulling her hair back to open her face to his, pressing her against the elevator wall, his mouth insistent and insatiable, his right hand moving over her, trying to feel her body under her thin dress. He pulled at her hem and his fingers moved up to find her, and she collapsed against him unable to breathe when they found their mark.

Someone was ringing for the elevator. Joseph groaned. He moved away from her, his eyes black and haunted. He pulled her coat up onto her shoulders. She rolled into the corner of the elevator, pressing her face in it. She couldn't imagine how she'd regain control of herself. He picked up her gloves and handed them to her, then straightened his clothing.

He pulled the "stop" button out, glanced through the tiny round window to see where they were, and then pressed the button for the third floor.

Joseph glanced at her once, and then left her alone in the elevator.

Frances pushed herself away from the corner and wiped her mouth with her gloves. She ran her fingers through her hair. The elevator didn't stop at any other floors, and she took a long breath before getting off when it stopped on the sixth. She pushed the door open and the hall was empty. Her hands were shaking when she tried to push the key into the lock of her apartment.

The door behind her opened. She spun around and Mrs. Kramer was standing there in the doorway. She wore a beautiful red dress and black velvet high heels. There were pearls at her ears and a diamond bracelet

78

sparkled at her wrist when she raised her hand against the doorjamb. Her salt-and-pepper hair curled softly around her face and there was high color in her cheeks. Frances knew the woman was attractive, but she'd never seen her look as lovely as she looked at that moment.

"Oh, I'm sorry…did I frighten you, Mrs. LaCorte? I heard the elevator and thought my husband was on it. He's been gone…"

"I think he's talking to someone in the lobby," Frances managed to say, but she couldn't look at the other woman any longer. She looked down at the key in her hand. "I saw some people talking down there…I thought it could have been him."

"That explains why he's taking so long. I worried that he was outside in the snow without a coat. I don't want him to catch a cold."

Frances shook her head no and turned to unlock her door again.

"Merry Christmas, Mrs. LaCorte. And have a good New Year if we don't see you."

She was so goddamned nice, this woman who stood between Frances and happiness. She was so concerned about her husband…the only man Frances had ever loved…the one man that Frances couldn't live without. She was so goddamned…*there*.

"You, too, Mrs.…Kramer…" Frances had to close her eyes when she said it. The name stuck in her throat.

She pushed her door open and rushed into the apartment. She fell back against the door, nauseated and trembling, and then she heard footsteps…his footsteps…coming from the staircase.

She heard his wife say, "Joseph Kramer, you had me worried…talking in the lobby all this time. Thank God Mrs. LaCorte came up and told me where you were. I thought it was you on the elevator and…"

"I'm here, Martha. Not to worry," he said, his voice husky…heavy.

"You're flushed," his wife said to him. "Are you sure you're all right, Joseph?"

"I'm fine…fine…I walked up, that's all. I'm winded."

Frances heard the door to their apartment close. There was silence in the hallway…silence in her apartment…but inside her head there was a great and frightening wail of frustration and defeat.

Spring 1962

6C

WILLIAMS

Eamon and John carried their tennis rackets on their shoulders as they entered the building. Both were dressed in white tennis sweaters. Eamon had changed into long navy blue slacks, but his friend still wore his tennis shorts and shoes.

They met Frances LaCorte at the elevator. She smiled and nodded at them.

"How are you, Mr. Williams?" she asked.

"I'm wonderful, and you?" He couldn't remember her name for the life of him. He knew it started with La, but no matter how often he looked at the little name card on her mailbox, he just couldn't seem to remember the rest of it.

"It's a beautiful day," she said. "I wondered when spring would finally come. It was a long winter."

John's smile was dazzling, as it always was when he spoke to attractive women. "It's a day made in heaven. Isn't Easter this Sunday?," he asked, looking at Eamon, who nodded. "Perfect for Holy Week…brings me right back to my childhood and I knew we would be getting out for more than a week for Easter. Remember, Eamon?"

"I remember." Eamon laughed. He was always in a good mood when John was around. The other man's charm and love of life were contagious.

They all entered the elevator, and John reached out and took Frances's hand. He said, "We haven't met…I'm John Sullivan."

"And I'm Frances LaCorte," she said, giving Eamon a chance for redemption.

"I apologize for not introducing you to my friend here, Miss LaCorte. How rude of me…but then I always hesitate introducing him. I'm afraid people will hold it against me."

They laughed. "He seems harmless," Frances told him, pretending to eye the other man critically.

"Don't bet on it," Eamon told her.

The elevator stopped at the fourth floor and a resident that Eamon didn't know opened the door and said, "Going down?"

All three of them answered "No" and then laughed again. The man waved them off, "I'll walk down … it will do me good."

The door closed and John looked over at Frances again. "He'll walk."

She smiled, "It will do him good."

They chuckled again, enjoying the private joke, and then left the elevator together when it stopped.

"Have a good day…or rest of your day," Frances LaCorte said to them as she unlocked her door.

"Nothing will top meeting you," John said, flirting outright with her. Eamon noticed that she blushed a little before entering the apartment.

Eamon shook his head as he led his friend to his apartment. "You just can't help yourself, can you?" He threw his keys on the hall table and leaned his tennis racket against the wall.

"She's an attractive lady…sexy," John said.

Eamon realized that he had called her Miss but it occurred to him now that she had introduced herself as "Mrs." when they met years ago. He winced and said, "Damn, I think I called her miss."

"You did," John said, throwing his tall, lanky body onto the sofa and placing his arm behind his head as he stretched one leg out on the couch.

"She's not…a miss, I mean…she's a Mrs."

"She's got a husband?"

Eamon shrugged, "Somewhere…but not in that apartment. She's divorced I guess, or a widow. I don't know the story."

"Well, whatever she is, she's a hot commodity…"

"Shut up," Eamon said. He threw the newspaper at his friend. "Make yourself at home…I'm going to the john…sorry, the head."

The other man groaned and covered his eyes with his arm now. "Will someone please tell me why does everyone insist on calling the toilet a john? I mean, don't people realize that there are men named John?"

Eamon was still smiling when he went into the bathroom. He washed his face and combed his hair. He had taken a shower at the tennis club, but he still felt the need to freshen up. John kept the top down on his Impala all the way from Forest Hills, and Eamon felt like his head had been whipped up in a blender. He combed his hair and brushed his teeth.

Eamon took off his sweater and put it in the basket with the other clothes that had to go to the dry cleaner.

"Where are we going for dinner?" he called out to John.

"Oyster Bay?"

Eamon took out his navy blazer and gray flannel slacks. "I'm wearing a yellow shirt," he said.

John appeared at the bedroom door. "Of course you are...let me guess, with your navy blazer and grays." He was holding two of Eamon's Waterford highball glasses filled with ice and Scotch. He held one out to Eamon and they clinked. "To your health," John said, the corners of his hazel eyes crinkling. He was tanned, long, lean...handsome.

When they looked into each other's eyes, Eamon's belly tightened and his breath came a little faster. "To your health, Johnny."

6B

SOMMER

"Mrs. Sommer, wait until you see the Easter outfit Paige bought for me! It's soooo pretty, and so grown up."

Germaine sat in her rocking chair after letting the little girl into her apartment. "It is?"

Audra placed a Macy's shopping bag onto the sofa and pulled out a navy blue jacket dress. The short jacket covered a white bodice with tiny navy blue polka dots. There was a bow at the neck that matched, and a thin red patent leather belt circled the waist.

"My goodness, that is grown up," she told the little girl.

"I know! And wait, look what else." Audra took out a pair of short white gloves, a pair of red Mary Jane patent leather shoes, and white socks trimmed in navy blue polka dots.

"Everything matches! But here's the best of all." Audra pulled out a white pillbox hat. "Paige says it looks just like the kind of hat that Jacqueline Kennedy wears. It's all the rage."

Germaine laughed out loud. "Well, you will have to go to the Easter Parade on Fifth Avenue and show that outfit off on Sunday...you'll be in the in Rotogravure."

Audra frowned and looked at Germaine for a long time before asking, "What's a roto...thing."

Germaine laughed again and hugged the child. "It's a special section of the Sunday newspaper that has photos. Every Easter they take photos of the most beautiful hats on the most beautiful women who are walking in the Easter Parade."

"Oh, well, that's not going to happen because we're going to my aunt's house for Easter and she doesn't live on Fifth Avenue."

"Well, we'll just have to make sure your Daddy takes lots of pictures of you so that we can all remember how beautiful and grown up you look this Easter. Come have a cup of tea with me and some Lorna Doones."

They went into Germaine's kitchen and she put the water in the kettle and lit the stove. "Did you enjoy your shopping trip with Paige?"

"My sister is the best sister in the whole wide world," Audra said, climbing onto one of the chrome chairs at the table. "She took me to Macy's and she bought all those clothes herself with her work money. And then we went to lunch in Rockefeller Center, and we met her boyfriend and went into Saint Patrick's Cathedral. It still has purple velvet on the statues there, but they were getting ready for a big Mass tonight."

"Holy Thursday Mass," Germaine said.

"Right, and then her boyfriend bought us ice cream. I had so much fun, Mrs. Sommer. I wish Paige was home with me all the time and not just on holy days and weekends."

Germaine was wounded, but she tried not to show it. It was only normal for the child to love being with her older sister. Germaine knew she was an old lady...not nearly as much fun. But didn't she do everything Audra wanted to do? Didn't she shower her with love and kisses, take her to the park and let her play outside? Didn't she buy her Chatty Cathy and make pretty clothes for the doll? And when the Chatty Cathy doll was abandoned for the new grown-up doll, Barbie, didn't Germaine sew beautiful ball gowns for the doll? Gowns that matched the prom dresses that Paige wore that season to her proms? Anything Audra wanted, Germaine did for her.

Could it really be true that blood was thicker than water? As far as she was concerned, Audra was as important to her as her own grandchildren were...or would have been if she'd been allowed into their lives. She loved the child as much, surely.

There was a knock at the door, and Audra said, "I'll get it, it's just Daddy."

It was her father. Germaine heard the commotion when he picked Audra up and gave her big kisses all over her face. If the child lacked other things, it wasn't affection. She got plenty of that from both her parents and her sister. It was as if she was a doll—a living doll—that they all claimed as their own. Germaine heard the man ask, "And how come you weren't outside waiting for me like you usually are when I come home from work? It's a beautiful day."

"I had to show Mrs. Sommer my Easter outfit. Paige took me shopping, Daddy, and she bought me clothes, and shoes, and we had lunch..."

"Where is Paige now?" he asked.

"She dropped me off and went to her boyfriend's house. She told Mommy she's having dinner there tonight and Mommy said it was all right. And you know what else, Daddy, we had ice cream and went to..."

"Okay, okay, honey, get your stuff and let's go."

Germaine came from the kitchen and said, "I just made her a cup of tea,

Mr. Walsh. Will you stay and have one with us…it's all made…and she loves her tea and Lorna Doones."

The big man looked a little surprised, and Germaine knew it was because she had never invited him to stay in all the time she'd been babysitting his daughter. Normally, on nice days she brought Audra down to the street at this time of day because Audra loved to wait for him outside and then run to him and throw herself into his arms when he appeared at the corner. He always had a few pieces of chocolate in his pockets or a stick of gum to give her. When they all got to the sixth floor, Audra would go into their apartment with him. Germaine's work was done…although taking care of Audra was anything but work. It was the joy of her life. And on the days when they weren't downstairs, he'd just ring the bell or knock, and Audra would take his hand, he would thank Mrs. Sommer and they'd go home. He rarely came into Germaine's apartment after work.

When Germaine would ask him to fix something for her, which didn't happen often even though he was always happy to help her out, she would just thank him and he'd leave.

"I'd love a cup," he said, smiling.

His frame looked too large for the chrome chair, and he seemed to fill up the kitchen with his bulk. He was still in his work clothes, but his hands were clean and he had changed into a clean shirt at work.

"Do you have to work tomorrow?" Germaine asked him.

"No, they give us Good Friday off. My wife is home, too."

"Three day weekends are always nice."

He nodded and put two spoonsful of sugar into the cup and some milk and sipped gingerly at the hot tea, while Audra dipped her Lorna Doone into the cup and quickly put the dissolving cookie into her mouth.

"I thought you'd be out playing on a beautiful day like this," Mr. Walsh said to his daughter again. "It must be 80 degrees out there… and it's only April."

"No, I was busy today doing grown-up things with Paige," she said to him. "She bought me a beautiful dress, Daddy."

"Where'd she get the money?"

"She said it was from her paycheck from work. She worked overtime at the store so she could buy herself and me new Easter outfits."

Germaine noticed that his eyes changed. They looked darker.

"Since when is she buying your clothes? I thought she turned her whole paycheck over to her mother?"

Audra's eyes changed too. "Are you mad, Daddy?" She looked worried. "I don't care about playing outside. I don't have that many friends anyway." She sounded so sad.

"What do you mean? You have friends," he said, picking up a cookie and handing it to her.

85

Audra sighed, "Not really. The girls across the street don't like me that much. They'll only play with me if they don't have each other to play with. Camille—she's older—and she tells them, 'Don't play with that dumb Polack.' So now they don't want to play with me. They leave me out."

"Polack? You're not a Polack," Mr. Walsh said. "You're Irish. Why does she think you're Polish?"

Audra looked up at him. "I don't know, Daddy...what's a Polack, anyway?"

He waved the question away with his large hand. "It doesn't matter. They don't have to play with you if they don't want to...you're better 'n them, anyway. At least your mother thinks so."

Germaine tried to defuse the issue when she saw how angry Mr. Walsh was becoming. He was in such a nice mood when he walked in, and she was alarmed at how quickly that mood was changing. The last thing Mrs. Walsh needed was his acting up at Easter.

"They're just children, Mr. Walsh. You know how kids are."

"I don't want my little girl called any kind of names...especially by the likes of them."

"No, of course not," she said calmly. "I spoke with Camille's mother myself and told her what happened. She said she'd take care of it."

"I'll go over there and give them a piece of my mind. Who does that kid think she is?"

Audra said, "I have to go to the bathroom. I don't feel good."

Germaine knew that the child was upset. She always complained about her stomach when her father's temper flared and she thought he was going to fight with someone—especially her mother or sister. She watched as the little girl ran into the bathroom. Mr. Walsh looked annoyed. "She gets sick a lot. I wonder if she has an ulcer. I had ulcers...had half my stomach removed because of them. I was only in my twenties."

Germaine wished she had never offered this man a cup of tea. She tried to smile at him and said, "She'll be all right. She just gets upset easily. She's such a sensitive little girl. And she hates when you are upset."

"What do you mean by that?" he asked, his face turning a dark red now.

"Only that she's so attached to you."

He pushed his cup away from him. "Why doesn't she have friends on the block? When I was growing up, we were never in the house. She hardly plays with anyone."

"She has some friends, Mr. Walsh. There's that lovely little girl that she plays with...Hannah. Audra is just a shy little thing and...tender, you know...she has a tender heart. Her feelings get hurt easily, and that just makes the other kids want to tease her more."

"The only friend she has is Jewish? No kids from school?"

Germaine ignored him. "Have a little more tea."

"What about school friends?" he asked again.

Germaine was amazed. Was this first he realized that his child was lonely?

"Again, it's just hard for her to make friends. But there are a few…"

"It's her mother's fault she's like this." He wagged his finger at Germaine. "Her mother and my step-daughter think they're better than everyone else, and it's rubbing off on my daughter. Before I know it, she'll be looking down on me like they do."

Germaine was alarmed now. His mood was getting darker by the moment. "No, no, that's not it at all. She's afraid of her own shadow and of hurting anyone. She doesn't feel like she's better than anyone, just the opposite, Mr. Walsh. She's timid, and the other kids take advantage of that. They'll all grow out of it. She'll probably be the most popular girl in high school when the time comes. That's how it is."

"My other daughter wasn't like that," he declared. "she always had friends around."

Germaine was puzzled. "Your other daughter?"

He looked surprised that she didn't know. "I had a wife and little girl before I met Eleanor. Both are dead. An accident."

Germaine had never heard about him having a first wife or a child from another marriage. Eleanor Walsh had kept that a secret and even Audra had never mentioned it. Germaine didn't know what to say except, "I'm sorry. I know what it's like to lose a spouse…a child."

"It tore my guts out," he admitted. "I've never been the same. You don't know how much you will miss your child until you don't have her. You don't know how much you love them until you can't be with them. Especially at the holidays…like now…seeing how excited Audra is about Easter…my other child was only six when they were killed."

He swallowed hard now, and downed his tea in a gulp. "I loved them, my wife and girl, more than my own life."

Germaine felt sorry for the man suddenly; his grief seemed so genuine and pitiful. And didn't she know this kind of pain herself? Didn't she feel this way about her daughter…her grandchildren? "Well, of course, you have Paige and Audra, they're your little girls, too."

"I love them…*both* of them. But Paige never warmed up to me. She was poisoned against me by her grandmother—that woman always disliked me."

"Paige isn't your daughter?" Germaine was astonished.

"No…she's from my wife's first marriage. The family was outraged when Eleanor got a divorce, convinced her to leave the kid with them and get a job in New York. Paige lived with them for five years. When Ellie and I met and I asked her to marry me, Ellie's mother blew a gasket. They didn't want her to remarry—her being Catholic and all—and they didn't

87

like me, said I wasn't good enough because my parents were immigrants...poor as Church mice...peasants, her mother called us. Poisoned Paige against me. No matter what I do, she just doesn't warm up to me. She's like that with everyone, though. Aloof...snooty. She doesn't have many friends either...blames me for it because we lost everything and have to live here...in a one-bedroom. She wants privacy, she says. She wants peace...as though anyone has peace in this crummy life."

Germaine was astonished...Eleanor Walsh divorced...she never would have guessed. "How old was Paige when she came to live with you?"

"Seven. I admit that sometimes I feel cheated...it's not easy raising another man's daughter. It hurts. I look at Paige and wonder about my own little girl. They were the same age. I know one thing, my daughter would have given me the love Paige won't. I try to be a good stepfather...I gave her whatever she wanted when I had it...well, her mother did anyway. Her own father doesn't have anything to do with her, hasn't seen her since she was a year old."

Mr. Walsh stood up just as Audra came out of the bathroom. Her eyes were red from crying. Germaine led her into the living room and said, "Don't forget your grown-up Easter outfit, darling." She took Audra's hand and they walked together to the sofa. Germaine started to put the clothes back into the shopping bag, chatting happily about how pretty she was going to look in it, trying to distract the child. It was no good. The thrill of her new clothes, the excitement of Easter, was gone from the little girl now. She knew as well as Germaine did that her father was boiling up inside, and Germaine also knew that Audra blamed herself for it because she told him about Paige buying the outfit and about the girls not liking her.

"You know what," Mr. Walsh said from the hallway. "Would you mind keeping her a little longer, Mrs. Sommer? I think I'll go down to the Erin Pub and have a beer...just to celebrate Easter. I won't have another chance all weekend."

Audra's whole body tensed and fresh tears came into her eyes. "Please don't go, Daddy. Stay with me. Let's watch TV together." She ran and took her father's hand. "You don't have to go to the Erin. Please just stay home with me. We can watch whatever you want on TV. I think there's an old movie on at four o'clock on Channel 9—Fred Astaire, I think; you like old movies with Fred Astaire. And Mommy's coming home a little early today, remember? We were going to the spaghetti restaurant tonight. Don't you remember, Daddy? Please stay home with me and watch television."

Audra's pleas were falling on deaf ears. The man was wallowing in ...what?...self-pity?...anger?...but Germaine clearly realized now that it had nothing to do with the girls teasing Audra.

She wasn't certain why he was acting this way. She wondered if it had anything to do with his talking about his first wife and child...remembering them just as Easter was approaching. Or maybe it angered him that Eleanor had never told Germaine about his other family. He seemed wounded when she acted surprised about their existence.

But why did he need to take it out on the lovely family he had now…the sweet girls that were in his life? Why couldn't he see what he had and how happy he could be if he just let himself be happy?

"I'll be back in time, honey," Mr. Walsh said, picking up the little girl by her elbows and kissing her cheek. "I'll be back long before Mommy comes home, and then we'll go to the spaghetti restaurant."

"No you won't!" Audra wailed. "You don't come home until late when you go to the bar."

He put her down on the floor firmly and what Germaine considered a little too hard. "That's enough. You stay here with Mrs. Sommer. I promise I'll come home early and I never break a promise to you."

He walked out of the apartment and pulled the door closed behind him. They could hear him walking down the staircase, trying to make as quick an escape as he could. Audra just stood staring at the door, her shoulders hunched forward and her head down. The crying had stopped. It hadn't worked anyway. She was powerless to control her daddy when he was like this.

"He's lying. He always breaks his promises," she said to the closed door.

6E

KRAMER

Only a few more days, and they'd be on vacation, their first vacation together since before Joey died. Martha took her third load of laundry from the washing machine in the basement of Ashley Hall, and placed the wicker basket beneath the door of the dryer. As she was putting the wet clothing into the dryer, she heard the elevator stop and someone step out of it.

Martha kept to the business at hand. The person behind her stopped walking and there was silence. Martha glanced behind her shoulder, but couldn't see who it was. She closed the dryer, put her quarter into the slot, and pushed it in. The dryer started up. She turned, saying, "The washing machine is free. I'm finished with it."

Mrs. LaCorte stood in front of her, holding a pink pillow case stuffed with dirty laundry. The woman looked shocked to see Martha.

"Mrs. LaCorte, how are you?"

Martha's neighbor swallowed hard before she answered, "I'm well, thank you. Um…I'll just come back later."

"No, don't be silly. The machine is free, and the rest will be dry in fifteen minutes. It's a light load. Come…come on."

Mrs. LaCorte stood looking as though she didn't know what to do.

"Really, I'll be finished in a few minutes…throw the clothes in." Martha reached over and opened the washing machine for Frances.

"I forgot my quarters," Mrs. LaCorte said then, starting to turn back toward the elevator.

"Ach, don't go all the way back up to the sixth floor. Here, I have a coin purse full of them. You'll give them back later."

Martha counted out four quarters and put them on the side of the machine. "I've forgotten my change purse plenty…and twice now Mrs. Walsh had been down here and gave me her quarters. We all help one another out…we're neighbors. And if you don't pay me back, I know where you live," she said, laughing at her own joke.

Mrs. LaCorte approached the washing machine slowly. Apparently she had sorted the laundry before coming down, because she placed all her whites in the machine and put the half-full pillow case on the floor. She sprinkled powder over the load, put a quarter in the slot, and closed the washing machine door. It started to load with water.

"So, how was your winter?" Martha wanted to know. "You'll be celebrating your high holy days this weekend?"

Mrs. LaCorte's lips turned up into a nervous smile. "Easter? Yes."

"Are you a religious woman, Mrs. LaCorte?" Martha asked, throwing the clothes from the basket onto the folding table. She took one of Joseph's undershirts in her fingers to fold it.

Mrs. LaCorte sat down on a gray metal folding chair near the washing machine. "No, not really. I was raised Catholic, but since my divorce…"

"Ah, yes, I understand," Martha said. Martha was surprised, though. She had thought that the woman was a widow.

"But I go to Mass with my family on Easter," Mrs. LaCorte told her. "My mother always has an early Easter dinner, brunch really."

"That's nice," Martha said, continuing to fold and not looking up. "It's good to be with family on holidays."

They fell silent then. Finally Martha said, "We're going away to the Catskills for a few days on Sunday; a little vacation. It's been years, but now with Joseph retired, I insisted. He keeps himself so busy—busier I think than when he worked—and I thought he was sick during the winter…so sullen and dark circles under his eyes. He wasn't himself. I was convinced he was dying." Martha didn't know why she was going into such detail about her personal business, but she'd held it all in for so long, and now that she knew Joseph wasn't sick, wasn't dying, she wanted to let it all out.

It was just a month ago that she fell off the chair in the kitchen when she was changing the winter curtains to her yellow Swiss dotted curtains for the spring, getting ready for Passover. She hit her head on the counter. Joseph came running from the bedroom and picked her up and put her on the chair. The blood was worse than the cut, but he insisted they go to the doctor.

Dr. Haber had to put two stitches in it…nothing too bad. She sent Joseph out of the examining room because he was fussing over her too much. When they were alone, and Dr. Haber was working with the needle, she found the strength to ask him, "What's wrong with my Joseph? What disease does he have?"

"Disease?" Dr. Haber asked her, standing back. "Joseph has a disease?"

"Don't you know?" she asked, surprised.

"He was here last month with a cold, but other than that, he's as healthy as an ox."

"You can tell me; *he* won't, so I need *you* to tell me," she persisted, convinced that Joseph must have told their doctor to keep it a secret. "You don't know what torture it is not to know what it is and how long he has. I'm losing my mind, doctor. I need to know. I can't sleep, I can't eat..."

Dr. Haber put the needle down and took Martha's hand. "How long have you been thinking this?"

"Since Hanukah...late December."

"Martha, three and a half months you've been putting yourself through this hell?"

He opened the door of the examining room and called to his nurse. "Get me Joseph Kramer's chart." The doctor picked up the needle and began to work on Martha's wound. He said nothing, just worked in silence. The nurse came in and placed the folder on the counter and left again. When the doctor finished stitching Martha's head, and had placed a bandage over the cut, he washed his hands and then picked up the folder. He held it out to her.

"Here, look for yourself. There's nothing in there."

She took it from him, but didn't open it. His word was enough. "Maybe he's going to another doctor?"

"He's not going to another doctor, Martha. He's not sick. He's not dying...right now anyway. I don't know what made you think it, but the man is well."

She sat up and handed the folder back to her doctor. "Then what's been wrong with him? He isn't the same, Dr. Haber. He's thinner, he has the dark circles, and he doesn't want to make love anymore." Martha had blushed deeply when she said the last, but she had to tell the doctor why she thought her husband was ill...maybe dying.

Dr. Haber leaned against the counter and crossed his arms over his chest. "Martha, sometimes when a man retires, he starts to face his own mortality. He feels useless...old...unwanted. All men are different, we all handle things differently. Your husband worked hard from the time he was a boy, always with the numbers and the responsibility of an entire business payroll and budgets, and what all else I don't know. What can we expect? He should just turn it off because someone says, 'Hocus pocus, you're now retired?' No, it can be very difficult for men sometimes. Maybe he was suffering from a little depression, I don't know. But he's not sick. I checked him out when he came in with the cold. I did blood tests, prostate exam, an EKG...I would know, Martha."

Just as Dr. Haber finished his last sentence, there was a soft knock on the door. Dr. Haber opened it. Joseph was standing there, his hat in his hand. "Is she all right? I've been worrying in the waiting room."

Dr. Haber swept his arm around to show Joseph that Martha was fine, sitting up, a bandage on her temple. Both men looked startled when Martha let out a dry sob, loud enough for everyone in the waiting room to hear it.

"Martha?" Joseph asked, alarmed. She didn't know how to answer him...how to explain this great and overwhelming relief she felt and why it was choking her.

For the first time in eight years, Martha gave into tears—a great tide of tears—they welled up and flowed out of her.

She cried so hard, she couldn't breathe.

Dr. Haber pushed Joseph toward her and said, "Hold your wife, Joseph. She's put herself through hell and back in the last three months. Hold her and tell her you're fine...she's fine...life is good. And for God's sake, take her on vacation. How long has it been? Go to the Catskills...have a few days of rest and relaxation. Take her out of those same four walls. Enjoy your life, you schmuck. Be happy you're retired. Stop scaring the hell out of your beautiful wife."

Martha had clung to Joseph then, and he held her tenderly, hushing her, consoling her. "What is it? What's wrong?"

Martha felt so foolish that she had convinced herself that he was dying. She didn't want to tell him, and she was relieved that Dr. Haber hadn't done so.

"It doesn't matter," she said finally, wiping her face. "I'm fine now."

"But Martha, you're so upset...he said you put yourself through hell..."

"It doesn't matter," was all she could tell him. The tears passed and she began to laugh at herself. And then the laughter took control, just as the crying had. She laughed so hard, that Joseph started to laugh with her, even though he didn't know what he was laughing at.

"You're acting like a meshuggeneh," he said, shaking his head, and placing her sweater around her shoulders.

"I *am* crazy...I am a crazy woman, Joseph," she told him. She put her arms around his neck and kissed his lips.

"Martha, not here," he said, worrying that someone would walk in on them. It made her laugh harder.

Remembering it now, as she folded their clothing, Martha touched the healing scar on her temple and smiled.

"You're going away?" Mrs. LaCorte asked in a very low voice.

"Just to the Catskills. A resort there...five days, that's all. Just to get away together."

Mrs. LaCorte looked away. "I didn't know you were going."

"Well, you wouldn't, of course," Martha said. She was puzzled. Poor lady, she must be so lonely. Such a nice looking woman, too. Maybe when they got back from the Catskills, she'd introduce Mrs. LaCorte to one of the widowers she knew. She said she wasn't religious…so, who knows? She knew a lot of mixed marriages that survived.

The dryer stopped, and Martha started to walk over to take out her clothing. She tripped over the pillowcase and accidentally knocked it over onto its side and a few items of clothing fell out. Mrs. LaCorte jumped up and scooped the fallen clothes up and stuffed them back into the pillow case. She pulled it against her chest as though it contained gold.

They looked at each other…Martha's eyes met Frances's eyes.

Clarity came quickly and painfully for Martha.

6D

ALLCOCK

Danny jumped up from the bed. "What the hell is going on?"

The uproar from the hallway awakened both of them. Vera pulled on her robe. "I can't imagine. Do you think the building is on fire?"

Danny took her hand as they rushed to the door. He threw it open and stepped out, at just the same time Eamon Williams did. They looked at each other, and then at where the screaming was coming from.

"Please, Brendan, please stop," Mrs. Walsh was begging her husband, who had Paige by the hair and was trying to pull her back into the apartment. Mrs. Walsh was trying to place herself between her daughter and her husband. The girl was dressed in her street clothes, but Mrs. Walsh was in her nightgown. She was begging. "Let her go. Just let her go. She'll come back inside."

Walsh was pulling at the girl's hair, but Paige was pulling back with all her strength. She held his hand with both of hers, her head was bowed, she was nearly bent in half, but she was fighting back, trying with every muscle to get away from him.

He seethed, his face was red. "Get in here! You're not leaving this house."

She continued to pull away from him. "Let me go. Let me alone." The wail resounded against the marble walls and floor. "You bastard...you lousy son of a bitch...let me alone."

"What did you call me?" he roared and swung her around. When he did, he lost hold of her hair and she reeled and lost her balance. Her forehead landed hard against the marble wall. Her knees buckled, and Danny thought she looked dazed, but she regained her balance. Walsh looked surprised, and leaned over to help her up, but she kicked out and caught him in the knee. He grabbed at his leg, swearing at her.

"Walsh, what the hell..." Danny shouted.

But Vera grabbed his arm and said, "Don't...Danny be careful."

Walsh reached out again for the girl, but she flinched out of his reach. He turned and grabbed his wife. "No!" Eleanor said, covering her face and head with her arms.

"Okay, you want to go," he said to the girl, "then go...get the hell out." He pushed his wife across the hallway. "Take your mother with you. I'm finished...do you hear me? I'm finished."

Eleanor tried to stay on her feet, her arms flailed as she strained to find something to hold on to, but he was too powerful, and she fell hard onto the floor, smashing her elbow and shoulder against the cold marble. Paige ran to her mother to help her up, but by now Eamon Williams had moved out of his apartment. He took the girl's arm and pulled her out of harm's way while Danny helped the older woman off the floor. Bruises had already started to turn dark on the fair skin around Mrs. Walsh's eye and there was a bloody cut on her cheek and one on her hand.

Vera took her other arm as she got to her feet. There was a pause in the hallway as Walsh looked around. He could see that he was outnumbered. "It was an accident," he said to them. When they just continued to stare at him, he backed away from the crowd, over the threshold of his apartment, and slammed the door closed.

"Audra!" Mrs. Walsh breathed. "Audra...oh my God, Brendan, let her come out to me." She wriggled free of Danny and Vera's hands and ran to the door. She banged on it. "Brendan, let me in or give me Audra."

"Go to hell," they heard him say from inside.

Mrs. Walsh placed her forehead on the door and lowered her voice. She was quiet now, controlling her breathing, her voice plaintive. "Come on, Brendan...open the door. Let me in. Audra must be frightened. Our little girl must be so scared."

Paige shook Eamon off her now. "Momma, stop it! Don't plead with him!"

Mrs. Walsh turned toward her daughter. "Paige, be quiet! I have to get Audra out of there."

"He won't hurt her. You know that. Don't give him the satisfaction of pleading with him."

By now Mrs. Sommer and Bridget Riordan were in the hallway. Mrs. Sommer held her robe tight around her throat; her eyes were wide with fear. But Bridget Riordan let her door slam behind her as she walked past the little crowd, past Paige, and right up to Eleanor Walsh. Danny noticed that she was carrying a billy club. She pulled the woman away from the door, and then pounded on it with the club.

"Walsh," Bridget said. "You'll be openin' that door in two seconds, or I'll be breakin' it down meself...and your head with it. Let that child out of that apartment this minute, ya thick, gin-guzzling bullocks! I called the police. They'll be here in minutes, and you're not wantin' that sweet baby of yours seein' you being taken away in cuffs, are ye? D'ye want her watchin' them drag you into the paddy wagon?"

There was a long silence. Bridget banged harder on the door with the club. "Let that little girl out of that flat or I'll bring this club down on your fat head meself before the cops get here!"

Then they heard the lock turn slowly. Eleanor Walsh put her hand to her mouth, and steadied herself. "Be careful," she whispered.

Bridget wasn't the least bit afraid. She stood solid in her spot, legs spread a little, hands on her hips, the billy club clutched firmly in her right fist. Danny would have smiled at the little Irish woman's stance if it wasn't so dangerous for all of them at that moment. There was no telling what Walsh would do...who he would lash out at when he opened that door. Danny pushed Vera behind him and stood ready.

But when the door opened a crack, it was Audra. She was barefoot and in a pink ruffled nightgown. Her eyes were wide and frightened, her hair hung around her face and shoulders. Bridget grabbed her and pulled her out of the apartment. Brendan slammed it shut behind the child and the noise reverberated through the hallway. There were people from the floor below standing at the bottom of the staircase, looking up, mumbling to one another. One called out, "What's going on up there? We've called the police."

Everyone ignored it. Bridget handed the little girl to her sister. Audra flung her arms around Paige's waist and buried her face in her sister's stomach.

Bridget said, "Take her into my apartment."

"No," Vera said. "Come in here to mine. Come on, sweetheart." Vera took Paige's shoulders and led both of the girls into her apartment. Danny took their mother's arm. "Mrs. Walsh, come inside," he said.

She lifted her head, and looked around the hallway. All eyes were staring at her. She crossed her arms over her chest, realizing suddenly that she wasn't wearing a robe.

Then her eyes met Danny's. He smiled gently and nodded. "Come on in ...the girls are in there with Vera."

"I'm so ashamed," she whispered. "I'm so embarrassed."

"It's okay...come on...come with me," he coaxed her and she started to move with him.

Then she looked at Bridget. She asked, "Did you really call the police?"

"I did...and he belongs in jail. Don't be feelin' sorry for him. He can't be doin' this to you and your little girls. He's got to stop."

"He doesn't mean to...something must have happened today to upset..." Mrs. Walsh began to say then stopped when she saw the furious look in Bridget's eyes. She looked away and went with Danny toward

97

his apartment.

Eamon Williams patted her on the shoulder as she moved past him. "You'll be okay now, Mrs. Walsh. Don't worry."

Mrs. Sommer left her apartment door, took Mrs. Walsh's arm, and went into Danny's apartment with her. Bridget stood in the hallway with the billy club held out at an odd angle. It was just Danny and Eamon in the hall with her now. Eamon smiled at her and indicated the club with his head. She shrugged. "A woman livin' alone needs some protection."

"Remind me never to get on your bad side." He chuckled a little. "Are you going back inside?"

"No, I'll stay here until the cops arrive. I want to see them take him away, and I don't want him to slip out before they get here."

Just as she said it, the elevator came to the floor and the door opened. Three officers stepped off and took a long look at Bridget standing with the billy club.

"Not me," she said. She indicated the Walsh's apartment with the club. "In there…he's mad with the drink and he was beatin' up his wife and daughter."

"Are they still in there?" one of the cops asked her.

"No, they're in my apartment, over here," Danny said.

One of the officers went into the Danny's apartment, while the other two went to the Walsh's door. One of them banged on it, and said, "Police, let us in."

The other cop rang the doorbell at the same time.

Bridget said, "He's in a terrible rage."

"Does he have a gun?" the officer asked her.

She shrugged. "I doubt it, though I'm not sure."

"All right, ma'am, get back into your apartment now. All of you, get out of the hallway. We'll take care of this. We'll get your statements in a few minutes."

They glanced at each other and went into their apartments. Inside Danny's apartment, Audra was sitting on her mother's lap, crying softly. They were on the couch, and Eleanor's hand had been bandaged—he assumed by Vera.

Vera had filled a towel with ice and was holding it on Paige's forehead. He noticed that Vera's hands were shaking as she tended to the girl. Mrs. Sommer stood off to the side of the couch, her eyes fixed on Audra.

"So what you're telling me is that he was out drinking and came home about a half hour ago," the cop said to Mrs. Walsh.

"Yes."

"What started the fight?"

"Nothing started it…he just started the minute he walked in the door. A few minutes later, Paige came home."

"Where were you?" he asked Paige.

"At my friend's house."

The cop looked at her for a long minute. "Kind of late for a girl your age to be coming home. Are you sure your father wasn't just reacting to that? Fathers worry about their daughters being out…did you come in after your curfew?"

Paige straightened her back. "My stepfather didn't even realize I wasn't home until I walked in. He was already arguing with my mother. I tried to stop him."

"Did you mouth off to him?" the cop asked. "Did you sass him? What did you do to make him so angry?"

"Are you serious?" Vera asked. She took the towel with the ice away from Paige's forehead. "Look at this kid's head…are you trying to say she deserved this? You're blaming the victim here." They looked at Paige's forehead. There was a goose egg on it that had turned purple and was oozing blood.

Eleanor said, "No, that was an accident. He didn't mean for her to get hurt."

"There's no victim, ma'am…it's a domestic dispute," the cop said to Vera.

"You can't be serious," Vera said.

Danny moved over to stand next to his wife. He put his arm around her shoulders. "Honey, take it easy…"

Vera looked at him now. "I won't take it easy! This is horrible. Do you see how he's treating her? How he's interrogating her? He's supposed to be helping her."

Paige took the towel from Vera's hand and placed it on her forehead, as though resigned. "No," she said to the cop in a flat voice. "I didn't do anything to make him angry. He doesn't need anything to set him off when he's been drinking. It could be something that happened a week ago…a month ago…ten years ago."

Mrs. Walsh spoke up then, "I called her at her friend's house to tell her he was on the warpath. I told her to stay out late. I was hoping she wouldn't be in until after he'd fallen asleep. I was trying to spare her. Unfortunately, he stayed out later than he usually does, and when I called to tell her, she'd left for home already. The timing was all wrong."

"What was he angry about?" the cop asked Mrs. Walsh again.

She just shrugged and looked tired. "Whatever it was, it was something that happened before he got home."

"It's my fault, Mommy, because I told him that the girls across the street won't play with me," Audra said from her mother's arms. She put her hand on Eleanor's cheek to turn her mother's face to hers. "And because I told him that Paige bought my Easter outfit today. I think it's my fault, Mommy.

I made trouble."

Mrs. Walsh wrapped her arms tighter around the little girl and drew Audra's head against her shoulder as though to comfort her, but at the same time she asked, "Oh, honey, why did you tell him that? You know how he is. You have to think before you say anything to him. Now look at what's happened...look what you've done."

Paige sat up in her chair and took the towel away from her face again. "No, baby," she said to her little sister, shooting an infuriated look at her mother. "You're not to blame for this...it's not your fault. Don't think that. Tell her, Momma, that it's not her fault. She's only ten years old. She should not feel guilty...tell her, Momma."

Eleanor looked at her older daughter for a long moment, and Danny could see that there was some sort of challenge going on between them. Then Eleanor said to Audra, "No, of course not, it wasn't your fault, honey."

Mrs. Sommer shook her head and looked as though she was going to cry. Danny said, "How about something to drink? Why don't I make some coffee?"

Vera smiled at him then, knowing that Dan wouldn't know how to put on a pot of coffee if someone paid him. "That's a good idea; I'll make some," she said, "and how about some hot chocolate for Audra?"

Just then, they heard another commotion in the hall. Audra threw her hands up over her ears and hid her face in her mother's shoulder. Paige jumped up from her chair and moved over to her mother's side of the room, standing slightly in front of her mother and sister, defensive... protective.

The cop stood up, too. "Don't panic. We won't let him near you. We might arrest him."

"What do you mean?" Danny asked. "You might arrest him?"

"Well, as I said, it's a domestic dispute, and..."

Paige spoke up. "Arrest him for drunk and disorderly conduct...the whole apartment house will attest to that at this point. Give us tonight to get out of the apartment. If you don't arrest him, he'll be worse than before. He'll blame us for the police being called. He'll blame us because the neighbors got involved. Please. I'm begging you. You can arrest him for drunk and disorderly conduct and keep him overnight."

The cop looked at Paige. "You've been through this before? You know the routine?"

She nodded. "Yeah, I know the routine."

Eleanor Walsh said, "Ah, Paige, don't make them arrest him. You're exaggerating. He'll just go to sleep."

"Mother! You know what he'll do if they don't take him. How can you say that?"

"And you know what he'll do tomorrow and the next six months if we let them take him." Eleanor's voice was almost a shriek now.

"Ma'am, that's out of your hands," another officer said, walking into the room. "We're taking him in. I can't calm him down. He took a swing at me."

Vera gasped. "Do you mean to tell me that you can arrest him now because he took a swing at one of you, but you can't arrest him for beating his daughter and wife?"

The cops looked uncomfortable. Then they heard Walsh calling out.

"Ellie! Eleanor, get out here. Tell them to let me go. I didn't hurt you on purpose. Paige...Paige, it was an accident. I'd never hurt you...you know that. Come out here; tell them that."

Audra started to whimper again. "Mommy...Mommy, what are they doing to him? Are they hurting him? What are they doing to Daddy?"

"Nothing, honey, be quiet. It's all right," Eleanor Walsh told the little girl. She put her bandaged hand over the child's ear and held her head tightly against her shoulder so Audra couldn't hear what was going on in the hallway.

"Momma, if you go out there to him, I'll never forgive you." Paige said, pulling the towel of ice away from her head again. "Look at me." Her entire forehead was swollen and purple now. One eye was beginning to swell shut.

Walsh's voice came from the hallway again. He was crying now, begging, "Eleanor, please help me."

Eleanor Walsh closed her eyes. "Dear God, help me. Holy Mary, Mother of God, please, help me."

The officer who had just come in turned and went back out, shouting, "Get that asshole out of here, please. Shut him the hell up."

"Momma," Paige said, warningly. "Momma, don't do it. I can't take it anymore. When will it stop unless you stop it. Don't do it."

"I won't," Eleanor said to Paige. "I won't ever let him do that to you again. I promise you." She started to cry.

Paige knelt next to her mother. "It's okay...don't cry...but no more, Momma. Promise you won't bail him out tonight. You have to promise me."

"I do...I promise, Paige."

"And we'll move out tomorrow, right? Before he gets home?"

"Yes, yes, of course. We'll go to the YWCA until I can find a place of our own."

One of the cops said to Danny, "Can we have a statement from you?"

Danny nodded. They walked into the kitchen and the cop asked, "Does this happen often?"

"No...not this bad. It never came out of their apartment before, anyway." After seeing Walsh at his worst, Danny wished he didn't have to get involved…for a moment he thought he'd call his father and ask for the family lawyer's number, and then he remembered, he couldn't call his father for anything.

"Can you arrest him without our statements?"

The cop nodded. "For the night…or until she bails him out."

"Yeah, well then I think I'd rather not give a statement. If you let him go tomorrow, he could come after my wife."

The cop shrugged. "It's up to you."

"Then he will be released tomorrow?"

"We can't keep him longer unless it's something other than a domestic…"

"Dispute…I know."

"Hey, man, if she bails him out, he'll be back before morning."

"She's not going to do that. She just promised her daughter."

The cop sighed and looked away. "Twenty to one he'll be back in the morning, they'll both still be here, holding hands and kissing, and they'll pretend nothing ever happened. The guy won't drink for a week…maybe two…and then it will all start over again."

Danny shook his head. "No."

"Yes. I've seen it over and over. Look, for the record, I can't guarantee it, but this guy isn't going to come after you or your wife. This is personal…between him and the wife and girl. He's probably the nicest guy without the drink in him. Give him a chance and he'll convince you that his wife and daughter are abusive to him."

The other cop came into the room. "The kid needs to go to the emergency room, Mike. I put a call in for the ambulance. She can barely see out of her eyes now. I think she's got a concussion."

Danny looked at the cop named Mike, "And you're telling me he'll be out in the morning? He put his daughter in the hospital, but he'll be out?"

"All right, buddy, are you going to give me a statement or not? I'm not here to argue with you about the law…or how married people act."

"No…no statement."

Mike the cop went into the living room and Danny followed him. "Mrs. Walsh," he said, "your apartment is empty now. He's gone. Do you want to go get some clothes and go to the hospital with your daughter? That eye of yours doesn't look all that great, either, and the cut on your hand might need a stitch. It's bleeding through the bandage. How'd you get that cut?"

Eleanor looked down at her hand as though trying to remember. "He didn't mean it. He threw his fork, but he didn't mean to hit me."

The cop sighed loudly. "Yeah. Well it should be looked at. Do you want to come with your daughter?"

"Yes, of course," she said. She stood up, holding Audra. Danny reached out and took the little girl in his arms. She was as light as a bird, but her whole body was trembling.

The ambulance technicians arrived and brought a stretcher into the apartment. Paige groaned. "Oh, please, I don't need that."

Danny put the little girl on the couch next to Mrs. Sommer who held her arms out for her.

The cop took Paige's arm and gently led her to the stretcher. She sat down and the ambulance people swarmed around her, looking into her eyes with flashlights, taking her pulse and blood pressure, listening to her heart.

"Really, this isn't necessary. You're scaring my baby sister," Paige said, worrying about Audra who had buried her face in a pillow on Mrs. Sommer's lap. "If you take us to the hospital, who'll take care of her? We can't leave her alone. I'm really fine."

Paige looked so young suddenly…so powerless…and frightened. Danny felt that he had betrayed her by not making a statement. By the look on her face, the kid would spend the rest of the day in the hospital, longer if she had a concussion. How could her mother move out as she had promised? Where would they go?

And what if the cop was right? What if the mother bailed him out…took him back? She'd obviously done it before. Suddenly Danny realized that the girl knew that's exactly what would happen. Just as the cop knew it. She'd been through it all before…how many times, he wondered? How many times had the mother promised it was over, and then put the kid right back into harm's way?

Danny walked over to the stretcher and hunched down next to Paige. "Hey, Paige, don't argue with them, okay? Just lie down and let them help you. Audra is fine. I promise we'll take care of her. Mrs. Sommer is here. Doesn't she babysit for Audra?"

Paige nodded.

"Okay, then she'll be fine. Don't worry about her. Let them take care of you. You're the one who needs taking care of right now."

"My mother…"

"She's getting dressed. She's going with you. You'll be together at the hospital."

Paige closed her eyes. Her face was white under the bruises. She continued to hold the ambulance attendant off.

Danny said "Are you afraid? I'll go with you if you want me to. Do you want me to come?"

She shook her head no. "No, thanks, I'll be okay. Please don't be nice to me, Mr. Allcock."

He was taken aback by her request. "Why?" he asked her.

"Because you'll make me cry."

Danny smiled at her and helped the ambulance attendant put the blanket over her. He tucked it under her chin as they strapped her onto the stretcher. "What's wrong with that?" he asked her.

"Because I'm afraid that if I start crying, I'll never be able to stop. Not for the rest of my life."

1963–1969

When lights go out…

Fall 1963

```
ST. PATRICK'S
SCHOOL
1898
```

Germaine stood with the parents of Audra's fourth grade classmates and the other classes at Saint Patrick's School. They crowded around the tall, wrought iron gate that enclosed the compound—the school building, the convent, the rectory and the back of the Church. It was chilly, and Germaine hunched down deeper into her coat. The cold was starting to seep into her bones these days, especially her arthritic knees. She wondered how long she'd be able to walk to the school to get Audra. But that wasn't important now. That wasn't today. Today was a bad day, and she needed to get the little girl and bring her home immediately.

One of the sisters came to the locked wrought iron gate. The nun's face was somber; her eyes were red.

"The children are at the Church," she told the crowd. "They're saying a rosary for the President. They'll be brought out here in the schoolyard as soon as they're finished."

The nun carried black, white, pink and blue plastic rosary beads in her hands. There had to be fifty or more. She unlocked the gate and allowed the parents inside, handing out the rosaries as the adults filed past her. "Won't you pray with us as you wait for your children?"

When everyone was inside and all the rosaries were handed out, she pulled up the larger beads that hung from her waist and made the sign of the cross with the heavy black and silver crucifix. The parents did the same with theirs.

"I believe in God, the Father Almighty, maker of heaven and earth..." she began.

The adults huddled together in the chilly November afternoon and mumbled the words of the prayers they had learned as children, the first prayers they had taught their own children, the prayers that their parents and grandparents and great-grandparents had prayed before them. The go-to prayers of every devout Catholic, practicing or not, when disaster struck...prayers that also belonged to the President of the United States.

Germaine wondered, as she recited the familiar words, was the rosary being said all over the country—the world—at this moment? Were all the voices blended into a single voice, asking for mercy for the man who beat all odds by becoming the first Catholic President of the United States...the youngest man, with a beautiful wife, and a sweet little family...a man who was now lying in a hospital in Dallas, Texas, fighting for his life? Tears stung her eyes and she held the beads closer to her chest as she fingered them. Hail Mary, full of grace...save our president...don't let him die...protect him...the Lord is with thee...

The hum of the recited prayers was going on too long. All she wanted was for Audra to come out of the Church so she could hug her and know she was safe. The mothers who surrounded her wanted the same thing—all of them had run to the school the moment they heard the report on the radio or the television. A mother's response to a national disaster—get the children in the house, lock the doors, keep them safe in an unsafe world.

The children came out of the side door of the Church in lines, two by two, boys on the left, girls on the right, and by class, their coats on and buttoned up, carrying their school bags. The first graders came out first, then the second and third. Germaine watched for the fourth grade, for Audra's frizzy blond hair. The children were quiet this day. There was no end-of-day exuberance. They were stunned. Most of them didn't understand what had happened. How could they?

Germaine wondered how do they do this...these nuns? How do they keep these little children so organized, so obedient—sixty-five in Audra's class alone—and only one nun to keep the chaos at bay?

The pastor, Father Brosnahan, followed the children out of the Church. The schoolyard was overcrowded now as more parents arrived to retrieve their children. Get the kids, get them home, keep them safe.

The usually smiling Father Passarella moved quickly through the lines of children, his face solemn. He whispered into the pastor's ear. Father Brosnahan looked down at the ground, frozen for a moment.

Then the pastor climbed to the top step of the school stoop. Sister Thomasina, the principal, stood on a lower step. He cleared his throat a few times, then lifted the bullhorn to his lips.

"This is one of the saddest days in the history of our country," he said, stopping to clear his throat again. Germaine wondered how there could be such silence amid so many human beings. Even the children didn't make a sound as they watched the priest try to gain control of his emotions.

"We just got word that President John Fitzgerald Kennedy, the President of the United States of America, has died of a bullet wound to his head." His voice cracked. He lowered the bullhorn and added without it, "He's gone…may God have mercy on his soul. May God have mercy on us all."

"No!" a woman screamed, and then sobbed, "No…please don't let it be true!"

A hum went through the crowd, people started to weep, and women clung to one another, leaning against each other to keep from falling to their knees in grief.

Germaine was not one of them. She pushed through the crowd of shocked and mourning adults and broke through to the lines of children. Most of them were too young to understand the importance of that moment, but some of the eighth graders were sobbing and holding one another just as the adults were doing.

She walked directly over to the line where Audra stood, and grabbed the little girl's hand. "Come on, honey," she said.

"But Sister didn't dismiss us," Audra whispered, pulling back into the line. "I can't go yet."

Germaine held Audra's hand tightly in hers, "It's all right. Let's go, I want to get you home. Enough of this."

The child lived with enough drama at home. She didn't need more of it here.

"Mrs. Sommer," Sister Thomas Mary stood in front of Germaine, blocking her way. "We haven't dismissed them…"

"Consider her dismissed," Germaine said. "I'm taking her home right this minute."

They were the first to walk out of the line and to the gate. Within seconds, the other mothers, fathers, and grandparents did the same thing. They held their children tightly.

"Hurry," Germaine said to Audra, and they walked a little faster, in spite of Germaine's painful knees.

"Mrs. Sommer, what is going on?" Audra whined. "Why were all the sisters crying? And why was Father crying? I don't understand what is going on?"

Germaine didn't answer her. The child had to have heard what happened, it just couldn't register with a ten year old.

"Mrs. Sommer, what does it mean that President Kennedy is dead?" Audra was almost out of breath because of the hurried way that Germaine was pulling her. "Mrs. Sommer, you're walking too fast."

Germaine slowed down then. She squeezed Audra's hand. "I'm sorry, honey."

"Will you tell me what's happening?"

"It's just something sad that happened."

"You mean the President? Because he died?"

"Yes, honey."

Germaine had been through this before...in 1914 when she was a young girl and the first World War broke out—a war against her parents' first country, the country where they were born and lived until they were almost adults—and then again in 1939, against the same country, another brutal war. Americans of German descent were suspect, and God forbid they spoke German or English with a German accent. Some lost their jobs, some lost their homes. It was starting again. What country this time? Was it the Russians...the Chinese...Cuba? Not Germany...surely not Germany again.

Would we be at war by the end of the day? Would air raid sirens be screaming in the night?

Germaine let go of Audra's hand and pulled the child close to her hip and they walked. Would the bombs and the guns and tanks be brought to this country this time? Would the children be annihilated from the face of the earth with atom bombs? War would be different now. America had changed that, in Japan, and it didn't make the world safer, it made the idea of war more fearsome—terrifying. Didn't we just go through this fear last year during the Bay of Pigs? We all held our breath then...and now we'll hold our breath again. When will this stop?

Where were her grandchildren? Were they home...were they safe? Her grandson was old enough to be made to fight...was he already fighting? In Viet Nam? In Cambodia?

Germaine and Audra were approaching the corner where Audra's favorite candy store was. The owner, Mr. Schwartz, stood in the doorway, his usually bright smiling face like stone now. A radio sounded behind him.

Germaine walked up to him. "Mr. Schwartz, we'd like some licorice, please; some of the long red strings."

"You haven't heard?" he said to her.

"I've heard..." she answered and moved beyond him and into the store. She let Audra's hand go, and the little girl ran into the store, directly to the counter that displayed all the penny candy.

Mr. Schwartz followed them in. "It's a tragedy," he said.

Germaine looked at him firmly. "We won't discuss it."

He frowned. "Not discuss the most important..."

"Audra," Germaine said. "Tell Mr. Schwartz what you want...you don't have to get the 'spaghetti' licorice as you call it. Is there anything else you want?"

Audra chose the licorice, but she also wanted Turkish taffy, and Germaine said it was fine, she could have both. Mr. Schwartz put it all in a little white bag and rang it up on his cash register. Germaine paid him. She could feel his eyes on her, but she refused to look at him.

Germaine took Audra's hand and led her from the store without saying another word to him. People were gathering on the sidewalks now; neighbors wanted to share their shock and grief, tell what they had heard on Channel 2 or Channel 7 and Channel 4. Germaine could hear the names they were throwing around as she and Audra passed by...*Ron Cochran said that ...Walter Cronkhite actually cried...he was dead by one o'clock their time...they tried a tracheotomy...Connolly is in emergency surgery...it's Castro, no one can tell me different...they've been after him since the Cuban Missile Crisis...we should bomb those commies off the goddamn map.*

Germaine continued to walk, pulling Audra behind her, one block more, a half block, their building was in sight, just get us home, just get us up to the apartment, away from the street, safe...safe.

There were residents of Ashley Hall in the lobby and the courtyard, groups of them, huddled, chatting, crying.

"Did you hear, Mrs. Sommer?"

"Mrs. Sommer, are you all right?"

"Mrs. Sommer, the president has been killed, don't you know!"

Germaine pulled Audra closer to her side. "Just keep walking," she said.

They entered the elevator and Germaine was relieved that it was empty. She let go of Audra and walked into the corner of the lift, leaned her shoulder into the wall, facing the corner and away from Audra.

"Why are you acting so strange?" Audra wanted to know. "I'm scared. Is mommy home yet? Did she get out of work early? Maybe Daddy did; he's probably home by now, don't you think so?"

The elevator stopped at the sixth floor and Audra rushed out first, but instead of going to Germaine's door to the left, she ran to the right, to her own apartment and started to bang on it. "Daddy? Daddy? Are you home?"

The door opened and he stood there, filling the doorway with his bulk, and then he got down on his knee and pulled his little girl to him. She started to cry and he rocked her and hushed her, stroking her hair gently. Then he pulled back and with his coarse swollen thumbs, brushed her hair away from her face and told her not to cry. "I'm here, baby. I've got you."

Germaine's stomach turned. She stood in the middle of the hallway, holding the little white bag of candy.

Brendan looked up at her. "I guess they told them at school. She's shaking like a leaf."

Germaine didn't answer. She threw the bag of candy at the floor, turned around on her heel and went to her apartment.

"Mrs. Sommer? Hey, Mrs. Sommer, are you all right?" She could hear him calling her, but she just unlocked the door, went inside, and let the heavy metal door slam closed behind her.

Still in her woolen coat, Germaine sat down at the kitchen table and put her head in both her hands. There was a high pitched alarm screeching inside her head. Corky put his front paws on her leg, whined for her attention, then got down and sat staring at her.

She could not understand what was wrong with her head. She could not understand what was wrong with Audra…with Eleanor Walsh…with the infuriating, bullying…generous and helpful…Brendan Walsh. Who were these crazy people?

Her own family never treated her with concern and compassion the way Eleanor treated her; it was as though she was Eleanor's own mother. And that man…anything she needed…anything at all…he did it for her. Doctor, pharmacy, store, her sister's in New Jersey…she had only to say she was going somewhere and he got his car keys and met her in front of the building, car running, giving up his parking space when spaces were so sparse.

She wanted to like him, but she couldn't. He was a brute, a bully with his family—that little family she had come to love so much. And yet his wife stayed with him. His little girl cried for him every time something upset her or she was frightened. What madness was this?

Entering into the lives of these people, or rather having them enter into her life, three years ago, was one of the most important things that had ever happened to her…and one of the most disastrous. All boredom was gone; but all peace had vanished since then, too.

Right now…right at this horrid moment when the world was going crazy…she wished she'd never met them, never heard their names, never known they existed. Why couldn't they have moved away after that night he was arrested? Why didn't Eleanor take the money she had offered her that night and gone away, found herself another place to live where she and her girls would be safe and live in peace?

Eleanor would only take $10. That's all she wanted of the $2,000 that Germaine offered her that night. "I'll return it in the morning," Eleanor had said, as the police waited to take her in a squad car to the emergency room. The ambulance with Paige in it had left minutes before. Germaine had Audra in her apartment, already settled down on the sofa in soft sheets and the afghan tucked around her, Corky lying against the little girl's side.

"Why? Why won't you take this and get away before he kills one of you?" Germaine had held out the money she had taken from her hiding place and tried to force it into Eleanor's hand.

"No, Mrs. Sommer, please. I won't take your money. Just take care of Audra until Paige and I get back from the hospital. That's all I need you to do right now. Take care of my baby tonight."

"Do you think I can't afford it? You're wrong, I can; I don't need it. I'm giving it to you. It's not a loan."

"Please, the police are waiting for me. Thank you, but I don't want it. Just take care of Audra for me. I'll be back as soon as I can."

Audra had slept on the couch that night and throughout the morning. Germaine didn't awaken her. At around ten in the morning, Eleanor rapped softly at the door of Germaine's apartment. "Is she all right?" Eleanor asked as soon as Germaine opened the door.

Germaine nodded and opened wider, letting the woman in. The skin beneath Eleanor's left eye was purple and yellow, and her right hand was wrapped in an ace bandage. The last time Germaine had seen her, the night before when the police were taking her to the hospital, she was hurriedly dressed in a housecoat over her nightgown and hard-soled slippers, but when she arrived that morning she was dressed in a lavender crepe dress with a matching coat piped in black, a pink hat and black patent leather high heels. She wore a pearl necklace and pearl earrings.

"I can't thank you enough for taking care of Audra for me. Was she a good girl?"

Germaine was dumbstruck. The woman acted as though she'd been on vacation…not in a hospital holding the hand of her teenaged daughter who had a concussion and two black eyes…not in a hospital being x-rayed and bandaged herself. She looked and acted as though she was getting ready to go to a garden party.

"How is Paige?" Germaine asked. "I've been worrying about her…about both of you…all night, all morning."

Eleanor's face changed; she looked away. "They admitted her. She has a concussion, but she'll be fine."

"What are you going to do?" Germaine asked her in a whisper.

Audra continued to sleep on the sofa, and Eleanor went over and sat on the edge, ignoring Germaine's question. She stroked the little girl's hair and back. Audra opened her eyes, cried, "Mommy!" and threw her arms around Eleanor's neck. "Oh, Mommy, Mommy, Mommy. I missed you."

Eleanor held Audra tight and rocked back and forth, murmuring, "My baby, my sweet baby."

"Mommy, where's Daddy? What did they do to him?"

Eleanor had taken both of Audra's cheeks in her hands and kissed Audra's nose. "He's fine, honey. He's home…do you want to see him?"

"What?" Germaine could not believe what she was hearing.

Again Eleanor ignored Germaine and continued to speak to Audra. "Oh, that daddy of yours; he got himself in trouble last night, didn't he? But the police gave him a good talking to, just like I do to you when you misbehave. I drove over to pick him up and brought him home. He's very sorry, Audra. He didn't mean to get so mad. He just couldn't help himself. You know that, right?"

Audra nodded, but Germaine could see in her eyes that she didn't know it. She was confused, bewildered…just as Germaine was.

"Are you mad at Daddy?" Eleanor asked the child. "I hope not, because it would upset him if you are. We don't want to upset him again, now, do we? When we go back to our apartment, we're not going to mention last night, are we, honey? He's sorry... right? And just like when you or Paige do something wrong and you say you're sorry, I forgive you and we don't talk about it anymore."

Germaine had had to sit down. She felt weak...sick to her stomach.

"I won't say anything to him, Mommy. I promise."

Eleanor hugged the little girl again. "You're my sweet baby. Let's get your slippers on and go home. Was it fun staying at Mrs. Sommer's house? Did you have a pajama party with Corky?"

Remembering it now, at this very moment, on the day John Fitzgerald Kennedy had been shot and killed, Germaine wanted to pick up her sugar bowl and throw it across the kitchen, against the wall. She wanted to hear it crash into smithereens. She wanted to throw things...dishes...anything. For two years she had lived with that scene in her mind, dreamed of it, remembered it at the most unusual times of the day.

Astonishingly, she didn't relive the scene from the night before that...Paige trying to get free of the big man's hand, Eleanor in her nightgown, begging that he let Paige go, him grabbing his wife and throwing her to the marble floor.

That she didn't relive in her mind for two years. Just the scene of the well-dressed bruised and bandaged woman holding her little girl on her lap and delivering in the most subtle way a very clear message that when daddy misbehaves, we forgive him, take him back, and don't throw it in his face in fear that he'll do it all over again. Which of course, he will anyway.

Germaine remembered that while Eleanor was helping her child put on the slippers to go home, she had decided that her relationship with the Walshes was over. No more babysitting. She wanted nothing to do with them. It was all too offensive and confusing. She loved the little girl too much to know that the child was going to withstand her father's fits of tempers again and again, without stop. She liked the older girl too much to bear the thought of what that lovely girl—almost a woman really—was going to have to withstand. It was a kind of madness that Germaine wanted nothing to do with, in spite of the joy and pleasure Audra brought her. She'd get over it...she got over not having her grandchildren in her life...she got over the death of her husband...her precious daughter...she'd get over this little girl...not much more than a stranger to her.

When Eleanor had stood up and started to leave that Good Friday morning, she had the audacity to smile at Germaine. "Thank you again, so very much, for your help last night. Audra has a little Easter gift for you. She'll bring it over on Sunday morning before we go to Mass."

"Don't bring it over," Germaine had said to her.

Eleanor was alarmed. She glanced down at Audra and then back at

Germaine as though to say, don't upset her. Her eyes begged Germaine not to say anything. The panic in Eleanor's face silenced Germaine.

She had followed them to the door, and when Audra ran ahead to their apartment, eager to see her father, Germaine grabbed Eleanor's arm and whispered. "I mean it. No more. Find another babysitter, Mrs. Walsh. I'm finished with the lot of you."

What had happened after that morning Germaine found out through Bridget Riordan.

Paige had never seen Audra in the beautiful grown-up navy and white jacket dress with the red patent leather belt that she had bought for her little sister. She didn't see her sister in the red Mary Jane shoes and white socks with navy polka-dots, or the white pillbox hat that looked like Jacqueline Kennedy's. She spent two days in the hospital, and when she left it, she went to her aunt and uncle's home. They came for her clothes and her books. Eleanor took a week's vacation to take care of Audra during her Easter week holiday. It worked out fine since she wanted to wait until her face and arm healed before going back to work. Germaine heard all of this from Bridget Riordan one day when Bridget stopped in to see how Germaine was doing after that disquieting Holy Thursday.

Paige never came back to live at Ashley Hall. But she did come back one afternoon a week later and rang Germaine's doorbell.

When Germaine looked through the peek hole and saw it was Paige, she decided not to answer the door. Paige knocked softly then, and Germaine could tell that the girl was leaning into the crack between the door and the doorjamb when she whispered, "Please let me talk to you, Mrs. Sommer."

It was a plaintive request. Germaine had unlocked the door and opened it a crack. "Are you alone?"

The girl had nodded, and Germaine opened it wider. Paige was wearing a blue dress covered by a beige spring coat and sunglasses. When she removed the glasses, Germaine saw that the entire top half of her face was still black and blue, but the swelling was gone.

Germaine couldn't help herself then. She reached out and took the girl in her arms and held her tightly. "Please...please tell me you aren't moving back into that apartment."

"No, I'll never do that. I will never go back."

Germaine had let her go then and led her into the living room. Paige sat on the edge of the sofa, just the way her mother had the morning she came to pick up Audra.

"She needs you, Mrs. Sommer."

Germaine just stared at Paige.

"My little sister...she needs you...she has stability when she's with you. God only knows who my mother will find to babysit. She had horrible babysitters...before you, before we lived here...none of them cared for

Audra the way you have. You know how quiet, how sensitive she is. It's hard for her, Mrs. Sommer. With you she was safe…you accepted her just as she is. She's so sweet; she's very innocent. Please don't blame her for what her father does; she shouldn't be punished for his sins."

Germaine continued to stare at Paige. It was as if she'd lost her ability to focus. She didn't know what to say; she didn't know how to say anything. For a week she had sat in the apartment, leaving only when Corky needed to go out, and she'd take the stairs and wait around corners to make sure no one was moving in the lobby or hallways. She didn't want to meet them. She didn't want to see the little girl who had become so much a part of her life.

Paige continued to speak. "If it's because you're afraid of my step-father, please don't be. He'll never bother you. On the contrary, he'll want to win you over, make you see that he's really a nice guy…" Paige stopped and swallowed hard. "It's not just him, anyway. It's my mother, too. They're both good people, I know that's true, but sometimes I think they're poison for each other. She seems the innocent, but she pushes his buttons—almost as if she wants his wrath. They both have such anger inside them…they're both hurt in ways that we'll never understand. I'm sick of trying."

Paige raised her palms. "I'm asking for Audra. I'm not going to be around to give Audra what she needs, to protect her…I did, you know; I did the best I could to protect her, to give her as normal a childhood as possible in that crazy, maniacal home. I love her. I couldn't love her more, Mrs. Sommer, but I can't do it any longer. I have to leave."

"Take her with you," Germaine had said. "Take her away from them."

Paige closed her eyes and shook her head. She pulled her coat tighter around her as though trying to shield herself from the statement. "Don't you think I would? I'm seventeen years old. I'm going have trouble supporting myself, let alone my little sister. I can't take her. And if I did, as much as Audra loves me, she would want to come home to her mommy and daddy."

Paige had held up her hands in supplication. "She's just a little girl, Mrs. Sommer. To Audra, they aren't the complicated…crazy people…that you and I see. They are her parents. My mother is her mommy, the nurturer, the person who cooks special meals for her and tucks her in bed at night. That man is her daddy…right or wrong, at this stage in Audra's life the sun rises and sets in him. Audra is his own child, his baby, and he wouldn't hurt a hair on her head…not physically anyway. He's too oblivious to realize what he's doing to her mind…to her little heart…when he drinks and acts up. It will come…the fear of him, then resentment, even revulsion…when she's old enough to realize how he is, and how other fathers aren't like that. But not yet. She's just too young to understand."

Paige had jumped from the sofa then, crossed the room, and fell on her knees in front of Germaine. "I'm begging you, please, Mrs. Sommer. Please take care of her again. Let her snuggle on the couch with Corky. Give her tea and cookies in the afternoon, pick her up from school and take her to the park. Let her have a normal life in the afternoons, before her idiot parents come home from work."

Paige grabbed Germaine's hand. "She needs you. Do you realize how important it is when a child needs you? Do you know how wrong it is when a child needs someone but no one will help? It's the worst thing in the world, Mrs. Sommer. It's the worst betrayal for a child."

Paige quieted, let go of Germaine's hand, and sat back on her heels. Corky jumped down from Germaine's chair and curled up on Paige's lap. He licked her hand and then placed his snout on her wrist with a sigh. She smiled sadly and stroked his head and velvety ears before saying, "My mother is going to be desperate to find a babysitter when her vacation is over. Who will she find, Mrs. Sommer? Will anyone love her the way you do?"

Germaine knew that this young woman—for that's what she was suddenly, no longer a teenager, but an adult with a great burden on her shoulders—was right. Audra did need her.

"All right," she had said. "I'll tell your mother tonight."

Paige covered her face and wept with relief. "I don't know what to say; how to thank you."

"You've said enough…you've said plenty. There's nothing else you can say."

Paige kissed Germaine on both cheeks when she left. She slipped out of Germaine's apartment and tiptoed to the stairs. Germaine understood why…she was avoiding her family just as Germaine had been doing.

And so, that night, Germaine rang the Walshes' doorbell, and Eleanor opened the door. The worried look in Eleanor's eyes broke Germaine's heart. How could such an intelligent, well-bred woman find herself in such an impossible life? How could she not want to get out of it? How could she not want to get her children out of it?

"I've changed my mind. I miss her terribly," Germaine said.

In the three years that followed, there were still blow ups and drinking and fights…but not as frequently. Wednesdays mostly. The neighbors stopped calling the police or complaining to the landlord. It didn't seem to do anyone any good. No one on the sixth floor wanted to see them evicted because of little Audra.

The days after the loudest sessions, Audra said nothing when Germaine walked her to school. She tried to ask the child about it, tried to find the right words to show the little girl that it was safe to talk to her, that she would comfort her, and even protect her from it when she could, but Audra was well trained. What went on in that apartment was to stay there.

Even at her young age, Audra knew what the word loyalty meant, and she would not betray the loyalty she had pledged to her mommy and daddy.

After a few months, Paige started to visit the Walshes' apartment. If she didn't forgive her mother for betraying her and staying with Brendan, she made some sort of peace with her, and there was a kind of uneasy truce between Brendan Walsh and Paige. Germaine knew Paige only came because she missed her mother and her little sister, and he was part of the package, so she put up with him, but only when she knew he hadn't been drinking. She came for Sunday dinners, and eventually for holidays, but never in the evenings, and almost always with the young man she was dating.

Paige was working and going to school at night. She found a studio apartment on the other side of Astoria, and sometimes Audra would go there to stay with her.

Over the years, Germaine had come to realize how insightful Paige was. Audra needed her mother and father. She loved them, she turned to them, she relied on them, and it thoroughly frustrated Germaine. She had tried so hard to show Audra that the child was safer with her...not them...and yet there it was—today—when Audra was frightened...when Germaine wanted nothing more than to bring her to safety and protect her from harm...from a crazy world...the child ran away from her...ran to him. How could he, a man who acted like a misbehaving child himself, be able to protect her...in an insane world where a President of the United States could be killed?

For two cents she'd pack her suitcase, grab Audra, and get the next bus to Canada.

The president was dead...John Kennedy was dead...the world was in crisis...again. There would probably be a war.

Germaine put her head down on her arms on the kitchen table. She was too old. She'd seen too much of this. She didn't want to think about it. She didn't want Audra to think about it. She didn't want Audra in a world like this.

6D

ALLCOCK

I can't believe it…I just can't…not him.

Vera sat on a kitchen chair directly in front of the Emerson where she could change the channels without getting up. She held a box of tissues in one hand and a glass of water in the other. She didn't even bother to throw the tissues in the waste basket…they were scattered on her lap and on the floor around the chair.

She heard Danny open the apartment door, and she jumped from the chair and ran to him. He held her tenderly. "Poor darling," he said. "I knew you'd be like this."

Vera was so miserable she couldn't answer him. It just felt so good to be in his arms, to be comforted by him.

"Vera, honey, don't take on so," Danny said, pulling away a little and wiping a tear from her cheek.

"I can't believe it," she told him, blowing her nose.

"I know…I can't believe it either."

"His wife is covered in his blood."

"How do you know that?"

"They said it…they're getting ready to fly him back to Washington." Fresh tears and grief welled up in her. "Oh, Danny, what kind of world are we living in?"

"That's the question, isn't it?"

Danny let go of her, and Vera went back to the chair. She changed the channel to CBS, then to NBC, while Dan went into the refrigerator and took out a can of beer.

"You came home early," she said, without taking her eyes from the television screen.

"I skipped class…I figured there wouldn't be much going on tonight, and I knew you'd be a basket case."

Vera felt wounded and looked at him sharply. "Not tonight…of all nights," she said.

"I'm sorry, honey. It's just that you know I wasn't as much of a fan."

"Yes, Danny, I've heard you say it many times," she said. "But even you Republicans have to be upset by this…God, Dan, he's the President of our country. He was shot down in the street!"

Danny moved over to her shoulder, watching the TV from behind her, and stroked her back. "I am, baby. I really am. I don't think anyone—even my father—is happy about this. Well, maybe Lyndon Johnson…"

Anger surged up in Vera now, replacing tears. "I can't believe you'd make jokes today. What kind of man are you?"

Danny was her husband and she loved him, but when his *vedy, vedy* country club Republican upbringing reared its ugly head, she wanted to slap his face. "How dare you!" She saw him fight back a smile, and it made her even angrier. "Forget it. Sometimes I think God forgot to put a heart in you."

"Aw, come on, Vera. So I've never worshipped at the altar of John Kennedy, but I do have a heart and I feel really bad about this. And I'm telling you the truth."

Vera felt better then. She changed the channel three times before she settled on NBC. Frank Magee was announcing that Air Force One was arriving at Andrews Air Force Base.

Danny picked up the other kitchen chair and sat down next to Vera. Together they watched the cameras focus on the plane that carried the dead president's body. Suddenly men appeared on a lift that hid the door of the plane. They seemed to be struggling with something, and then the head of the casket appeared.

Vera choked and covered her mouth with her tissues. Danny leaned forward, his elbows on his knees, the can of beer between his hands. She knew that the reporters were all talking, explaining what was going on, a man, then a woman, then a man again, Vera couldn't focus on what they were saying…only some words seemed to be distinguishable…dark, shiny…glistening in the lights…bronze, I think…

Then the lift started to move down, and in seconds the casket was being lifted off and Jacqueline Kennedy appeared, surrounded by men.

Vera stopped crying when she saw the First Lady. The president's beautiful widow was still dressed in the suit she'd worn all day…the clothing she was wearing when he was shot and fell into her lap. "Holy Mother of God," was all Vera could say.

"Jesus," Danny breathed, as solemn and moved as Vera was. "It's really just hitting me now," he said very quietly. "Look at her. And now she's got to go home and tell her little kids about this…it's really just hitting me—all of this—it's real suddenly."

Vera watched as Jackie tried to open the door of the ambulance, but it was locked, and men were ordering it to be opened for her. She stood for a moment, seemingly composed, then stepped into the ambulance and it drove away.

"Danny," Vera said shaking her head. "What sort of world do we live in?"

"A scary one," he answered.

"You know, they were saying on the news before that one of the last things President Kennedy said in the speech he gave there—before the motorcade—was, 'This is a very dangerous and uncertain world.'"

Danny turned away from the television to look at her. He reached over and took her hand. "I love you, honey," he said.

"I love you, too," she said, crying again. "I'm so glad that you're in law school. Men like you, good men like you, need to make this a better world…a safer world for our children."

He smiled at her and reached out to touch her cheek. "Even if I'm a Republican?"

She smiled back and nodded.

"Hey," he said, pulling her hand up to his lips and leaving a kiss on the back of her fingers, "I'm going to run out and get a pizza for dinner. I don't want you cooking…stay there and watch the news. Remember important things so you can fill me in when I get home."

He grabbed his keys and walked to the door, then turned to look back at her, "And open that bottle of Merlot we have in the cabinet…the one we got last Christmas that we never opened. I think we could both use a little wine."

Vera watched him leave. She stood up sluggishly, and went over to the cabinet to get out the dishes and wine glasses. She set the table and opened the wine to let it breathe…Danny had taught her about that…letting wine breathe, and chilling white wine to just the right temperature, and using different glasses for white and red. She couldn't care less, but it was important to Danny…a leftover from his childhood days in his family's perfect home.

She wondered if it had been the right thing for him to skip classes. There were probably going to be important discussions in college circles about the assassination. But then, wouldn't the professor and other students want to watch television and see all that was going on? She tried to recall which professor Danny had right now…she struggled to think…was it the guy Danny always called a commie?...or was it the other one, the one who had gone to Yale and spouted a lot of the same opinions Danny's father always did? She could never really tell which one he disliked more.

Danny was in his second year of City University of New York Law School. The week after the incident with the Walshes he told her he wished he could go to law school.

"I've always wanted to do something that would make a difference in the country, maybe even in the world. I never really thought of law school, though. But now I realize that I would have loved it. Not just business law like my father would have wanted me to study, but the kind of law that helps people like Mrs. Walsh."

The laws were skewed…a cop can't arrest a man who beats his wife, but he can arrest a guy if he takes a swing at someone else. Something just wasn't right about that.

It was Paige, though, that had gotten to Danny the most. "For crying out loud, Vera, the guy was back in the apartment the next day, but the kid was still in the hospital with a concussion. Something about this stinks to high heaven."

But there was no money for law school. She knew Danny would never go to his father for the money. They were barely making ends meet as it was with his job as a sales associate at Saks and hers as a junior secretary. He was expecting a promotion and raise; after all, he was a college graduate. And so was she, although at Katz Communications, women were only good for stenography and typing, education or not. But neither one of them thought Danny's raise would cover law school.

And then Vera's grandmother died. After the funeral when the family was having lunch, Vera's father took her aside and said, "Your grandmother had some money…a life insurance policy…not a lot, but you were her beneficiary."

Vera couldn't believe it. "Why?" she had asked her father. "Why me? Why not you?"

He had shrugged. "She did it when you were born. There were two— one to bury her with a little left over for your mother and me—and another for the first grandchild."

"Papa, I don't feel right taking it," she had said.

"Take it," he said. "It was what she wanted. I just need some information and the check will be sent to you."

"What about my sisters?"

Her father shrugged and sat down beside her then. "Your mother and I talked and we're going to give them what's left over from the other policy. They don't even have to know about yours. We don't want them to know. You were her eldest grandchild. It was her choice."

Vera decided at that very moment that she was going to get married in the Roman Catholic Church, even if she had to drag Danny to the priest. If her parents could do this for her, she would do that for them…and for herself, because the truth was that she wanted it. She had always wanted it.

She didn't tell Danny about her conversation with her father.

The day after her grandmother's funeral, she made a nice dinner, and half way through it she said to her husband, "Danny, I want to be married in the Church."

He had looked up at her over his pierogies, onions, and fried cabbage—a tribute to her grandmother—and said, "Why?"

"Because it's important to me." She waited, holding her breath. She waited for his anger, the argument about why they didn't need organized religion to tell them they were man and wife.

"Okay...let's do it."

Vera had sat in her chair and stared at him. She thought for a moment that she had only imagined he said it. "Danny..." was all she could say.

"I mean it, Vera. If it's what you want, then let's do it. Who the hell am I to tell you what you should and shouldn't want? I couldn't care less about being married in my church, but if it's important to you, what right do I have to tell you that you shouldn't feel that way? Get it set up. Let's go."

Two days after Danny and Vera had their marriage convalidated by Father Gallagher in a simple and quiet ceremony in her parents' church, Vera found an envelope in their mail box from Liberty National Life Insurance Company. She didn't open the envelope. She carried it up to their apartment and put it on the table. She didn't know how much it was. It wasn't hers. It was Danny's...his tuition for law school.

When he came home from work, she met him at the door. She handed him the envelope, saying, "I don't know if this will cover your tuition, honey, but this money is for you to go to law school. Promise you'll use it for that. Make a difference in the world, Danny."

It was $1,000...a fortune...and Danny took the entrance exams, went to the interviews, and was admitted to CUNY for the following semester. He worked all day, and attended classes at night.

Danny would make a difference in this country...for women like Eleanor Walsh and children like Paige and Audra. Things had to change.

President Kennedy had wanted to be a part of that change, but now that dream was over.

No, not over. There was always hope. There had to be.

She finished setting the table and went back to her chair in front of the television. A photo flashed up on the screen. It was a photo of Johnson taking the oath of office as President of the United States on the airplane. Lady Bird was on his right; Jackie on his left.

Vera sobbed aloud, "Look at her face...dear God, look at Jackie's poor, sad face."

6E

KRAMER

Martha rocked in a steady rhythm back and forth in the toile-covered chair, head down, staring at the carpeting. The news was on but her ears were not tuned to the television.

Her grief wasn't about President Kennedy...or about the elegant Jackie...not even about the two tiny children in the White House who were about to find out they were fatherless. It was sad, yes, and in a few days when she would watch the dead president's funeral, she'd feel that familiar lump in her throat. But not at this moment. At this moment, Joseph was late coming home. She knew, as only a wife who was cheated on knows, that he was seeing *her* again.

This time she would tell him she knew. This time she would make them move so far away that he'd never be able to meet the *korvah*—the whore—again. Or this time she would leave him and never return. No silence...no pretending this time. Not even for the sake of their grandchild.

Joseph Kramer the third.

How the fates play games, Martha had thought so many times in the last two years. She didn't want to think it was God, although she'd heard Christians say He has a wry sense of humor.

On the very evening that Martha saw Joseph's blue Oxford shirt fall out of Frances LaCorte's pillow case in the laundry room, and knew with profound awareness that her husband was having an affair with the LaCorte woman, her dead son's illegitimate child came into their lives.

Even now, two years later, she remembers all of it as though in a dream. She never finished folding her clothes that evening in the laundry room in the basement of Ashley Hall. When she tripped over the pillowcase and the shirt fell out—the very shirt she had been searching for all day in order to wash and iron it for their long awaited vacation—the shirt with JK embroidered on the cuff, which she had ordered from Bloomingdale's as a gift for his last birthday—she put all of her clean clothes into her basket unfolded, left the load of clothes tumbling in the dryer and walked to the elevator.

The LaCorte woman sat on the folding chair, holding the pillow case against her chest, and watched in silence as Martha carried her basket of clothes into the elevator. Neither of them spoke.

In a stupor, Martha entered her apartment, put the basket on the floor in their entry hall, walked into their bedroom and sat on the edge of their bed.

No, Joseph hadn't been dying...Joseph wasn't doing research for a book...Joseph wasn't always playing chess at the club.

Joseph was sticking his schlong in the woman across the hall.

"Martha," he had called from the kitchen. "Martha, are you back?"

She heard him trip over the basket of clean clothes in the hallway.

"Martha?" he called again.

He appeared in the doorway of the bedroom, carrying the basket, his eyebrows raised.

"What are you doing?" he asked. "You left this in the hall."

Martha could only stare at him. Her Joseph. The only man she'd ever loved. The father of her dead son. The man she lived and breathed for every day of her life for all these years...for almost her whole life.

"Martha?" he asked again. "Are you all right? You look funny."

Funny...I look funny. Martha began to laugh, not with mirth, but with irony. *Funny, I look.*

What does a heart attack feel like? Is it like an elephant sitting on your chest? Does it steal away your breath? Can you feel your pulse everywhere in your body? Please let it be that way. Yes, let me be having a heart attack and let it take me right now, immediately, no chance to speak...no chance for him to say anything to me ever again.

The buzzer from the lobby rang. Joseph turned to look back, then put the basket on the bed next to Martha, saying, "Who could that be?"

He walked to the intercom, pushed the button, and asked, "Who's there?"

"Mr. Kramer?" a woman's voice spoke back.

"Yes," he answered, annoyance edging his voice.

"Mr. Kramer...um...can...*may* I come up? You don't know me, but I knew your son, Joe."

From somewhere out of the fog that surrounded Martha, she heard her son's name, and her back straightened.

"Joe?" Joseph asked, then he said, "Yes, yes, come up." He pushed the buzzer to open the lock on the lobby door.

Joseph came back into the bedroom. "Did you hear?" he asked.

Martha nodded.

"Who do you think she is?"

Martha shook her head slowly, staring into space.

Joseph paced in front of her. "Who could she be?"

Martha said without even knowing what she was saying, "How the *fuck* do I know?"

Joseph inhaled hard and long. Martha had never said that word before. Never.

He bent down in front of her then. "Martha, what is it? What is wrong with you? Does it have anything to do with this visitor?"

For the first time since coming into the apartment from the laundry room, for the first time since realizing her husband was being unfaithful, Martha looked into his eyes. He looked confused; he looked concerned.

Tell the bastard...tell the lying cheat now.

But before she could say another word, the doorbell rang. He didn't move. Martha didn't move. Their eyes were locked in a hold that neither one of them could break. The doorbell rang again.

"Come," Joseph said, taking her hand and pulling her to her feet. "Come. Let's see who this is."

She allowed his touch; his gentle tug. She followed behind him and stopped in the living room while he continued to the door. Her chest still ached, her breathing was still shallow, her world was still in pieces around her.

"Mr. Kramer," the woman said, her voice clear now. "My name is Janice Farron. I knew your son when he was in the service. I was in the Woman's Army Corps at the time. I'd like a moment to speak with you."

Joseph stood aside and held the door open wider. Martha saw a tall, elegant dark haired woman walk through it. She wore a navy blue suit and a beige hat and gloves. A pin made of pearls and sapphires decorated the shoulder of her suit jacket, but other than that, she was unadorned. She was beautiful...a *shiksa goddess*. Joseph indicated that she continue into the living room where Martha stood in the center.

When the woman saw Martha, she smiled nervously. "Mrs. Kramer?"

Martha nodded. Joseph said, "Miss Farron, won't you sit down? Can we get you something to drink?"

Martha continued to be rooted in the center of the room. Joseph touched her shoulder, "Martha, come and sit down."

He pulled her with him to the sofa while the strange woman sat in Martha's favorite chair. Martha felt stiff, unyielding, doped.

"Nothing to drink, but thank you," Janice Farron said, taking a deep breath. She moved her pocketbook over between her thigh and the inside of the chair's arm. "This is not going to be an easy conversation for any of us, so let me just get to the point and...and...well, just let me say it."

Joseph sat down next to Martha and indicated with his hand that she should begin.

Janice bit her lip and Martha noticed that the stain of her red lipstick clung to the woman's front tooth. Martha stared at it as the woman continued to speak. "I knew Joe when we were both stationed in Germany...before he went to Korea." She paused, seeming to expect them to know that, as though waiting for them to say something about it...*oh, yes, he mentioned you....Janice...of course, he wrote about you.*

But they didn't because Joey hadn't mentioned her in any of his letters or phone calls. Janice continued. "Joey and I were going to be married."

Martha could sense more than see Joseph's head rise and stare at the woman. "Miss Farron, Joey never mentioned..."

"No, I don't suppose he did. He told me he wanted to wait until he came back from Korea to tell you. He wanted you to meet me in person before we told you." She smiled nervously again. "He was a little worried I think because he was your only son...and I'm not Jewish...and all."

Neither Martha nor Joseph spoke.

"But I had hoped that perhaps he wrote a little bit about me..." Janice looked at her hands. "Anyway, you know what happened. He never came back."

Martha saw tears in the woman's eyes and she could tell that they were genuine. But Martha still could not find her voice.

"Well...that's..." Joseph started, not sure what else to add.

"I...I should have come to see you right away...I should have introduced myself to you immediately after his death. I couldn't get leave at the time, though. I had to stay in Germany, but I should have written to you to tell you about me...about our being in love. There was so much I wanted to write to you about Joe, and so much I would have loved to hear about him from you...about his childhood, his high school years...his life before the service."

"We would have welcomed any letter about our Joey," Joseph said sadly.

"But then something happened to me..."

"Oh?" Joseph prodded.

The woman took a breath to speak, but then closed her mouth. Her eyes, still watery with unshed tears, darted around the room.

"She was pregnant," Martha said. It came from somewhere down deep in her body. She had no idea how she knew it, but she did. She had no idea what her voice sounded like when she spoke the words.

Joseph and Janice Farron both looked at her in surprise. Then Janice nodded. "I was...with Joe's baby."

Martha closed her eyes and clenched her hands into fists. She didn't know what the woman was going to say next, but she readied herself for it.

"I had a little boy, Mr. and Mrs. Kramer. I named him Joseph after your son...his father."

Joseph jumped up and paced around the room, one hand on his back and the other over his mouth. The woman watched him in silence. It took him a long time before he asked, "What happened to him? Did he die in childbirth?"

"No, sir," Janice said, looking down at her hands, tears choking her now.

"Well, what happened to him? You gave him away? You gave him up for adoption?" Joseph sounded desperate.

"No...no...I didn't. He's with me. He's downstairs in the car with my father. I've been raising him on my own with my parents' help. I guess I was afraid to share him...I don't know why I didn't tell you. I didn't want you to think I wanted you to support him. Oh, God, can you ever forgive me?"

The heart attack passed. Martha could breathe again. The elephant was gone. The fog was gone. She saw the woman named Janice Farron sitting in the chair across from her, the same chair that she sat in every day reading, embroidering, doing crossword puzzles, when her life was whole. She felt so light at that moment that she wondered if perhaps she really had died of the heart attack and her soul was floating around them.

"Martha?" Joseph said.

"Sit down, Joseph," Martha said firmly. She wasn't dead. He heard her and sat beside her again. "How do we know you're telling us the truth?" she asked Janice.

"All you have to do is take one look at him, Mrs. Kramer. You'll know." Janice smiled.

"He's...what?...six?" Joseph asked.

Janice nodded, "He's six years old."

"Our grandson," Joseph whispered. "Our grandson, Martha..."

Martha turned to look at him for the first time since the woman had entered their world. She saw how pale his face had turned. She saw the tears brimming in his eyes.

"Why are you here, Miss Farron," Martha asked levelly.

"I can't bear it anymore. I can't bear your not knowing about him...*knowing him*. I've grown up a great deal myself in this last year, for many reasons, and I've lost two loved ones to death now, and I see things more clearly. As a mother, I realize how much pain you both must be in since Joe's death. And here I have kept this wonderful child from you for God only knows what reason. My parents have been hounding me to reach out to you, but I've been so stubborn...so...*afraid*."

"Of what?" Joseph wanted to know.

"That you could take him away from me. I know, it's ridiculous...my parents have assured me that you can't, but I've been such a child myself...so afraid that there's some kind of loophole you could use...that you'd know how to work the law...or..." she held her hands up unable to explain further. "I live for him," she offered simply.

Martha heard Joseph sob once, and then again, and finally he placed his head in his hands and wept. A part of her wanted to comfort him. Another part of her mind thought, *"You don't deserve this, Joseph Kramer. You don't deserve this goodness to come to you. Not tonight of all nights...not ever."*

"Miss Farron," Martha began.

"Please...please call me Janice."

"Janice...may we meet him...little Joseph?"

"I'm so relieved that you want to. Of course, you can. He knows about you. My father and I have been telling him in the last few days that he has another grandma and grandpa. We took the chance that you would want to meet him."

"And your mother? His other grandmother? Has she also been telling him?"

Janice shook her head. "She died three months ago...of cancer. She asked me to do this when she was on her deathbed. She told me she would never rest in peace until I did."

"It took you long enough," Joseph said, still weeping but angry now. He blew his nose in his handkerchief.

"I know," was all Janice said.

"Go and get him...bring your father. We'll have tea...or would you rather coffee?" Martha asked her.

"Tea is fine," Janice managed to say, jumping up and moving toward the door.

When she was gone, Martha said to her husband, "Go and wash your face, Joseph. You don't want your...grandson...seeing you cry...all red faced and ugly."

Joseph stood at the same time she did, and he took her into his arms. "Martha...Martha...our grandson...our son lives through our grandson."

She didn't return his hug. His embrace felt like hot irons around her. She hated Joseph Kramer at that moment. But he would not know. He would never know, because it would ruin their new world with Joseph Kramer, III.

The LaCorte woman stole something very precious from her, but she could not have this... this moment...this new chapter of her life. This was a reprieve from losing her husband...this was a stay of execution of a marriage...come at the oddest time, but here nonetheless.

It seemed that Joseph felt the same way. After the night they met the sweet faced tintype of their son, Joseph stopped going to the "synagogue" or the "library" or the "club." He was home every day and when he wasn't at home, he was with Martha or with their grandson, making up for six lost years.

He whistled when he shaved in the morning, and he started singing in the shower as he used to. He started to eat better again and gained some weight. They went food shopping together, and they went to the movies in the afternoons. And they started to make love again.

It started that night, the night they met their grandson; the night Martha found out that he was having an affair. Martha decided they would be lovers again. It took place after they met little Joey, and knew the moment they laid eyes on him—just as Janice had promised—that he was their son's child...after they talked and drank tea and ate Martha's pound cake with the little boy and his mother and Grandpa Farron...after Joseph walked their new family members to their car.

Martha stripped off her clothes in the kitchen and met Joseph at the door of their apartment. She waited with her eye at the peephole until the elevator came to the sixth floor. He walked off and she saw him hesitate between the two doors. He stood looking first at their door, then at *hers*, then again at the door where Martha stood naked, watching him.

Don't do it, Joseph.

He didn't. He turned toward their apartment, and Martha took several steps backward. He unlocked the door and came inside. His eyes were bright with excitement. They had a grandson...their beloved son's child. Martha could see that he was barely able to contain his joy.

It took him a moment to realize she was standing in front of him naked, her fingers on her breasts, her head back slightly, sensually.

"Martha," he had breathed. "What are you doing?" The door slammed shut behind him.

She went to him, knelt in front of him, and unzipped his pants.

"Martha, what are you doing?"

He tried to push her hands away, but she had ahold of him and she uncovered him, and put her mouth over him...he swayed...and gasped...his long arms reaching out to grab the walls on each side of the hallway. "Martha...what..."

She used her mouth, her tongue, her hands until he lowered himself to his own knees and grabbed at her buttocks and breasts. "Martha." He groaned as they fell down together on the floor of their hallway...near their door...ten feet away from his mistress's door...and Martha rolled on top of him and absorbed him into her own body while she ripped his shirt open and pushed at his undershirt to lay bare his chest. Her mouth worked her way around his chest and her tongue played with his nipples, then travelled down his belly.

He thrust up into her...but she pulled off, causing him to groan and look at her in surprise. She lowered onto him again—very slowly—*she would be in control of their lovemaking*—and she allowed his thrusts again and again until he gasped and his whole body quivered.

When he was done, she said to him, "Now it's my turn."

And Martha made him do everything to her that she had done to him. She demanded it...and he did it, hungrily, gently, passionately until both of them convulsed at the same time and lie spent on the floor of that hallway that was only ten feet away from his mistress's door.

Martha had never had an orgasm until that night.

She insisted on more of them, every day, every week...from that night, through their short vacation in the Catskills, and beyond in their new life as grandparents. Sometimes he would laugh and beg her to give him a break, saying, "I'm an old man, Martha...a *grandfather*, you know...yet you make me perform like a teenager. You'll kill me."

But he would never say no to her.

How many times had she said no to him in the years they were married? How many times would she say yes but act like it was a burden...a job to be endured? How many times had she pushed him into the arms of the LaCorte woman?

The night little Joey stepped into their life, Martha's life with Joseph started over. She would make sure he was pleased...sated...didn't need any other woman...didn't have the energy for any other woman.

In the two years since that night, she had often wondered if there had been other women before the LaCorte whore. Had he been a cheater for years? Had there been *shtupm* with other women throughout their marriage? Did he have quickies during lunch when he was working? Did he have women at work, secretaries...stenographers... or prostitutes *after* work? He came home late often when he was working full time...was he with women, not ledgers?

Martha decided not to drive herself mad thinking about it. And anyway, she didn't think he did. She decided that the LaCorte whore was the only one...and Martha took care of that. She took care of it, she was sure of it. For two years, she was certain the LaCorte whore was out of their lives.

But now, suddenly, things were different.

In the last two weeks Joseph was distant again, not as willing in bed when she seduced him. Then she caught him in a lie. He told her he was going to take Joey out to a football game. He got tickets to the Jets at Shea Stadium. Oh, how wonderful she thought that was! Joseph and his grandson...just like when he would take their son. How good for both of them.

When she called Janice the afternoon of the Jets game to set a date for them to go shopping for Hanukah and Christmas gifts for Joey—Thanksgiving was only a week away, and the holidays came quickly after that—Janice asked how Joseph was.

"Didn't you see him when he picked up Joey?" Martha asked.

"When?"

"Today…for the Jets game."

"They didn't go to a game today, Martha," Janice said, sounding confused. "Joey is here…do you want to say hello?"

Martha's head felt as though a vice was pressing on her skull. "No…not now." She hung up the phone. Her body was icy…too stiff to sit down.

She left the apartment and rang the doorbell of the apartment across the hall. There was no answer. She rang the bell over and over again, her finger pressed against it constantly, until Mrs. Walsh opened the door of her apartment and peeked out.

"Is everything all right, Mrs. Kramer?"

Martha just stared at the door behind which she believed her husband was making love to the LaCorte whore.

"Mrs. Kramer," Eleanor Walsh said quietly, "I don't think Mrs. LaCorte is at home. I met her in the elevator just a little while ago…she was going out."

Martha could not find her voice. She continued to keep her finger on the doorbell.

Mrs. Walsh stepped out into the hall, letting her door close a little behind her, but not shut tight. She said very gently, "Maybe I can help? Is there anything you need?"

Martha just shook her head and pressed on the bell…twice, three times, a fourth time.

"How about a cup of coffee? Would you like to come in for coffee…or a cold drink? I just bought a pumpkin pie at the bakery. Maybe you would like a pot roast sandwich…I have some left from Sunday dinner…then we could have the pie and coffee? Mrs. Kramer? "

Martha shook her head and backed away from the LaCorte woman's door, continuing to stare at it. Her arm, hand, and finger were still out in front of her as she backed away. As she passed Mrs. Walsh, the other woman took her hand and enfolded it in both of hers. "If you need anything, I'm right here. Just ring my bell or call me—you have my number, right?"

Martha nodded.

"Are you all right, Mrs. Kramer? Can I help you?" Mrs. Walsh persisted.

"Why?" was all Martha could ask. "Why?"

Mrs. Walsh shook her head, her eyes filled with tears. At that moment, Martha realized that Eleanor Walsh knew everything…she knew about

Joseph…she knew about the LaCorte whore. How many others on that floor knew? How many in the building?

She said nothing to Joseph when he came home that night. She would wait until she knew what and how to say it. She would leave him…go to Ozone Park…get an apartment near Janice and Joey. She wanted to…she had begged Joseph to go many times throughout the last two years…but he would say the apartment they were in was affordable, rent controlled, accessible to the subway to go to see Joey. It would be foolish to move.

She wondered at the time if it was it because he didn't want to leave the whore across the hall…but, no, that was over…she had believed it was over. She was certain of it. She knew it.

But now…what about now?

She'd leave.

She had come to love Janice. The young woman was a devoted mother and good daughter to her widowed father. She was a good woman, and they got along fine. Janice was the kind of daughter-in-law she had always wanted, despite the fact that she was a Christian…who cared? Janice always celebrated the Jewish holidays the best she could so that Joey would know…would *understand* his father's heritage. And she did it before they had met…before she brought the boy to meet Martha and Joseph.

Yes, Martha would leave Joseph and move nearer to Joey. She could take care of him after school. The hell with Joseph Kramer. He was nothing to her…nothing. He was filth. A pig. He could have the whore across the hall and she could have him.

Martha had carefully rehearsed what she would say to him; over and over in her mind she composed her farewell speech. On Friday morning, on November 22, five days after she found out he had lied to her—two days after she had found a new apartment—Martha packed her clothing in the two suitcases they owned. She wanted it done before Thanksgiving so that there would be no pretending on the holiday. Janice had invited them for Thanksgiving dinner…Martha would be there…*without* Joseph. He was no longer welcome in the world with their grandson. He could stay in his world with the whore.

She'd tell him about the shirt she'd seen two years before in the LaCorte whore's laundry. She'd explain how the fates had saved him that night and that she had given him one chance…had granted him a reprieve…because they had a grandson they never knew about. She gave him a second chance…that *one* time.

And that time, without even knowing he had a choice, he had chosen Martha. He had chosen his grandson.

But he was different again. Oh, yes, he was changed. He was *filthy* again. She knew.

Jack Kennedy was shot and killed on the day Martha Kramer was going to tell her husband all of this …that she knew about the whore. On this day that the President of the United States was shot and killed, Joseph, too, would lose the life he thought was his.

Like JFK, Joseph wasn't going to be given a choice.

6A

RIORDAN

"A son of Ireland, he was, Bridie," Bridget's mother cried into the phone from across the Atlantic Ocean, from Abbyknockmoy. "And the wee ones…just babies…fatherless now."

"It's tragic, Mam," Bridget said. She was still stunned by the news. It was the middle of the night in Ireland, but her mother called three times that evening, wanting all the news that she couldn't get in Ireland. Bridget was trying to get it all straight in her own mind.

"Come home, Bridie…come home. Don't stay in that terrible place that kills its own President."

"You know I can't do that," Bridget said.

"You can, indeed. No one knows…not a word said to me in all this time from anyone. And you know they would if they knew. He's gone himself."

"His father isn't. I took his father's money and went to England to…do what I did. His father knows. God only knows who else is privy to all the sordid details."

"Who cares? So you went to London and gave the baby up for adoption…it happens all the time. It's a scandal sure, but it's not that uncommon."

Bridget rested her head back against the side of her day bed. She was on the floor, the little television in front of her, her back against the bed that doubled as a sofa in her small apartment.

"I can't," she said into the receiver.

"When will the funeral be?" Her mother changed the subject, really more interested in the assassination than in her daughter's life. "Where will they lay him out?"

"He'll be in the East Room of the White House for a while, they say," Bridget told her mother. "Then they'll take him to the Capitol. But you'll see all of that, I'm sure. It will be broadcast all over the world."

"What will she wear, do you think?"

Bridget smiled, rolled her eyes, and shook her head. All the details. It was the Irish way. She could picture her mother, green chenille robe with its large collar, pin curls in her graying red hair, her skin scrubbed pink with a hint of shine from the wrinkle cream. "Black," she answered.

"Oh, don't be bold, Bridie. Of course, black."

"Other than that how would I know what she's going to wear?"

"Chanel? Cassini? That's what I mean."

Bridget sighed. "Oh, darlin', you amaze me sometimes. Your guess is as good as mine. We'll find out soon enough. Now why don't you get some sleep? It's the middle of the night for you. Go to bed."

"I'll never sleep...not a minute. It's all too upsettin'. Too shockin', it is."

"I know, Mam, but you have to get some rest. There'll be stuff on TV for days about it. And whatever you don't see over there, I'll make sure I catch you up on it. I promise."

There was silence for a moment, then, "Bridie?"

"Yes, Mam."

"I wish I could see you. I miss you so much it hurts inside me something fierce."

Bridget felt the familiar burn of tears behind her eyes. She swallowed hard. "I know, Mam. Me, too. But I'm all right. No worryin'...right?"

"I'm a mother...I'll worry 'til the day I die. It's a mother's lot in life."

Bridget smiled and put her lips to the phone, wishing her mother could feel their warm press on her thin cheek. "Go t'bed, Mam. I love you."

"Don't forget to call if anything important happens...and if you find out what she'll be wearin'...*who* she'll be wearin' I mean."

Bridget laughed out loud now. "I'll have to rob a bank to pay for the telephone bill if I do that. G'night, m'lady...sleep well."

Bridget placed the receiver on the pink princess phone on the floor next to the bed. She closed her eyes. This self-imposed exile was more difficult than she imagined it would be. She ached for home.

She took a wad of money out from under her mattress. It was wrapped in aluminum foil inside a Wonder Bread bag. More than ten thousand dollars now. A fortune.

Every week she added to it from her meager pay check. And there was more in the bank, in the savings account she'd opened the day after she moved into Ashley Hall. This was her secret stash...just in case the stock market crashed again and there was another Depression.

She didn't know what it would buy her. A ticket back home where she longed to be maybe...and a little dress shop in Galway City. Ah, that would be good.

But how? She could never return, for she'd never be able to receive the

Eucharist again, and they'd wonder why. And she'd never go to confession with what was on her soul...not there...not here...not anywhere. Not with The Lie and The Sin that threatened to smother her almost every day of her life.

6C

WILLIAMS

Eamon sat on one end of the sofa while John Sullivan sat on the other side. They watched the six white horses pull the caisson from the White House to the Capitol on Eamon's television. The cortege followed—each member somber, grief-stricken—each one isolated in his or her own personal mourning for the man in the coffin. Mrs. Kennedy's face was barely visible beneath her black veil, but the faces of her brothers-in-law, Robert and Teddy, were immobile. They looked blank.

The funeral was all that was aired on every station. Only Channel Nine carried something different…the movie "PT109"…but in the United States on that day, all other television came to a halt.

The two men watched in silence for an hour.

Then Eamon said, "You know, Barry was beaten to death last week."

"Not now," John said, closing his eyes.

"He was…they found him in an alley behind the bar."

"I know that, all right? I don't want to talk about it."

"No six white horses for him."

"Eamon, please…"

"No mourning widow…no riderless horse…Barry's brothers never even came to New York to claim the body. They said something like 'keep it' when the morgue called them."

John sighed and crossed his legs.

"If anyone were ever to find out about…"

John jumped to his feet now. "You want to have this out *now?* Of all the moments in our lives…it has to be now?"

Eamon shrugged and turned his face toward the window, looking out at the brick façade of the brownstone across the street. He felt sick to his stomach.

"Jesus, Eamon…we're very careful, very cautious. Don't we go on

137

double dates? Don't we talk about 'chicks' whenever we're with friends—the other kind of friends? No one knows. Honora was just saying the other day that we're just two carefree bachelors, but we'll get "hooked" one day. And we're almost as close to Honora as we are to each other, for God's sake. She'd suspect if anyone would. No one knows...no one even suspects."

"Mrs. Walsh across the hall does." Eamon said this very quietly.

John stopped short. "What?"

"She came in the other day...she needed the new telephone number of the landlord and I told her I had it, so I asked her in while I looked for it. I thought she'd wait in the hallway while I went into the bedroom to get the number. When I came back out, she was here in the living room, her back was turned away from me, but she was staring at the mirror over the television console."

John spun around and looked at the elaborate gold framed mirror. The reflection of his portrait...an oil painting Eamon had commissioned three years earlier and had hung over his bed...was clearly reflected in the mirror. In the painting, John was dressed in his smoking jacket, a cravat at his throat, a book in one hand. It was a stunning image of him...he always thought that the painter had captured who he truly was. But he always worried about it being on Eamon's wall. Eamon promised he'd never show anyone the portrait. He would take it down whenever the superintendent had to do any work in the apartment and whenever Eamon had company.

John covered his eyes now. "Did she say anything?"

"Not a word. But I saw it in her face...the revelation, you know. She's not a stupid woman."

"Christ," John hissed. "Will she tell her husband, do you think?"

Eamon leaned his head back against the sofa. "I have no idea."

John sat down on his side of the sofa again, but leaned forward, his elbows on his knees. He was quiet a long time. "She won't," he said finally.

"Really? And how do you know this?" Eamon asked.

"I'm serious, Eamon. The few times I've spoken with her in the elevator and once in the lobby when I was waiting for you, I realized that she's vulnerable, maybe a little crazy because she stays with that husband of hers, but she's not malicious. She's not the type. She seems to have a little class. She's intelligent...educated."

"Yes...and *queers* have never been hurt by classy, intelligent and well-educated people, have they?"

The statement wounded John. Eamon saw it in his face. Certain words, certain expressions, were not allowed by John. They could be what they were...he and Eamon...but he refused to allow a label to be put to it. His philosophy was to act "normal," and no one would ever know. And above all things...don't call it what it was...not ever. Not in front of him, anyway.

They both went back to watching television, but neither of them paid attention. The coffin was brought into the church, the reporters droned on in narration, the coffin was brought out, placed back on the caisson, the funeral procession started again.

John reached over and took Eamon's hand and squeezed it.

SALVATORE'S PIZZA

BROADWAY

Danny Allcock entered the pizza place at the corner of Broadway and 30th street and ordered a large pizza, half sausage and onions. It was the second time in four days that he'd been there: the night Kennedy was assassinated, and now the day of the funeral. There was no getting Vera away from the television on either day.

"Give me fifteen minutes," the pizza guy said. The man's face was covered with a thin layer of flour. Danny realized with surprise that there were tear tracks through the flour on his cheeks. The Italian flattened, threw and docked his pizzas while he glanced from time to time at the small television on the high counter that surrounded his prep area. Right after Danny ordered, the man threw down a wad of pizza dough on a floured counter, looked up at the television, shook his head, spoke in Italian, and sobbed.

Danny walked toward one of the booths to sit and wait. He saw Brendan Walsh in a booth in the corner. The man was dressed in a black suit, white shirt, and a blue and green striped tie. A black hat lay on the seat beside him. His black dress shoes shone on the pizza shop's linoleum floor. Brendan also glanced at the TV and then shook his head, his face contorted with grief.

"Mr. Walsh," Danny said, thinking that maybe something *else* had happened in the world. "Is everything all right?"

Walsh looked at him as though he was insane. "The president..." he started to say, pointing to the television.

"Oh, yeah, of course," Danny said quickly. "It's just that you look...you're all dressed up, and I wondered if..."

"I went to Mass this morning for him. No work today."

Danny nodded.

"Sit," Walsh invited him, pointing to the seat across from him.

Danny hesitated a moment, then slid into the booth.

140

"It's terrible," Walsh said.

"It *is* terrible," Danny agreed.

"The kids...babies...I can't help but think of my little Audra. What if something happened to me?"

Danny looked away thinking that they'd probably be better off.

"It's a tragedy. My wife couldn't even make lunch..." Walsh explained.

"My wife either," Danny told him.

"Death is a terrible thing, Allcock."

Danny nodded, but didn't add anything. He wasn't all that familiar with it himself. Three of his grandparents had died before he was born, and his maternal grandmother was still living. He couldn't think of a funeral he'd been to in his life except for Vera's grandmother's.

"A death like this can eat away at you," Walsh continued. "Any kind of surprise death...unexpected death, I mean. It's hard to ever get beyond it."

"I guess so," Danny agreed.

"My father died when I was two years old—no one was ever sure why, he was alive one day and dead the next—and my mother was pregnant and lost the baby from the shock of it. I don't remember much about my father, but I remember the day he died, as young as I was. Bits of it, you know? Then when I was a kid...just twelve years old...my older brother came home from work sick as a dog. He was working in construction, and it was two days before Christmas when Billy got sick. Cold December that year. Lots of rain and sleet that week alone. Billy was only seventeen. He was an apprentice—an ironworker."

Walsh's eyes filled with tears as he spoke about his brother. He leaned over a glass of Coke he'd been drinking, and put both of his large hands on the glass and his elbows on the table. "He was just a kid himself, but he was the oldest, and after my father died Billy became the head of the family. He had to work or we all would have starved. My mother took in washing, and did some work for the landlord, so we had a roof over our head, but the pay was next to nothing. Billy went to work out of the sixth grade, and then my other brother, Hank, did the same. I did what I could...going to the subway stop with an umbrella on rainy days to offer to walk people home for a nickel...selling papers...stocking shelves. Stuff like that. It was the Depression, you know, so there wasn't much work anywhere. There weren't many nickels to go around."

"Tough life," Danny said, interested now.

"My life was cushy compared with Billy's. He worked all day in construction, and then swept up in a bar and grill at night, doing dishes, taking out the garbage. Anyway, he got real sick that Christmas. Came home from work with a high fever. Mom usually gave us a whiskey in boiling water when we were sick. She did that for Billy, and put him to bed with mustard and flannel on his chest, but it didn't help this time. By the next day, Christmas Eve, she knew this sickness Billy had was different…worse. She could tell he was sicker 'n usual. Hot as hell, he was."

Walsh looked up from the dark syrupy soda. "I can still remember feeling the heat from his body in the bedroom when I stood at the doorway. That's how hot he was. The whole room felt like fever. And raging, like he'd lost his mind or something. And he cried…Billy never cried…but that week, when he slept, he cried like a little kid. Mom told me to run to the clinic and fetch a doctor. The clinic was about five blocks away. I ran as fast as I could. The only doctor there that day was a woman doctor."

Now Walsh bit his top lip. Danny saw his hands begin to tremble…the soda vibrated with it. "I asked if there was a man doctor, and they told me no, it was Christmas Eve, if we wanted a doctor this was the only one."

Walsh pushed the glass away from him and sighed. He leaned back against the red leather seatback. "What did I know? I brought her home with me. She was nice…real nice, you know…kept telling me not to worry…she was a good doctor and she'd take good care of my brother. I wish you could have seen my mother's face when the woman doctor walked into our flat behind me. 'What is this?' Mom said to me. But the woman doctor walked right past her and into Billy's room and started to examine him."

Walsh stopped talking then when he heard the narrator start to speak on the television about Jackie Kennedy lighting the candle at the president's grave. Danny and Walsh watched for a long minute; then, after the First Lady stood and started to walk away, tripped, and was caught by her brother-in-law, Bobby, Danny asked, "Mr. Walsh, what happened to your brother?"

It looked as though Walsh was having difficulty coming back to the story. His eyes were glued to the drama on the television when he answered. "He died that night. The woman doctor said it was only a bad cold, gave my mother some pills, and left. Two hours later, Billy stopped breathing. Never took another breath. One minute after midnight…Christmas morning."

"Jesus Christ," Danny said.

"My mother never forgave me…never. Not for the rest of her life. When Billy died, she turned to me and slapped my face and said, 'It's your fault. You brought that woman doctor here…I told you to get a doctor, and that's what you brought home. You killed your own brother.'"

Danny was astounded. He couldn't think of a thing to say to the tall man on the other side of the table. They sat in silence a long time while Danny searched for the right words to end the awkward hush. Even the television was silent as the cameras displayed the dead president's family walking away from the grave.

Danny found his voice and said, "Look, Walsh, your mother was just upset. She didn't mean it...she couldn't have meant it."

"No? Whenever she'd introduce me to someone new she'd say, 'And this is Brendan, my youngest, he's the one who brought home a woman doctor who killed his brother on Christmas.'"

Danny decided to keep his mouth shut. What could he possibly say?

Walsh shook his head and took a drink of the cola. "She never said, 'This is my son who fought in the war, then worked his way through college and became an architect, and never stops giving me money to live on.' I tried to make her proud of me...I wanted her to forget what I did that one Christmas Eve."

"Walsh!" shouted the pizza guy. They both looked over and the man placed two pizza boxes on the upper counter. He started to ring up the amount of the pizzas on the cash register.

"Right here," Walsh said, standing up. He reached out to shake Danny's hand, and Danny took it. "Sorry if I talked too much."

"No, no...thanks for...telling me."

Walsh smiled a small smile. "Death's a tough thing...and this..." he indicated the television with his free hand, "brings memories up in your mind...you know. I guess it's the shock."

Danny nodded.

"You got family?" Walsh asked him.

Danny nodded again.

"That's good...I don't know what I'd do without mine. My wife, my kids...I'd be lost without them. You probably feel that way, too, about yours. Stay close to them, Allcock. They'll get you through the tough times. Look how those Kennedys are stickin' together...takin' care of Jackie and her two babies. That's what families do. Families stick together."

More surprised than he ever would have imagined, Danny felt a lump form in his throat. He looked at this man and wanted to hug him, comfort him. Just an hour ago, he couldn't stand the guy...looked down on him. Yet, he knew now that this man had gone through more pain and sadness in his life than he could imagine. He realized that things aren't always black and white...that maybe fate—circumstances—made a person what he became...right or wrong. Maybe that was true of his parents, too. He wondered about it. He never tried to understand them...know them.

He watched Walsh pay for his pizzas, push an extra dollar bill at the pizza guy, and then put his black fedora on his head before taking another look at the television. He shook his head sadly before leaving the shop.

6E

KRAMER

Joseph sat alone in his living room. The television wasn't on...he had no desire to watch the funeral. The apartment was tomblike in its silence. No aroma of cooking from the kitchen, no clatter and clinking from where Martha would be puttering around.

He felt very, very old.

He got the news on the day the President of the United States was killed. He remembered feeling as though it was a fitting thing...to learn you have pancreatic cancer on a shocking and infamous day.

Well, I'll never forget when I learned, he had thought when he left the doctor's office—the oncologist Dr. Haber had referred him to.

To top it off, it was the day his wife accused him of cheating on her, took her packed suitcases, and left the apartment, with him following behind her five blocks to the elevated station, begging her to listen, to hear the whole story.

Martha never even looked at him.

She was staying with Janice and Joey until the first of the month when she'd move into her new apartment. She was staying with their grandson, surrounded by people who cared about her...and who, at this point, probably wouldn't spit on the ground in front of him.

"But it's over...it's been over for two years," he had said to Martha again and again in the ride down the elevator, in the lobby, in front of the building and for five blocks, until she walked up the metal stairs to the token booth. "Martha, for two years, I haven't been with her. For two years, it's been only you."

Martha was deaf for all she reacted to his plea.

"You lied about the game," she had said the moment he walked into the apartment that day, the day the President was assassinated. There on the television was the coffin, the blood-soaked widow, the ambulance taking the coffin away. And she said, "You lied about the game."

"The game? What game? Martha, what are you talking about?"

"The Jets game. You were with the LaCorte whore, weren't you?"

The name was a blow like none he had ever felt since they got the news about their son's death.

"You preferred to be with her than with your precious little grandson...your dead son's child. No, your whore was more important to you."

His legs wouldn't hold him. He grabbed for the back of his desk chair and sat down, staring at her, his mouth agape with shock.

Here he had thought that it was he who would shock and devastate Martha with the news from his doctor on this day. He was going to say to her, "I have cancer, darling, but I'm going to fight it...I'm going to fight it and live...for you and for our little Joey." That was what he had been planning to say to her as gently as he could.

He never got the chance to say it. Her bags were already packed, her coat and hat and purse placed on the arm of the sofa, waiting for him to return so that she could tell him she knew about Frances...his Francesca...the woman he had not lain with in more than two years, but whose face and voice still haunted him every day, every night.

"I knew it two years ago," Martha had said to him. "I saw your blue Oxford shirt in her laundry by accident, and I knew. But Joey came into our lives...and I changed...I changed because I believed you were worth changing for...worth fighting for. I thought I'd won...I thought I had you back."

You did, Martha, my love, my sweet. You had won. You did. I left her the night Joey came back into our lives...the night you made love to me as you had never made love to me in our life together.

"But you are a pig...a rutting, no good, dirty scum-sucking pig."

Yes...yes...that I am...I was...but not now. Now I'm only yours. Only Joey's grandpa.

"I know that you will rot in hell...I know it in my heart...but I only wish I could see a little of it. I wish I could see you suffer."

Stay and that may come to be. You can stay and watch me suffer with cancer. Will that do?

But he never said any of this to Martha. He begged her to stay and listen, to believe him that his affair was long over, that he lied about the game because he had to have tests and he didn't want to worry her needlessly until the results came back and they knew for sure. He begged her to forgive him, to forgive him, to please, please forgive him.

Three days he sat in the apartment alone, in silence, not eating, not showering, in the same clothes he wore the day the president was assassinated...the day he found out cancer was eating away at his organs...his bones. Why? What was he waiting for? For her to walk through the door and they could start over again?

Martha? Are you coming home?

He picked up the phone three times. He'd tell Janice to tell Martha that he had cancer and that's why he lied about the game. He hung up before he finished dialing. What was he doing? He was pathetic, and it would look pathetic to do this.

How easy it would be to go across the hall and ring Frances's bell and collapse into her arms again. How much he needed to feel kindness…to feel comfort…to be kissed on the forehead and told that he was loved. How easy. How hard.

He broke her…his Francesca. Yes, her heart. He broke her heart. But more than that, Joseph knew he broke her…the woman she was. He would never forget that when they met for lunch six days after little Joey came into his life, she seemed to know exactly what he was going to say. They met in their favorite restaurant in Manhattan. It was a miracle he could get away from Martha for the afternoon…she hadn't let him out of her sight since Janice brought Joey to meet them that first night. And the shock, the happiness and joy of it all, had changed Martha. She came alive as she had never been before, even before their son's death. She was insatiable, wanting him, loving him, smothering him. It was a Martha he had longed for, and it was a Martha he finally had. The woman he had always loved had come alive and loved him back as he had always wanted.

As planned, they went away to the Catskills together, and it was like a honeymoon. They held hands, wrapped their arms around each other when they walked on the trails, and sat touching on the bench overlooking the lake. Martha laughed like a young girl, and truly listened to him when he spoke to her. And what plans they made for the future, for their new life with little Joey in it. All the things they would do with him…the way they would treat Janice so that she would learn to love them and never want to keep the boy away from them again. They would make her father their best friend and surround all of them with love and acceptance. They'd even go to church with them…Methodist was it?…if that's what it took. If Janice were to fall in love again and marry, they would accept the new man in her life; make him like them, too. Nothing would be too hard to do or to take if they could have their grandson in their lives.

But he had to talk to Frances. He had to explain and to tell her about little Joey and how he could do nothing to jeopardize this new and important relationship in his life. As if a miracle happened, Janice called and asked Martha to babysit with Joey for the day. Martha expected him to go with her, but he said, convincingly, "No, darling. You go. Make him know you and then he'll get to know me and then us together. Bond with him, don't share him with anyone right now."

It had worked, and she left to go to Ozone Park. He called Frances at work and asked her to meet him for lunch and she agreed without hesitation, but with an odd edge to her voice.

When he slid into the chair across the white linen-covered table from her, the look on her face told him that she already knew.

"Frances…" he had begun, reaching over to take her hand, but she kept it on her lap.

"Frances?" she asked. "Not Francesca?" Her voice was hoarse…tight.

"You must listen," he had begun, but then he couldn't find the right words. She didn't help him. She just sat staring at him, her back straight and stiff, her hands still on her lap.

"My son had fathered a child before he was killed and his mother brought him to our apartment last week to meet us. It is a miracle, Frances. A miracle…Martha and I are overcome with joy."

Frances had moved just a little at the news, shock showing on her face, but she remained with her hands hidden, her back straight.

"Frances, please understand what this means to me. Please try to accept that I cannot take any chances that Martha will find out about us. I can't choose you over my grandson. I just can't. I don't know how else to say it."

"Martha doesn't know about us?" That was all Frances said. Nothing about little Joey being alive and coming into his life; nothing about the shock of this strange woman coming to his door with this news. And then she repeated it, leaning forward now. "Joseph, Martha doesn't know about us?"

"No, no, but I can't take a chance that she will find out…not now…I just can't, Frances…oh, my poor darling, I'm so sorry."

"Joseph, I'm asking you again, Martha did not find out about you and me?"

"How would she? No, did you think that was what I was going to tell you? No, she doesn't know…I wish you could see her now that we have a grandson. I wish you could see how she has come alive from it, as though she's been in a tomb all these years, and someone unlocked that tomb and she's free of it…free to live again…to love again."

Frances picked up her glass of water and drank until it was empty. She placed the stemmed glass back down on the table very gently, deliberately not slamming it down. She did not look in his eyes when she asked, "You are telling me that we cannot be together anymore? Because you have a grandson? Not because Martha found out about us?"

Joseph had never felt so low…so despicable…in his life. He had had terrible moments during the years of this affair…guilty, agonizing hours when he couldn't look at himself in the mirror. But no matter how bad it had been before, looking at Frances now, and hearing her repeat to him what he was trying to tell her, was the worst he'd ever felt. He covered his eyes with his hand.

"Will you forgive me?" he had asked her after a long time.

"No...I will never forgive you, Joseph. If I live through this, and I'm not sure that I will survive this, I will never forgive you or speak with you again. Do not speak to me if you see me in the hallway. Do not get on the elevator with me ever again. Do not even walk on the same side of the street. In return, I promise I will not do any of these things either."

"Will you move away?" he asked, hoping that she would say yes...dreading it at the same time.

"No, Joseph, oh no, that would make it much too easy for you. I will stay and, unless you move away, I will torture you with my presence. I will be there...just beyond your reach...always, just beyond your reach. Martha, too, will know that I am there."

"Why would Martha care? I told you, she doesn't know." Then as though icy fingers were squeezing his heart, he wondered if she was planning to tell Martha about their affair. "Oh, Frances, please...please, I beg of you...don't tell Martha..."

Frances smirked. "No, I am not going to tell her. But I am going to hate her, and she'll know it."

He wondered how she could be so cold, speak so cruelly. They had shared such a wonderful love, such long, heartfelt conversations. They weren't strangers, and they weren't just lovers. They were friends...soul mates. They finished each other's sentences now, and shared each other's thoughts. She knew what he would say before he said it; he knew what she would do before she did it.

"You are so hurt," he said.

"Did you think I wouldn't be?"

"I knew...of course. But, Francesca, a grandson...God has given me a gift I never expected. My dead son's child...it is like looking in my Joey's face...I cannot turn my back on that...on him."

"And we couldn't enjoy that gift together?"

"No, we could not. Martha would never allow it. And this relationship with my grandson's mother is too new...I cannot bring scandal to it...I am afraid to try. She might run from us...from me. I need to get to know him...to get to know her...and for them to get to know me without this dishonor hanging over me."

She didn't speak. He tried to reach out for her again, and again she didn't move. "Please try to understand, Frances, my dearest."

"Your dearest? I thought I was your dishonor...your scandal."

"You are deliberately misunderstanding me."

"Joseph, I have only one more question. If Martha had found out and confronted you...if there was no surprise grandson in the mix...if Martha said to you that she knew about us and you had to make a choice—her or me—would you have left Martha and come to me?"

Joseph studied her face. He could not...would not...lie to her. How easy it would have been to tell her yes, if there was no little Joey, he would go to her. It would ease this pain for her, he knew that. But he could not be dishonest with Frances. He owed her honesty. "No...she is my wife."

For the first time since she had entered the restaurant, Frances's spine bent, she grabbed her stomach and bowed her head. It was at that moment Joseph knew that he had broken her

"Go," she whispered, holding on to the table with one hand. "Please, Joseph, go."

"Frances..."

She shook her head. She didn't look up at him. He stood. He wanted to touch her, to hold her in his arms, but he knew he should not do it.

He left the table, went to the Maître d' and gave him a twenty dollar bill. He glanced back, and Frances was still sitting in the same position. Bent. Broken.

What have I done?

He had asked himself that question then, and he asked it again now, sitting in the silent apartment without his wife...without his grandchild.

He asked it again.

What have I done?

Eleanor Walsh stood on one side of the elevator while Frances LaCorte stepped into the corner on the other side. They didn't speak. They hadn't spoken for years...not even small talk, not about the weather, not about banal things that people mention in an elevator to bridge the silence.

Frances noticed Eleanor glance at her with a judgmental once over. She'd seen it before. It infuriated her. She was in a bad state of mind anyway. It was almost Christmas, and she dreaded being alone again during the holidays. She looked at Eleanor again, at the shopping bags she carried from Macy's and Gimbal's, which were probably filled with gifts for her children. How dare the woman look at me that way when she had a family...a man who cared about her, such as he was.

"Mrs. Walsh, have you ever been in love?" Frances asked, unable to stop from speaking.

The other woman ignored the question, although she looked surprised by it.

"Have you ever loved someone you shouldn't have? Oh, forgive me, of course not, not the upstanding Mrs. Walsh. I have to tell you that I'm sick to death of your scorn. You don't even pretend to tolerate me. Well, here's a little tidbit for you...I can't stand the arguing and racket that goes on next door to me two nights a week...when that jerk..." Frances stopped speaking. She didn't want to go that far...she was immediately sorry. It wasn't the woman's fault; she didn't like it either. But Frances was so sick of Eleanor's contempt.

Eleanor lifted her chin and looked away, but not before Frances saw tears fill her eyes.

"No," Eleanor said without looking at Frances. "I have never loved another woman's husband if that's what you're asking me."

Frances didn't acknowledge the statement. She was immensely sorry she'd said anything. She started to reach out to press the button for the next floor so she could get out and walk the rest of the way. Eleanor reached over and took Frances's wrist to stop her from pressing the button. "But I have been the wife whose husband fell in love with another woman—just so you know that I have some knowledge of what you're talking about."

Frances pulled her hand away from Eleanor's grip.

"I know what it's like to feel betrayed. I know what it's like to wonder why my husband preferred another woman to me...the doubts...the feeling that I'm unlovable...the annihilation of my confidence...the end of trust...of dreams...of...of happily ever after."

Frances couldn't believe Eleanor was saying all this, and although she knew what Brendan was, she never would have thought he cheated.

"I know what it's like to be left with a baby to support, while he goes off to a new life...with a new wife."

"Mrs. Walsh...let's forget..." Frances didn't understand, but she wanted to end the conversation.

"My first husband," Eleanor continued. "Not Brendan."

"Look," Frances said, backing into the corner again. "I'm sorry. I don't know why I said anything. I just can't stand you judging me."

"Yes, Mrs. LaCorte, I do judge you. I can't help myself. I see the pain in Mrs. Kramer's eyes, and I know it by heart. You put it there."

"I fell in love with him."

Eleanor raised her eyebrows. "How lovely for you. Well, she's cleared the way. She's gone...have fun."

Frances felt the air leave her lungs and Eleanor must have heard or sensed it because she spun to look at her.

"What do you mean?" Frances was surprised by her own voice...it sounded as though it came from someone else.

"You don't know? He didn't tell you that she left him a month ago? Hmm...that's interesting. Why wouldn't he tell *you*?"

Frances didn't care that the woman across from her was being sarcastic; she needed more information.

"Why?"

"Why what? Why did she leave? Or why hasn't he told you?"

"Please," Frances breathed, closing her eyes. "Why, Mrs. Walsh?"

Eleanor sighed and looked down. Frances wasn't certain if Eleanor was annoyed or embarrassed...or maybe even a little remorseful.

"I don't know why she left. I do know that I found her in the hallway ringing your doorbell one night. She was almost catatonic with pain. She rang that bell for five minutes, until I came out and told her I'd seen you go out. I saw raw emotional agony on her face. I recognized it."

Frances raised her eyes to Eleanor. "I didn't want to hurt anyone...I never wanted to..."

"Save it."

"Please hear me."

"Mrs. LaCorte, I don't think I'm capable of hearing you...I don't understand and nothing you say will help me to understand. It's too close to what I went through; Mrs. Kramer's hurt is my hurt. But it doesn't matter now, he's free. What obstacle is there?"

"A wife he'll always love," Frances said, knowing it was true. "And a grandson."

The elevator stopped, but neither of them moved to open the door and leave.

"I loved him," Frances offered once again. "I loved him with all my heart."

"Yes...so did *she*...with all her heart."

Eleanor left the elevator.

Frances remained, even as someone else rang for it and it started to move.

Spring 1965

Saturday was Bridget Riordan's cleaning day. There wasn't much to clean, but she went at it as though her flat was about to be visited by the Pope. First the bathroom, scrubbed until every inch of soap scum was off the tiles. Then the bathtub; it had years of scratches on its surface and was worn in numerous spots, but she'd make sure that it was clean even if it looked shabby. The tiny sink, the white ceramic faucets, the glass shelves in the medicine cabinet, and finally the commode...every inch of the bathroom shone by 9 o'clock on Saturday morning...every Saturday morning.

She tackled the kitchenette then, always annoyed by the grime that came through the tiny window above the stove and cabinets, even in winter when it was closed. Where did the soot and dust come from, she'd wonder every week. There was always a layer of dust on the few pieces of furniture she owned, and the hardwood floor at the edges of her area rug would look dull until she wiped it down with her dust rag. It took all of two hours to clean the tiny apartment, and it would have taken less if Bridget didn't make such a production of it.

She was on her knees, finishing up the floor, when the doorbell rang. She stood, stretched out her legs to straighten her pedal pushers, and checked to make sure her sleeveless blouse hadn't come unbuttoned in her efforts with the floor.

It was Mrs. Sommer's face in the peephole.

"You're a sight for sore eyes," Bridget said, opening her door. "You're dressed up like the Queen of England."

Mrs. Sommer waved her hand at Bridget. "No, I'm not at all. I just needed a hand finishing up the zipper of my dress, though. I just can't seem to reach it like I used to...the arthritis in my arms, you know...and Mrs. Walsh and Audra are not home."

Bridget pulled the older woman inside and closed her door. "Turn around and let me see..."

The dress was a heavy deep purple crepe that was high in the back. Bridget finished zipping it up and turned Mrs. Sommer around to look at her. The dress was stylish, considering that it must have been fifteen years old or more. It was cut into a v at the neckline, and a silver and ruby brooch decorated the bottom of the v. It hung a little too loosely on Mrs. Sommer, and Bridget thought that Mrs. Sommer must have had a lovely figure when she first purchased this dress. She was thinner now and not as perky in the right places as she once was. It was obvious that the elderly woman had just had a permanent, too. Her white hair was in tight rows of curls.

"Where are you going to, wearin' a grand dress like this and your hair all done up?"

"An anniversary party at Steinway."

"Steinway Street, is it?"

"No," giggled Mrs. Sommer. "No, at the plant...the Steinway factory...pianos."

Bridget had no idea what she was talking about.

"You've never heard of Steinway pianos?" Mrs. Sommer was shocked.

"Well, of course, I have...but what has that to do with you?"

"I worked there...at Steinway...for many years after my husband died. I retired—a little early—just before I went to Arizona to be with my daughter."

"It's here? In Astoria? The Steinway factory?"

"It is. A beautiful complex. It was its own city, really, when it first opened. We lived there, my daughter and I. We lived in their housing when I worked there."

"What did you do?" Bridget wanted to know, curious, and offering Mrs. Sommer a seat at the table.

"Well, I did several things. At first, I worked in the factory after my husband died. Staining the woods...beautiful woods they use, you know. When they realized I spoke fluent German, they promoted me to the offices. I would communicate for them with the factory in Germany...Hamburg. There were only the two factories, there in Hamburg and here in Astoria, but ours was the parent office. They taught me how to type, so I'd type letters and orders in German that needed to go to Hamburg and translate orders and other communiques when they came in from Germany. It was a good job. It helped to support me and my little girl."

"You speak German? I had no idea? And you write it, too?"

"My parents were from Germany…and my husband came here to America from Berlin when he was a child. We all spoke German…and English, of course. I still have relatives there, and I write from time to time. Not much anymore. After the war things changed."

"So, what's the anniversary about?"

"Well, every five years, a group of us who all retired at the same time get together to catch up and have dinner. It's not really an anniversary, exactly, but we call it that. And it is always on the anniversary of the day I retired…so that makes it a real anniversary for me if not for all of them."

"That sounds lovely," Bridget said.

"It is lovely…to be with old friends…but we don't bother except every five years. They all have their own lives. My old boss at Steinway always pays…he arranges for the meal to be served to us in their private dining room. Most of us worked thirty years or more—through the second World War."

"Were they nice…the people at Steinway?"

Mrs. Sommer thought the question over. "Yes, I suppose. Of course, it was work, not fun…and the bosses I had were stern. Germans can be stern sometimes, you know. But we understood one another, and they were kind to me. My Eunice never got sick, not even a cold, when she was a child, so I rarely had to take time off to care for her once she was in school. They appreciated that. She was given free piano lessons by another woman who worked there, and when she was a teenager, she worked in the factory, too, testing the pianos. She was quite a pianist, my Eunice. She played so beautifully that people would stop working to listen to her. It got so that the boss only wanted her to test the pianos…after the day shift or on the weekends because she was in school. It was a good place to work. The pay was decent for a woman. My last boss—the one who buys dinner for us— was a good man. He's retired now, but he always remembers and joins us. I think he once had a crush on me…but he was married and I had a child to take care of. I wasn't interested."

"Being a German company must have created problems during the war, no?"

Germaine Sommer leaned back in her chair, remembering. "We made very few pianos during the depression, and then the war came. It was an American company—even though there was a factory in Germany and the company was owned by Germans—so there were some difficulties in alliances, of course. The factory in Hamburg was bombed a few times by Allied forces, almost destroyed. But here in the United States—right here in Astoria—we built some things for the soldiers and sailors. We actually made little pianos, we called them GI pianos, that could be carried by four men. They were used on ships, and I had heard that they were even dropping them by parachutes where soldiers were so they could have music." She laughed and shook her head. "They had to lay off a lot of workers during that time. But they kept me on…I was useful because of my German."

Mrs. Sommer smiled tightly at Bridget. "It wasn't always a good time for Germans here during the war…both wars. Things would happen there, in the factory, with some workers not understanding that the company was mostly American. And I would sometimes be called names…Nazi even or Nazi sympathizer…and my daughter, too, in school—high school by then. I was afraid sometimes during the war…mostly for her. I made certain we never spoke German in public or even in our apartment in fear a neighbor would hear and be suspicious of us. It didn't take much, you know." She sighed. "But we made it through."

"I'm sorry," Bridget was compelled to say.

Mrs. Sommer shook her head. "No, don't be. We weren't interned like the Japanese people. Some were, I guess, but not most of the German-speaking people. There were too many of us. People are ignorant sometimes. We learn to live with it. Mrs. Walsh and I are always telling Audra not to chime in when the new people at the end of the block are being teased and made fun of…the Spanish who moved in."

"You mean the Cubans?"

"Whatever they are…Mrs. Walsh heard that some of the Italians and Irish who own homes here were harassing them, and Mrs. Walsh wants to be sure that Audra doesn't go along with the other little girls. It's the way it is, when new people come. People don't understand them and are afraid. That doesn't make it right."

"But you weren't new…you were an American."

Germaine laughed, a little too bitterly. "I was German suddenly to everyone else…spoke German, had a German name. That's the way of it."

"How many years did you work there?"

"Thirty-two."

"Do you have a pension from them?

"No."

"All those years…in one place."

"Yes," Mrs. Sommer said. "Many years. I'm grateful for them…I supported my child because of them. Paid for her college education with my pay from that job."

"But nothing to show for it except a dinner every five years?" Bridget was unbelieving.

"I'm alive…I fed myself and my child…I have a home here—a roof over my head—a little money. Clothes. That's something. Remember, I'm a woman, Miss Riordan. I was lucky to have work. Just a high school diploma and yet they hired me."

"No they were lucky to have you, Mrs. Sommer, and I think they knew it. At least, I think your boss knew it and that's why he buys you and your friends a dinner every five years. Women don't realize how valuable they are to a business...how good they make their bosses look...and men who realize it keep it firmly under their hats."

"It's true. But it won't change. I applied for a promotion once...I was doing the work anyway...but they gave it to a man. They said he had a family to support. I suppose they didn't consider my daughter a family to support." Mrs. Sommer looked away through Bridget's window lost in thought for a long moment.

Then she looked at the thin silver wristwatch that decorated her arm. "Oh, and this...he—my boss—gave me this when I left."

That too was a little too loose, but Bridget noticed it was elegant...expensive. Indeed, that boss must have admired Mrs. Sommer a great deal.

Mrs. Sommer stood and said, "It's a man's world. It will always be a man's world."

Bridget shrugged and walked her neighbor to the door. "We'll, see," she said, patting Mrs. Sommer on the back. "We'll just see about that."

Fall 1965

The elevator in Ashley Hall was between the fifth and sixth floors when the lights went out and the elevator stopped, one of millions of electrical machines and appliances across the Northeast United States and Canada that stopped working. From Buffalo to the eastern border of New Hampshire and from New York City to Ontario, a massive power outage struck without warning and the "world" went dark.

Eamon Williams and Frances LaCorte didn't know that, however. All they knew was that they entered the elevator on the first floor at 5:27 p.m. and seconds later it stopped suddenly and went dark and silent.

"Hey," Frances said. "What's going on?"

Eamon couldn't see her in the pitch blackness. "Good question." He felt for the panel of buttons and pressed every one that his fingers came to. He knew the alarm was down at the bottom right corner of the panel and he counted down and over until he found it. He pressed three times. Nothing. No sound.

"Shouldn't an emergency light go on or something?" Frances asked.

"I thought so," he said.

"This is a little scary, isn't it? I have a recurring dream that I'm in this elevator and it slips and starts to plummet down and crash. I always wake up before it hits the bottom...this is too much like a dream come true for my taste."

Eamon sighed, "Yes, I'd say so. I wonder what's going on."

He felt for the door and tried to pry it open but it wouldn't budge.

"Well, I'm not too embarrassed to start screaming," Frances said, and Eamon could hear panic in her voice.

"No, it's all right. They'll get us moving shortly. Don't worry."

"But if the alarm isn't working..."

"It's okay, let's just wait a few minutes. I'm sure they'll know. It's 5:30.

People are coming home from work now, so someone will ring for the elevator and realize it's not moving. They'll get Biermann...and if he can't fix it, he'll call the elevator maintenance company, and we'll be out before you know it."

"Mmm, if you say so. Okay. I promise I won't go psycho...yet."

They stood, each in their own corner, silent for a long time. Their ears strained to hear any movement...any voices. Before long they did hear apartment doors opening and then closing. Soon there were voices.

"See...it didn't take long," Eamon said to Frances. "Hello," he shouted. "Hello...we're stuck in here, in the elevator. Can someone call Biermann?"

"In here," Frances joined in. "We're stuck in the elevator. Here...yoo-hoo...in the elevator."

But no one seemed to hear them.

Eamon said, "Wait...let's listen...there seem to be a lot of people out there talking..."

Voices faded in and out, but they heard a woman say, "There isn't a light anywhere ... I looked out the window and it's completely black out there. Not a light in sight...only the moonlight."

The words gave Eamon a chill.

"Mr. Williams, did you hear that?" Frances asked him, panic back in her voice.

"A blackout, I guess," he said, trying to keep his voice very steady.

"So what does that mean for us?"

"The electricity has to come back on in a few minutes. Stop worrying."

He felt the elevator move but it was Frances walking into the middle. "Hey, out there," she shouted. "We're stuck in here. Can somebody please get us out?"

They stood listening, but the voices from the two floors—one above and one below—came and went away again. Then they heard Audra Walsh's voice call out. "Daddy, do we have candles for Mrs. Sommer?"

"Audra!" Eamon shouted now. "Audra...we're in the elevator."

There was no sound, no movement. Then they heard Brendan Walsh say, "This is all I can find. I don't know where your mother keeps the candles. I know she has some votive candles that she uses to light in front of the statue of the Blessed Mother, but for the life of me I can't find them. This flashlight's batteries are going to go out soon and I don't know where she keeps the batteries either."

"They're in the junk drawer in the kitchen, Dad," they heard Audra say and then her footsteps moved away from the elevator.

"No!" Eamon shouted. "Audra! In here! Can you hear us?"

"Daddy, come out here again, please."

They heard Brendan say, "Wait, I'll be right there. I'm looking for the batteries. Is she all right? Mrs. Sommer?"

159

"Yeah, she's all right. But I think I hear something else."

Eamon and Frances started shouting at the same time. "In here! We're stuck in the elevator!"

"Daddy, someone is in the elevator!" they heard Audra shriek.

"All right, all right, calm down, baby. What are you saying?"

Again, Eamon and Frances started to call out.

"Who's in there?" Brendan asked, unable to distinguish their voices because they were shouting at the same time. "How many of you?"

Eamon reached out and touched Frances's arm to silence her. "Mr. Walsh...this is Eamon Williams and Mrs. LaCorte is in here, too."

There was silence for a long moment, and then Brendan said. "Okay, don't worry. What floor are you near?"

"Between five and six."

They heard him trying to open the outer elevator door on the sixth floor.

When the elevator was working, the inner door slid open between the outer wall of the elevator and the shaft wall, and that unlocked the door to the hallway when it was in place. Unless that lock was pushed open, the outer door wouldn't open without a special tool. It was what prevented people from falling to their death in the elevator shaft. Eamon heard Walsh tug on the handle again. "The idiot...he can't open it that way."

"Well, at least he's trying and he knows we're in here." Frances was reassured.

Eamon ignored her, "Walsh," he called out, "call Biermann, please."

"There's a black out, Williams. All the telephone lines are busy. I'll take the flashlight and see if I can find Biermann. Sit tight."

Eamon leaned against the wall of the elevator again. Neither he nor Frances spoke to each other. Then they heard Audra call down.

"Mr. Williams, I'm still here. If you're scared, I can stay and keep talking to you. You're not alone...I'm here."

Eamon smiled. She was a big girl now, about thirteen. She still wore her hair long, but curly hair was just not the style anymore. He had overheard Audra and her mother having an argument about how the girl would ruin her hair if she continued to iron it and sleep on beer cans. It had made him smile. He felt as though he'd watched the child grow up...he had watched her grow up. He noticed that she was wearing light pink—almost white—lipstick the last time they were in the elevator together, and if he guessed right, a little powder and mascara. But she still had a baby face.

"She's growing up," Frances whispered as though reading his mind.

"I was just thinking the same thing. She's a teenager now."

"She's still very shy, but she's always polite."

"Would her mother allow anything different?" Eamon asked, and they both chuckled.

Then Audra called out again, "I have a transistor radio. I'm going to go get it so let you know what's going on, Mr. Williams. Just wait for a minute; I'll be right back."

"We might as well sit down, Mrs. LaCorte." He slid down until his backside rested on the floor. His suit would need cleaning, but what the heck? He could tell that Frances LaCorte was doing the same thing.

"Please call me Frances. We've lived on the same floor of this building for years. Enough of the formality. After all, we may be spending the last few minutes of our lives together here in this coffin."

"Now, enough of that," Eamon said. "We're stuck…but we're safe."

"By the way…Eamon…I heard that your mother died a few weeks ago. I meant to slip a sympathy card under your door, but I keep forgetting. I'm sorry…I'm very sorry about your loss. Was she very ill?"

"No, actually, she died in her sleep…an embolism, they think. Painless they tell me."

"That's something to be grateful for. Were you very close?"

Eamon leaned his head back against the elevator. "Yes…my father died when I was ten; she raised me by herself. I had no siblings, so it was just her and me."

"I'm so sorry," Frances said again.

Eamon thought about the wake. The only family that came was a distant cousin of his father's from Pennsylvania. They only had older relatives, his mother's sister who was in a nursing home, and a few of her cousins, but no one else. His mother's friends—those who could get to the funeral home—came and paid their respects, and of course, John was there with him, and that was his salvation. It got him through the wake and the funeral services…and then the burial. At the luncheon afterward there were Eamon's closest friends, mostly men he and John knew, their friend Honora, and a few women from his office in the bank. Some had their husbands with them.

He was still going through her things, trying to sort them out—what to keep, what to give away, what to throw away. Honora helped him with this chore; she knew what were treasures and what was junk. The house, the one he had grown up in, was already listed for sale. John and Honora helped him get it in shape—just a lick and a promise, as John would say. Good enough. Honora hung new drapes and curtains, and bought rugs and towels. It was in a nice neighborhood in Forest Hills. The real estate agent said it should sell quickly. Lots of New York City firemen and their families lived in the area. Eamon knew that. His father had been a fireman in New York. The word that it was for sale would go out quickly and a young fireman and his family would buy it. That's how it was in those neighborhoods.

"What did she look like?" Frances asked him.

He thought it an odd question. "When? At the end?"

"Not necessarily...when she was young, when you were growing up."

He pictured his mother when she was young. For the first time in his life, he saw her as a woman, not just his mother. It surprised him. "She was beautiful. She had fair skin, and the bluest eyes. She kept herself well, you know. She got her hair done every Thursday afternoon, and wore a net over at night so it stayed perfect. We didn't have a lot of money, but enough, and she bought good clothes for herself and for me. She made sure I was dressed very well. It was almost an obsession. In the end, it was a source of embarrassment for me—I was the butt of jokes for it—but I never blamed her. She meant well. It was important to look your best, she used to say, 'People judge you by how you are dressed, Eamon.'"

"She was right," Frances said.

"Yes."

"And you still dress elegantly, Eamon. She taught you well."

He didn't thank her.

"Your friend, the one who comes from time to time, have you known each other all your lives?"

"Yes, since we were in grammar school."

"Are you very much in love with him?" She asked this very quietly.

He was stunned by the question, and deeply alarmed. She knew. How did she know? But he didn't hear any sarcasm or revulsion in her question. He chose not to answer.

"I was in love...with the wrong person," she said. Now her voice was sad.

Again, Eamon chose not to acknowledge what she said. He knew, of course. He imagined that most of the people on that floor suspected the affair, but he had actually seen Kramer with her in a restaurant in the city. It was in the lobby of a hotel. They were just paying their check, and he watched from the bar as they walked to the hotel elevator and got on together. When he saw them in the same place two weeks later, he told John that they had to stop meeting at that bar. He didn't want to embarrass them, and he didn't want to be embarrassed if they found out that he knew. There was enough awkwardness in his life at Ashley Hall. He still couldn't look Mrs. Walsh in the eye since she had seen John's portrait in his bedroom. He wasn't certain, he could be imagining it, but he detected a difference in her husband's attitude toward him since then, too. Nothing threatening, as he had feared, but a difference. He wondered how many people knew about him and John. He thought they were so clever...or at least, John did.

"He left me for his grandson."

This time the pain in her voice prompted a response from him. "I'm sorry, Frances."

"He thought his wife didn't know until she told him...but she did know. She knew for two years before something set her off and she left him. She lived with him...slept with him...for two years... knowing and never saying it to him. Of course, during those two years that she knew, he wasn't with me anymore. But she knew about me...about our affair. She just didn't tell him she knew. They pretended I didn't exist because they had a newly found grandson."

Eamon pulled his knee up and placed his arm over it. He wished Audra would come back. He didn't want to hear any more about the affair...or the end of it. The man was sick, probably dying. He was a skeleton...his skin hung on him these days. Eamon wasn't sure what kind of cancer Kramer had, but over the last two years, he had gotten thinner and sicker. He wondered what Frances thought of that...she couldn't help notice. The wife never did come back. If Frances was so in love with him, why didn't she go to him, help him while he was sick?

"Did your mother know?" Frances asked.

The question confused him.

"About you?" she prodded. "And your friend."

He didn't answer her.

"I'm sorry...none of my goddamned business."

No, he thought, *it isn't any of your goddamned business*. "Yes, she probably did, but we never spoke about it," he finally answered.

"Even though you were close?"

"You just don't go to your mother and say, 'Hey, Mom, I'm a homosexual. I love a man, and you're never going to have any grandchildren even though I know you want them.'"

"You probably could have told her. She loved you."

"It was a conversation I chose not to have."

"But as you say, she probably knew anyway."

"Probably doesn't count. She could continue to pretend that she had raised a normal young man who was just playing the field until he found the right woman. She used to call me her playboy son... as I got older she'd refer to me as an 'established bachelor.'"

"Then what makes you think she knew?" Frances wanted to know. She wanted to know too much.

"Because she stopped asking John to come for dinner at her house. She'd known him from the time he was in the first grade...he was like another son to her...Christmas, Thanksgiving, birthdays...he was always there with us. And then all of a sudden she called me up at the bank and said, 'Don't bring John for dinner on Sunday. I don't want him.' She told me she didn't like him anymore. She said she thought he was a little 'weird' and not a good influence on me."

Eamon remembered that he hadn't argued with her. He knew it would hurt John, but there was nothing that could be done. If he fought his mother, she'd have to say it out loud, and none of the three of them wanted it said out loud.

Audra interrupted the conversation. "Mr. Williams? Mrs. LaCorte? I'm back. I found the transistor and some more batteries. It's a blackout all over the Northeast. No electricity anywhere, even in Canada. I'm a little worried about my mother. She would be on the subway now. Maybe she's stuck in the tunnels. They say there are hundreds stuck in the subways, and in elevators—like you guys—and they don't think the electricity will come back on for hours."

"Oh, brother," Frances said.

Eamon was suddenly very, very weary. "Where is your father?" he called up to Audra.

"He hasn't come back up. He went to look for Mr. Beirmann...but he probably got stopped on other floors by people needing his flashlight. No one seems to have candles or flashlights."

"All right, Audra. Thanks for the update."

They sat in silence again. Every once in a while, Audra would call down to them, "Are you both all right?"

"No sign of your father? Of Biermann?" Eamon would ask her.

"Not yet. But they'll come, Mr. Williams. Daddy won't forget you."

Another hour passed, or so it seemed. They had no way of knowing the time. Eamon couldn't see his watch in the dark.

"Eamon, do you think he's dying?" Frances asked.

"Who?"

"Joseph."

"Yes, I do. He has cancer."

"He looks like death already, doesn't he?"

"Yep...he's a sick man."

"I want to go to him, but I just can't."

Eamon didn't answer her...he didn't think she wanted an answer.

"I know that he sees his grandson...I actually saw him going into his apartment with the boy not long ago. She must have relented...his wife I mean. At first she wasn't going to let him have anything to do with the kid. But the boy's mother talked to her...told her it wasn't fair to the little boy."

"How do you know all of this?" Eamon asked her.

"Mrs. Walsh. When his wife left him, Mrs. Walsh reached out to him. She made him dinner a few times a week because he was getting so thin. She felt sorry, not just for him but for his wife, and I guess, a little sorry for me, because she'd tell me things. She wasn't real sympathetic toward me, though. Her first husband had left her for another woman, so she has no love for the other woman in anyone's marriage. She made sure I knew that. But she's got a good heart. She's a romantic, I guess...she's probably a sucker for love stories. It's not that she was minding our business, but I think Joseph was kind of using her as a go-between...and she let him... I don't know. Maybe not."

"They're a complicated lot, those Walshes," Eamon said.

As though on cue, Brendan Walsh bellowed down to them, "Okay, Williams. I'm coming."

"He's coming?" Eamon echoed to no one in particular.

They heard the hall door to the elevator shaft open. They felt the elevator vibrate, then heard someone jump down onto the top of the elevator.

"God almighty," Frances breathed. "He'll kill us."

"Hang on," they heard him say. His voice was clearer now, not muffled as it had been when he was on the other side of the door in the hallway. A small amount of light shone through the little round porthole in the elevator door, reflecting off the concrete wall from above them. Eamon could see Frances's face now.

There was the sound of scraping above them. They could hear Walsh grunting with effort, then a bang of metal against concrete, and Walsh swore.

"Mr. Walsh, is everything all right?" Frances called up to him.

"Yeah, I'm trying to pry off the trap door."

Eamon almost laughed. "The trap door...I never even thought of it."

"Yeah, well it wouldn't have done you any good," Walsh said, his voice straining against whatever he was doing above them. "This damn thing is rusted shut." With that, the elevator lurched a little and the trap door above them gave. Walsh shined the flashlight down onto them. They couldn't see him because the light blinded them.

"You okay?" he asked.

"We are now," Frances said. "How does it feel to be a hero?"

Walsh laughed, a hearty, good natured laugh. Eamon joined him, more with relief than with humor.

"Okay, you first. Give her a boost, Williams."

Eamon took hold of Frances's arm and said, "I'll bend over and you put your foot on my hands. I'll lift you up to Walsh. Hold on to the wall until you get your balance, and then reach your arms up to him."

"My purse."

"I'll hand it up to Walsh after you're up there."

Frances took off her high heels and placed her foot in Eamon's hands. He hoisted her up and in a second she felt Brendan Walsh's hands grab her and pull her up. She sat on the edge of the hole then pulled her legs up. Walsh held her arm until she was in a standing position. He moved the flashlight up to the hallway door, about five and a half feet above them.

"It's not too high...think you can do it? Audra and Joseph Kramer are up there to help you. I'll push from down here, and they'll pull you up."

"They can't...neither one of them is strong enough," she said, aghast.

Joseph's voice came to them from above. He peeked into the shaft, and his face was illuminated by the flashlight. "It's okay, Frances. I still have some life in me. Audra is skinny but strong, aren't you?"

Audra looked down at her then. "Sure, we'll be able to help."

"Okay, get ready," Walsh said, bending down, indicating that she should stand on his shoulders.

"I'll fall down the shaft," she said then, truly afraid.

"You're not skinny enough," he said laughing. "There's not much room between the elevator and the wall. Just be careful."

Frances took a deep breath and put each foot on a shoulder. She gasped as he stood up, and she reached out and found the metal riggings that supported the elevator. He turned so that she was facing the doorway and she let go of the riggings and grabbed at the two hands that dangled from the hall above her. They were Joseph's hands. She knew those hands. They were bonier, but they were his hands. He grabbed hard and pulled. Audra then grabbed at the back of her dress and helped to pull her up until her waist was bent over the edge of the shaft and the floor. Mrs. Sommer held the door open while Joseph and Audra continued to pull Frances all the way over the edge and into the hall.

Audra wrapped her arms around Frances in an embrace. "I'm so glad you're safe," she said.

Frances laughed, "Yeah, me too, honey." But she was still holding one of Joseph's hands and she squeezed it tight. She could barely see his face. There were only two candles lighting the hallway. "Thank you," she said to him.

In the shadows, Joseph nodded and squeezed her hand again. They all laughed when Brendan Walsh called out, "Heads up," and first her purse and then each of her high heels flew up and into the hallway.

There was a commotion when Brendan Walsh helped Eamon out of the elevator—a little swearing from Walsh, and couple of grunts from Eamon—and then Joseph moved into action again to help the elegant man over the edge of the doorway and into the hall. This time Frances helped the same way Audra had, grabbing Eamon's suit jacket and pulling hard until he was lying on the floor next to them.

"Okay," Eamon said after catching his breath. "I'd like to know how we're going to pull Brendan out of that shaft."

They all knew what he meant...the big man had no one to lift him up from below while they pulled him out.

"Don't worry," Audra said, "Daddy will get himself out."

Sure enough, Walsh started to pull himself up on the riggings. When he was even with them, he said, "Now what?" with a big grin. They all laughed.

Eamon shook his head, "You're going to have to jump, Brendan."

"Yeah…okay…get ready. Make sure you catch me and pull me in."

Eamon stood holding on to the doorway of the shaft. "Come on, jump and I'll grab you. Joseph, get on the other side."

Brendan did as he was told. His shoe slipped off the edge when it made contact, but both Joseph and Eamon grabbed an arm and steadied the large man until both his feet were planted on the marble floor.

Eamon didn't let go of his arm. Instead, he held Brendan's elbow with one hand and shook his hand with the other. "I can't thank you enough."

The men looked into each other's eyes, then Brendan looked away, a little embarrassed. "It was nothing…when I was an architect, and a building I designed was going up, I did that kind of stuff all the time. I walked on beams twenty stories up at the construction site—nothing to the left or right of me."

"Well, I'm very, very glad you were around," Frances said, kissing the big man's cheek and giving him a hug.

Joseph closed the door to the shaft and said, "How do we keep people from opening this now and falling in?"

Audra ran to the door of her apartment, "Daddy, give me the flashlight. I'll make a sign and we can put a chair against the door."

"Here," he said, handing her the flashlight. "Be careful."

Audra disappeared into the apartment, taking the light with her. The others could see one another only through the dim candlelight.

Mrs. Sommer said, "Let's hope Eleanor gets home all right. I wonder where she is?"

Brendan looked worried at the mention of his wife's name. "If I knew, I'd go out to look for her. But there are too many places she could be. I'm best staying here with Audra. Maybe she'll call…if the lines open up. I'm worried about Paige, too. She works in the city now."

"The lights will go on soon, surely," Joseph said.

"By the way," Eamon said. "Where's Beirmann?"

"Drunk as a skunk in the basement," Brendan answered. "I took some of his tools from his workshop to get you out." He smiled wickedly, "And I left them all on the roof of that elevator. He'll be looking for them for a year."

Eamon laughed out loud, as did Joseph.

"All right, then," Mrs. Sommer said. "I'm going in. I'm exhausted after all this excitement."

Joseph picked up the two candles and gave one to her. She led the way for Eamon; his door was right next to hers. She held the candle out until he unlocked his door and they both disappeared into the darkness of their flats. Brendan went into his apartment after saying good night to Joseph and Frances. He looked embarrassed again, eager to escape.

Joseph held the other candle near the lock on Frances's door so she could see enough to put her key in it.

She did so and then looked up into his gaunt face, all the more haunting in the flame of the candle. His eyes were so sunken they looked like empty sockets in the eerie light. She looked away and closed her eyes.

He asked, "Do you have a flashlight?"

She nodded. "I keep it in the drawer next to my bed."

He nodded. He started to turn away from her. She reached out and touched his arm. "I'm sorry you're ill, Joseph."

He looked back at her then. He smiled. His teeth looked too large for his deflated face. "Me too."

6B

SOMMER

Germaine sat in her chair and grieved.

Her little Corky was dead. He was all curled up on her bed this morning, just as he always was, but he didn't wag his tail when Germaine sat up. He didn't lift his head to watch her limp into the bathroom. He didn't jump down and wait for his leash to be fastened to his collar. He stayed curled in a ball.

"Corky," she called to him. "Audra will be here to walk you in a minute. Don't make her late for school, now. Come on, boy."

No reaction. No movement. Little Corky was gone.

The doorbell rang as she expected. How would she tell Audra? She heard the girl put the key in the lock; she had a key now so that she could let herself in when Germaine's arthritis was too painful to get out of the chair. The tables had turned; the little girl she had babysat all those years was now her babysitter.

"Mrs. Sommer?" Audra called. She appeared from the hallway dressed in her Mother of Christ high school uniform. She was so tall now, with a woman's figure...even the loose green weskit couldn't hide that fact. The nuns tried, but little girls grew up and their womanhood showed through the unattractive plaids and long skirts and knee socks. Audra had the waist of her skirt rolled up so that the hemline was way above her knees. The green knee socks might hide her slender ankles, but she found a way to show off her thighs.

"Where's Corky?" Audra asked, looking impatient. "I have an algebra test this morning and I want to study with Mercedes in the cafeteria. I have to leave early."

Germaine swallowed hard. She couldn't say the words, they were too painful. She pointed to the bedroom.

Audra frowned and walked through the living room to the bedroom.

She saw Corky on the bed. "Hey, Cork, come on boy…let's go out…"

Audra turned around to Germaine. "Why isn't he moving?"

Germaine shook her head, and for the first time, tears spilled from her eyes and down her cheeks.

Audra looked horrified suddenly. "Oh my God, no!"

She ran from the apartment and within a minute, returned with her mother. Eleanor was dressed for work, all but her high heels. She didn't say anything to Germaine. She went into the bedroom. Audra stood at the doorway, her shoulders hunched, her arms across her chest.

Eleanor said. "Audra, go get the empty box in my closet—the one that my new hat was in."

Audra left again. She returned with the hatbox and a crocheted blanket she had made with Germaine's help. Germaine could see that the girl was crying so hard she could barely breathe. She put the box on the bed and placed the blanket inside it, spreading the corners out beyond the edge of the box.

"Do you want to pet him one last time?" Eleanor asked her.

The girl shook her head and covered her face now, convulsed in sobs.

Germaine watched from her chair as Eleanor picked up the stiff little body and placed it gently into the hat box. She pulled the corners of the blanket up and over the body of the dog, covering it completely. She then put the top of the box back over the rim. When she stood up straight, Germaine could see that Eleanor was crying now, too, although she tried to hide it.

"Mrs. Sommer," she said coming out with the box. "Do you want me to take him?"

"Where?" Germaine managed to ask.

"I'll take him over to the vet's office. They'll take care of him for us."

"It's too late, Mommy. He's dead," Audra said, confused.

Her mother smiled sadly. "It's okay, honey, the vet knows what to do now."

Audra went over to Germaine and sat on the arm of the chair. She leaned down and put her head on top of Germaine's. "I'm sorry he died, Mrs. Sommer. I loved him, too. I loved him so much."

Germaine reached out and patted the girl's bare knee. It was going to be so lonely without his gentle little presence.

"I don't want to leave Mrs. Sommer," Audra said to her mother. "Let me stay home with her today. I'm too sad to go to school anyway, Mom."

Germaine could see Eleanor thinking it over. "Oh, but your grades…don't you have an exam…"

"I'll make it up, Mom. I'll make it up next week. Sister Anecetus will understand…she's a really nice teacher."

Eleanor thought some more, and then nodded. "Okay, go change out of your uniform and I'll call the school."

She put the box down on a chair and picked up the receiver of Germaine's phone. She dialed the high school, explained that there was a death in the family and Audra would have to miss school, and then hung up. She walked over and stood in front of Germaine.

"Are you all right?"

Germaine was miserable. It hurt down to the core of her being. He was just a dog…but he was her family. He licked her face when she was sad, he did tricks to make her laugh, and he made her get up every morning to live another day because he had to be fed, and walked, and loved. He gave her life purpose. He was such a happy little friend. And he was a connection with Audra…he tied them together.

"Mrs. Sommer," Eleanor said, taking her hand. "I'm sorry this happened to you. I know it's hard to lose a pet…it's happened to me…and it's okay to grieve. Don't be embarrassed."

Eleanor handed Germaine a wad of tissues that she had in her pocket. Germaine wiped her face and blew her nose. "I'm going to miss him."

"Of course, you are. We all will…but especially you and Audra…you were so kind to share him with her. He was her childhood pet…and that's because you shared him. We're all going to miss him. Brendan will be heartbroken, too."

Germaine nodded. "He did love him…he always called him the little rascal."

Eleanor smiled, "Yes, he did, didn't he? That's because he loved him."

Germaine blew her nose again. "Thank you for letting Audra stay home with me. I don't think I could be alone today."

"No, of course not, and she wouldn't be able to concentrate at school. You stay together and mourn little Corky. By tomorrow you'll both feel better."

Audra returned in jeans and a light blue sweater. She had stopped sobbing, but her face was red and her nose was still running.

Eleanor handed her a ten dollar bill. "Honey, order pizza at lunchtime, have it delivered. I'll get dinner for Mrs. Sommer tonight. And make her a cup of tea now, and some toast—put a little butter on it. She likes marmalade, there's some in our fridge. You take good care of her, okay?"

"I will, Mom," Audra promised.

"Okay, I'll call you later."

Eleanor picked up the hat box and left the apartment. There were fresh sobs from Audra then, and Germaine cried into her tissues. He was gone officially now.

After Audra made Germaine tea and toast, she went into the bedroom to make the bed for Germaine. There was some soiling on the bedspread, where Corky had lain, and so she stripped the bed and put the sheets and

171

blankets in a basket. She remade the bed with clean sheets and found another blanket—the light weight blanket Germaine used in the summer—and put that on the bed.

They watched television the rest of the day. After the game shows, Audra found an old movie and they watched it together. It was a silly movie, about a leprechaun and a businessman in New York City, with lots of slapstick, and Audra seemed pleased when Germaine laughed a few times.

They ate their pizza and each drank a glass of cola. Their moods lightened a little. But by late afternoon, Germaine felt ill. She was having trouble breathing. She didn't want to alarm Audra, so she tried not to show it. She went into the bathroom and sat on the toilet for a long time, trying to catch her breath. Her chest felt strange, and there was a pain under her arm and in her jaw.

She decided to lie down for a little while. She was certain it was the shock and strain of Corky's death. She told Audra she was a little tired and would lie down on the sofa. "Don't let me sleep too long, or I won't be able to sleep tonight," she said.

"Okay, Mrs. Sommer. Do you want anything? More tea?"

Germaine shook her head and lowered herself onto the sofa. Audra covered her with an afghan and got a pillow from the bed to put under Germaine's head.

"I'm going to go back to my apartment, Mrs. Sommer, so you can sleep. I'll come back in an hour. Is that all right?"

Germaine wished she could just catch her breath. The pain would go away if she could only breathe. Maybe she shouldn't let Audra leave her alone.

The doorbell rang, and Audra left Germaine to answer it. Germaine heard another young girl's voice at the door. "What happened? They told us someone died?"

Germaine recognized it as Mercedes' voice, one of Audra's closest friends from school.

"Well, yes, sort of," Audra said. "It was Corky, Merry. Our little Corky was dead this morning when Mrs. Sommer got up."

"Ohhhh, noooo," and suddenly there were tears again, and the girls were holding on to each other. Mercedes was well acquainted with Corky since she was with Audra in the apartment after school almost every day. She and Audra would walk Corky together when they got home, still in their uniforms, full of gossip from the school day.

Mercedes lived at the end of the street in one of the flats in the row of brownstones. There were four Cuban families there...they had all escaped Castro's regime and were related. Mercedes told Germaine that they had left beautiful homes and big cars to live here in the United States, mostly in poverty since they had nothing now. The girls had met on their way to high school the very first day, although they had seen each other before. Knowing they were going to the same school now bridged the chasm that being white and being Latina in 1960s New York had created.

They traveled on the elevated subway together to the end of the line, and walked to the school. They were in different homerooms, and were only in one class together, but at the end of the day they found each other and came home together. Germaine liked Mercedes. She liked the girl's gentle ways, her intelligence and compassion. She was happy that Audra had her friendship. She enjoyed sitting in her living room listening to the girls giggle and share stories over their homework.

But this day she couldn't enjoy them. She wanted to call out to the girls. The pain was worse. She knew she needed help.

"How is she?" Mercedes asked, and Germaine knew the girl meant her.

"So sad...she's so sad, Merry," Audra answered.

"Audra," Germaine tried to call, but she couldn't breathe in enough air.

"Can I talk to her?" Mercedes asked.

"She's sleeping."

"No...come," Germaine tried to say. The pain was growing stronger, spreading across her chest now, to her back.

"Well, let me leave a note for her. I'll go into the kitchen and write it."

The girls went into the kitchen, and Germaine pushed herself over, trying to stand. She rolled off the couch and fell with a loud thump. The girls glanced in to see what caused the noise. They saw her on the floor, straining for air.

"Oh, God," Audra screamed.

They both ran to her, tried to get her up off the floor, but she was dead weight. Germaine grabbed Audra's sweater. "Call...help ..."

Mercedes jumped up and grabbed the phone and dialed 911. Each spin of the rotary dial seemed to take forever. It was new...this emergency call number. It had just been initiated, and the kids in high school were being trained to use it in cases of emergency.

"Hello? Yes," she said into the phone. "We need help. A woman is sick, she's passing out...I don't know exactly...she's about seventy-five years old, I guess...she can't breathe...her mouth is kind of blue...I don't think so...Audra, is she choking on something?...no, she just can't breathe. She's grabbing her chest...we don't know what to do. Please help us," Mercedes shrieked. It was the last thing Germaine heard. The pain stopped. She looked up into Audra's frightened face before blackness crept over her eyes.

♦♦♦♦

"Germaine? Come on, Germaine, come back to us...come on, open your eyes."

The voice came out of the darkness. A strange voice. Germaine had never heard it before. She was hurting again, only now it was because someone was pressing on her chest over and over, pushing air into her. She opened her eyes, and there were faces over hers.

"That's it, dear...come on out of it."

"Is she all right?" It was Audra's voice. She sounded so panicky and young. Germaine wanted to tell Audra that she was fine, but she couldn't.

"She's awake again, anyway."

Germaine tried to push those pressing hands away, but she had no strength in her arms. Suddenly, they stopped, and there was movement, she was being rolled somewhere, and then more strange voices, more people touching her, prodding her, calling her name. All the while, she wanted to call out to Audra and tell her to get her purse. Her Medicare number was in it, and her other insurance card. She wanted to tell Audra to call Eleanor; she'd know what to do. But she couldn't. There was something hard and plastic over her mouth and nose. She wanted to move it, she touched it, but someone took her hand away.

"It's all right, Germaine. It will help you to breathe easier. It's just oxygen."

The hand was warm, and it squeezed hers and made her feel better...assured.

She heard Audra again. "I have her wallet here; it has some important cards in it."

"Go to the admissions office in the lobby. They'll take all the information."

Germaine was relieved to hear what Audra said. Then she gave up. She couldn't fight the machines and the people around her. She was too tired. It would all sort itself out. She needed to rest now.

But they wouldn't let her. They cut her clothes off, and attached things to her chest. She could feel the weight of wires all over her...on her legs and her stomach. There were strange beeps and motors were running.

Just leave me alone. Please just let me sleep.

"It's okay, Germaine. Hang in there...we'll be finished soon. You're doing fine."

What's wrong with me? What happened to me?

More movement, more rolling, more bright lights passing over her closed eyes, more new voices, more questions she couldn't answer, more sticks in her arm.

She stopped trying to hear what the voices were saying. She just wanted to rest. She wanted to sleep. She wanted to fall into the black velvet behind her eyes that kept calling to her.

◆◆◆◆

"Germaine...Mrs. Sommer..." The voice was very familiar this time. She struggled to open her eyes, and after a few tries, they did open. Eleanor was standing over her, her face soft and smiling, and Germaine felt Eleanor holding her hand.

Germaine's mouth was dry, it felt like her lips were glued together.

"Here, dear, take a sip of water." Eleanor lifted Germaine's head in one arm and held a straw to her lips with another. Germaine took the straw into her mouth. The water was cool and comforting. She could feel the cold liquid moving down her throat…down her esophagus.

"Better?" Eleanor asked.

Germaine nodded. She tried to move, but she had no energy.

"Stay still, dear. You've had a terrible time. Just rest." Eleanor placed Germaine back down onto the pillows.

"Am I in the hospital?" Germaine asked.

"Yes, dear, you've been here for four days. You had a heart attack…it was the shock of losing Corky, I guess. I'm sorry I wasn't home … I should have stayed home from work that day. I should never have left you when you were so upset."

Germaine shook her head. It ached something terrible, especially when she moved it. It felt like shards of glass moving in her brain. "I had Audra," she managed to say.

"Wasn't she wonderful?" Eleanor said. "She knew exactly what to do…both she and Mercedes were wonderful. I still think of her as a baby, but she showed me what a grown up girl she's becoming. She took care of everything. She brought your insurance cards, your money, she took your jewelry off you and put it in your purse. She rode in the ambulance with you, did you realize that? She wouldn't leave your side. I'm so proud of her."

"Not surprised," Germaine mouthed with her cracked, dry lips.

"No, I guess not. Sometimes I think you know her better than I do. God knows, you've been with her more in the last eight years than I have. It's been a blessing to have you in her life."

Germaine was too tired to answer now. Eleanor squeezed her hand. "Get some more rest, dear heart. You'll be good as new in a few days and back home with us. Sleep. The nurses know to call me if you need anything. And your sister and brother-in-law are coming tomorrow to see you. Their son is driving them over."

Germaine did what Eleanor told her to do. It was such blessed relief not to struggle to hear, to speak, to understand. She let herself drift back…back…back into the darkness.

♦ ♦ ♦ ♦

"Germaine…wake up now. We didn't come all this way from New Jersey to watch you sleep."

Germaine opened her eyes to see her sister standing at the side of the bed. She turned on her back and took a deep breath. "Thank you for coming," she said

"Well, of course we came," Gertsy said. "Why wouldn't we? I'm just glad you're getting better. What a scare!"

Germaine smiled. She lifted her body up with her arms. It was a struggle, but she did it. "Fred, lift the back of her bed—the crank at the bottom—just get her up a little higher," Gertzy took charge. "Not too high, now."

Germaine's brother-in-law moved to the side of the bed now. "How you doing, Germaine? You better now?"

"I think so."

"Good, good," he said, patting her shoulder. "We were worried." He still spoke with a slight German accent.

"Aunt Germaine," Fred said, leaning over to plant a kiss on her cheek. "You gave us quite a scare." He placed a bouquet of flowers on the night table. "Everyone sends their love. These flowers are for you...to brighten the room a little."

Oh, why did they come? Germaine didn't want to make small talk. She wasn't ready yet. She wished Eleanor hadn't called them.

"Well, we just don't know what we're going to do with you," Gertzy was saying. "Fred, pull that chair over for me please, my legs are killing me. Anyway, we just don't know who will take care of you when you get out of here. I can't care for you, myself. And there's no money for nurses, is there? No, how could there be...well, we'll have to figure something out. That nice Mrs. Walsh said she'll take care of you, but doesn't she work? And the little girl...Audra, isn't it?...she goes to school. So I don't know how they can. This worry about you is enough to give *me* a heart attack."

Gertzy leaned in from her chair then and lowered her voice. "How about a nice nursing home, Germaine? Shall we look into one for you? Fred thinks it might be a good idea."

"No!" Germaine found her voice for the first time in five days. "No nursing home. The doctor said I'll be all right. And the Walshes will take care of me...I'm not going to a nursing home."

"It's just for a few months...until you're well again."

"You and I both know that once you put me in there I'll never get out of it. No nursing home, Gertzy."

Germaine was angry. She didn't need this now. Gertzy was the last person she needed right now. They all heard the beeping of the machine above her head start to get faster.

Fred leaned over now and took Germaine's hand. "Don't upset yourself, Aunt Germaine. No need to make any decisions now while you're still mending. Stay calm."

"I'm only thinking of you," Gertzy said, wounded, ignoring her son. Her dyed brown hair fell to her shoulders and accentuated her fleshy jowls.

Germaine hated that Gertzy kept her hair so long at her age.

"Well, stop thinking of me. You never do much of it other times." Why was she speaking this way? It was as if someone else was speaking from inside her...she was never hostile like this.

"How can you say that? What do you mean by that, Germaine?"

"I won't ever make that decision," Germaine told her sister.

"No...no...let's not worry about it," Fred said.

"Well, she has to be sensible, Freddie," Gertzy said, her voice cold as ice now.

"Mother, let it alone for now, please." His own voice was just as icy.

Germaine had always liked Fred. He was Gertzy's eldest...her only son. Good head on his shoulders...always very serious and level-headed. But none of this was any of his business. He never did anything for her in all these years. He wouldn't even come to pick her up on Christmas and Easter or for Sunday dinners at Gertzy's. He was always willing to drive her to the bus stop at night... but never all the way home to Astoria. She always ignored how much it hurt her feelings, but today she didn't feel like being nice. She was tired...she was, what?...she couldn't find the word...what was she?...she was...she was...*scared.*

"I'm tired," she said aloud.

"Okay, we'll go," Fred said quickly.

"We will not. We just traveled an hour to get here, and she wants us to turn around and go back already?"

"Yes," Germaine said, closing her eyes and turning her head away from Gertzy.

There was a stunned silence in the room, until Germaine heard the patient in the bed on the other side of the curtain chuckle. Was the stranger in the other bed chuckling at her?

"Aunt Germaine," Fred said softly. "We'll go now. I'll take Mom and Dad out for a nice lunch...how about a Manhattan cocktail, Mom? Wouldn't you like that? There's a great restaurant on the way back to Jersey. Very swanky. You'll love it."

"Well, all right, we'll go. Might as well let her rest. But this was just a wild goose chase...we should never have come...and you taking time off from work, Freddie. A whole day lost." Gertzy stood up. She gave Germaine's cheek a perfunctory brush with her lips. "I'm sorry you had the heart attack, Germaine. I am. But you know it isn't my fault. Don't take it out on me."

"Let's go, Mom," Fred said firmly now. He leaned over and kissed Germaine. He whispered in her ear, "Don't worry...it's going to be fine."

Her brother-in-law patted her shoulder again. "Get better, Germaine. Get better soon."

Germaine nodded, but she continued to look away from them.

"I'll call you," Gertzy said.

Don't bother.

"Have Mrs. Walsh call me if you need anything...not that I'd be able to get anything for you from New Jersey, but if there's anything I can do from there..."

"Mom," Fred said.

Please just go.

Then there was silence in the room, and Germaine took a deep breath of relief. She wasn't going to a nursing home. She'd give herself another heart attack—one that *would* kill her—before that would happen.

Spring 1968

29TH STREET
AND 30TH AVENUE

"Mr. Kramer, how good it is to see you out and about," Vera said when she saw Joseph Kramer standing on the corner. "You look wonderful."

Joseph smiled at Vera. "Don't you know that it's not nice to lie, Mrs. Allcock? Oh, but such a pretty little liar you are, it's okay…I forgive you."

"I'm not lying. You do look better. You have some color in your cheeks, and you're outside, walking around. You *are* better."

He fell into step with Vera, who pulled a wheeled metal cart full of groceries.

"It is such a lovely spring day, and I was bored. I thought a little walk would be good for me," Joseph told her. Then he said, half asking, half declaring, "You've been shopping?"

"I have, Mr. Kramer. I'm hosting a dinner for my husband's family."

"Oh?" Joseph said, noticing that the tall, slender woman slowed down so that he could keep up with her.

"Yep. My husband passed the bar exam yesterday. He called his parents and invited them over to celebrate."

"Isn't that nice," Joseph said,

"I'm a nervous wreck, Mr. Kramer," Vera confessed.

"Why is that?"

"Danny was estranged from his family after we were married. He wouldn't have anything to do with them. Well, they started it, actually. They didn't think I was good enough for him, and all of that."

Joseph cocked his head, letting her know he was interested.

"Around the time of President Kennedy's assassination, Danny called his father. I don't know why, but I was really happy that he did. I guess the call didn't go all that well, though, because Danny didn't call him again. He acted funny when I asked him how the call went. I assumed that his father was still…I don't know…negative…about me. Then his mother called him at work about two weeks later. She invited us to their club for dinner."

Vera looked over at Joseph now and leaned into him. "Their club, Mr. Kramer, is *very* exclusive...I've never set foot in a place like that in my life."

"You would give a place like that class, Mrs. Allcock...you would make it sparkle with your beauty and charm."

Vera laughed heartily at that. "You're an awfully nice guy," she said, touching his shoulder with hers. "Well, anyway, Danny told me that he wanted to go to dinner alone. He wanted to have a good heart-to-heart talk with his parents before he exposed me to them. I was a little hurt...I thought he might be ashamed of me. But I had to trust him. As it turned out, he didn't want it to be a 'set-up,' you know?"

"No...what do you mean by a set up?"

"He was afraid that they wanted to embarrass me in some way, I guess. To make him see how inadequate I was compared with how he was raised."

Joseph shook his head. "They couldn't...you are many things, Mrs. Allcock, but inadequate isn't one of them."

Vera smiled. "Thank you. You're very kind."

"It's the truth. Okay, so, tell me the rest."

"Well, he let them know in no uncertain terms that night that I was the love of his life and that they were going to accept me and treat me with respect. If they couldn't, then everything would go back the way it was...with all of us not having anything to do with one another."

"What did they say?"

"I don't know what they said exactly. I do know that he explained to them that I was helping to put him through law school and that my family may not be wealthy and on a 'who's who' list of Americans, but he loved me and he had come to love my family, too."

"Good for him!" Joseph said.

"Well, almost two years went by, and they called once or twice, but no invitations, so I don't think it went all that well. But when Danny graduated from law school, he called them to tell them, and they were very excited and happy. They said they wanted to meet me and celebrate. So now that he's passed the bar exam, I wanted to invite them over to a little dinner here at our apartment. I told Danny to call them."

"And Danny said yes."

"No, he said, 'God, no!'" Vera and Joseph laughed together then.

"But I persisted. It's too important a day for him. His parents deserve to be a part of it, Mr. Kramer. And it's time for them to meet me. I put my foot down and told Danny that if he didn't call and invite them, I would."

"Why not a restaurant?" Joseph wanted to know. "A neutral territory?"

"This is where we live...this is how we live. I'm not the least bit ashamed of it anymore. It's a nice building...a small, but nice apartment. And I'm a good cook...sort of."

"It will be good," Joseph said, thinking it over. "This will be a good thing."

Vera sighed as they turned into the courtyard. "I certainly hope so, Mr. Kramer. I have only one worry—Mr. Walsh."

Joseph nodded. "Well, it's not his usual night to go out, Mrs. Allcock."

"Yeah, but with my luck…"

6B

SOMMER

Germaine sat in her chair and stared at the television. There was a rerun of "I Love Lucy" on, but she wasn't paying attention. She was straining to listen to Audra and Mercedes who were in the kitchen doing their homework.

"He'll be home in a few minutes," Audra said, her voice hard. "God, I hate him."

Mercedes was shocked. "No! You shouldn't say that. He's your father, Audra. Don't say that."

"He's an idiot."

"Audra...stop."

"Last night, he came home drunk, as he usually does on Wednesdays—and lately it's been Mondays, too. I always pretend to be sleeping when he comes home. I sleep on the pull-out couch in the living room. If I pretend to be asleep, my mother can tell him to be quiet and he doesn't yell as loud...it works sometimes. I don't want to have anything to do with him when he's like that. I could be sound asleep, but as soon as I hear his key in the lock, my stomach goes into a knot and my heart starts to beat so hard I think he can probably hear it. I have trouble keeping my breathing steady."

"What does he do?" Mercedes wanted to know.

"Nothing to me...never to me. He'll just give me a kiss on my cheek...but I could throw up with the smell of beer and whiskey on his breath. I don't let him know I'm awake. Then he goes into the kitchen and starts throwing pans around, like he's going to cook dinner for himself. God, Mercedes, it's like eleven or twelve o'clock at night! My mother works all day. He makes so much noise to get her out of bed. I can't even imagine what the neighbors think."

Germaine listened, but there was silence in the kitchen for a long time. This was the first time she'd heard Audra talk about what went on in that apartment on the nights that Brendan Walsh came home drunk. In all these years, Audra had never shared a story like this with her.

"So then my stupid mother comes out of the bedroom in her nightgown and robe and says, 'I'll make you something, Brendan. I saved dinner...I'll heat it up.' It makes me sick, Merry. Sometimes I think I hate her more than I do him. How can she put up with this? Why doesn't she get us away from it? She's so weak...she acts so smart and strong all the time, but when he's drunk, she's pathetic."

"She's married to him, Audra. She's a good Catholic."

"Oh, baloney...she's a divorced, remarried Catholic. She's going to go to hell anyway...she'd be better off leaving him."

"Audra, don't say that...she won't go to hell."

"Yes she will...she's living in sin. She's got a huge sin on her soul because of it. You know that. We learned all about divorce in religion. That's why she keeps it a secret."

Mercedes ignored what Audra was saying about the state her mother's soul was in. "She's just keeping the peace by cooking for him."

"Well it doesn't work," Audra said, her voice hard and angry. "As usual, last night he starts picking on her, dragging up things that happened during the week...things we never even thought were a problem...and he picks and picks and picks. She's real quiet, trying to calm him down, trying to appease him. 'I'm sorry, Brendan...I didn't know that would upset you...come on, Brendan, don't be mad...' It made my stomach turn."

Germaine heard Audra throw a book on the table before she continued. "Before you know it, his voice is raised, and he throws the plate at the wall. The food goes all over and the plate crashes into smithereens. I couldn't stand it, Merry. My body just exploded. I went berserk, you know? I jumped up and flew into the kitchen and I told him to stop...to just shut up. I called him a name, but I can't even remember what I called him. By the look on his face and my mother's, it must have been bad. I knew I was acting like a crazy person, but I couldn't stop. I thought that this would be it...the night he'd come after me, like he always went after Paige...that finally *I'd* get it...but no. He gets up from the table, goes over to where my mother is sitting on the other side of the table, and he grabs her hair on each side of her head and starts banging her head against the wall, saying, 'Look at what you did...you turned my little girl against me...you did this...you made her call me that name.' Then he looks at me and says, 'This is your mother's fault.'"

Germaine closed her eyes and felt tears pressing against her lids.

Mercedes asked, "What did you do?"

"I got down on my knees and begged him to stop. I told him I loved him and I didn't mean what I said...I told him I was sorry, Merry...I begged him. I would have done anything to make him stop hurting her. I wanted him to hurt *me*...I wanted him to come after me...I feel so guilty that it's always my mother or my sister but never...never me."

There was a long silence in the kitchen again. Finally, Mercedes said, "Because hurting your mother hurts you more and he knows it, Audra. That's how he controls you."

Germaine pulled the afghan up higher on her chest. It was almost summer, but Audra's story sent chills through her.

"And then he starts crying," Audra said with a sigh. "He whines, 'I don't want to hurt you, honey. I don't want to hurt your mother...I love her.' I want to vomit when he starts that up."

Just as Paige had predicted years earlier, Audra was getting more and more resentful of her father. She barely spoke nicely to him anymore. She used to run into his arms when he came home from work; now she glared at him and acted morose around him. There were no hugs and kisses, no big bear hugs. She was gloomy and removed when he was in a room. And she wasn't much better around her mother.

Things had changed, and Germaine worried about the girl and where this anger and belligerence would take her. There were so many stories about drug abuse and teenagers now...didn't Audra tell her that they were selling drugs right in the cafeteria at school, right under the nuns' noses? She told Germaine that if she wanted to "do" drugs, she just had to bring the money to school with her.

Audra had told Germaine about the girls who passed out in class and about ambulances coming to the school to take them to the hospital, and how the girls never came back to school after that. She talked about kids who stood outside the school gates after school and tried to get the girls to buy pills as they were leaving.

Audra seemed normal every day when she got home from school, except for the underlying hostility toward her parents. She never tried to hide what was going on at school. She talked about it openly. Her speech was never slurred, her eyes were always clear, and Germaine could tell that Audra wasn't drugged. She was making more friends, nice kids. Yet, she knew that it was often the troubled, unhappy kids who tried to find an escape by taking drugs. It would break her heart, but it wouldn't surprise her if Audra did came home bleary eyed. The girl seemed miserable all the time now.

Germaine and Eleanor talked about it frequently...about how they had to be aware of any change in Audra's behavior. Eleanor was strict with the girl, but very loving. It didn't matter how many hours she worked in the day, Audra's friends were always welcome in their apartment, and Eleanor cheerfully prepared dinner, even when she didn't expect them. She always had enough food, and was always hospitable to Audra's friends—boys or girls.

Sometimes it amazed Germaine.

"I keep them close, even though they don't know it," Eleanor would say to Germaine. "I watch them, know them, earn their trust, listen to their conversations, and look for signs. I don't know how else to protect Audra from falling in with the wrong crowd."

There were days that Germaine wanted to shake Audra and say to her, "Do you realize what a good mother you have? Do you realize what she does for you? How she worries about you?"

But Germaine never did. She knew that Audra's life was anything but normal, and Audra's story today made that even more evident to Germaine.

Give him his due, when Brendan was sober, he was always as hospitable to Audra's friends. He encouraged her to bring friends home. He was a lot of fun when the kids were around. He teased them, he played practical jokes, he drove the kids wherever they wanted to go and he even paid for all of their movie tickets sometimes. He drove them to Rockaway on weekends, and sometimes to Coney Island, to Nathan's, for hot dogs and fried shrimp.

When he knew the girls were at the apartment, he stopped at the bakery on his way home from work and bought cookies or Audra's favorite pie. A few times he brought home Beatles albums—which he called those 'damned Bugs'—and Rolling Stones records, and they'd put the records on the turntable in the stereo console and he'd dance with them in the living room. He loved to dance, and although he preferred the fox trot, he let the girls teach him how to Twist and gyrate around in the newest dance craze. Audra's friends loved him.

Germaine sighed and leaned her head back against the chair. She was tired of agonizing over Audra and Eleanor...she was weary of hating and liking and then hating Brendan Walsh, over and over again.

Since the heart attack, Brendan couldn't be more attentive to Germaine. He drove her to every doctor's appointment, and to every blood test. Eleanor did all the food shopping and cooked dinner for Germaine every night. When they went out for dinner, they insisted she go with them or they brought dinner home from the restaurant for her.

In the beginning, when Germaine was first released from the hospital, she asked Eleanor to help her hire a nurse. Eleanor was a little surprised that Germaine had the money for a private duty nurse, but she didn't ask any questions. Eleanor made some phone calls, and together they interviewed a few women until they found one they both liked.

The nurse came every day for a month, until Germaine was strong enough to get around by herself. The nurse arrived at eight in the morning and stayed until Audra came after school, and then Eleanor checked in several times during the evening and helped Germaine get ready for bed. Every morning before she went to work, she came to help Germaine get up and dress. With the Walsh's help, Germaine was able to avoid the nursing home Gertzy was so eager to put her in. She was still recuperating, and not what she once was, but she was living in her apartment, as independent as possible. It couldn't have been that way without Eleanor and Brendan.

"Sometimes I want to pack my suitcase and just go and live with my sister," Audra was saying in the kitchen. "Paige would let me. I know she would. I actually mentioned it to my mother. She was furious. She said that it was bad enough that Paige had run away from home...how could she ever survive if another of her children ran away from her? She told me others have it worse...that I'm an ingrate... if I went, I would ruin Paige's life."

"Oh, Audra, how awful...she should not have said that to you," Mercedes said.

Germaine heard Mercedes sigh deeply. Germaine sighed, too.

"Well, I don't think it's nice what she said to you. I think she's wrong," Mercedes said. "But I'm still a fan of your mother's. She's always there for us. She never minds when we're all in the apartment when she comes home from work. She's gotta be tired, yet she always cooks for us. She's the only mother I know who you can actually have a conversation with about all kinds of things—the Vietnam War, Civil Rights, hippies...even sex. She understands us...our generation. I think she hates the war in Vietnam as much as we do. And remember how she tore into your superintendent when he wouldn't let Genevieve Boyer come into the building with the rest of us because she's black? She was furious—reminded him that things were changing in this country, and a girl of any color was welcome in her home. It's so easy to talk to her about the Civil Rights Movement; she's read so much about it, and she is able to present so many different sides and opinions. She cares about it, even if she doesn't always agree with some of it...like the Black Panthers...and rioting and stuff like that."

Germaine knew that Eleanor was particularly worried about some of the activities going on in the projects a few blocks away. There were problems all the time at the park there...the same park that she used to take Audra as a child, just a few years before. Audra played with the children there then, but now there were tensions that Germaine couldn't understand.

Mercedes continued to plead Eleanor's case with Audra. "Look at how she came to the school to see the principal, and demanded that the Gaelic Daughters Club and the Daughters of Italy Club be disbanded and a new club be instituted for all the students because you told her that Genevieve and I weren't allowed to join the club. Remember how she went to the school, pretending that she'd seen a lawyer and that the clubs were discriminatory and that the school, being Catholic and all, should be an example in social justice? She was brilliant that day, wasn't she?"

Audra joined in now. "She demanded that they let us start the *All*

American Melting Pot Club!" The girls convulsed in laughter then. Germaine smiled at the sound of it. The storm was over...Audra's anger defused...for now.

The doorbell rang, and Germaine saw Audra go to the door. Germaine heard the lovely young Mrs. Allcock say, "I got this lemon pie for Mrs. Sommer when I went shopping today. Is she doing better?"

"She's really good now. Do you want to see her?" Audra asked.

"No, just give this to her. I'm rushing around today. I have company coming for dinner tomorrow and I have tons of things to do."

"Okay," Audra said. "Thank you. Mrs. Sommer will love this pie."

A moment later Audra came into the living room with a lemon meringue pie, all smiles and cheeriness. She wore bell-bottomed jeans with flower patches on them and a blue peasant shirt, an outfit that her mother criticized incessantly—saying it just wasn't ladylike, it looked like she was wearing rags—yet it was Audra's favorite outfit. "Look what Mrs. Allcock gave you!" Audra said. "Doesn't it look delicious?"

Germaine wished she was strong enough to get up from the chair and hug the teenager. She loved her so much...and it hurt so much to hear what she had been telling Mercedes. She wasn't supposed to be eavesdropping, so she couldn't say a word about it.

"It looks wonderful," she said to the girl.

"Want a piece? I'll make you a cup of tea to have with it."

"Let's all have a piece and a cup, shall we?" Germaine said.

Audra nodded and went back into the kitchen. Mercedes said she couldn't stay for pie and tea. She had to get home. She gathered her books and tied them together with an elastic cord and came into the living room to say goodbye to Germaine.

"I'm really glad you're feeling better," she said. She had an accent—just a hint—which endeared her to Germaine even more. The child had worked so hard to become an American, to fit in, just as her own German-immigrant parents and husband had.

Germaine reached out and took the pretty, dark-haired girl's hand. "And I'm really glad that you're Audra's friend."

Mercedes understood. Germaine could see it in her eyes. The girl nodded, kissed Germaine's cheek quickly. "And I'm glad that she has you, too," she whispered in Germaine's ear. Mercedes left the apartment just as the kettle started to whine.

Germaine listened while Audra poured the tea and sliced the pie, then Audra appeared with two plates and china tea cups on a mahogany tray. She put it on the coffee table and brought one of the plates to Germaine. The clear yellow curd looked cheerful against the white meringue, and Germaine smiled as she took it from Audra.

"I put a little milk and a spoonful of sugar in your tea...just the way you like it."

"Perfect," Germaine said. "Just leave it here on the table next to me. I'll wait until it cools a little."

Audra took her pie and sat on the sofa. She rolled her eyes and moaned. "I looovvve lemon meringue."

Germaine took a bite of it herself and nodded. "Mm, it is good, isn't it?"

Audra looked up at the ceiling. "I wonder if they have freeze dried food that tastes like lemon meringue pie...you know, for the astronauts? Imagine eating a piece of pie on the moon? I still can't believe that a man actually walked on the moon, Mrs. Sommer. It's amazing, isn't it?"

Germaine nodded her head. "It is, Audra. It's amazing. I cried when I watched it on TV."

"I'd love to walk on the moon. I'd be a woman astronaut if I was smart enough."

They ate in silence for a little while, and then Germaine said, "Audra, I heard you tell Mercedes about last night."

Audra looked surprised that she had been overheard. It was a while before she said, "It's okay, don't worry about me."

"I am worried."

"It's just the way it is...I've got to get out of that apartment. I'm going to switch to the commercial course next year. I'll take typing and steno. Paige thinks it's a good idea. She said then I'll have some skills when I graduate. There's no money for college anyway. I know Mom always says she wants me to get a college degree, but she knows we haven't got the money. As far as I'm concerned, it would only be worth it if I could go away to school, to board, and get away. But the money's not there and I would never get a scholarship. I need to work so I can get my own apartment as soon as possible."

Audra sighed and reclined on the sofa. She balanced her pie plate on her flat stomach. Looking up at the ceiling, she said, "I wonder what it would be like to live in a normal house...to have my own bedroom where I could study...to be good in school so I could get a scholarship...for life to be easier. I want to do well. My teachers are always saying I don't apply myself, but I think I do. I try to study, but I just can't pay attention, you know. I just can't seem to focus on anything...except English...and I love to read. I feel like I'm somewhere else when I read a novel. But I hate studying. Without a college degree I'll be a nothing for the rest of my life. I'll never have a really good job and my own home...a home like Donna Reed or Father Knows Best. That's the kind of life I want, but it will never happen."

Germaine said then, "Do you remember when you were in the eighth grade and you stayed after school right before Christmas to help the teacher decorate the classroom for the Christmas party...what was her name?..."

"Sister St. Catherine," Audra said, still staring at the ceiling.

"That's right…and I was worried because you were so late and I came to the school to see where you were? You were annoyed because you felt that I was treating you like a baby?"

Audra groaned. "Yes, I remember."

"Well, before you knew I was there, when I got to the door of the classroom, you were sitting at a desk and Sister St. Catherine was sitting at another student desk and you were talking. I overheard what she said to you."

Audra looked puzzled. "You did? What did she say?"

"She asked you if you were pleased that you had gotten into Mother of Christ…and that she had highly recommended you to be accepted in that school because she believed in you."

Audra sat up then, remembering. "Yeah, I remember. But she didn't mean it."

"Why would she say it and not mean it?"

"She felt sorry for me."

"No, Audra, she believed in you…she saw your potential. A teacher knows what a student is capable of. And she would not risk her reputation by recommending you for the Diocesan High School if she thought you weren't capable. You don't realize it now, but when you're older you'll understand how wonderful that nun was to you…what a gift she offered to you."

Audra looked very sad then. She shrugged. "I guess."

"Don't guess…know. You can be a someone, honey—you *are* someone—even without a college education…but do what Paige told you to do. Once you have an office job, you can go to school at night. Don't give up on yourself."

"I guess it's rude to say this to you after what you've just gone through, and how hard you fought to live, to survive your heart attack, but if I had a heart attack, I wouldn't fight it. I'd welcome it. I don't even want to get up in the morning…especially this morning. It's too hard to face the day…and some nights." Audra put the plate of half-eaten pie on the tray again. She sat staring into space.

The expression the girl wore was one of resignation. No sixteen-year-old should look like Audra did at that moment. If only her parents knew what they were doing to her…they loved her, wanted the best for her, yet they couldn't see what they were doing, how they were hurting her.

"Don't feel that way. Don't ever feel that way. Life is tough sometimes, almost unbearable, but it's always worth living. Good days follow bad days. You know that. Look at Paige's life…how hard things were for her, and how happy she is now. She has that beautiful little baby girl, and a good husband. That's what's in store for you. In the meantime, you have dances at school that you'll go to, and basketball games and you'll have a boyfriend before long. There's nothing like a first love. Oh, Audra, my dear girl, you have so much to live for."

Audra didn't answer. She didn't believe what Germaine was saying…not today anyway.

She gathered the pie plates and empty tea cups and carried them to the kitchen. Germaine heard her wash them and put them away in the cabinets. When she returned, she had her books in her arm and said, "I guess I better go home to my apartment. Dad will be home in a few minutes. Mommy asked me to start dinner for her tonight. You okay if I leave?"

Germaine nodded.

"Okay…I'm going then."

"Audra," Germaine called before Audra closed the apartment door behind her.

"Yes?"

"Tell me again not to worry about you."

There was a pause, and then Audra said, "Don't worry about me." Germaine heard the door close. She looked beyond the curtain which was lifting gently in the spring breeze. It was dusk and she could hear the increase of traffic noises from the street below when people arrived home from work.

Voices speaking in Italian drifted into the room. Most of the neighbors living in the well-kept brownstones across the street were Italian. Germaine didn't speak a word of it, but she loved hearing the melodious language as the children greeted their fathers and mothers when they arrived home, obviously happy to see their parents after being under their grandmothers' care all day. She knew many of them from when Audra played with the little girls across the street.

Many of them knew about her heart attack…she guessed they saw the ambulance taking her away, and they sent Germaine get well cards, and cakes or cookies. She thought about how many thank you notes she had to write since her heart attack. There had been so many acts of kindness by the neighbors both inside the building and outside.

Even Joseph Kramer, as sick as he was, brought her flowers twice.

She heard very little from Gertzy, or from Gertzy's children. No thank you cards to write there.

It was Eleanor who called Gertzy when Germaine was being released from the hospital. She assured Gertzy that a nursing home wasn't necessary. They had secured a private duty nurse, and the money wasn't an issue at this point. "But there won't be any left afterward," Gertzy had said to Eleanor. "What's the sense of having a will if there isn't anything to leave?"

Eleanor had ignored the question, but had told Germaine about it.

"She's worried about her children not getting an inheritance from me," Germaine had said. "They weren't in the will anyway, but she doesn't need to know that."

Eleanor had laughed. Even Germaine laughed when she said it. No, her money was being left to her grandchildren wherever they were. Her lawyer would find them…he assured her he would. And some of it would go to Audra.

She started to drift off to sleep with the muted noise from the street flooding the room, the soft spring breeze from the window caressing her face. It was a lovely, light sleep, disturbed when she felt a touch on her shoulder. She opened her eyes and Brendan was standing over her. She hadn't heard him enter the apartment.

"Mrs. Sommer," he said. He stood back a little, smiling at her. "We got a surprise."

Germaine shook off the sleepiness and looked around. Eleanor sat on the sofa, still in her office clothes and high heels, Audra stood leaning against the wall, looking sullen and bored, and Brendan stood with his work jacket just slightly unzipped at the neck.

"You ready? You ready, too, Audra? Get over here. Come and see the surprise I have. It's for both of you…"

"Daddy, *puleese*, I have homework to do…"

Eleanor looked sternly at her daughter. "Don't talk to your father that way. Get over there right now."

Audra pulled herself off the wall and went toward Germaine's chair. When she sat on the arm of the chair, Brendan pulled the zipper of his jacket down a little farther. Two pointy, furry ears stuck out, then two emerald green eyes, a black nose and a pink mouth against white fur and long white whiskers, and finally two tiny black paws appeared at the edge of his jacket.

Audra gasped. Germaine didn't know what to think.

"A kitten!" Audra said finally. "Daddy, a kitten…is it ours?"

"Yours and Mrs. Sommer's." Brendan Walsh was smiling from ear to ear.

Audra jumped up and reached out, gently removing the kitten from her father's jacket. It was tiny—no more than eight weeks, Germaine estimated—and it mewed and placed its tiny head between Audra's jaw and her shoulder. It was completely white except for its front paws and the tip of its tail.

"Oh, Daddy, I love it. What's its name?"

"Sooner," he answered.

"Sooner?" Germaine asked.

"Sooner or later I'm going to regret this."

They all chuckled. Germaine didn't want a cat, but she had to admit it was adorable. More than that, it made Audra smile as she hadn't seen the child smile in months.

She knew the arrival of the cat was Brendan's way of apologizing to his daughter for his behavior the night before...his way of showing her he wasn't a tyrant...that he was sorry. It seemed to be working.

Audra ran to him and kissed his cheek and thanked him. Germaine looked over at Eleanor. There was a sad smile on the woman's lips, and a look of relief mixed with frustration in her eyes. How easily Brendan could bribe Audra to forgive him for beating her mother...Germaine felt angry for a moment, angry and protective of Eleanor. And then she realized, as she had come to realize many years before, that it was a situation that she would never understand. Being angry and exasperated over Eleanor did Germaine no good. The Walshes were a roller coaster ride...one that she had decided to stay on...for Audra's sake...maybe for her own, too.

Today she'd thank God for this kitten that brought squeals of happiness to the girl she loved and worried over.

"Will she live with us?" Audra asked her mother.

Eleanor shook her head. "If Mrs. Sommer will agree, why don't we let the kitten live here with her. It will be good company for her now that Corky is gone. You have to promise, though, Audra, that you'll clean out the kitty litter box every day for her and feed the cat until Mrs. Sommer is all better."

"I promise...oh, Mrs. Sommer, I promise...I'll take really good care of it...and maybe sometimes it could sleep in our apartment with me, Mommy?"

"It's up to Mrs. Sommer...it's really her kitty."

Germaine reached up to pet the little cat, and Audra placed it in her lap. It was purring loudly and looked up into Germaine's face with curiosity. Its green eyes looked too large for its little head.

"Hello," she said to it. The kitten seemed to look into her soul. She looked at Eleanor, "I guess it's all right. If Audra is happy, then I'm happy. We need to find out if it's a boy or a girl, I guess...and rename it."

"It's a girl," Brendan said. "Call her whatever you want."

"Do you want to call her Corky?" Audra asked, and Germaine could tell she really didn't want that name.

"No...no, Corky was Corky. This is a new friend. She needs her own name. Why don't you think of a name, Audra?"

"Princess?...no, not Princess...she's so sweet...hey, sweet...what about Sweetiekins? Sweetiekins Sommer!"

"If you like it, then that's her name. Sweetiekins...I think I like it."

The kitten curled up on the afghan on Germaine's lap, completely contented that she now had a name and belonged to someone.

Eleanor and Audra took the new kitty litter box out of a bag that Eleanor had bought after work and filled it with litter. Then they took the tiny porcelain dishes for food and water from the bag and filled them up.

Eleanor said, "Brendan called me at work to tell me he'd found the kitten near the job he's working at. I stopped on the way home from work and picked these up."

"It was a stray, then?" Germaine asked Brendan, who was sitting on the sofa now, smiling at the kitten.

He nodded. "Poor little thing followed me around at lunch time. I couldn't just let it starve, so I fed it part of my lunch—good thing I had a tuna sandwich—and it was still there when I got off at 3:30. It broke my heart. It's so tiny and alone. I couldn't just leave it there, could I?"

"No, of course you couldn't," Germaine said, stroking the warm little body in her lap. It was amazingly clean and white for a stray. She didn't believe a word he said. She knew in her heart that he had deliberately gone somewhere to get this kitten for her and Audra.

"I put it in my jacket and took it home on the subway. People must have thought I was nuts or something because I kept looking down into my jacket whispering to it."

Germaine just smiled. Audra came back from the kitchen and sat on the floor. She rested her chin on Germaine's knee and stared into the kitten's face. It leaned out and sniffed Audra's nose. "She's so pretty, Mommy, isn't she?"

"Yes, she has a very pretty face," Eleanor said, studying the cat from a distance. "Well, come on, let's get dinner and then you can come back over to see it and help Mrs. Sommer get into bed."

Audra petted the kitten, which still was curled on Germaine's lap. "We'll have lots of fun with her, won't we?"

Germaine nodded. "Lots. I have to count on you to take good care of her until I'm back on my feet."

"I will...I want her to love both of us like Corky did."

Germaine reached out and stroked the girl's cheek. "She will, honey. She'll love us both, just like Corky did."

"But it's easier to take care of a cat, don't you think? No walking in the rain and snow."

"That's true."

"It's a lovely pet that will let us give her lots of love and return it back to us...that's really all we need, Mrs. Sommer, right?"

"Oh, you are so right, my dear girl, giving love and getting it back is all we need."

6D

ALLCOCK

Bridget Riordan was just walking up the sixth flight of stairs when Vera Allcock flew out of her apartment.

"Oh, my God, what am I going to do?" Vera said to no one in particular.

Bridget was winded from the climb. "What? What's wrong?"

"The electricity is out and I have Danny's parents coming for dinner tonight. I can't cook...I have nothing to cook on...Oh, God, it's all gone wrong."

Bridget stepped up on the last step and tried to control her breathing. She eased her rear end down onto the second step of the flight going up to the roof. Her mini-skirt pulled up higher on her thigh, but she was too tired to care and too winded to worry about modesty.

"So that's why the elevator is not working," she breathed.

"Of all the days..."

"Okay, okay," Bridget said, putting her hand up. "Let's think this through."

"There's nothing to think through. The night is ruined."

"Vera, let's think this through," Bridget said to her neighbor reasonably. "Can ye get take out for 'em?"

"How will they see what they're eating without lights?"

"Good point, that," Bridget said frowning. "Well, why not just explain and take 'em out for dinner?"

Vera winced and flounced down next to Bridget. "I wanted them here, in our apartment, to see that we're happy and that it's not a dump. We've gotten nice furniture and wall-to-wall carpeting, and everything is perfect...well, no, not perfect...but it's nice. They need to see that I can make Danny happy, you know? That I'll be a good mother to their grandchildren."

"One dinner in your apartment will tell them all that, will it?" Bridget said, smiling now.

Vera huffed and put her head in her hands. "No...but I wanted to impress them. I've waited so long to meet them and have the opportunity to..."

They heard Joseph Kramer's apartment door open then. "Is everything all right with you two?" he asked, peeking out at them.

"Is your electric out, too, Mr. Kramer?" Bridget asked.

"No...only the front of the building it seems...one circuit only."

Vera stamped her feet on the floor. "I knew something would happen."

Mr. Kramer came over to them then. "What is it, Mrs. Allcock?"

"My in-laws...the dinner..."

"Tonight's the night? Oh, well, that is a problem I suppose."

"I suppose," Vera said mournfully.

Audra Walsh stepped out of Mrs. Sommer's apartment then. "We don't have any electric in Mrs. Sommer's apartment," she said to the three of them. "But there's electric in ours."

"That seems to be the case," Bridget said.

"I'm bringing Mrs. Sommer over to my apartment until her lights come back on," Audra said, then looking at them, she asked, "Why are you all out here in the hallway?"

Bridget explained Vera's problem to Audra. Audra stared at the miserable Vera for a long time.

"Well, our oven is working...so is Mr. Kramer's oven and stove. Why can't you cook your dinner in our apartments? My mother won't care, what about you Mr. Kramer?"

"No, if she needs my oven, it's hers to use." He smiled gently at Vera when he said it.

"That still doesn't solve the problem of no lights—no way to see. And they'll have to walk up six flights of stairs...no, no, no...no...no..."

"The flights of stairs we can't resolve," Mr. Kramer said, "But I have many candles—I have two silver candelabras, in fact. And Martha always keeps," he looked away then, "kept tapers in the house to use in them. You can have them to help light your table."

"Oh," Audra said excited, "that would be beautiful. And my mother has some pretty candle holders, too—for the rest of the apartment. It would be filled with candlelight...that would be so romantic."

"Yes, indeed it would," Bridget agreed. "And just in case you missed a piece of dust when you were cleanin', your mother-in-law wouldn't see it!"

Mr. Kramer laughed at what Bridget said. "Do you have china and crystal?" he asked Vera then.

"Nothing nice, just some dishes we got at Woolworth."

"I have Martha's wedding china. You might as well use it and you can use her silverware."

"Mrs. Sommer has the most beautiful crystal glasses…they're from Germany," Audra said, thinking hard about how she could contribute. "There are water goblets, wine glasses, and champagne saucers that all match. She always says she wishes she could have a dinner and use them again. I know she'd let you borrow them."

"I haven't a decent thing to lend you," Bridget said, gloomy at the thought.

"And my mother has a gorgeous white damask linen tablecloth that belonged to my grandmother," Audra continued. "We only use it on Christmas, and then Mommy has it dry cleaned and puts it away until the following Christmas. She'll definitely let you use that."

Vera almost looked happy, as though their suggestions were possible, then she shook her head, "No, I can't borrow all of this from you…and the candlelight thing won't work. We still have the issue of the elevator not working."

"It will work," Audra said, insisting. "The whole thing will work."

Mr. Kramer touched Vera's shoulder. "Come on, get the food and bring it into my apartment. We'll start to cook it."

Just as he said it, the elevator gears started to crank and they heard it moving in the shaft. Vera jumped up and ran into her apartment saying, "It must be back on…the electricity is back…"

A minute later, she came out again, looking crestfallen. "Not in my apartment."

Bridget got off the stair and unlocked her door. She tried her lamps and ceiling lights. Nothing.

"No, but they did get the elevator on, so it's probably only a matter of minutes before the rest of the lights come on," Bridget reassured Vera.

"There won't be enough time to get the roast cooked," Vera said.

"Come…start cooking in my kitchen, then you can transfer it to yours if you want," Mr. Kramer said. He smiled at Vera kindly, reassuringly.

Bridget liked the man; she always had. It hurt her to see how thin and wasted his body had gotten in just a short time; and it hurt her to know that he was suffering alone. She had no idea why his wife had left him. It always bothered her. They seemed so happy when they were together. She'd seen them with their grandson when he visited, walking hand-in-hand, all three of them, laughing. They doted on the little boy who seemed to have shown up out of nowhere. Bridget was shocked when she'd heard that Mrs. Kramer had moved out. The only thing she could think of was that his wife just didn't want to deal with his illness, whatever that was…probably cancer…and she must have panicked. Still, that was a horrible reason for a wife to leave her husband.

She knew Mrs. Walsh looked in on him and fed him from time to time.

Bridget had seen her carrying a plate of food into his apartment one night. A few days later, when she was on the elevator with Mrs. Walsh, she asked about Mr. Kramer. Mrs. Walsh didn't let on what was wrong with him, or if she knew why the elegant Mrs. Kramer had left, but Bridget could tell that Mrs. Walsh was concerned about him.

Then Mrs. Sommer had the heart attack, and Mrs. Walsh seemed to take over her care completely, especially after the nurse left. It didn't seem fair that Mrs. Walsh had two people to care for on that floor.

Audra helped, though, and Bridget was impressed at how dutiful the girl was to the elderly Mrs. Sommer. The blond-haired, blue-eyed shy little girl she'd met on her first day at Ashley Hall was now a tall, willowy teenager. Where had the time gone? She'd been here in this country for six years, yet it seemed like yesterday that she found this building. After all that time, she barely knew anyone—just a passing conversation here and there, a few visits with Mrs. Sommer before she had the heart attack, and an insignificant friendship with Vera that had started when they were both worried about the elderly woman. They visited her at the hospital on the same evening by coincidence, and decided to go out for coffee afterward. Since then, they'd had coffee or a glass of wine in each other's apartments twice.

It amazed Bridget that there were seven apartments on this floor of the building, all side by side, and the people in them separated by just plaster walls, and yet none of them ever really got to know one another. Everyone was so anonymous in New York…living within inches of one another, yet they could be miles away for all they got to know one another.

It was so different in Ireland. Everyone knew everyone else…everyone stopped by each other's homes almost daily. She missed that. She missed everything about Galway…about Ireland. She wondered if she'd ever get used to living in America.

Maybe there were places like Ireland here in America…friendlier places…places where people visited and chatted and knew everything there was to know about one another. But she'd probably never get to know where they were. It seemed she would never have a chance to leave this tiny world she'd created for herself.

"Come…" Mr. Kramer said again to Vera. "We'll help you carry your groceries into my apartment. Audra, you go get your mother's tablecloth, then Miss Riordan will help get Mrs. Sommer's glasses. We'll set everything up in my apartment. That's where you will entertain your relatives tonight."

"No, I couldn't," Vera said, shaking her head. "That's just not right."

"It's as right as rain," he said, smiling brightly. "There's more room in my apartment. They don't even have to know it's not yours, if your husband doesn't mind."

Bridget was intrigued. She started to chuckle. "Well, from what I've heard, Mr. Kramer, yours is the nicest apartment in the building."

"Where did you hear that?" Mr. Kramer asked.

"Biermann…I can't remember why he told me, it was years ago."

Vera raised her eyebrows. "Really? It is?" It was very tempting. "This is just too kind, Mr. Kramer."

"We'll do it!" Audra said. "First I have to bring Mrs. Sommer into my apartment so she isn't in the dark."

She disappeared into Mrs. Sommer's apartment, while Joseph Kramer led Vera into his. "But where will you go while I'm entertaining in your apartment?"

Bridget said, "We'll go out for dinner…how about it, Mr. Kramer, would you go on a date with me?" She was pleased that she had found something to offer.

He turned around slowly to look at Bridget. She wondered then if he was strong enough, or well enough, to go out. By the expression on his face, she realized that he was wondering the same thing, but he smiled. "It would be an honor, Miss Riordan. I'll pick you up at…" he looked at Vera.

She shrugged, and then suggested, "Six-thirty? My in-laws are arriving at seven."

Joseph Kramer turned back to Bridget, "Six-thirty, then?"

Bridget answered with a curtsy, "Six-thirty, Mr. Kramer, is perfect.

They had only an hour and a half to get all of this done and out of Vera's way. When Audra had Mrs. Sommer settled in the Walsh's apartment, she rang Bridget's doorbell.

"Can you help me get Mrs. Sommer's crystal? The glasses are all the way at the top of one of her cabinets. I can get up on the step stool and hand them down to you."

Bridget followed Audra into the other apartment and together they pulled out four of each sized stemware. They hadn't been used in quite a while and there was a film of dust on them, so Bridget filled the sink with hot sudsy water and washed them while Audra dried. When they were finished, the crystal sparkled.

"Gorgeous," Bridget said, holding one up to the light. "Absolutely brilliant."

Audra put them all in a box she had brought from her own apartment. They walked them over to Mr. Kramer's apartment. The door was open and they let themselves in.

There were no dining rooms in the apartments at Ashley Hall, but the living rooms in the three room apartments were very long and narrow. Mrs. Kramer had set up one end of the room near the kitchen with an elegant antique mahogany dining room table, six matching chairs, covered with green damask that matched the drapes in the room, and a matching sideboard. The breakfront was farther into the room on another wall.

Without the leaves in it, the table was perfect for four people and didn't take up much room. The rest of the apartment was decorated with fine antiques, porcelain lamps, and a tufted sofa covered in coffee-colored silk, two club chairs sat opposite the sofa on the other side of a cherry wood coffee table. A large Oriental rug lay beneath the seating arrangement, and another was under the dining room table and chairs.

Bridget was amazed and truly impressed by the lovely room. She thought, this is the way every apartment should look in Ashley Hall...elegant, subtle, tasteful.

Vera and Mr. Kramer had placed the padding on top of the table and were just putting the Walsh's white tablecloth on top. Mr. Kramer went to the breakfront and took out two silver candelabras. He handed one to Audra and one to Bridget and then opened one of the drawers and took out a box of white tapers.

"Open the sideboard doors," he instructed Vera. "The china is in there...use the Havilland...I've always thought it was the prettier set. But if you like it better, you're welcome to use the Lenox."

Vera and Bridget looked at each other, then bent down and opened the doors of the sideboard. Inside were two sets of china, carefully sorted and separated. Vera reached in and took out one of the delicate plates. The white porcelain was decorated on the rims with violets and green leaves with the slightest accent of pale blue. In the center there were two birds on a branch.

"Oh, my..." said Vera.

"Holy Mother of God..." breathed Bridget.

Audra inhaled loudly.

Joseph smiled when the three women looked up at him. Vera asked, "Are you certain...you're absolutely sure...that it's all right for me to use these tonight? Won't Mrs. Kramer..."

"Mrs. Kramer doesn't live here anymore, so we do not have to worry about what she would say or think. She left...the apartment, the china, the silver, the furniture...and me. It gives me pleasure to see you use it on this most important of occasions." He placed his bony hand over his chest to emphasize his words.

Bridget and Vera took a service for four out of the sideboard—dinner plates, salad plates, bread and butter, cups and saucers—and stacked them on the table.

Mr. Kramer said to Audra, "The silver service is in a drawer to the left in the kitchen cabinet. It's in a wooden box."

"I think I suddenly believe in fairy Godmothers..." Vera said, then laughed and added, "I mean, fairy Godfathers."

Mr. Kramer sat down in one of the chairs. "I'll just sit and read the paper while you ladies set the table."

"Flowers," Audra cried out. "You need flowers on the table…it just doesn't look right without them."

Vera reached into her jeans pocket and pulled out a five dollar bill. "Audra, can you run down to Broadway and get some for me?"

"Sure…I'll get some that match the plates. It'll be *gargeus*, absolutely *brilliant*." She said this with an imitation brogue, mimicking what Bridget had said about the crystal.

"You scamp…" Bridget said, faking annoyance. She snapped a linen napkin at the girl. "Get on wit 'ye."

Audra left the apartment laughing.

When the table was set, Bridget went into the kitchen with Vera to help prepare the side dishes. The aroma of the roasting beef made Bridget's stomach groan with hunger. They worked together preparing the vegetables and Bridget put the dinner rolls on a cookie sheet to be warmed, then placed a stick of creamy yellow butter on the Havilland butter dish.

"They'll love it…all of it, Vera. You'll see…there is nothing to worry 'bout."

"I wish I could believe that. I called Danny to tell him what was going on and I could tell by the sound of his voice that he was worried. He was worried to begin with…now he's downright panicky, but he tried not to show it. He just kept saying over and over, 'Kramer's place? Are you sure that's a good idea?'"

"How did you answer him?"

"I told him I don't know if it's a good idea…I do know it's the only idea anyone had."

Bridget patted Vera's shoulder. "Go get dressed. I'll finish this up."

Vera turned to leave, and then spun back. "I hate to ask you this, Bridget, but the bathroom…it looks like it hasn't been cleaned in a while…you know, a single, older man living alone…I don't know if I'll have enough time to get dressed, finish dinner, and …"

"I'll do it…go…I'll take care of it."

Bridget looked under the kitchen sink and found some cleaning products. There were brand new rubber gloves still in the box…apparently Mrs. Kramer hadn't had a chance to use them before she bolted on the poor old gentleman in the living room. She donned the gloves, grabbed some rags and the cleaning solutions, and started for the bathroom.

Joseph jumped out of the chair. "Here now, I'll do that. I didn't think of it before, but of course, she would want a clean bathroom."

"Sit down…I never met a man yet who could clean a bathroom proper."

"You shouldn't have to…"

"Now, there's no arguing with an Irishwoman…didn't you know that?"

He smiled and sat down again. He looked exhausted and she wondered if he would have the strength to go out for dinner after all. She went into the bathroom and started to scrub the bathtub first, then the sink and toilet, and finally the tile floor. There was a vial of medicine on the sink and she opened the medicine cabinet to put it inside. Every shelf in the cabinet was covered with medicines...large vials and small containers, with names she never heard of before. Obviously, these were keeping Mr. Kramer alive. But what if the mother-in-law looked in? How would Vera explain that?

Bridget finished cleaning and ran to her apartment. She got some things from her own medicine cabinet, some fresh Ivory soap, her best towel set, and a chenille throw rug that matched the towels, and ran back into Mr. Kramer's bathroom. She used the box she and Audra had brought over with the crystal glasses to hold Mr. Kramer's medicines, and replaced them with her makeup, a razor, a tube of toothpaste and a comb. She even brought over a bottle of aspirin. When the cabinet was finished, she replaced Mr. Kramer's towels with her own and opened the bar of soap. She threw the rug down onto the tiles.

Bridget stood back and admired her work. "It's a miracle," she said chuckling. She put the box of medicines and his towels in one of the closets in the hallway, returned the cleaning products to the kitchen, washed her hands, and went back into the living room to sit in the chair near Mr. Kramer.

"Well, it's as good as it's gonna get, and that's pretty good, if I say so."

Audra ran into the apartment then with a bouquet of flowers wrapped in paper. She showed them to Bridget and Mr. Kramer. "Aren't they lovely?" she asked. "And all the right colors."

"There's a short crystal vase over there in the breakfront," he told her. "Martha uses that for the table."

She and Bridget went into the kitchen, filled the vase with water, cut the stems of the flowers, and arranged them carefully.

Vera walked in, dressed in a rose colored silk sheath and black high heels, just as they placed the flowers in the center of the table.

Her eyes lit up when she looked at the table. "It looks absolutely elegant."

"Indeed," Bridget said proudly. She put her arm around Audra's shoulders. "The lass has excellent taste in flowers, now, doesn't she?"

"Hello? Audra? Mr. Kramer?"

Audra jumped, "That's my mother...in here, Mommy."

Eleanor Walsh appeared from the hallway. She was carrying two cut crystal bowls, one larger than the other. "I just got home and Mrs. Sommer told me what was going on...I wondered if you could use these bowls, Mrs. Allcock? They belonged to my grandmother. In fact, they're Galway Crystal." She looked at Bridget and smiled. "Good things come from Galway, isn't that right, Miss Riordan?"

Bridget smiled warmly and nodded.

"Yes, Mrs. Walsh, they're perfect," Vera told her. "There weren't enough bowls for all the vegetables I'm serving. And the large one is perfect for the salad. You have all been too kind."

"Mommy," Audra said, taking her mother's hand and leading her to the table, "doesn't it look beautiful? Your tablecloth is perfect under all of the dishes and flowers and crystal."

Eleanor hugged her daughter to her laughing. "You always did enjoy a beautiful table setting, even when you were a tiny little girl. Someday you'll be married like Mrs. Allcock and you'll invite Daddy and me over for dinner just like this."

Bridget's eyes met Vera's, and Bridget smiled reassuringly.

Vera sighed then. "If my food tastes half as good as this table looks, I'll call it a successful night." She didn't mean it. The food and the decorations had little to do with the success of that night and Bridget knew it.

"Audra and I will be right next door if you need us," Eleanor said to Vera. "Don't worry." She reached out to take Vera's hand. "They will love you. Trust me."

Bridget walked over to Mr. Kramer, "Are ye still up to going out, or should we order in...I still have no lights, but we can eat a pizza by candlelight."

"No, my dear, we made a date and I have no intention of breaking it. I made reservations at the Oyster Bay."

"You did? When?"

"Before, when you asked me out on a date."

Bridget laughed, "Well, I'll go freshen up and meet you at the elevator in three minutes."

She gave Vera a quick kiss and whispered, "They're idiots if they don't fall in love with you within the first five minutes."

Vera's eyes welled up. "It's been eight years, Bridget...what was I thinking?"

"You were thinkin' it's about time, and it is. Good luck."

She left and walked across the hall to her apartment. It looked so small compared to the Kramer's. She went into the bathroom, washed her face, brushed her teeth, and applied fresh powder to her nose. She ran the comb through her short curly dark hair. Bridget stared at herself in the mirror. Plain, she thought. Just too plain. She smeared lipstick on her mouth and was still disappointed.

She went to her jewelry box and took out pearl earrings and a pearl necklace...gifts from the past that she had tried so hard to forget. Gifts she hadn't worn before now, afraid they'd burn through her skin.

She looked in the mirror again. Not as plain, she thought now. And they aren't burning holes in me. She laughed at herself. She changed the flats she was wearing for her good high heels and admired how they looked.

What in the world was she doing? Pearls and high heels and all of that? He'd called it a date. She chuckled to herself.

"Well, he's an older man…he's dying…but a date's a date after all."

6E

KRAMER

Danny had rushed home, turned on all the lamps in the apartment to see for himself that there was still no electricity, and then went to Kramer's door. Vera opened it. She looked as nervous as he felt and their eyes held for a long time. It took him a full thirty seconds before he really looked at her. She looked beautiful.

"Wow," was all he said.

"Wow good?"

"Wow great."

"Come inside and see…I think this is going to work." Vera led him deeper into the apartment, directly to the table.

"Vera, this is terrific. Where'd you get all these dishes and glasses? I mean, this is *impressive.*"

"All on loan, I'm afraid, but your parents don't have to know that. I put away all of Mr. Kramer's photographs, and replaced them with some of ours. The rest…well, let's hope they believe I have such good taste."

"But our apartment number is on the bell downstairs…they'll come up to…"

"Audra thought of that and switched the names. I don't know what I would have done without all of them…and they seem to have had so much fun helping me." Vera placed her hand on her stomach. "I'm really nervous, Danny. Do you think we'll get through this?"

Danny looked at his wife and wondered how he had ever lived without her. She was so vulnerable, yet so capable, so accommodating. He didn't know why this dinner meant so much to her, why she even cared if it was successful or not. His parents had been rotten to her, rejected her from the beginning, and yet here she was, working like a dog to make it perfect, dressed like a movie star, and acting as though royalty were coming to dinner.

"We'll not only get through it," he said, taking her in his arms, "we'll make them regret how much they've missed all these years. Vera, honey, I'm so proud of you."

He pulled her closer to him. He had loved Vera when he married her, but it was nothing compared to how his love had grown. She'd sacrificed so much for him...given so much *to* him.

The doorbell rang and Vera jumped out of his arms. She looked terrified for a split second but then took a deep breath and said, "Okay–get the buzzer and let them in downstairs. I'll get the hors d'oeuvres. We're on..."

"Hey, Vera...one thing before they come up."

"Yes?" she cocked her head.

"I was offered a job in the law firm today...the firm I wanted...great job...good pay...the one that does a lot of pro bono work for domestic abuse victims...so we're moving...soon. As soon as I'm settled in and know that all is going well, I want to look for a house in Long Island ...four bedrooms, three full baths, two walk-in closets, a pool in the back yard...oh, yeah, and white wall-to-wall carpeting...in *every* room except the kitchen. That's what you want, right? Good. I love you with all my heart...now get the hors d'oeuvres."

6A

RIORDAN

The electricity was back. Bridget unlocked her apartment door and asked Joseph in. It sounded as if Vera and Danny were still entertaining in Joseph's place. When they stepped off the elevator, they heard laughter coming from behind his door. Joseph gave Bridget the okay sign with his fingers, and they both giggled.

Although her flat was small, she had carefully decorated it over the years she'd lived in Ashley Hall...two comfortable chairs, a small table with two chairs, and her day bed that filled in for a sofa. She had sewn silk drapes in a sage color for the windows and hung lace panels underneath them. Matching lace panels were hung on the French doors to the kitchenette.

"Sit, Joseph," Bridget said, putting her purse away in her closet. "Shall I pour us a glass of Port while we wait?"

She opened the doors to the kitchenette and took two wine glasses from the shelves in the cabinet. She poured the ruby liquid into them and handed one to Joseph, who nodded with a smile. "It was a good dinner, wasn't it? The scallops I ordered were good, anyway," he said.

"It was indeed. The seafood was exceptional...I've never eaten there before. I pass it all the time on my way to the station, and I've wondered about it, but never went inside. It's a nice restaurant...chic..."

"It was one of Martha's favorites." He shook his head and frowned. "There I go again. I occupied the entire conversation tonight with stories about her, haven't I? You must be bored."

"No, I'm not at all. I'm honored that you told me the whole story, Joseph. Naturally, I wondered what had happened...you two always seemed...shall I say it?...happy...contented, anyway."

"In case I didn't mention it, I loved her...love her still. The affair was something I just can't explain...not a fling, not that at all. I cared deeply for the woman. She understood me as Martha never had, and I truly believed that I couldn't live without her, which is why I never ended it. But I knew, too, that I couldn't live without Martha. And here I am...living without both of them."

"You still won't tell me who the 'other' woman was?" Bridget teased him gently.

"No, that's something I won't do. She's a special person. I was so wrong, Bridget. So wrong on so many counts. But I'll tell you this, I was not still in that relationship when Martha left me. I hadn't been with that woman for two years...not since the day little Joey came into our lives. And I'll tell you that I'd never loved Martha more than during those two years. She was the woman I had married...the one I had lost when our son was killed in the war. She came back to me that night that we met Joey, the night we found out that a part of our son was still living. I'm not saying that it was her fault that I strayed. It wasn't her fault. It was a fault in me...a need I had that I couldn't control and should have...but I think I missed Martha, you know? I felt so lonely after I retired. I felt I had nothing...not even Martha who lived with me, cooked for me, cleaned for me...but stopped connecting *to* me."

They sat silently for a long time. "So, Miss Riordan, I've done all the soul searching and confessing tonight. It's your turn. Let me go back to my apartment feeling as if I wasn't a complete bore. I listen well, too."

She smiled at him. "Not much to tell."

"What brought you to the United States? You're young and alone, and I can tell by some things you said tonight about Ireland that you're homesick."

"I am that," she admitted, sipping from her glass. "I miss home something terrible."

"Then why not go back?"

"I can't ever do that," Bridget said. She knew she was squirming in her chair and she tried to stop.

"Why? Did you commit a murder? An escaped convict are you?"

Bridget wanted to smile at his joke, but she couldn't. It was too true.

He picked up on her mood immediately. "I'm sorry. I was prying. Let's change the subject."

"It was a sort of murder," she said then, realizing that she didn't want to change the subject at all. She wanted to spill all that she'd held buried deep inside her to this man she hardly knew, yet felt safe with.

"You had an affair...so did I. With a married man from where I grew up. We'd known each other our whole lives long. Where I come from, everyone knows everyone else their whole lives, ye see."

Joseph nodded but said nothing.

"I didn't even love him." Bridget shrugged, trying to remember why she had fallen into his arms one night when his wife was away visiting her cousin who was having a baby. "I was home from university, you see. A holiday it was. We met at the pub…everyone goes to the pub…and we got to talkin' at a quiet table after most of the others had gone home. We talked about school days when we were kids, and his work, and me being in university. He wanted to know all about it. He thought that was excitin' and grand. Most women don't go, but I wanted to be somethin'…I wanted to make somethin' of meself and all of that."

Bridget related it as though none of it mattered, but oh, how being the first in her town to go to university in Dublin had meant so much to her…to her parents…her family. Some of her friends had scoffed at her about it, accused her of being uppity, but Bridget was determined. She wanted to learn everything she could. She wanted to read every book ever written; every poem, every essay. She longed for knowledge. As the first year of university unfolded, she wanted more…and more…she just couldn't get enough of it. She'd never been happier in her life.

Joseph stared into his Port. The fact that he wasn't looking directly at her made it easier to talk to him. She wondered if he knew that.

"Anyway, he was the son of a very successful merchant in Galway…a few miles from the village. He worked in the family business, y'see. It would be his one day. He wasn't happy, though. Said he was bored. He said that I excited him…made him want more out of life…made him hunger for learning just being with me. Oh, Joseph, it was heady talk he gave me that night. But the *more* he wanted turned out to be more of *me*—and not my mind. Honest, Joseph, I don't even remember how we got into his house. It isn't that I was drunk, because I wasn't…not with the beer, surely…but drunk with being flattered…being wanted by someone so handsome and charming as he always was…and the next thing, we were on the floor of his sittin' room, and my clothes were off…God, why am I tellin' all of this to you?…and we were doin' it. An hour later, he handed me my clothes, thanked me for a grand night, and asked me if I was going to tell anyone. He looked like a scared little boy."

Joseph asked, "How old were you?"

"I was just eighteen…himself was twenty. He'd been married about six months, I guess."

Joseph shook his head again. "Babies…you were just babies."

Bridget sneered, "Sure, we were. Speaking of babies…I got pregnant from that one foolish drunken night."

Joseph looked up at her now. She nodded. "Yeah, realized it two months later, and I went to see him in Galway. He wasn't in the store, but his father asked me into his office; he was nice as can be. He was always a bit of a blowhard, the old man was, and very impressed with himself, and all of that. He sat across this big mahogany desk that was imported from France—he made sure to point that out to me—and asked what I wanted with his son. I tried to tell him it was just a friendly visit…old school chums and the like…but he wouldn't buy it. Apparently, there had been other 'ladies' comin' around from time to time for 'friendly visits' with the same problem I had. The father could spot us a mile away."

"What did he say to you?"

"He said, 'Let's get down to business…I'll write you out a check for a hefty amount, you go to London, where I'll make an appointment for you with an excellent doctor I know very well, all expenses paid in a beautiful hotel, and everything will be fine and taken care of. You'll let my son alone, go back to university—though I just don't understand why a girl needs an education—and it all will be in the past, with only your future to look forward to with the extra money I'm giving you.' He wrote the check, handed it to me, and led me gently and firmly out of the store. He even had the audacity to kiss me on the cheek as though he were my long lost uncle."

Bridget felt woozy telling the story. "I went to London, I stayed in the fancy hotel—it was a fine hotel, indeed—and I saw the doctor. I was so naïve. I thought…I *really* thought…that he'd be my physician until the baby came and then he'd help me put it up for adoption and I'd be living in that beautiful hotel the whole time. An inconvenience, sure…my education would be put off a little while…but I could live with all of it."

"And is that what happened?" Joseph asked.

"No, that wasn't in the plan a'tall. It was an abortion. The doctor did abortions for wealthy women, got them all fixed up, and then sent them on their way. Oh, he was nice all right…very gentle, very intelligent…*very* persuading."

"You had an *abortion*?" Joseph asked, and although he tried, he couldn't keep the shock from his voice or his face.

"I did, Joseph…the murder you were talkin' about earlier."

"I'm so sorry," he whispered. She looked for judgment on his face, but couldn't find any.

She lifted the pearls at her neck, "When I returned to the hotel, a package was waiting for me…the final pay off."

Bridget thought she was going to cry, but she swallowed hard and willed herself not to.

"Next thing I know, me mother is calling me at the hotel in London askin' me if it's true. How did she find out, I asked her. Seems the father tells a discreet family member—not about the abortion, mind you, he wouldn't ever be attached to that kind of scandal, but that there was a tryst and the girl lost her virginity and got herself pregnant. The relative, in my case it was my aunt, runs to the mother to tell her, and the next thing, the girl involved—girls, I should say, for there were three I've heard—never want to return to face the scandal and the shame they've brought onto the family. That's what the money is for...their escape to another place...in my case, another country. My mother thinks I gave it up for adoption."

"The father's as bad—no he's worse—than the boy who uses all these women as though they're toys."

"Yes, but don't you see, the boy—and isn't that a laugh...boy, indeed—can still trot around as though he's as pure as the snow because the father knows that the girls and their mums won't tell another living soul because of the shame. Only, it backfired on him. The priest found out, and the boy and his wife had to move away. Finally, they're the ones who were banished in shame." Bridget ran her fingers through her hair. "I don't gloat over the wife...she's innocent and as much a victim."

"How did the priest find out?"

"One of the other girls—the one after me, it seems—was dumb enough to go to confession before she left for London."

"I thought that a priest cannot divulge what he's heard in the confessional?"

"He can't...but an old biddy sitting in the church and eavesdropping on all the confessions heard the whole thing and started to wag her tongue about it. Next thing, the mother of *another* girl goes to the priest, telling him she *suspects* that it happened to her daughter as well. She demanded to know what the priest was planning to do about it. This wasn't in the confessional, you see, so now the priest's hands aren't tied anymore."

"And did the village find out about you, too?"

Bridget shrugged. "I don't know. My mother says no...and my aunt would never in a million years tell. She's a saint, she is. I think people must wonder, though. My mother has said to them that I decided not to finish university because a company in London offered me a good job in their offices in the United States. It was an offer I couldn't turn down. How can anyone believe that, though? I don't know...I guess people are gullible."

Joseph reached out and placed his hand on top of hers. She was trembling and he saw it. His gesture to comfort her touched her heart. "It's all in the past, Bridget. We make mistakes, and we move on from them. You are very young. You have your whole life ahead of you. Don't let this one mistake..."

"This one mistake, Joseph, was a whopper. I'm a Catholic, for God's sake, and I committed a crime. It's against the law. I would have been fine givin' the baby up for adoption. Why did I let them talk me into the other?"

"Because you were young; you were frightened and impressionable."

"I wonder sometimes, when I'm lying in the dark in the middle of the night...was it a girl?...a boy?...was its hair the color of mine...did it have me mother's smile, me dad's sense of humor? Would it have grown up to be someone really special one day? Where's its soul now? Is it in Limbo because it was never baptized?"

Bridget had to stop speaking for a moment. Then she said, "It's just been legalized in Great Britain, you know."

"What?"

"Abortion...it was a crime then, when I had it, but not now."

"See, Bridget, then it really can't be a crime. It can't be a criminal act one year and the next year be legal. If it isn't murder now, it wasn't murder then." He wanted to sound convincing.

Bridget tried to laugh, but the sound she made sounded more like a stifled sob. "You don't believe that any more than I do, Joseph. It will take a lot of talking and a lot of legalese before people really don't think it's a crime...that it isn't the act of a mother murdering her child." Those words caught in her throat. "God help me."

"It's done all the time...*all* the time," Joseph offered kindly. "It's a compassionate thing. It doesn't seem right that a woman has to give up her life for a child she doesn't want...it will be legal here one day...one day soon."

"Yes," Bridget said with a sigh. She finished the wine. "I wonder though, does that make it right? I'll have to live with it. I know that. And I should move on, I guess...but...one thing I'll never do is feel that it was a good and righteous thing to do. Maybe someday we'll all see it that way, but I can't. Not yet, I can't."

Bridget had cried over leaving Ireland, over not being with her mother and father, and over not being home where she belonged. She had cried over losing her chance at an education. And she had cried over living in this tiny apartment, constantly worrying about someone coming through the window at the fire escape. But she had never allowed herself to cry over the abortion. It was much too big. It was much too terrifying. And she didn't cry now, but it took all she had in her to control it. Speaking at that moment was impossible, and she knew that tears were filling her eyes but she wasn't going to allow them. She wasn't going to allow a single sob.

Joseph was very patient. He sat as a witness to her silent grief. He asked no questions; he didn't try to have a conversation. He was just there. He was there for as long as she needed.

Finally, when Bridget managed to smile at him, Joseph said to her, "For what it's worth, I don't think you are a murderer, I don't think you committed a crime, and I do think you're beautiful...inside and out. That may not help you...but I'm a dying man, and I see things differently than I ever did before. I see things a little more clearly—I see how things happen, and we just can't change what happened once they are done. Your Catholic faith allows for forgiveness. Doesn't it encourage your seeking it? So seek forgiveness, then—it's a gift your faith gives you—and take it and hold that forgiveness to your heart. And don't worry what the priest says to you in that confessional—you've said it all to yourself a million times, haven't you?—and once he gives you...what's it called?"

"Absolution."

"Absolution..." he said the word slowly, rocking a little as he contemplated it. "Absolution...I like the word...it's a good word." Then he continued, "Once he gives it to you, you're forgiven. You're right in your God's eyes again. Am I correct in that? Yes? Yes, I thought so. And so never mind what others think—who cares what others think—*fuck* them—only God matters...only the fact that you received this...this...absolution."

The profanity made Bridget smile again...even though fresh tears clouded her sight. It sounded so odd to hear this gentleman use a vulgarity. He did it so matter-of-fact. She knew she should be offended, but she couldn't be. In this one evening, they had shared so much. They had bared so much of their souls to each other. She hadn't known that strangers could do that.

This was a Jewish man—she'd never even met a Jewish person before moving to the States—yet Bridget felt as though she'd just been to the confession he had encouraged her to seek. She felt washed...cleaner than she had in years. Of course, Joseph Kramer was right. She needed to make good with God, and that's what mattered. Maybe then she would be able to live with what she'd done. She needed to go to confession...if only she knew of a *Jewish* priest, someone like Joseph.

She looked up at him. Joseph smiled gently. She understood why his mistress had fallen in love with him. And she understood even less now how his wife could have left him.

"Thank you, Joseph."

"You're welcome, Bridget Riordan," he said, leaning forward and patting her cheek. "You are very welcome."

6E

KRAMER

"Mrs. Kramer, it's Eleanor Walsh. I'm calling because I think you should come home. Your husband is very, very ill. He can't get out of bed...he can't eat...he won't go to the hospital. I called his doctor and the doctor told me to call you and tell you to...he asked that you come. He thought you could talk Mr. Kramer into going to the hospital."

Joseph lay in his bed with his eyes closed. He could hear everything Mrs. Walsh was saying, and although he wanted to call out and tell her to stop, to leave Martha alone, he couldn't. There was no strength in him. They all acted as though he was sleeping...in a coma or something...but he could hear every word they were saying. He just couldn't speak to them. He couldn't respond. It took too much effort...too much energy. This dying thing was harder than he thought. Why couldn't he just go to sleep? Why couldn't the dark come and just envelop him as he had thought it would?

"Oh, thank you, Mrs. Kramer. Thank you. I'll stay with him until you get here. He wrote a note saying that no one was to call an ambulance, and I didn't want to go against his wishes, but now...please come quickly....what's that?...oh, no, Mrs. Kramer...I don't think you should bring your grandson. It wouldn't be good for him to see your husband like this. I won't even let my Audra in here. Okay...I'll see you then."

Joseph tried to reach out, but his arm wouldn't cooperate. His body was failing him. He wished his mind would. He felt Eleanor Walsh enter the room again and sit on the chair beside his bed. She took his hand and squeezed it, whispering, "I hope you won't be angry with me. But you need her...and she's going to need to be here with you."

Was she right, he wondered? Did he need Martha now? He needed her for the last two years...but now, now that he was dying once and for all, did he need her? What would she say to him? What did he want to hear her say?

I forgive you. Yes, that would be nice. I forgive you and I love you. He would like that. He would like to hear her say that. And he would want to say *And you, my Martha, were the love of my life…no one else.* But could he say that? Was it true? Did he not love Francesca? He did. He burned for her during those years. Burned for her body…her kindness…her attention. Yet, it was always Martha in his heart.

"Mrs. Walsh?" he heard someone familiar call from the living room.

Martha? Already?

"Mrs. Walsh…may I come in?"

No, not Martha. Frances…Francesca.

"I don't want to intrude, but…"

Eleanor Walsh's voice changed just the slightest bit. It was harder than it had been a moment before when she was talking to him…and before that when she was talking to Martha on the phone. He could hear the difference. It saddened him. *Don't treat her like that* he wanted to say but couldn't.

"Yes, of course. Come in. You need to know that his wife is on her way, so please, I beg you, don't stay more than a minute. I'll go into the kitchen for some water. Let me know when you're leaving."

Joseph heard one woman abandon the chair and another sit down. He wanted to bridge the silence that crept into the room, but he couldn't.

"Joseph," she said finally. She was crying. "I'm sorry. Forgive me."

No…no…no…that was not the way it was to go. He wanted to ask for the forgiveness. He struggled, and his arm lurched out. She grabbed his hand and put her lips to it.

"Me…" he was able to get out through his cracked lips. "me…"

"You what, darling?"

It was no use. He couldn't form the words. He couldn't say it to her.

"Joseph…I know now that the whole thing was just an impossible situation. I should have told you that a long time ago. I know that hurting Martha for our own sakes would have ruined what we had. Our guilt would have destroyed whatever love we felt. I know that now. Please…please…know what I'm saying, hear what I'm telling you. I should have been more gracious…if I loved you as I professed, I would have let you go with more kindness. I was selfish…I was brutally selfish. And when she left you, I should have helped you in some way."

Oh, please, let this agony stop.

"I can't stay. I don't want to be here when she arrives. I just want to say…oh, my dear, dear Joseph…forgive me."

"Mrs. LaCorte," Eleanor said from the doorway.

Joseph wanted to shout out to them both, but nothing would come, just a gurgling in his chest.

"He's agitated," Frances said. "He's trying to move."

214

"Go now," Mrs. Walsh said gently. "Go...and...and...I don't know what to say...I don't know what you want to hear...but be at peace. Try to be at peace, Mrs. LaCorte."

Yes, Joseph thought, relieved that she was being kind to Francesca now, telling her what he would want to tell her if he could. *Yes...yes...*

"I'm so sorry for..." Frances was crying harder. He couldn't bear it. His chest tightened and his throat ached.

"Mrs. LaCorte, please. Don't say it to me. I don't think you can say it to anyone but him...and please, don't go to his wife now or after...let her alone. Okay? Believe me, it won't help her. You may think it will, but in the end, it won't help you either. Let sleeping dogs lie, as they say. She needs to heal...she needs a great deal of healing...and your apologies won't help her heal. That's something I know firsthand. It will just rip the scab off her wound. Trust me with this."

Joseph agreed in silence. Martha wouldn't handle an apology from Frances well.

Mrs. Walsh continued to speak to Frances. "You fell in love, you did what you did, you can't take it back...let them alone and forgive yourself. That's what you have to do now. You gave him something he must have needed at that time...you were there when he needed you...and that's a good thing, I suppose. I was a jilted wife, so I'm having problems saying this gently. I don't want to hurt you...I want you to heal, too. I know Mr. Kramer would want that."

Yes...that is what I want.

Joseph could tell that Mrs. Walsh was moving closer into the room. Was she touching Frances? Was she embracing her when she asked, "Can you do that, Mrs. LaCorte?"

"I can," Frances whispered.

Joseph sighed and stopped struggling beneath his covers. He was so tired. There was a final touch from a soft hand, and he suspected it was Francesca's hand, then it was gone and there was silence in the room again.

She had been so beautiful. She had filled that hole in him that his son's death and Martha's detachment had created. Yes, Mrs. Walsh was right. But at what cost did he allow that hole to be filled...at the cost of his marriage...of Martha's happiness...of his own in the end...and Francesca's.

He felt something cold on his lips and he jumped. "Sh," Mrs. Walsh said. "It's just a cool cloth for your lips, Mr. Kramer. They're so warm and cracked. I wish I knew how to make you more comfortable. I'm sorry you're hurting."

Joseph managed to shake his head no, but he knew the motion was very small. Did she understand that he was trying to tell her not to worry about him? He wasn't hurting. The pain was going away.

There were more voices in the apartment. Voices he couldn't pinpoint.

Voices that bothered him. Mrs. Walsh left him alone in the room. He heard her say "Mr. Biermann" and then "but his wife will be here soon" and then he heard someone ask, "How long do you think...should we put an ad in the paper for the apartment?" Oh, yes, it was Biermann and the wife. Joseph felt angry for the first time, but it was no use. He couldn't show it. He couldn't yell out *get the hell out of my home...my wife's home...go away. Let me die before you rent this place out.*

"This is not the time or the place, Mrs. Biermann," Eleanor Walsh said.

Oh, she could be so firm...so hard sounding when she wanted to. Good. He was glad.

"I think you'd better go now. His wife will be here in a few minutes. You can discuss it with her...but not tonight. This is a bad time. I should think you'd know that."

No more voices then...just silence...silence...silence. He felt his body relax in the silence but his mind was still darting from one thought to another.

"Honey, I don't think you should go in..." Mrs. Walsh was saying then.

"Mommy, I really like him. He's so nice. I feel so sad. I wish I knew some Jewish prayers so I can pray for him, Mom."

Little Audra...not so little now...but still just a girl. It's nice to have someone grieve for him. He doesn't want her sad...but to have someone so young and tender care is nice.

"Prayer is prayer, darling," Mrs. Walsh told her daughter. "They pray to the same God, the same Father, so that's who you can pray to for Mr. Kramer. Pray for Mrs. Kramer, too, Audra."

"Okay, I'll go back in the hallway and wait for Mrs. Kramer. Let me know if I can help, Mommy."

"I will, honey."

Silence again...blessed silence...dark and comforting silence.

"Joseph."

My Martha.

"Joseph, it's me."

He felt her take his hand and put it to her cheek. *She's forgiven me? She's touching me...holding my hand...she's forgiven me. Absolution.*

"Joseph, I want you to go to the hospital. Will you do that for me?"

No, my love. Let me die here in our bed. Just let me feel you beside me, holding me.

"Joseph, please, darling...Dr. Haber said that they can make you more comfortable there. They can give you pain killers in an IV and they will take good care of you. I'm going to call an ambulance now so that we can take you to the hospital."

Joseph pulled at her hand...pulled it down onto his chest...he didn't know where the strength came from. "No...no...stay here. Stay with me...

216

home…" *Was that me? Did I speak? Did she hear me?*

"Oh, Joseph, I don't know…I don't know what to do."

"Stay with me…" Joseph still did not know where the words were coming from…were they coming from him? Was he able to speak after all?

"Yes, I will. I won't leave you. Not here or at the hospital."

Joseph opened his eyes and looked into her face. It hurt him to see how anguished she was. "Here, Martha…stay."

Mrs. Walsh said from behind Martha, "I can't believe he's talking. He hasn't said a word since this morning."

"I think we'll wait before we call the ambulance, Mrs. Walsh. He doesn't want it, and who am I to make him do something he doesn't want to do? I'll just stay here with him. If he gets worse, I'll call them."

"Call me first, please. I'm right next door."

He heard Martha speak, but he couldn't understand what she said. She moved away from him for a few minutes and then returned. She laid a cool cloth on his head.

She didn't speak for a long time. Martha just sat beside him, and he knew that she was lost in her own thoughts. He fought hard to speak to her and finally, he said, "I wasn't cheating when you left…"

Martha said nothing, just moved the cloth on his head around to the cooler side.

"Martha…" his voice sounded like a croak even to himself.

"It doesn't matter now, Joseph. Don't worry about it."

Again it took Joseph a long time to speak. "It matters…to me."

"I know it, Joseph. I knew it about six months after I left…when I found out you were sick. Dr. Haber told me…you had told him the whole story. So, I've known."

She knew? Yet, she didn't come home?

"Joseph, when I left you, I built you up in my mind to be a monster…it was the only way for me to survive leaving you. I had burned this image of you and…and…her…into my mind. I tortured myself—on purpose—with visions of the two of you in bed together. You became an ogre…a cheating no good bum…and then when I found out about the cancer, I couldn't seem to put who you really were back into focus. And…if we speak the truth…maybe you weren't cheating then, but you *had* cheated with her before then…before Joey came into our lives."

Martha stood up and moved to the bedroom window. He tried to follow her with his eyes, but she moved too quickly, and it hurt his head. She stood a long time, saying nothing. When she spoke again, she told him, "Joseph, I wanted to continue to hate you…I didn't want to forgive you…I was sorry you were sick, but I thought it was a just punishment for what you'd done…it's a terrible thing to feel that way, Joseph. It's a horrible thing. I didn't know that I could be such a cruel woman…I didn't know such meanness existed inside me. I hated myself for it...but I hated you more. Nothing could ever be the same with us, and I knew it, so I stayed away from you. I didn't want to watch you get sicker and suffer. That would have been more cruel for you...I thought so, anyway. I convinced myself of that."

"I love you," Joseph managed to say. "Martha...did you hear?"

There was a very long pause before she said, "I heard."

He had used up all his energy. He couldn't manage to speak another word. His head throbbed, his chest hurt. He tried to say he was sorry...he should have said it first...now he couldn't...he just couldn't do it.

"Joseph," Martha said, coming back to the bed and lying down next to him. He felt her head on the corner of his pillow. He wanted to reach out and take her in his arms. How he wanted to feel her against him, take comfort from her warmth...forgiveness. "Joseph, I'm lying," she said. "I'm lying, Joseph...I didn't hate you. I always loved you. I couldn't come back because I couldn't face that you were sick and I would lose you completely. I'm a terrible coward, Joseph. I've always been a coward. I should have confronted you when I first found out about the LaCorte woman, we could have hashed it out, fought, then made up, and it would have been behind us. But instead I was afraid. I kept it all inside...I'm a foolish woman. A cruel and foolish woman. But Joseph...my Joseph...my husband...I always loved you. I lied before. I lied to myself. I want you to know I love you."

Joseph cried. The tears welled up behind his closed lids and his chest constricted and he started to sob. It was a dreadful sound. He knew it himself, but he had no control over it. He was sobbing, but it sounded like he couldn't breathe. Martha jumped up off the bed and ran from the room. "Mrs. Walsh...Mrs. Walsh! Come...come!"

Joseph tried to stop...he tried to breathe normally...but now he couldn't. He was suffocating...gasping...he was scaring himself. Blackness started to shroud him. He needed air...*just open a window...just get some air.*

He felt arms move beneath his shoulders and knees. He tried to open his eyes to see, but he couldn't.

A man's voice said, "Eleanor, get the corners of the blanket and wrap them around him. That's it, tuck him up in it. Audra, ring for the elevator, honey—hurry."

"What are you doing?" Martha asked, her voice high-pitched and frightened.

"I'm bringing him down to meet the ambulance. They have to get oxygen into him and the sooner the better."

Joseph felt the man tighten his grip around him and he was lifted against a hard chest. *Brendan Walsh?*

Walsh cradled him gently, as though he were a child. Joseph wanted to be embarrassed, but strangely he wasn't. He felt protected in the man's massive arms.

"It's okay, Kramer. I'm going to take care of you. Don't be afraid."

Walsh held Joseph tighter to his chest. "Try to breathe…just try to breathe. It's going to be all right. Relax…I got you…I got you…don't be afraid. You're a good man, Kramer…I don't know if I ever told you that…but you are. I always admired you. Except for the other thing…well, that's not important, now. Just breathe until we get you to the oxygen."

Joseph allowed himself to relax in Brendon Walsh's arms, and suddenly it didn't seem to matter if he could breathe. The sobbing stopped, replaced by a rattle in his throat. Breathing wasn't all that important. He allowed his head to loll over onto the other man's hard shoulder. He was warm…he was safe in Walsh's arms, and it seemed all right for him to just let go…let go…just let go and let the blackness settle over him…a peacefulness…a place of no pain…no sadness…no thoughts but one: *I never would have thought…who would have ever thought…I'd die in Brendon Walsh's arms?*

OTIS

It was by coincidence that they all ended up at the elevator at the same time; all but Martha Kramer and Frances LaCorte. They stood silently, one by one arriving within seconds of one another, as they waited for the lift to come from one of the upper floors to the lobby.

They acknowledged one another with a nod of the head...a few smiles... Brendan Walsh and Eamon Williams held their fedoras in their hands; Dan Allcock didn't wear one as was becoming the fashion among younger men. The women all wore black.

Joseph Kramer had just been buried.

The elevator arrived, and Brendan opened and held the door. The ladies entered first, then he indicated that Dan and Eamon should follow before he stepped on to the elevator and allowed the door to close behind him.

No one had thought to push the button for the sixth floor and they all stood wondering for a second why the elevator hadn't moved. Dan pushed it with a grin, and the automatic door closed.

"The prayers were so beautiful." Audra was the first to speak.

"Yes, they are beautiful," Eleanor agreed.

"Mrs. Kramer looked so sad," Audra said.

"Of course, she would, honey," Eleanor told her daughter. "The grandson is the spitting image of Mr. Kramer. He's a handsome boy."

There was silence again, until Eamon said to Brendan, "You did a good thing, Walsh. I heard that they were able to get his heart beating again because you saved them some time by carrying him downstairs."

"Not good enough," Brendan mumbled.

"He lived another hour...long enough for Mrs. Kramer to see him once more in the hospital and kiss him goodbye. She told me she'd never forget you for that. And you were there with her when he died... she wasn't alone, and that meant the world to her."

Brendan pursed his lips, looked down at the floor, and said nothing. Eamon knew that Walsh had been shaken by the whole thing. Eleanor had told Eamon that since the day before yesterday, when Joseph Kramer died, her husband had agonized over whether he had done the right thing. Maybe he should have left Kramer in his bed. Maybe carrying him down wasn't the right thing to do. He wanted the guy to live, not die in his arms. It was eating at his gut.

Eamon reached over and touched Brendan's shoulder. Their eyes met for a second, then they looked away, both slightly embarrassed.

"She'll be sitting Shiva," Eleanor said, "I don't know if she mentioned it to anyone else, but she said everyone was invited tomorrow. She was worried that she may have forgotten to tell everyone."

"Not tonight?" Vera asked.

"No, tonight is for the family and closest friends."

"We covered all her mirrors for her yesterday," Audra told them. "The Jewish people do that, you know. They shouldn't be able to look at themselves in a room where they pray during mourning, or something like that."

Bridget smiled at the teenager. The day before, she had rung the Kramer's bell to deliver a platter of cold cuts and fresh rye bread. She was surprised when Audra answered the door. Apparently Bridget wasn't the only one in the building who brought food. When Eleanor and Audra brought a brisket over to Martha Kramer, the widow asked if Audra could stay to answer the door for her. Martha was exhausted and couldn't get any rest because of the callers who brought food. Her daughter-in-law hadn't arrived at Ashley Hall yet, and Martha was alone. Audra was happy to stay and help.

Audra led Bridget into the apartment and Bridget gasped when she saw how much food was on the kitchen table and on the counter tops. Audra had explained to Bridget that she was also helping get the apartment ready by covering the mirrors and doing other little chores Mrs. Kramer needed done. Bridget stayed for an hour to help Audra while Martha rested in the bedroom. Audra was full of questions about Ireland and what kind of customs they had for funerals there.

Bridget had answered, "Oh, an Irish wake can be an experience, it's true."

"Why?" Audra had wanted to know.

"Well, there's some that does a lot of keening."

"What's that?"

"A sort of wailing," Bridget said, smiling. "Some people pay women to come to the wake and cry loudly, sometimes they sing sad songs or poems. Everyone watches over the dead body, and cries, even if they didn't know the person well. But there's lots of fun, too. Drinkin' and lots of food and the like. People tell funny tales about the dead person. Your family is Irish;

didn't your mother tell me your father's people are from Ireland? You've never been to one of their wakes?"

Audra shook her head no. "Both of my grandfathers died before I was born. My father's father died when my father was only two years old. My grandmother died when I was really little, about four or five, so I didn't go to the funeral. My mother didn't think it was appropriate for children to go to a funeral. I do remember though that the night she died we were in her apartment, I think it was in the Bronx, and my father was sitting in a corner of the kitchen on a step stool. He was kind of hidden between the refrigerator and the wall. He was crying and I went over to him. He took me on his knee and cried harder, and I wiped the tears off his face every time one dropped onto his cheek. One by one I wiped them off his cheeks. I didn't know why he was crying and it sort of scared me, but I didn't ask him. I just kept wiping the tears. I guess I thought if I wiped them away, he wouldn't be so sad. I remember it like it only happened last week."

It didn't seem all that long ago that Bridget moved into Ashley Hall and met the wee curly haired girl in the lobby. Now Audra was in high school, with a boyfriend. They saw very little of each other, just in passing and rides on "Otis" as Audra used to call the elevator, but Bridget had watched her grow up. She was still the only child in the building—the only teenager at this point. Bridget had played the conversation they had about her father on the day his mother died over and over in her mind, picturing the tiny child wiping tears off her daddy's cheeks. Bridget found it hard to imagine the burly Brendan Walsh crying like that. She had only seen him at his best when he was sober, or at his worst when he was not.

They left the elevator when it stopped, and Bridget touched Audra's arm when she passed her. She felt a fondness for Audra that she couldn't explain. Audra smiled shyly at Bridget.

The inhabitants of the sixth floor of Ashley Hall left the elevator in silence. There was the briefest pause before they walked to their own apartment doors. No one said goodbye. No one said a word. The sound of keys jingling and locks turning echoed against the marble floor and walls.

They were all anxious to escape from the other sound in the hallway— the unconstrained weeping coming from Frances LaCorte's apartment.

6G

LaCorte

Frances lay on her bed all day, unable to eat, unable to stop crying. She had called in sick the day before, the morning after Joseph died, and stayed in her bed for two days.

Why had she let him think she hated him all those years? Why was she so cruel? He had broken her heart, but he had never made her any promises...she knew from the beginning that he was married, that he held his vows sacred. She had no right to treat him that way. She had no right to expect more from him.

She had wanted to hate him. From the moment they met in the restaurant that last time, before he had said a single word, she was ready to hate him. Frances was certain that Martha knew about the affair. She had seen the reaction Martha had when Joseph's shirt fell out of the pillowcase that night in the laundry room. She watched in horror as Martha recoiled from it and backed away, her hand gripping her crepey throat as though she couldn't breathe.

Frances was deeply disturbed that the secret she and Joseph had been keeping was revealed that way. The woman had looked at her with such...what was it?...shock...then grief...intense grief...then derision...scorn and revulsion, as though Martha was looking at the devil himself.

But there was some relief, too. Now Martha knew. Now the woman who stood between Frances and happiness knew what was going on and maybe...*just maybe*...she'd leave him. Excitement grew in Frances, even as she watched Martha grab her laundry basket and run to the elevator, a strangled moan coming from her as she ran...even while Frances felt remorse and fear that Martha was going to confront Joseph. She remembered thinking that maybe there would be a scene. She should have dreaded it. She didn't. She felt excitement that finally...*finally*...something would be resolved. She would fight for him...and she believed she would win.

It was quiet on the sixth floor when she returned. She listened and heard nothing coming from the Kramer apartment. She wondered, should she go and ring the bell and have it out once and for all, or should she wait...wait until Joseph summoned her?

She had decided to wait, and she let herself into her apartment. She sat at the kitchen table waiting for Joseph to ring the bell and tell her, "Okay, Francesca, she knows. I'm free. We're free." But there was nothing that night. She heard people in the hall, and ran to look out the peephole, and she saw a young woman with an older man and a boy going into Joseph's apartment. How could they have company tonight of all nights? Wasn't Martha screaming at him? Wasn't she weeping, threatening to kill him, or at least threatening to leave?

Frances backed away from her door and waited. She carried a kitchen chair closer to her door so she could hear. The guests left. She heard them leaving. She heard Joseph's voice speaking to them as they waited for the elevator. She couldn't hear what they were saying, but she knew he went down with them. It was his custom whenever they had company...to walk their guests—Martha's and his guests—to the lobby to say goodbye.

And when she heard the elevator come back up, she tensed and stood up from the chair waiting for Joseph to ring her bell. When he didn't, she went to the peephole and looked out. He stood there, between the two doors, contemplating. *Come to me*...she had longed to say aloud. *Come, Joseph, my love. I'm here. We'll handle Martha together. Now that she knows, we can be together.*

But Joseph only glanced at Frances's door, then turned and went into his own apartment. She heard him say, "Martha, what are you doing?" and then the door closed behind him.

What was she doing? Was she going to kill him? Was she holding a knife or a gun? Would she hurt him?

Frances unlocked her door and tiptoed on bare feet into the hallway. Her head felt strange, foggy...fearful. What could she do to protect him with a locked door between them? *What was Martha doing?* She listened at the door.

The noises were unmistakable. The sounds from the Kramers' apartment—sounds that were right there, right behind the door—were familiar. She knew them well. She'd heard those noises come from Joseph time and time again. She was well acquainted with the sound of Joseph Kramer's orgasms.

Frances backed away from the door as though there were electrical currents coming from it. She bolted back into her own apartment, slammed the door as hard as she could, and threw herself on her bed, screaming into the pillow until there was no strength left in her. She hated him. *Hated* him. But she hated Martha Kramer more. How dare that bitch seduce him when she knew full well that he belonged to Frances? How dare she? How dare *he*?

And they went away the next day. Just as they had planned...just as Martha had told her before...before the damned shirt fell out of the pillowcase. They were gone several days, and Joseph didn't call when he came home. Frances waited...one day...two...four...then suddenly he called her at work and asked to meet her for lunch.

Frances knew what he was planning to say to her. Lunch was not necessary. But she agreed anyway.

No, Joseph's telling her that their affair was over was no surprise. What was a surprise was the fact that he didn't say that Martha knew about it. No, he was breaking up with her because some new-found grandson had come out of nowhere and he was choosing this child...this stranger to him...over her.

She wanted to get some comfort from the fact that Martha wasn't the one who won. Yet, Martha did win. The fates were on her side. The very same evening...the very same day Martha found out about the affair...the boy came into their lives.

Yes, Martha had won.

Comfort came later when Frances thought about how Martha knew now that she was living just feet away from the apartment in which Joseph took Frances to bed. Just a coin toss from where Joseph buried his face between Frances' breasts and thighs, even while Martha was in her own apartment thinking he was at the club, or the synagogue, or playing chess with his friends.

Frances took great comfort from knowing that every time Joseph left his apartment, Martha would wonder: is he going to her? Is he going to place his body over the red-headed vixen across the hall and move himself deep inside her over and over until he quivered and moaned. Would he be covering Frances's mouth with his own? Oh, yes, Martha Kramer must be frantic with worry every time Joseph was out of her sight.

Less comfort came from the thought that Joseph must be longing for her. How could he not? Frances knew that he was as connected to her now as he was to his wife. She knew that he loved her. She knew that she was a fever in him...he could never get enough of her when they were together. And it wasn't just the sex. It was a melding of the minds, of the hearts, and of their souls. Frances wasn't just his mistress; she was his life too. And it didn't please her when she thought that he must feel as though a piece of himself was missing now. It *should* please her, but it didn't.

The only way for Frances to live with this disaster in her life was to stay in that apartment—across from the Kramers—and make life miserable for Martha, even though only the two of them knew that was the case, and to make Joseph think that she detested him for choosing his grandson over her. It was a twisted and dysfunctional way to live, but it was the only way Frances wanted to live.

Two years she had lived that way. And then, suddenly, Martha was gone. Moved out. Joseph was alone. Frances's moment had come. All that she had waited for…longed for…was there, ready for her. He would take her in his arms and into his life completely and they would have whatever time was left for them. They could move away, far way, maybe to California.

Yet, something told Frances that it would not have worked that way. Not that she couldn't forgive him. She could forgive him…had in fact done so already. No, that wasn't it. It was more that Frances knew he had moved on…had moved away from her emotionally. So they were there, living a few steps away from each other, and yet nothing. She didn't make a motion toward him. And he didn't make a motion toward her. It wasn't over. It would never be over for *her* anyway. She didn't think it was over for him either. Yet they stayed apart—separated by a ten foot hallway.

Vera Allcock told her about Joseph's illness. It was on the elevator one morning as they both left for work.

"Have you seen Mr. Kramer? How thin he is already? He was only just diagnosed six months ago. His clothes are hanging off him."

The buzz started in Frances's head. It was so loud that she couldn't understand how she could hear Vera Allcock talking.

"I think it's appalling that his wife has left him because he's sick. I can't imagine why else she would have left him. They were always together…walking with their grandson, going to his school and to games…and then suddenly, poof, she's gone."

Frances looked for a sign that Vera knew about the affair and was goading her, but none was there. Obviously, Vera was one of very few on the sixth floor who didn't know.

"I just feel so sorry for him. He looks so gray and weak."

Frances found her voice when they were almost at the first floor. "I didn't know he was ill."

"Cancer, I think it is," Vera said, shaking her head sadly.

"I haven't seen him in a long time."

"You'll be shocked when you do see him," Vera told her.

The elevator stopped. Vera stepped out, but Frances couldn't move. She said something to the other woman, but she wasn't certain what she had said. Something about forgetting her wallet or her subway tokens, and she had to go back up. She let herself into her apartment and just made it to the bathroom in time to vomit. She was on her knees, sobbing and vomiting for a long time.

Joseph...Joseph...Joseph...Joseph...Joseph...Joseph...Joseph...

She sat on the floor of her bathroom and moaned for him as though he were already dead. Then she got up, straightened her clothing, fixed her makeup, combed her hair, and left for work. Joseph Kramer *was* dead to her.

The only time they spoke after that was the night she got stuck in the elevator with Eamon Williams...the night of the blackout. After Brendan Walsh rescued them, they were alone in the hallway for a moment, and he held a candle for her to find her key and unlock her door. He didn't really look like Joseph by then. It even appeared to her that he had become shorter, although she knew that wasn't the case. But his voice was the same, and she closed her eyes and spoke to him just so that she could hear his voice...and remember who he was once...who he was *to her* once.

"I'm sorry you're ill," she had said.

"Me too," was all he had replied as he left her at the door. He didn't know, because it was too dark, that her eyes were closed when she spoke to him and that tears slid down her face, to her neck, beneath her collar.

Audra was in the hallway the night Joseph died...before he died. She was between his door and her own, and she was crying. Frances barely spoke with the girl most of the time. In all the years they lived right next door to each other, she rarely had a conversation with her. And she avoided Eleanor. Frances knew that Eleanor not only knew about the affair, but held great contempt for Frances because of it. Eleanor's attitude made it very clear. Yet Eleanor always made sure to let Frances know what was going on with his health...surprisingly not with malice.

"What's wrong," Frances had asked the Walsh girl. She wondered if her father had done something terrible to his wife and that was why the girl was alone in the hallway crying.

"Poor Mr. Kramer," the girl said. "He so sick...he is so very sick..."

Frances felt the strength leave her and she had all she could do to remain standing.

"How do you know?" she managed to ask.

"My mother is in there with him. She brought dinner to him, but he was in bed and couldn't speak."

Frances knew she alarmed the Walsh girl when she breathed in a loud, ragged breath and dropped her purse. The girl stopped crying and stared at her.

Frances left her bag on the floor of the hallway and walked into the Kramer apartment, wooden, heavy, her body stiff. Eleanor met her in the living room.

"May I see him?" It was difficult to say the words. And how ludicrous it was that she had to ask permission from Eleanor Walsh...who was Eleanor to stand in the doorway and block her? It should have been Martha. It should have been his wife. *That* Frances could handle...but not Eleanor Walsh.

Eleanor let her in but with many warnings that Martha was on her way. Eleanor begged her to be brief...as though only Martha mattered. Only *Martha*'s grief was important...was real...was acknowledged.

Yet, there was sympathy in Eleanor Walsh's eyes. Frances saw that as well.

Frances knew that Joseph heard her. He knew that he was being forgiven, that he was still loved by her. At the very end of his life, he knew they were reconciled. She told him she loved him. He couldn't say it, but she knew he was telling her the same thing.

She tore herself away from the side of his bed. She didn't know where she got the strength to leave him.

Eleanor Walsh was kind to her then. She put her arm around Frances's shoulder to lead her out of the room, but Frances could barely remember what the woman said to her. She knew that there were words of comfort. Eleanor asked her not to say anything to Martha...it would have been too cruel at that time...and Frances understood that Eleanor was talking about healing...not just Martha's healing, but Frances's as well.

As she walked out of the apartment she heard the elevator stop. The door opened and Martha stepped out. They stared at each other. Not a word was exchanged between them, but Frances saw the question in Martha's eyes: had Frances been in there with him? And Frances's eyes answered. *No...he is yours.*

She was on the roof of Ashley Hall when Brendan Walsh was carrying Joseph down to the arriving ambulance. She was standing on the ledge, in bare feet, her arms outstretched, the pain unbearable, and the knowledge that it would be over in just a moment was overwhelmingly satisfying. This would be the only way she could be with the man she had truly loved. If there was an afterlife—and she believed that there was—then their spirits would leave their bodies and be joined there. If she couldn't have him *here*, she'd have him *there*.

And just as she was ready to let herself go...to fly into the night...she saw the red flashing lights, and she heard—even from six stories below her—Brendan Walsh shouting to the ambulance attendants that the man in his arms was dying and to help him...to help Joseph...please don't let him die...please help him to breathe. Help this man, please help this man.

She would have landed right there, where they stood putting Joseph on the stretcher. Perhaps she would have landed on top of them. She and Joseph would have died together in the same place. And wouldn't that have been just…wouldn't it have been righteous…wouldn't it have destroyed Martha Kramer?

But she couldn't jump. There was something so plaintive…so *compelling*…in Brendan's plea that Joseph should not die, that it just seemed wrong to make him suffer the shock of her death on the concrete sidewalk beside him.

Why would she care what Brendan Walsh thought?

She didn't know why. She just did. She couldn't do it to him. He sounded so frantic, *so desperate* to save Joseph. Even up there on the roof, so far above, she could hear the emotion in his voice, the way his voice cracked when he pleaded with the ambulance attendants to save Joseph.

It made her…*no, it wasn't possible*…but yes, it did…it made her feel love for him because he was so concerned about her Joseph. He wanted to save Joseph's life. He *tried* to save Joseph.

He failed.

Brendan Walsh would never know that he *did* save a life that night. He saved Frances LaCorte's life.

She'd never forgive him for it.

Summer 1969

Vera finished cleaning the hardwood floors and stood back to look. They shone. There wasn't a spot of dirt, dust, or grime anywhere in the apartment.

It looked different now that it was empty. Most of their furniture had been given to Goodwill. Danny insisted they buy new things for their place on Long Island. Once they found the house they wanted, they selected each piece carefully, and paid for it without going into debt. The closing on the house had been the day before…the furniture was being delivered today, and a thrill coursed through her thinking about it.

Danny had left her an hour before, taking all their clothes, a couple of lamps, boxes of pots and pans and the few things they did keep. They each had a car now. He insisted on that, too, since they'd be living in the suburbs without any public transportation. She wanted to stay and clean the apartment so the Biermanns couldn't gossip about them.

"Knock, knock," Bridget Riordan said pushing the apartment door just slightly ajar. "Are ye still around?"

Vera leaned the dust mop against a wall and said "Still around."

Bridget came all the way in then. "I saw the door was just open a crack and I wanted to say goodbye to ye."

Vera reached out and took the other woman in her arms. "Oh, I'm going to miss you, Bridget. Really, you're just about the only one—well, you and Mrs. Sommer. You've been good to me."

"Are ye excited?" Bridget asked, her eyes shining with pleasure for her neighbor.

"I have butterflies. As soon as we're settled, we want you to come out and see the house and have dinner with us. It's such a lovely house.

And we're going to fill it up with children! We've waited long enough."

Bridget laughed heartily. "Well, now, that's the way it should be. And your in-laws?"

Vera sighed but smiled at the same time. "We're still a little cautious around each other. I think they feel that it was my fault that they were estranged from Danny—I don't think they see their own fault in it—but we're all willing to let it go. I have no intention of ever getting into it with them. I'm hoping that we can all just agree to disagree and move on. We'll never all see eye to eye anyway. I'm just grateful that they've come to accept me...if not like me."

"Are your parents happy about you movin' out on Long Island?"

"Not extremely...my mother's been crying every day for the last week, saying she'll never see me anymore. But she knows that's not true. My father is just such a gentle man, and he's relieved that Danny and his parents are talking again. He only wants what is best for us. My sisters are coming out tonight to help me unpack and put curtains on the windows. They're going to stay for the weekend."

Vera felt bubbly, she was so happy. She couldn't believe it was actually happening. So it wasn't Connecticut. Who cares? It's going to be her home, a real house, with windows that allow the sunshine in, and that's all she really cared about. That and Danny.

"What about you?" she asked Bridget.

"What about me?"

"When will you get out of this hell hole?"

"Aw, it's not such a hell hole. It's a nice building. I would like to have taken your apartment though—havin' a bedroom would've been nice. But Biermann rented it out so fast I never had the chance to ask."

Vera looked around and then said, "I don't even have a chair to offer you."

"I don't need it. I'll let you get back to your cleanin'."

"Promise you'll come see us," Vera said.

"Sure. I'll bring Mrs. Sommer with me if she can make it. Poor old thing seems to get frailer every day. And what with Audra having a boyfriend now, she hardly ever goes in to see the old woman. It's Eleanor and Brendan that's been watching over her. And I've been doin' my best, too."

"I saw Audra and the boy in the elevator the other night. I think they were wishing they were alone. The ride up in the elevator is a great time to get in some goodnight necking."

Bridget laughed with Vera. "Yes, well, it's hard to think what poor Brendan feels about his little girl having a boyfriend...let alone thinkin' of her kissing him in the elevator. Worse yet, can you imagine being the boyfriend and having to come home to meet the giant Brendan Walsh? Audra is probably the safest girl in Queens. What boy would take advantage of her with the likes of him waiting home?"

They both laughed now. Vera said, "There was an awful row in the elevator recently between Audra and her mother. I wished I hadn't gotten on at the same time the Walshes did. Apparently, Audra wants to go to Woodstock...that concert in upstate New York everyone is talking about...and Eleanor was fit to be tied. Even Brendan looked afraid of Eleanor that night. He tried to defend Audra, and I thought Eleanor would bite his head off. He backed away from her and slinked into the corner of the elevator and left Audra to fight her own battle with her mother."

"What was the outcome?" Bridget asked.

"All I know is that as they walked into their apartment, I heard Eleanor tell Audra that she'd send her to reform school in Philadelphia before she'd ever allow her to go to Woodstock...she had a few choice names for the 'kind of girls' who'll be going and she'd see Audra locked up before she allowed her to go. I think I heard Audra say something like 'I'm not a baby, mother,' but the door closed before I heard Eleanor's answer to that...thank God...I can only imagine..."

Bridget raised her eyebrows and said, "Time goes by so quickly. She was just a small girl when I moved in, barely eight. And it feels like just last week that you and I got to be friends, and already you're leaving. We lived on the same floor for...what now?...seven years?...and just started to talk to each other a year or two ago."

"I'm hoping that's not what it's like where I'm moving. I want lots of friends."

Bridget hugged Vera again. "And you'll have 'em. I wish you all the luck...and the friends...in the world. You and Danny."

Vera wanted to say thank you, but she was suddenly filled with emotion. She held back tears, but Bridget knew and laughed. "Oh, now, don't be a ninny," she said, kissing Vera's cheek again.

When Bridget left her, Vera carried her cleaning supplies out to the hallway. She went back into the apartment, checked that everything was clean, the cabinets were empty and the closets, and then walked over to fix a crooked blind. She looked out through the living room window one last time.

Some people were walking into the courtyard, coming home from work. She smiled. In the beginning, she hated this apartment, but now that she was leaving it, she felt sad. It was Danny's and her first home...they got through all the ups and downs of early marriage in this tiny place. It felt like a safe cocoon, albeit a dark cocoon. She worried now. Will everything be the same on Long Island? Or will we just have new worries and ups and downs to confront?

She suddenly thought of one of the darkest moments in her marriage, when she thought Danny was ashamed of her and that was why he wouldn't invite his parents over. That one evening long ago when she had imagined that he looked at her the same way his parents did, and she had run to the roof of the building, seriously thinking she didn't want to live if he felt that way. She also remembered how Mrs. Walsh had found her there, and how kind she was, how wise and generous she had been that evening. Vera knew that Eleanor Walsh was the last woman on Earth that a young bride should use as a model, yet that evening Vera was able to resolve her fears and deal with her husband because of Eleanor's counsel.

After that evening, she knew that if there was ever a need, she could turn to Mrs. Walsh. Luckily, there never was. She and Dan put all of that aside...settled into the apartment, small as it was...made it a home...a safe haven.

The apartment on the sixth floor of Ashley Hall seemed very safe just then, and moving to the new house seemed very forbidding.

The new house was a done deal, so she just had to go. Vera was very happy that Eleanor Walsh had given her a piece of paper with her phone number on it—just in case. She gave it to Vera with a lovely crystal vase as a house warming for the Allcocks' new home. "Audra wanted you to have a nice vase for flowers when you set your table," Eleanor had said. "We hope it will make you think of her fondly when you use it."

Vera would think fondly of Audra...but she'd also think of Mrs. Walsh with fondness, too. Wasn't Mrs. Walsh—proud and overconfident one minute, trampled and weak the next—the reason why her husband was practicing law now?

From her apartment window, Vera saw Mrs. Kramer walking slowly into the building. She seemed much older now that her husband was gone. How long was it? Six months? Vera had heard that she was keeping two apartments, this one and the one she'd been living in near her grandson before poor Mr. Kramer died. She just couldn't seem to make the decision to get rid of this one. Vera still wondered why Martha Kramer had left her husband. She doubted now that it had had anything to do with his illness. It was obvious Mrs. Kramer had adored him. Strange...people do strange things.

Vera closed the blinds. She took one more look around and then left Apartment 6D. She was off to white wall-to-wall carpeting.

Fall 1969

Eamon prepared the salad and put the bowl in the refrigerator to keep it chilled. He carefully placed two steaks on the broiler pan and seasoned them exactly the way John liked—coarse salt, a little pepper, and a dash of steak sauce—before the meat was place under the heat.

He put the gas on under the green beans and finished setting the table. He was still wearing his white shirt, his sleeves turned back to the middle of his forearms. He had taken off his tie and opened the shirt at the neck. He intended to run a comb through his hair before John arrived, but before he could get to the bedroom, the doorbell rang.

"You're early," he said, answering the door and letting John in.

"Too early?" John asked.

"Never." Eamon smiled and moved behind John to take his jacket. "Take this off. I put the steaks in. They'll be ready in a few minutes." Eamon lingered as he reached to take John's jacket from his shoulders. He closed his eyes and breathed John in. John leaned, just for a brief second, back into Eamon's arms.

They walked into the living room and Eamon placed John's suit jacket on the back of the desk chair. He watched John roll up his sleeves in the same way he had rolled his.

Eamon told John to come into the kitchen with him while he finished getting dinner on the table. John joined him so infrequently these days. Eamon was in high spirits, thrilled that John had called and asked to have dinner in his apartment. They had been too busy lately, unable to match schedules. That had never happened before, and being in John's presence now reminded Eamon that they had to make sure never to go this long again.

"We've got to get back to the tennis court," Eamon said as they entered the kitchen. "We haven't played in weeks. And you have to clear your calendar a little. It's been more than a month since we've been together." Eamon smiled over at John. "I've missed you."

"I've been busy...work, work, work. The agency has been nuts lately."

"All work and no play...and all of that," Eamon said, laughing.

"Am I a dull boy?" John was already seated at the table when he asked.

Eamon looked at him. Something wasn't right with John. They'd been friends...lovers...long enough for Eamon to know the signs.

"I'm not a dull man...right?" John persisted.

"No. Not dull...never dull...brilliant maybe." He flashed a bright smile at his friend, then took the steaks from the broiler and used a meat fork to place them on the plates. He took out the salad, put the vegetables in a bowl, unfolded his linen napkin at the same time John did and they began to eat.

Their conversation moved smoothly into politics, which was what they always talked about over meals.

"Johnson has to get us out of Viet Nam. It's a no-win war," John commented.

"Bobby would have," Eamon said, "if they hadn't killed him."

"Come on, Eamon, his brother got us into it in the first place. It's up to Johnson now."

They sat silently for a long while, then Eamon asked, "Is it me, or are you a little edgy tonight?"

John shrugged. "Got lots on my mind...and I hate this war. I hate even talking about it. Everyone is always talking about it. You can't put the news on without seeing protestors, and then those scenes from Viet Nam...kids shot up, copters hovering over them. It's never ending."

Eamon nodded in agreement. "Maybe the Tet Offensive will end it."

John asked, "How many people have to die in this war? They don't even want us over there...the south Vietnamese. It's none of our business. It's destroying our country. I was watching kids burning the American flag in Central Park on the news the other night, and I felt like spitting I was so angry. But something inside me wanted to be on the kids' side... they have the right...I mean, what the hell are we sending these kids over there for?"

"Sounds like you've been talking to Honora. Is our liberal friend wearing off on you?"

John looked up at him, studied him, then looked at his plate again. He shook his head and took a mouthful of the meat. They ate in silence for a few minutes. Quieter now, John said, "I feel like the world is upside down. You can't even go to a bar for a drink without having to hear about it...discuss it. Civil rights, girls burning their bras in public, guys burning their draft cards. Even at the club, it's the constant buzz of what's right about Viet Nam and what's wrong about this war. People you thought would be on the side of fighting are the very people who hate it, and vice-versa."

Eamon put his fork down. "You've been at the club?" he asked, trying to sound casual, but knowing that his question was accusatory.

John's neck became flushed and the red crawled to his cheeks. "Yeah...for a drink and dinner...a couple of times."

"Oh," was all Eamon said. It was all he could say. For as long as he could remember, John never went to the club without him, and he never went without John. He thought John was too busy lately, too tied up, work...work...work. Wasn't that what he said?

When their plates were empty, Eamon stood to clear the dishes. He came back to the table to take the bowls from the table, and John grabbed his wrist.

"Sit down a minute," John said to him, "I need to tell you something."

Eamon sat down and leaned back against the chair. He reached into his pocket and pulled out a pack of cigarettes and offered one to John, who shook his head no. Eamon lit the cigarette and took a long drag. "Okay, what's up?" he asked finally, letting the smoke stream out of his mouth and nose.

"We've been friends for such a long time, E."

Eamon laughed a little. "All our lives."

"And it's been one of the most important relationships in my life." John crossed his arms on the table and looked down. "The most important."

"You look serious," Eamon said, alarmed, although he didn't know why.

"I am serious. This is a very serious conversation we're about to have."

Eamon dragged on his cigarette again, flipped the ash into a glass ashtray on the table, and asked again, "What's up?"

John swallowed hard. Eamon saw his Adam's apple move up and down three times, before he said, "I'm getting married."

Eamon burst out laughing. "You had me going there for a minute. Honest, I thought you were going to tell me something devastating by the way you were acting."

John didn't laugh with him. The usual crooked smile didn't reach John's lips as it did when he was being playful or sarcastic. "Honora Morel," he said.

Eamon stopped laughing. After a long silence, he said "Stop it."

"Honora."

Eamon stood up and his chair moved hard against the wall behind him. "That's enough, Johnny. It's not funny anymore."

"Oh, God, it is, E. It's funny all right. Sometimes I laugh myself to sleep over it. Funny but true." He wasn't laughing when he said it.

Eamon walked into the living room, one hand on the back of his head and the other in his pants pocket. "You're not...I don't believe you."

John took a long time getting up and walking into the room where Eamon was pacing. Eamon noticed for the first time how tanned John was. He looked thinner, too. Eamon repeated, "I don't, John. I don't believe you're serious."

"Next month."

"Stop! Just stop, okay?" Eamon was facing the window. Night had fallen and it was dark beyond the glass panes. He could see himself reflected in the glass, and John standing behind him.

"People are starting to notice...the old confirmed bachelor act isn't working any longer. Even my parents were acting funny around me. I'm almost fifty...we're almost fifty...and...I don't know...I feel people looking at me..." he stopped speaking and shrugged. "I don't like it, E. I hate anyone thinking I'm a fag. It's terrifying. It's mortifying."

Eamon felt like his head was going to explode. "Mortifying? Mortifying? It's what you are, John Sullivan...you *are* a fag. You've been one since we hit puberty. When the hell are you going to admit it? When the hell are we both going to admit it?"

"Never, Eamon. And you know that we're never going to admit it. Not us. We're forever in that proverbial closet."

"Then we'll stay in the closet, but we don't have to get married to other people, for God's sake."

"I do." John said. "I'm getting married."

Eamon took a deep breath to calm himself. Then he sat on the couch, taking John's hand and pulling him down with him. "Let's talk about this...sanely."

John allowed Eamon to pull him onto the couch, but he shook his head and leaned back, pulling away from Eamon. "I can't talk about it with you, Eamon. I'm sorry, but I just can't."

"Honora is a beautiful woman. An educated woman. Are you really willing to ruin her life? When she comes to realize what you are—and she will realize it eventually—it will destroy her."

"She won't find out, Eamon."

"Don't fool yourself."

"We were away together last week...in Nassau. We had long luxurious nights in the same bed, and I can't tell you I hated them. I wasn't repulsed. I've never been repulsed by women, E. And Honora is a goddess...intelligent, sweet, giving...beautiful."

Eamon wanted to vomit. His body shook uncontrollably. "You son of a bitch," he whispered.

"Yes, I am, but that doesn't change the fact that although I'm going to marry Honora next month, I love you. I've always loved you, E. I will always love you."

"She's a communist," Eamon spit out, as though that mattered, as though it had anything to do with the fact that John was going to marry her.

"No...a socialist," John corrected. "She marched with Martin Luther King, she espouses Civil Rights in her classes at Hunter College, and yes, she's an activist. But it's one of the things that attract me to her. We have long talks—sometimes arguments—but it's stimulating. She's stimulating. And she's different. She's a feminist, I know, but she's so feminine at the same time. And when she presents her side of the story, it's fascinating. She can almost persuade me. Not always, but then that's what makes our time together so intriguing. She's brilliant. It draws me to her."

"That and the fact that her parents are millionaires and you'll get to benefit from the estate?" Eamon didn't want to say it, but he couldn't keep his mouth shut.

"That's not exactly fair."

"And it's not exactly wrong, either, is it? A beautiful, intelligent wife...long standing member of the club...well seated in the Upper East Side...artists...bankers...Wall Street execs. That's the life you've always wanted, John. Let's face it. Working class boy makes good...marries an heiress."

John jumped off the couch now, meeting Eamon's anger. "So what if it is? What's wrong with it? What's wrong with wanting a normal life?"

"It's not *normal* for you...for us...for guys like us, John. We're not that kind of normal, we're different."

"Why do you feel that we should go around bragging about that? I don't want to. If you do, fine, go ahead. But I don't. I want a wife, a home, and maybe children. I'm not too old, and Honora is only thirty-seven. We could start a family. I want children. I've always wanted children."

John knelt in front of Eamon now. He took Eamon's hands in his and looked up into his face. "Please, E. Please try to understand. I don't want this life...I want what the other...what other men...have."

"You'll never come back into this apartment again," Eamon warned him. "You won't leave your wife and come back to my bed. You have to know that before you do this stupid thing. I wouldn't do it to Honora...and I won't do it to myself."

"We'll always be friends," John said.

"You can't be friends after you've been lovers...get a grip, John. You're living in a fantasy."

"Eamon, I can't—I won't—let you out of my life. We're more than sex, you and I. We're friends...we are..."

"Soul mates? Isn't that what you used to say about us? Soul mates?"

John stood up and swore. "Damn you, Eamon. Damn you. *Damn you to hell.* We live in a straight world. Don't you know that? Don't you know that all these years we've been fooling ourselves...what we do isn't natural...it's twisted…perverse."

"Since when? Since you decided to get married? Because before then we were in love, John. We made love every time we were together."

"Shut up!"

"No, I won't shut up."

"Shut up, Eamon. We never made love. Damn, I don't even know what to call it. Lie to yourself if you want. But I'm finished with that. I'm finished with all of it."

Eamon's laugh was so acrimonious it surprised even him. "You're such a pathetic human being."

John took his suit jacket from the back of the desk chair. "Think whatever you will about me, Eamon. I'm sorry. I am. I do love you. But no one is going to look at me that way again. No one is going to intimidate me or make me feel like a…a…freak. I'm a man, Eamon. I'm a man…not a…not a…a sick twisted mistake of nature."

"Neither am I. And I don't have to marry an innocent woman to know that."

John put his jacket on. "I'm sorry…again and again and again, I'm sorry."

"You're sorry, all right. You're sick and you're sorry."

"Eamon…our friendship is important."

"Oh, yes, it would be, wouldn't it? If we stay friends and keep up the pretenses, then those people—the ones who may have wondered about us—will say 'that nice bachelor, John Sullivan, finally got hooked by a beautiful woman—his oat-sewing days are over—now we'll have to find a nice woman for that friend of his, too.'"

"Eamon, your bitterness is frightening."

"Your transparency is sickening."

"Eamon, we've always known something like this was going to happen."

"No…we didn't know that."

"I want you to be my best man."

"Oh, for Christ's sake, John, just get out. Just be that man you want to be and get out of here. I can't stand the sight of you. Go…be happy…be a man. Ruin that beautiful woman's life." Eamon covered his eyes with his hand and put his head back against the couch. "But that twisted perverse thing you were talking about before could become a rumor, you know. Just the right word in the right place, and this fantasy of yours will be over…and Honora will be saved." Eamon wondered about the words he was speaking. Could he do it? Could he actually do that?

"Eamon…" John's voice was pleading.

"Get out!" Eamon shouted. He reached out and found an ashtray on the end table and threw it with all his strength at John. It missed its mark and smashed against the gilt-framed mirror over the television console.

Both men looked shocked. They stared at the broken mirror for several long seconds as pieces of the mirror separated and fell to the top of the console. John's portrait was reflected in the few shards that remained in the mirror's frame, making him look deformed.

Eamon began to laugh. It started slow and low and then became hysterical. Soon the laughter turned to sobs. He bent in two, holding his head in his hands. "Get the hell out," he managed to cry out. "Please, Johnny, please, just get out. Leave me alone."

Eamon heard the apartment door close and he fell over in grief, sinking onto the floor, his knees pulled up to his chest, his hands covering his ears. He lay on the floor for a long time like that.

The sounds that emanated from his throat were monstrous...feral.

He had risked everything because of his love for John. He'd risked his career, his relationship with his mother, his happiness. It was all for John...for the moments they had together...the sweet, delicious moments they stole whenever they could...flashes of time that he never believed would end...time they devoted to each other ever since they were boys...boys who knew they would never want anyone else but each other. They had a pact, an unspoken pact, that they would be together until they died.

Why, Johnny?

Some other woman. Some other name...any other name. Not Honora Morel. No... God, no...not Honora. Their closest friend. The woman who loved them both, who danced with them both at the club, who teased them, prodded them into lengthy political arguments, laughed with them. The woman who enjoyed their company, their jokes, and their tennis matches. The woman they let into their lives...or let into their lives to a point. How often did they discuss the fact that if they ever told anyone about themselves, it would be her...she would understand and accept them no matter what.

Eamon adored Honora. He valued her. He respected her. But he never *wanted* her. Never in that way. How could John taint the love she had for them—it was for *them—both* of them. Not just for John. Her friendship belonged to both of them.

He would never forgive John. He would never forgive Honora. He would die hating them both.

He'd die hating himself, as he had always hated himself, for the one thing he couldn't change, no matter how he tried, no matter how he prayed, no matter how he agonized.

1970 TO 1972

The Exodus

Spring 1970

Germaine was drifting in and out of a doze when the banging started on her door. At first she heard it from a long way away...from deep in her drowsiness. Then she realized it was real.

The cat was curled on her lap, warm and secure, and only one of her ears moved in response to the noise.

"Sweetiekins, please let me up," Germaine said, pushing gently at the cat. "Come on, move over, let me up. Someone is at the door."

While she pushed herself to her feet, she called out, "Okay...I'm coming...who is it? Who's there?"

She moved toward the hallway, supporting herself on the wall as she walked closer to the door. When she opened it, Bridget was standing there, holding Audra up. The teenager's face was bruised and one cheek was scraped raw. Her lip was swollen and her knees were bleeding. Her school uniform was torn and smeared with grime.

"Let us in, Mrs. Sommer," Bridget said crisply, pushing into the apartment without waiting for Germaine to open the door wider.

"What in God's name happened to her?" Germaine was shocked by Audra's appearance.

Bridget didn't answer. She continued to lead Audra to the sofa. The girl wasn't crying. She wasn't speaking. She looked lost, almost as though she couldn't comprehend what had happened and where she was.

"She was attacked," Bridget said finally, settling the girl on the sofa and straightening to look at Germaine. "Thank God I heard her crying out as I approached the alley."

Germaine didn't understand. "What do you mean...attacked how?"

Bridget ignored her, "I need to use the phone. We have to call the police and then her mother."

"No!" Audra cried out. She grabbed Bridget's sleeve. "Please don't call anyone. Just let me stay here. I don't want my mother to know. I don't need the police."

Bridget looked surprised and walked over to the sofa to sit beside the girl. She took Audra's hands in hers. "Sweetheart, listen to me. You were just attacked. The police have to get this creep...look at how he hurt you. If I hadn't come along and heard, God only knows..."

"My mother will be very angry."

"Yes, but not at you, dear. She'll be angry that this happened."

Audra shook her head. "No...no...she'll blame me somehow. She has so much to deal with all the time. I don't want to upset her."

"She's going to know anyway, Audra," Bridget said. "One look at your face and legs and she'll know. Better to get the news to her right away. She'll want t'know why ye didn't call her. We've got to."

Audra started to weep then. Germaine went into the bathroom and found a hand towel and wet it. She carried it to Audra...her little Audra who was so hurt. She touched it gently to the girl's knees and wiped at the streams of blood that slid down her legs and over her torn pantyhose. Bridget had gone into the kitchen and came back with a towel filled with ice for Audra's face and lip.

"What will you say to her?" Audra asked Bridget. "What will we say to the police?"

"The truth, what else?"

Germaine's strength was sapped now and she sat down heavily in her rocking chair. "What happened, honey? Tell me what happened. Where is Mercedes?"

Audra lowered the towel filled with ice and put it in her lap. "Mercedes doesn't come home with me anymore. I was alone."

"And what happened?"

"I don't know. I don't remember. I was walking down the street, and then I woke up in the alley. Miss Riordan was standing over me."

"She didn't wake up...she was awake...she was moaning and rolling in the alley when I got to her. There'd been a man lying over her when I saw them and started yelling for him to get away from her. He jumped up and ran down the alley in the other direction."

Germaine was stunned. To think...to think...her Audra could have been killed...

"I'm shaking like a leaf," Bridget said. She held her hands out in front of her to confirm it. "Really, Audra, we have to call the police. This man must be caught. He could come back. He could climb the fire escape...No! We have to call and right this minute."

She dialed 9-1-1. The cat jumped up onto the back of the sofa and sniffed the top of Audra's head, then stepped down with one paw onto the girl's shoulder.

"Aw, now see, Sweetiekins wants to comfort you," Germaine said to Audra.

Audra started to weep again. "Mrs. Sommer, I'm scared. I don't want the police."

"No…no…dolly. You're safe now. You're here with me. We'll protect you."

The police were at the apartment within a few minutes. One officer sat in the living room while the other one stood leaning against the wall. The officer in the room had a pad and pen and asked Audra questions as gently as he could.

"Try to remember. Start from when you began walking from the station."

"I got off at Broadway instead of Grand. I don't know why…I wanted more time to walk before I came home, I guess."

"Did you see anyone following you when you got off the train?"

Audra shook her head. "No…not then."

"Okay. When? Did you feel you were being followed at all?"

Audra didn't answer, and Bridget, who was sitting beside her, said, "Audra, answer his questions. They can't help if you don't tell them everything."

"Yes…okay? Yes, I felt that I was being followed from a block away, but I ignored it."

"Did you know him?"

She shook her head no.

"He didn't look familiar at all?"

"I didn't look back. I just didn't. I didn't see him."

"All right. Then what happened?"

"Before I reached the courtyard of our building, he started to run. I could hear him running up behind me, but I thought he was going to pass me." Audra began to tremble uncontrollably. "I don't want to talk about it. Please don't make me…"

"Just calm down…you're okay now," the officer said. "Just try to remember as much as you can."

Bridget put her arm around the girl and held Audra's head to her shoulder. "Tell them, Audra. Tell them."

Audra buried her face against Bridget, unable to look at the man in the uniform across from her. "He grabbed me from behind. He just kind of swept me up and carried me to the corner of the building and down the alley. He had his hand over my mouth. I tried to get away, but I couldn't. My arms were pinned to my chest…I was still holding my books in my arms, like this," Audra demonstrated and then returned to her place on

Bridget's shoulder. "He was kind of carrying me because I couldn't get my feet on the ground to run."

"What happened when he took you into the alley?"

"We fell."

"To the ground?" the officer asked.

"Yes, to the ground," Audra answered. "My face hit the ground—the sidewalk in the alley is broken up. I think he tripped and I went down first and my face and knees hit the ground, but he still had my arms pinned to me and I couldn't break my fall."

Her voice was rising, becoming hysterical. Bridget stroked her hair and hushed her. "Give her a minute," Bridget told the cop. "Give her time to calm down."

They all sat silently for a long moment, and then Audra said, "I could feel my lip start to bleed...I could taste the blood and the dirt from the ground."

"What did he do then, Audra?" the cop asked her.

"He ripped my skirt. His one hand was still under me, still holding my arms tight, but his other arm was moving behind me. He was pulling at my clothes...you know?...my underclothes. He tore my pantyhose. I tried to cry out, but my face was pressed against the ground. Dirt was coming up into my nose and mouth when I tried to breathe. I started to cough on the dirt. I thought I was going to suffocate, and I moved up—I don't know how to explain—I guess I kind of bucked up and he fell off me. I tried to get up, and I was able to cry then, because my face was up out of the dirt."

"You saw his face then?"

Audra looked surprised at the question, and shook her head no hard. "No...no...no face. I didn't see his face."

"What color was his skin? Was he white?...black?"

"White."

"Do you know what he was wearing?"

"A shirt. A silky shirt, I think. It was a bright color...blue or purple. He had on jeans and boots with heels. I saw them when he ran away."

"Good, Audra. This is good information. Did he speak to you? Did he say anything?"

"Yes, but I don't know what he said. I was too scared. I couldn't focus."

"Did he have an accent?"

Audra closed her eyes and started to cry hard now. She grabbed at Bridget and hid her face against Bridget's blouse.

Bridget patted her back. "Don't Audra. You're doing so well...don't stop talking. Try to calm down."

"Audra, do you remember? Did he have an accent?" the cop persisted.

"Yes," Audra whimpered. "Yes."

"What kind of accent? Greek? Polish? Italian?"

"Spanish," she answered in a whisper.

"But you wouldn't be able to identify him?"

"No, I wouldn't. I didn't see his face. I couldn't."

"How do you know it was a Spanish accent? That sounds a little like Italian...there's a lot of Italians in the area."

"I know the difference," Audra said. "I was raised in this neighborhood with all the Italians...and I go to school with Cubans and Puerto Ricans. I know the difference between the accents."

They heard the other officer speaking in the hallway then, and Eleanor stormed into the room. "Audra!"

"Oh, God," Audra wept again. "Oh, God, she's going to be so upset," she said to Bridget and the policeman.

"Honey...my baby...what happened to you?. Look at your little face."

Bridget left her place on the sofa to give Eleanor room to get to her daughter. Eleanor took Audra into her arms and rocked her. "Oh my God...Audra, what happened? What happened to you? Who did this?"

The officer who was questioning Audra stood up. He held his hand out to Eleanor. "Mrs. Walsh, I'm Officer Carlin. I've been asking your daughter what happened. It seems that she's all right except for a few cuts and bruises. Try not to be too upset...she's shaken, but she's fine."

"Why were you alone? I told you not to come home alone. All kinds of things have been happening around here...all kinds of creeps hanging around the train station. Where was Mercedes? Was there no one you could walk home with?"

"No, Mommy. I told you Mercedes has new friends. There was no one else."

Eleanor pulled the girl closer to her. "You kids...you have no concept of danger. You walk around in those short skirts and think no one is going to look. You're asking for trouble. You walk down the street with your head in the clouds. I've told you to pay attention, to be on guard."

Audra closed her eyes and pressed her lips together. Her whole demeanor changed. Germaine noticed and wanted to defend Audra, but before she could say anything to Eleanor, the cop said, "Mrs. Walsh, do you think you could let me finish questioning Audra? I just have a few more questions."

"Yes, go ahead," Eleanor said, letting the girl go.

Audra leaned away from her mother and looked at Officer Carlin. "I don't know what else to tell you."

"I have to ask you this, Audra. We need to know. Did he penetrate you?"

"Oh my God!" Eleanor said, tears springing to her eyes. "God, no...Audra tell us he didn't do that to you!"

The officer held up his hand to still Eleanor. "Please, Mrs. Walsh, let her answer me."

"I don't know what you mean," Audra said. "What do you mean?"

The cop looked uncomfortable. Germaine wanted to put her hands over her ears and turn away. She couldn't bear the look on Audra's face…or on Eleanor's.

"I mean, did he touch you…down there…and did you feel anything…" he sighed before completing the question, "did you feel anything pushed up into you."

"Mommy," Audra cried now, grabbing at her mother. "Please don't make me do this anymore. Take me home."

Eleanor's eyes were wide with fear. She looked at the policeman. The officer lifted his palms and shrugged a little, letting her know that he had to ask these questions even as embarrassing as they were. She held Audra, and lowered her voice trying to sound calmer now. "Honey, you have to tell us. Did this man rape you?"

"Mommy, please…" Audra was sobbing now.

"Did he, honey?" Eleanor persisted.

"No…no, Mommy…he didn't…he tried…he wanted to." She was mortified and covered her face with her hands, "I was able to push him off me before he did that, and then Miss Riordan shouted and he stopped. He ran away then." Audra sobbed against her mother's chest. "I'm sorry, Mommy…I'm so sorry. I didn't know what to do. I didn't know how to get away. Don't be mad, Mommy…"

"Jesus, Mary and Joseph, honey. I'm not mad at you. I'd never be mad at you for this."

"Oh, God, Mommy, what will Daddy say? What will he do?"

Germaine saw that Audra was near hysteria now, and she felt powerless to protect the girl. She'd spent years trying to guard her, but at this moment she was completely helpless. She silently begged Eleanor to take control…to help the girl they both loved.

"Nothing…" Eleanor said, pushing Audra away from her now and looking into her face. "Your daddy will do nothing to you. You know that. I shudder to think what he'd do to this bastard if he ever gets his hands on him, though…I hate to think what I'd do to the son of a bitch."

Audra stopped crying. Eleanor's language had shocked her into silence.

Officer Carlin said, "Audra, no one is going to be angry with you. This isn't your fault. Do you hear me? I don't care how short your skirt was or whether you were alone. It was the middle of the day. You were coming home from school. You have every right to walk down your street without being attacked…and you didn't do anything to make it happen. It's important that you understand that." He looked at Eleanor then, and added, "I expect you and your husband to make sure she understands that."

"Of course…of course, we will. Why would we do anything different?"

Eleanor was irritated and defensive. She pulled Audra's long hair away from her face and tucked it behind her ear exposing the girl's scraped cheek.

"She needs to have that face looked at," Officer Carlin said. "I noticed that her tooth looks chipped…not too bad. The dentist can take care of that. And the wounds on her knees should be attended to. That alley is filthy and those cuts could get infected. She should go to the Emergency Room."

"I have a car. I'll take her myself. She's been through enough without being taken away in a squad car."

"Can I change first?" Audra wanted to know.

"No," Officer Carlin said. "Stay in your uniform just in case there's anything on it that will help us identify who did this. The hospital will know what to do with the clothing. Just bring a change of clothes with her to the hospital."

Germaine jumped up from her chair. "I have some of her clothes here," she told Eleanor. "She changed after school last week and forgot to bring them back to your apartment." She went into her bedroom and took the folded jeans and sweater from her slipper chair. It gave her something to do…some way to help her precious girl. She felt so helpless. Why did she have to get too old to meet Audra after school now? She longed for the days she went to the school and picked Audra up and they walked together, chatting about school and all the things that happened during the day when they were apart. She longed for the little curly-haired girl that was hers for such a short time. The child she protected. But Germaine couldn't protect her any longer.

Germaine put the clothes in a paper bag and handed it to Eleanor. They all started to leave together…the police, Eleanor and Audra.

Eleanor said to Germaine. "Can you leave a note for Brendan on our door? If he comes home before we do, he'll want to come to the hospital. He'll be frantic. Tell him I'm taking her to Astoria General."

"Yes, yes, I'll do it right away," Germaine said.

"Don't tell him too much. Just tell him she fell and got hurt."

"I won't say anything."

Eleanor looked at Bridget then. "Thank you for…" She tried to say more, but she couldn't speak.

"Mommy, please don't start crying," Audra begged her mother. "I hate when you cry."

"No, I'm okay. I'm fine." Eleanor wiped her nose with a tissue. "I'm fine, honey."

Germaine put her arms around Audra and hugged her tight. She whispered in her ear, "Don't try to protect your mother. You need her now…not the other way around."

Audra nodded and smiled sadly at Germaine.

"And come help me take care of Sweetiekins tomorrow. She misses you."

"I will, Mrs. Sommer. I'm sorry we got you upset today. Are you going to be all right? Is your heart okay?"

"Yes, yes. It's all fine. Just go to the hospital and let them fix you up."

Bridget and Germaine stood in the hall with Eleanor and Audra until the elevator came. They waved goodbye as the police officers held the door and Eleanor and Audra disappeared inside the elevator. Bridget told the police that if she thought of anything else, she'd call them, but she wasn't much help…she only saw the man from behind.

She turned when she and Germaine were alone. "Never a dull moment."

"Never, it seems."

"What do you think *himself* will do? Is it a night he's out late?"

Germaine shook her head no. "He'll be home soon…in a few minutes."

Bridget searched in her purse for her keys. "Well, I won't get much sleep tonight. I'll be jumping at every sound."

Germaine reached out. Her gnarled knuckles stuck out from her fingers when she touched Bridget's arm. "I don't know how to thank you. If anything happened to that child, I'd die."

Bridget patted Germaine's hand. "I know how much you love her. I just thank God I was home early today. I had a headache and decided to take the afternoon off. I was just in the right place, and I thank God for it. I must have been on the same train, but I got off the stop before she did. And I stopped at the market…dear God…the bag! I dropped the bag when I saw it happening and I never went back for it. My food's probably strewn all over the street by now."

"Let's go get it," Germaine offered.

"No, I don't want it. I just want to get inside and lie down. I'm not hungry anyway. It was only some ham and a tomato."

"It's all so coincidental, isn't it?" Germaine mused. "You coming home early, stopping at the market, and passing the alley at just that moment. It makes me cringe to think of it."

Bridget kissed Germaine's cheek. "Get some rest. Go sit with the kitty on your lap and you'll feel better."

Germaine did that, but first she wrote the note for Brendan Walsh.

◆◆◆◆

Audra didn't go to school the next day. Eleanor had an important meeting and had to go to work, and Audra didn't want to be alone. She stayed on Germaine's couch all day. Her father had gone into the alley after they got home from the hospital and gathered her books. Audra had them next to her, stacked on the coffee table, but she didn't open them. She stared at the television, but Germaine suspected that she didn't know what she was watching. The hospital had given her some pills to calm her nerves.

She looked glassy-eyed and detached. But it was her silence, her stillness, that bothered Germaine the most.

Germaine made her a sandwich for lunch, but it was untouched next to the books. She drank a half glass of cola, then left that on the coffee table too. Germaine couldn't think of what to do for Audra. She realized that letting her alone was probably the thing the girl wanted most of all, and so that's what she did. She didn't try to start conversations. She didn't ask questions. She let the girl stay on the couch without making any demands on her.

The cat didn't leave Audra's side. Between naps, Sweetiekins sat on top of Audra, kneading her blanket and purring loud enough to fill the room with the sound. Audra stroked the cat, smiling once in a while at it, and Germaine felt satisfied that this was all her precious little girl needed.

Audra's mouth was very swollen, and her face was scabbing over where it had been scraped on the ground. Her knees were sensitive, and when she turned to her side, she winced in pain.

Germaine crocheted in her rocking chair while Audra just glared at the TV. Then Audra said, for no reason at all, "I love you, Mrs. Sommer."

Germaine's heart could have burst with the pleasure of hearing the words. "And I love you, too, dearest. More than you'll ever know."

It was close to three thirty that afternoon when the bell rang. Germaine answered it, and Mercedes asked if Audra was there. Germaine let her in. "She'll be so happy to see you," she told Mercedes, patting her arm.

"I doubt it," Mercedes said angrily. She shook off Germaine, then stomped down the hallway and into the living room. She placed her hands on her hips when she saw Audra lying on the sofa. "Why?"

Audra didn't answer. She just continued to stare at the television.

Mercedes demanded once again, "Audra! Why?"

"Why what?" Audra asked.

"Why did you tell them he was Spanish? Why would you do that? You know what we go through down there. Every damned time there's a break-in, a car stolen, someone mugged, they start beating at our doors demanding to see our men. You know that. I told you that. Why, Audra? Why would you tell them the asshole who attacked you was Spanish?"

Audra's voice was very small when she said "Because he was."

"How do you know that? You told the police you didn't see his face."

"Because I do."

"Oh, yeah, right...because you do. You white girls are always so quick to blame the Puerto Ricans and the Cubans or the blacks and anyone else who doesn't look like you or sound like you."

"Merry, please don't yell at me," Audra begged, but her voice was still very quiet.

"Don't call me Merry. My name is Mercedes Anita Maria Conception, and don't Americanize it again with your stupid nickname."

Germaine was shocked at the way Mercedes was speaking. "But we've always called you Merry," Germaine said, looking from one girl to the other.

"Stay out of this, Mrs. Sommer. Audra knows what I'm talking about. She knows what I'm saying."

"No, I don't." Audra turned her back to Mercedes now and faced the couch.

"Don't you dare do that to me! Don't turn your back on me."

"Why not? You've turned your back on me...you suddenly have this need to be with your *Spanish* friends...to embrace your—what do you call it?—your Latin heritage? I'm just one of the bad guys to you now. How did you put it? We have nothing in common...I could never understand you?"

"What are you talking about? You're an idiot, Audra. So, I have other friends now...and yes, I like them better. But that's not a good reason for you to punish me by what you told the cops yesterday."

Germaine was upset. "Girls, why are you talking to each other like this? What is this about?"

"You want to know, Mrs. Sommer?" Mercedes turned on Germaine now. "You want to know what it's like being different in this country? We came here...we left everything we owned to come here, to escape Castro...to come to this America...this safe haven for all peoples from all countries. And what do we find? We find prejudice. We find racism. We find jobs that no one else wants. Why? Because our skin is darker. Because our tongue curls around the American language with an accent. We're looked down on. If we're Latin, we must be promiscuous, right? We're hot blooded, they say...we don't know how to behave. Well, they're wrong. You are all wrong. We are human beings...we're just as human as you white-breads. When one of us Latinas get raped or beaten, the police don't go banging on your doors to find the scum who did it, do they? No, it's different for you than it is for us. Sometimes the cops don't even come to ask us who did it...they don't ask what the rapist looked like or if he had an American accent. God forbid we should accuse a white man. But let one of you blond, blue eyed babies fall down and scrape your knees, then it's got to be a Latino...or rather a *spic*...that's what you call us, isn't it, Audra? You don't know who did this, but you immediately send them down the block to us, don't you? My aunt is sitting in our kitchen sobbing her heart out. They took my cousin away last night because of what you said. If my brother wasn't serving in Nam, they'd have taken him, too."

"Go away," Audra said.

"You'd like that."

"Go away."

"I don't have to do anything I don't want to do. I live in *America!*

Remember? I'm sick of this crap. I want you to tell the cops that you were wrong…that this guy who did this to you wasn't *Spanish* as you call all of us. My family is heartbroken. We're scared for my cousin. It's your fault, now do something about it."

"I can't, Merry…I mean Mercedes."

"Yes you can. Tell them that it wasn't my cousin. Stop lounging on that couch like a frizzy-haired, fat lump and do something to help him."

Audra turned back again, and this time she sat up. Her face was red beneath the scabs and scrapes, and it looked painful as she spoke through her swollen lips. "I didn't tell the police that it was *you…any of you*. I never said that. Instead of coming here and yelling at me, you should be thanking me, *Mercedes Anita Maria Conception*."

"Thanking you? What for? Why would I thank you? For telling the cops that it's one of those scum spics again?"

Audra stood up, her hands balled into fists. "It *was* one of those scum spics!" Audra screamed.

There was a long silent pause in the room.

"You're lying," Mercedes said, quieter now.

"No…oh, no, Mercedes Anita Maria Conception…I'm *not* lying. I lied *yesterday*. I lied to the cops. I told them I didn't know who it was…I didn't recognize him…that's when I lied, Mercedes Anita Maria Conception."

The storm on Mercedes's face receded and she backed away. "Stop! Don't say anything else. I'm leaving."

"Why? You asked me to stop lying, so why not stay and hear the truth?"

Audra's face was glowing red and she was spitting through her swollen, disfigured mouth as she spoke. She stepped around the coffee table. "I have plenty of truths to say, Mercedes Anita Maria Conception. You've changed. You can't even look at your friends who did love you and who didn't treat you different when you came into the neighborhood. It was okay for me to be white bread then. It was okay for me to share everything with you…all my personal fears and problems and wishes. I'm still the same person I was, Mercedes Anita Maria Conception…I'm still the same Audra Walsh." Audra pounded on her chest as she spoke. Then she reached out, her finger pointing at the other girl. "You're the one who has changed. You're the one who is prejudiced now…and bitter and mean. Your new friends have convinced you how horrible I am…*we* are…we who aren't *Spanish*." She emphasized the last word.

"I'm getting out of here," Mercedes said, turning and charging to the door.

"Girls, please, calm down," Germaine said, trying to reach out to stop Audra from following Mercedes. But Audra shrugged her off.

"You want to know the truth, Mercedes Anita Ma…"

Mercedes spun around, angry again. "Stop calling me that! Stop it!"

"You're right…I lied to the cops, Mercedes. I lied because I didn't want you to be mad at me. I didn't want to make your family suffer. I wanted to protect you. I told them I didn't know who it was. I told them I didn't see his face. But here's what I should have told the cops. I should have told them that it was your cousin. It was your sleazy, no good, ugly bastard of a cousin. I'm glad he's in jail. I hope they keep him there. He tried to rape me…he *would have* raped me if someone hadn't come to help me. He did this to my face. And I didn't tell, Mercedes; I didn't tell because I didn't want *you* to be mad at me. I didn't want *you* to be hurt."

Mercedes covered her face. "No, you didn't see him…you didn't know who it was…you said that. You told them that."

"But I *did* see his face, Mercedes. I did see it when I was struggling with all my strength to get away from him. He looked right into my eyes. He breathed his disgusting breath into my face. He spit at me before he ran away, Mercedes. He spit in my face, Mercedes! What did I ever do to him? We were friends…I loved your family. What did I ever do to make him hate me that much? I didn't deserve it. And I didn't deserve this from you and I'm not taking it from you anymore! Do you hear me? Do you hear me? I'm sorry I'm white, okay? I'm sorry I don't speak your language and that you *have* to speak mine."

Audra moved closer to Mercedes, saying, "I'm sorry your aunt is crying her eyes out. I'm sorry your father doesn't have a great job. But I'm sorry about a lot of things in *my* life, too. I'm sorry I have to sleep on a pull out couch and not have a room of my own. I'm sorry my father gets drunk and comes home and abuses my mother. I'm sorry I don't get good grades in school because I live with my stomach in a knot every day of my life wondering if this will be the night my father's coming home from the bar and if it's going to be the night he really loses it. Yes, Mercedes, I'm sorry. I'm sorry for my mother…I'm sorry for my sister…I'm sorry that despite what my father is…what he does…" her voice caught up in a sob, "I still love him even though I shouldn't. I'm sorry for the way people act and how mean they can be…I'm sorry…I'm sorry…I'm so *fucking* sorry all the *goddamned* time!"

Audra's shriek made Germaine feel ill.

"Audra…" Mercedes was reaching out to Audra then, her arms extended toward her friend to hold her…to comfort her.

"Don't touch me," Audra said backing away from Mercedes. "Just shut up, Mercedes Anita Maria Concep*tion*. I don't need you as a friend any longer. You see, I didn't know there was this big ugly difference between us until you started to show me…until your cousin, who I thought was a friend, hurt me and spit in my face. Why? Because *other* white people are mean to you? You've become just as insensitive and bigoted as the people you hate. Let me tell you some more truth, hatred is as ugly when it comes from *your* side as it is from mine. So go, okay? Go away and leave me alone."

"Audra, you have to tell the cops the truth," Mercedes said quietly but insistently. "You have to tell them who it was."

"Go away and leave me alone! I'm not talking to the cops again. I'm not going through that humiliation *ever* again." Audra walked slowly closer to Mercedes and pointed her finger at the other girl again. "But I swear, Mercedes, when they release him—that bastard of a cousin of yours—you tell him that if he ever comes near me again, I *will* tell my father. I'll tell him the whole story. And you better hope that the cops get to him before my father gets to him. You tell them that. My father will wipe the streets clean and shiny with him and then he'll cut off his nuts and feed them to him. You tell that scum spic that. Tell all your new friends that. I hate all of you now, and I won't protect you next time."

Germaine backed away from the girls and sat down on her chair. She felt weak and nauseated. Never had she heard such ugliness come out of Audra. Never would she have thought it possible.

Mercedes stood staring at Audra for a long time. "How can you talk that way?" When Audra didn't answer, she said bitterly, but her eyes were sad, "You have more of your father in you than you ever thought." Her eyes filled with tears.

"That's right. So what? Don't try to use my greatest fear against me to hurt me. I have a new fear now...less of being like my father and more of being like you."

Mercedes knew that there was no more that could be said between them. Mercedes left the apartment. She closed the door softly behind her. Audra turned and walked back to the couch. Her neck was covered with red blotches, her cheeks were shiny with perspiration. She lay down and covered herself with the blanket again. The cat settled on her stomach and Audra stroked its head and ears, her eyes fixed on the television.

Germaine expected tears...sobbing...recriminations. Even more anger.

Nothing. The girl just stared at the TV.

And Germaine stared at her.

The girl was gone. Her Audra was gone.

Summer 1970

They entered the elevator together, Eamon Williams and Germaine Sommer, after having gone to their mailboxes and extracted the envelopes from the long, narrow brass enclosures. They both shuffled through the mail in their hands, while they waited for the elevator.

Right after they stepped on, Germaine gasped.

"What is it, Mrs. Sommer? Are you all right?"

She didn't answer him. She dropped the mail onto the elevator floor, all except one piece which she began to open.

"Mrs. Sommer? You okay?" he asked again.

She read the letter and once again a small intake of breath made him reach toward her and take her arm to steady her.

"Bad news?"

Germaine closed her eyes and leaned back against the wall. "My granddaughter," she whispered.

"Sick?"

"No…she wants to come to see me."

He gave a sigh of relief. "Oh, well, that's fine then. You had me worried."

"Twenty-two years…it's been twenty-two years, Mr. Williams, since I've heard from her."

He studied the old woman, looking for signs that the shock was too much for her. He remembered that she'd had a heart attack just a few years ago. He leaned down and picked up her mail from the floor. "You dropped these." He handed them to her.

Twenty-two years, he mused, and wondered what had gone on that this sweet woman had been separated from her granddaughter for such a long time. She always seemed so unassuming to him…so devoid of trouble or bitterness. And he had never known that she had had children, let alone grandchildren.

"My daughter died, you see," Germaine said, as though she was reading his thoughts. "And her husband remarried...they lived out west, in Arizona."

He nodded as though he understood, but he thought that it didn't seem a good reason for not hearing from or seeing her grandchild in all that time.

"Did you not want to see them?" Eamon asked, unable to mind his own business.

"I longed to see them," Germaine said sadly.

"Well, so this is good news..."

Germaine raised her eyes to his. "Is it? I truly wonder."

Bridget Riordan was putting her garbage down the incinerator chute when she heard a man's voice ask, "Pardon...can you tell me if this is where I'd be puttin' the empty boxes and such? I just moved in and the super's wife told me that the garbage goes in here, but she didn't say about large things."

Galway. The brogue was unmistakable. Bridget closed the chute and spun around. "Who are ye?"

The man looked taken aback by the sharpness of the question. He murmured a little, then pointed to 6D—the Allcocks' old apartment. It was recently vacated by a tenant who'd taken the place after the Allcocks.

"I just moved...there," he said, continuing to point with one hand while holding stacked cartons in the other.

"County Galway is it, then?" she asked him.

He smiled broadly, realizing for the first time that Bridget shared the accent. "It is...I was born and raised in Galway City."

Bridget laughed and held out her hand to shake his. "The name's Bridget Riordan."

"And mine's Gallagher...Dermot Gallagher." He took her small hand in his. "It's good to know a fellow countryman in a strange place. I just arrived."

"Oh, you don't need to tell me that," Bridget said. "I can tell by the thickness of your tongue. You'll lose a little of it in a year or two."

"I never will," he said, flashing a white smile at her.

"Sure, that's what I said!"

"Well, I'm keepin' me brogue. I've been told it's a girl catcher here in the states."

Bridget laughed now. "We'll see about that, Mr. Gallagher."

"And the boxes?" he asked again.

"The basement," she told him. "There's a special closet in the laundry room where Biermann wants the boxes put. He'll cut them down and get rid of them. Come on, I'll show you where."

She rang for the elevator. "What brings you to the States?"

"Work for one thing…adventure for another."

"Adventure in Astoria, New York? Think again, me boyo."

"Go on, wit'ye. If you've never left County Galway in your life, then anywhere but there is an adventure."

"I guess…but don't expect too much. What kind of work are you doing here?"

"Computers."

"What, may I ask, is that exactly?"

He laughed. "The future, lass. I studied electronic engineering at University College. There was an American come to University to talk about a company called IBM and jobs that were going to be available and how computers were the future of the world—and I agree with him. I took him to the pub for a pint and we talked and here I am."

"You just graduated?" Bridget was surprised. Dermot Gallagher looked older than that.

"Yes…but I didn't go to University until I was more than thirty. I had to save up, you know. It's an expensive proposition, education is—books…a place to live…and the like."

The elevator arrived and they entered it together. Bridget took two of the smaller boxes he was carrying. "What's new in Galway City, then?"

"Nothin'…is there ever anything new in Galway?"

"You'll be missing it before long. The miles of endless granite and brick around here will have you dreamin' about the green of Ireland. You'll be smellin' the sea in your sleep, and wake up to the smell of car fumes. I promise you that."

Dermot studied her for a long silent moment. She blushed under his direct stare, and then she stared back. Tall and dark-haired, he was, with hazel eyes and a white smile and just the hint of a crooked tooth. His nose would have been straight but for the lump that was a tell-tale sign of a fist fight or two in his past. She liked the face.

"Will ye be me first friend in America, Bridget Riordan?" he asked her.

The elevator stopped and Bridget pushed the door open. She led him to the closet, pointed to where he should put his boxes, and then she placed the ones she carried for him on top.

"This is the laundry room," she said. "Come on, I'll show you the ropes. You'll need to get some quarters and keep them handy—I keep mine in a change purse, but you don't look the type to carry a change purse. A jar then will have to do, I suppose. You put the clothes in, dump a cup of soap on top—if you need bleach, you put it in this little hole over here—and then put the quarter in the slot, push it in, and the water starts. Basically it's the same with the dryer. If you want to hang your clothes, there's lines over in that room over there. But bring your own clothespins…there's never any in there."

He nodded at all her instructions as she gave them, and then she pointed to a door just off the laundry room. "There's a door to get out over there—the steps lead to the courtyard at the front of the building—just in case you need a quick escape. But it's locked all the time, so you can't get in that way."

They entered the elevator again, and he pushed the button before she had a chance to do it.

"Well?" He asked her, leaning over her with his hand against the wall.

"Well, what?"

"Will you be my first friend?"

"I'll see about it. Let's start with a pizza and beer for dinner…my treat as a welcome to America. If we get along over pizza, then I'll think about bein' your friend. But let it be clear, I'll stand for no hanky-panky from you. There's a man on our floor with fists the size of ham hocks, and we've become sort of begrudging friends. I know that if I gave him the word that you're not on the up and up, he'd take care of you good."

"What do you mean by begrudging?"

"It's what they call a love-hate relationship. He can be the nicest guy in the world, he'd give ye the shirt off his back, he would—that's what I like about him—but when he drinks…oh, brother, wait…you'll hear him. Wednesday nights, for sure…like clockwork."

"What about our other neighbors?"

They stood in the sixth floor hallway now.

"Nice…most of them quiet." Bridget pointed to each apartment door as she said, "A lovely old woman lives next to me, and a bachelor lives next to her. There's a woman rents the apartment over there, but she doesn't really live here. She was separated from her husband who died a couple of years ago. She keeps the flat, though I can't tell you why. Then there's the Walsh family I just told you about him—he has a wife and teenaged daughter. Next to them is a single woman—older than us, she is—and she keeps to herself. To be honest, I've been living here more than nine years, and I don't know much about anyone on this floor. And on the other floors I know maybe two people. It's not like Ireland at all."

Dermot looked around, taking it in. He pointed to the staircase.

"Up goes to the roof," Bridget told him. "I live in the apartment at the foot of that staircase. You'll find it's brutally hot in the summer here on the sixth floor, under that tar roof. No air conditioners allowed. The wiring isn't updated enough for them."

"Well, I don't mind the heat," he said. "What time for the pizza?"

"How about fifteen minutes?"

"I'll be waitin' at your door. Our first date."

"No, Mr. Dermot Gallagher…not a date. A welcome-to-America-get-to-know-ye dinner. If it was a date, I'd make *you* pay."

She let herself into her apartment, closed the door, and heard him laughing from the other side. It was more of a cackle and it made her smile. It stirred something inside her; something that had been dead a long time.

Bridget Riordan blushed again.

6B

SOMMER

"Eleanor, what should I do?" Germaine Sommer asked the woman she'd come to trust. "She wants to come here to meet me." Germaine held out the letter she'd received a few days before and handed it to Eleanor.

Eleanor read it slowly, then said, "I don't know what to say, Mrs. Sommer. Do you want to meet her?"

Germaine rocked in her chair. She was agitated, worried, and a little excited, too. "I do, I think. But after all these years, what would I say to her? What would we have to talk about?"

"Oh, my dear, that's not what you need to worry about. You'd talk to her just like you do to my girls, my Paige and Audra."

"Would I mention her mother, do you think?"

"Of course, you would have to. She was your daughter. Why wouldn't you?"

"I don't know…this girl was so young when…" Germaine rocked harder. "Why do you think she wants to meet me after all these years?"

"Because she has a hole in her heart."

Germaine was caught off guard by this statement. She expected Eleanor to say what she herself had been thinking, that the girl was looking for money, an inheritance. It had been worrying Germaine for days.

Eleanor smiled at her. "She's probably known you existed. For whatever reason she didn't or couldn't contact you. But she's a woman now, married …maybe with children of her own, and that makes a difference in a woman's life. It would make her curious about her own mother…and about you."

"Do you think I'll be a disappointment to her?" Germaine asked quietly.

"Have you been worrying about this? Why didn't you tell me about the letter sooner? I hate to think you've been sitting in here distressing over it and not telling me."

"I was afraid you'd talk me into seeing her, I guess, and I didn't know if I should."

"Of course you should, dear. She's your grandchild."

"My handwriting is so bad these days. Will you write to her for me?"

Eleanor looked down at the letter again. "You don't need to write. She gave you her telephone number."

"But it's long distance. It will cost me a fortune."

"I'll pay it for you," Eleanor said. "Just give me the bill when it comes in, and I'll take care of it."

"Will you? You're so good to me. I can afford it myself. I was just looking for excuses."

Eleanor asked, "Why don't we call her now? It's still early there. Let's see, it's seven here, so it's only five o'clock there."

Germaine just sat staring at Eleanor. She felt jittery inside.

"Shall I dial it for you?"

Germaine sighed and after a long time, nodded. "Will you talk to her first?"

Eleanor stood up and patted Germaine's hand. "Sure." She dialed the telephone number that was on the letter. Germaine held her breath while each number on the rotary phone took its time moving forward under Eleanor's pressure, and then back in place. Tich-a-tich-a-tich-a-tich

Eleanor stood with the receiver at her ear, waiting for an answer, and still Germaine couldn't breathe.

What does she look like? Does she look like my baby did? Does she look like me? Is she blond? What will I say? How will I start this conversation? She's a stranger...a stranger. Eleanor said talk to her like I would Audra...oh, but I don't even know this person...what in God's name will I say to this person?

"Yes, hello, may I speak with Mrs..." Eleanor looked down at the envelope on the coffee table where the return address was printed in a clear handwriting. "with Mrs. Carroll...oh, you are...well my name is Eleanor Walsh, and I'm here with your grandmother, Germaine Sommer. She asked me to dial your number for her. She was thrilled to receive your letter and couldn't wait to call you...yes, yes, she is. She's right here. Hold on one second..."

Eleanor held the receiver out to Germaine. She smiled broadly and whispered. "She sounds lovely. She can't wait to talk to you."

Germaine reached out tentatively. Her hand was shaking. "I don't know what to say..."

"Just say whatever you've dreamed you'd say if you ever had the chance to talk to her."

When Eleanor handed the phone to Germaine, she took Germaine's hand in hers—the phone between their palms. "It's all right, dear. This is wonderful. Be happy."

Germaine took a deep breath and said into the receiver, "Hello, this is your grandmother…I love you. I always have."

Winter 1970

The outer elevator door was closed, and Eamon noticed that the inside door was just starting to slide shut. He grabbed at the outer door quickly. The inner door immediately slid back. Eamon hadn't noticed that Audra and her boyfriend were in the elevator already.

"Oh…I'm sorry…" Eamon said.

Audra smiled. "It's okay, Mr. Williams."

He settled in place on the opposite side of the lift.

"Mr. Williams, this is my friend, Allen."

Eamon was surprised. She had barely spoken to him when they met in the hall or the elevator during the last several months.

It started when he had seen her the one and only time outside of Ashley Hall. He had just left the bank to go to lunch and was distracted by an anti-war protest near Federal Hall…just a block from the bank. The streets were full of the typical youths he was used to seeing protesting. Suddenly, there were construction workers all over the place, holding American flags and signs, chanting, "All the way USA…America, love it or leave it."

He saw the mounted police and cops in riot gear pushing back a line of kids; some of the cops were trying to get between the construction workers and the protestors. He was about to turn away, to continue to the coffee shop, wanting to get out of danger, when he noticed one of the mounted cops moved his horse next to a girl, accidentally shoving her down. Eamon got a glimpse of her face when she fell, and he knew it was Audra.

He ran over, pulled her to her feet, and dragged her back to the bank, through the glass doors. She tried to pull away, but he held her arm, saying, "Stay here."

"I need to go out there," she said. "My friends are…"

"No!" He said it firmly, pushing her against the wall of the bank, ignoring the stares they were getting. "I want you to think of something. Think about your mother's reaction when she has to come and bail you out of jail…or has to visit you in a hospital. Think about your father's reaction.

Did you see who those guys out there are? They're construction workers, Audra, with billy clubs and pipes."

She stopped struggling and looked at him. Her eyes filled with fear. "But I have friends out there…"

"Come with me." He led her to the other side of the bank, to another exit, and toward the closest subway station. "Go home, Audra. Go now. There will be other protests, just don't stay at this one." He shoved a token into her hand. She hesitated, not wanting to do what he told her, yet frightened by the shouts and screams from around the corner…torn in her desire to be brave and join her friends, yet afraid of her mother's reaction…her father's… if she was arrested. She looked like a little girl. She turned and ran down the stairs, away from him…away from harm.

The next time they met at the elevator in the lobby, she turned away and walked up the stairs. Ever since then, she would look away when they saw each other, and if he asked her questions, she'd give him one-word answers. It bothered him. He wasn't certain if she was embarrassed because she had been there—or because she had run away—or angry with him for interfering.

But here she was, all dressed up in a blue mini-coat and high-heeled white boots that stopped at her knees, looking more grown up than he'd ever noticed. She smiled at him. Gone was the shy, awkward little girl he'd known…gone was the wanna-be protestor of just months ago. Obviously, gone was her resentment of his interfering.

"It's a beautiful day," Audra said, making small talk, surprising him further by initiating the conversation. "We're going to the Village. There's an art show there today."

"Well, that's nice…I'm going to Manhattan myself. I'm standing up as Godfather for my friend's baby today."

Audra's eyes widened and she smiled brightly. "Really? That's so exciting. Is the baby your best friend's baby…the man who used to come here all the time? The man you used to play tennis with? My mother said that she'd heard he had gotten married."

Eamon was surprised that she remembered John and that Eleanor had heard of John's marriage. "Yes, Audra, it is. John Sullivan. They have a baby boy. They've named him after me—only they're calling him William Eamon, switching my last and first names."

"It must be really nice to still have the same friends you had as a child. Most of the girls I knew growing up around here have moved to Long Island or New Jersey. Almost every house across the street has new people in it. They're from Greece or Turkey…all over the world, actually."

"New York neighborhoods change like that. The houses look the same, but the faces change."

Everything changes, he thought. Little girls grow up. People move away.

Lovers become friends.

He and John—and Honora—were getting close again, mending bridges, learning to be friends as they once were…no, not as they once were…but friends nonetheless. He hadn't gone to the wedding, and Honora had been hurt more deeply than John. She thought it was because Eamon was jealous, but not in the way that was the truth. She thought Eamon was in love with *her*.

She called him almost every day before the wedding to tell him how sorry she was, to ask him to forgive her, she just couldn't explain why she fell in love with John and not him, but she would always love him as a friend. Then, when he continued to refuse to come to the wedding she became furious. "How can you break your best friend's heart?" she had asked him. When he had no answer, when he sat with the receiver against his ear and tears choking him, unable to speak, she hung up.

Six months after the wedding, she called again, saying, "We miss you so much, E. Please forgive us. We're going to have a baby, and we can't bear the thought of you not being a part of this child's life."

He didn't forgive them. But he couldn't live without them. And he wanted to be a part of that baby's life. John's child. A child that they themselves could never have together, but John's child nonetheless. A child that was also Honora's. And here they were offering to share that child with him. And so he pretended to forgive, and he was the first to visit the nursery at New York Hospital and see William Eamon on the night he was born…the first, after John and Honora, to look at the baby…John's baby…John's son. Standing at the nursery window, he vowed to love the child for the rest of his life. This boy would be the child of his heart.

His life would never be as it once was. What disturbed him the most was the fact that he and John could not look each other in the eye anymore. They never touched, even as other straight men did…not even a pat on the back…a warm handshake…nothing. Being in John's presence sometimes took Eamon's breath away—hearing his laugh, watching him smoke a cigarette could pierce his heart—but he was adept at hiding it. As long as they didn't touch and as long as their eyes didn't meet, they could keep up the pretense. Everything had changed…but then life always did.

He looked at Audra again. She smiled at him. In Ashley Hall she was the biggest change he could think of.

The elevator stopped.

"It was nice meeting you," the boyfriend said again as they walked out with Eamon.

He wondered how serious this relationship was. Would this be the boy Audra would marry one day? Audra…married?

Surprising himself almost as much as he did Audra, Eamon reached over and planted a kiss on her cheek. "I just realized that I've watched you grow from a tiny little girl into a lovely woman...I've lived on the same floor with you almost your entire life. I hope I didn't embarrass you just now, but I felt the need to give you that kiss. I'm proud of you, Audra."

He was rewarded with a huge smile and a giggle that sounded much like the once-upon-a-time little girl's.

6E

KRAMER

Martha put the small silver wine cup from her Seder set in the last box and looked around. It had taken her too many years to make this move. She didn't live in the apartment. She hadn't since she walked away from Joseph all those years ago. But she couldn't seem to get rid of it either. For Martha, Joseph was still around her as long as the apartment was there.

She could still smell his aftershave in the bathroom. She could feel his energy in the bedroom, the living room, in his chair. Yet, she couldn't bring herself to move back into it either.

Her apartment in Ozone Park, near her grandson and his mother, was a little larger. There were two bedrooms in it...so that little Joey could stay over with her sometimes. She had decorated it to her own taste—deliberately not incorporating any of Joseph's likes or dislikes. She had missed some of her things that she'd left behind—her Havilland, her silver service, her candelabras...her husband's love. But she never asked Joseph for those things...they were a part of her life with him. Martha felt that if she had asked for anything that remained in their apartment, he would have taken it as a connection...a fact that Martha still wanted to be attached in some way to their marriage. She could never let him think that, even if it were true.

Now, with money starting to dwindle a little and Martha not knowing what sort of care she'd need as she got older, she knew she had to get rid of one of the apartments. Ozone Park won. It was also rent controlled, and she had grown so fond of Janice and her father Ronald. They had truly become one family. Joseph was part of it for a while, those first two years, and then again, toward the end, when Janice insisted that they visit him and invite him for dinners on the weekend. Janice wanted Joey to know his grandfather, in spite of what Joseph had done to Martha.

"I like him," she had said to Martha, "and your son adored him. I want my Joey to know him, even with your problems. It's not fair to punish Joey, too. Please, Martha, this banishment has gone on long enough. He's very ill.

Please allow me to invite him over. Let Joey get to know his father's father."

And, of course, Martha knew Janice was right. She knew she'd been cruel. But at the time, she believed that he deserved it for his disloyalty...his duplicity. Martha relented, reluctantly...for Joey. But she never went to dinner when they invited Joseph.

Looking back, she was happy Janice insisted that Joey know Joseph. It showed what a good person Janice was...what a fair person. Since they'd come into Martha's life, they took good care of her. Oh, but she took care of them, too. She didn't mind their business. There was none of that. But she was always there for them, watching Joey, watching the little dog they bought for him, even though Martha herself wasn't crazy about dogs. And she smiled and crooned whenever Janice was dressed for a date with a gentleman. She couldn't help but pray that it wouldn't work out...and it never did...but she wouldn't let Janice know how happy she was whenever a suitor disappeared from Janice's life.

So, saying goodbye to Astoria was the best thing. He was gone. It was time to let go.

"Bub, how many more boxes?" Joey asked as he walked into the apartment. He was a strapping boy now—almost a teenager. He and Janice were spending the weekend helping Martha move her belongings.

"Just one. But come...come here...I want to give you something."

Joey wiped the perspiration from his brow with his arm and walked over to her. She held out a box. "This is yours. It belonged to your grandfather, and to his father before him. I found it the other night when I cleaned out his dresser."

Joey opened the box and looked puzzled. Lying on a velvet cloth was a pocket watch. He'd never seen one before then.

"What is it, Bub?"

"A watch...an old fashioned watch...but it's solid gold. It came from Germany. It was made there...long before the World War, the first World War. It's worth money. But it's worth more than that in sentiment."

"Wow," Joey said taking it out of the box and dangling it in front of him. "I don't know how I'll wear it, but I like it, Bub. I really do. It means a lot that you're giving it to me. It's not ticking, though," he said, holding it to his ear.

"It's old...maybe some oil or something...we'll bring it to a jeweler. I don't know, maybe it won't ever work...but you have it. It's yours." Martha smiled. "Keep it safe. It would have belonged to your father, but..." She rarely finished a sentence when speaking about her son, even all those years later.

Joey kissed her cheek. "I really like it, Bub. I think of Grandpa a lot. I think he'd like that you gave this to me. He was a good man. I know you were mad at him, and I don't know why, but I think he was a good man before then. Right?"

Martha cupped her grandson's cheek. She couldn't believe she had to reach up to that face now, that he was taller than she was. "Right. He was, Joey...a good man."

She looked up at Joey, who looked so much like his grandfather now that he was maturing. She saw Joseph's eyes...his smile...when she looked at her grandson. "When I was a girl—a teenager, I was—and we fell in love, and after we got married, I always felt like a princess and he was my knight in shining armor...more than forty years I felt that way. Even when I got mad at him...when he *made me* get mad at him...I still knew he was a good man in many ways."

Joey jumped then and lifted the hand that held the watch. "It just started ticking, Bub...all of a sudden it's working. I can feel it ticking. Listen..." He held the watch to her ear.

Tick...tick...tick...just like Joseph's heart sounded when they were in their bed together and she rested her head on his chest and he held her protectively—the knight and his princess. She could hear his heart beating like this watch...tick...tick...tick.

"It means Grandpa is happy that you gave it to me. He's letting us know from heaven," Joey said.

Such a Christian...he believes in heaven and the dead can make a watch tick...my grandson the Christian...still... Martha placed her fingers on the watch in Joey's palm and felt the rhythmic pulse. *Still... who am I to say my Joseph isn't telling us he's pleased?*

Joey put the watch back into the box and placed it on top of the last carton to be carried down to the car. His mother was waiting for them. "Come on, Bub. Let's get out of here. You look sad. Don't be sad. Mom's waiting for us. Everything's going to be okay. You'll see."

"I know...I know." Martha took a last look around the room...the nicest apartment in the building, the superintendent used to tell people. She was proud of that. Now it was empty. It had been a good home for her and Joseph...*before.*

She followed Joey out, and when the elevator came and the door opened, Frances LaCorte stepped off. The women stood frozen in place.

"Excuse me," Joey said, struggling with the heavy box, trying to pass Frances in order to go into the elevator.

Frances moved stiffly, giving him some room, but her eyes never left Martha. Martha walked over and stood in front of the other woman. Eyes met eyes. Martha saw that Frances was holding her breath. Then, inexplicably, Martha reached out and put her arms around Frances LaCorte and embraced her tightly.

The LaCorte woman had become a part of her life, whether she liked it or not…and good or bad, Frances had been a part of Joseph's life. He may have even loved her, though Martha hoped that wasn't the truth. But it was over now. She could forgive.

"Bub?" Joey called, trying to hold the elevator door open with his foot.

Martha let go of Frances. She joined Joey inside the elevator. Frances turned and watched.

The two women continued to stare at each other through the tiny glass window as the outer elevator door closed and the inner slid shut.

Summer 1972

They sat next to each other on the daybed watching "60 Minutes" on Bridget's small television. They'd just finished the Chow Mein and egg rolls they had ordered, and Bridget carefully broke open one of the fortune cookies and silently read the ribbon of paper.

"What's it say?" Dermot asked, trying to peek over her shoulder.

She hid it from him. "It's my fortune…ye have your own there." She handed the cookie to him.

"It says I'll be marrying within the year," he told her without opening it.

"Really?" she challenged him. "Are ye psychic in addition to all your other charms?"

"I don't need a Chinaman to tell me that."

She grinned and shook her head. "Well, you'll have to introduce me to your bride to be, Mr. Gallagher."

He wrapped his arm around her shoulders and buried his face in her neck. "You know her."

"That's enough," she told him, extricating herself. "Just because I'm allowin' you on my daybed, doesn't mean you've the right to take privileges. Keep your eyes on the telly, and your hands on the fortune cookie."

"You're a mean woman, Riordan. A mean and cruel woman."

She laughed, pushing him farther away, and started to say something, when he sat up straight and hushed her. He reached over and turned the TV's volume up.

"What?" she asked, surprised by his sudden movement.

"Sh…listen."

Mike Wallace was introducing the next segment. It was going to be about the war in Northern Ireland and the Irish Republican Army. After they listened to the tease, Dermot said, "Turn it off."

"Why? Don't you want to see it?"

"I don't. Turn it off…change the channel…anything. I want nothing to do with hearin' about it."

Bridget reached over and turned off the television.

They sat in silence for a long time. Dermot was moody now. Bridget reached out finally and took his hand. "Are ye okay, Dermot?"

They had an unspoken agreement not to talk about their pasts…although he was much quicker to share stories with her about his life in Ireland; light-hearted stories, about his family or his college days. But he never pressed her about why she was in the States, and he spoke little about his life before entering University. Bridget felt as though she was prying now, and wished she hadn't asked.

Dermot stood up and walked to her refrigerator. He took out a can of beer and drank long from it. "I did some things," he started to say, sitting down on a chair. Two red spots glowed on his fair cheeks now.

"Dermot…" Bridget didn't want to know anything about it.

"Bridie, we do stupid things when we're young and filled with a passion that we'd never do in other circumstances."

"Right," she said, trying to sound as though she was finalizing the conversation. "We do. And then it's behind us."

"Stupid things," he continued, "like being in the IRA and building bombs and the like."

She was silenced by this, yet her mind was working hard to come up with a way to change the subject.

"I was always good with my hands…with figuring out how to do…things…I could tie the tiniest wires together and fuse them…this wire to that, that wire to this…it's why I'm so good at the computers." He looked at her now. "I was good at building bombs and…"

"Dermot, please, I really don't want to hear this. I don't care anyway."

"I was responsible for some deaths, Bridie. You should know that."

"Why should I know that? I don't need to know that…anything like that."

"If we're going to be married…"

"We're just friends, Dermot. Nothing more."

He looked as though she'd slapped him in the face.

"I don't want to hurt you, but don't think that this is anything more serious than a nice friendship," she told him firmly.

"It's more than that, and you know it," he argued.

Bridget stood up now and paced across the room. "I know nothing more than that. Please don't ruin it by spilling your guts about things I have no need…nor interest…to know."

"I got out of it, though," he continued, hoping she'd listen to him. "I found out that one of my bombs killed a man who had twelve kids…a

273

merchant, he was, just trying to make a living. Something in my stomach turned."

"You didn't even live in the North of Ireland, for God's sake, Dermot. Why did you get involved in it?"

"I'll never stop hoping and praying for a united Ireland, Bridie...it's a just war, you know."

"I don't know anything. I live in the United States and I want nothing to do with it."

"You're an Irish woman."

She flopped down on the day bed again. "I don't care...I just don't care." She did, of course. There wasn't an Irish person alive who didn't have an opinion about a united Ireland. She knew that there were men in her village involved in the IRA, helping out, and she suspected her own father was one of them, but she kept out of it when she was there, and intended to stay out of it in the States.

"Bridie, let me just tell you, please let me just say it out and I won't talk of it again. I need you to know that I got out and never looked back. Before that man was...was killed...it wasn't all that real to me. I loved being a part of the whole thing, the secrecy, the knowledge that I was helping out. I never thought about the people, though I had to be hiding my head...I mean, what else were the bombs used for? Buildings...sure...but what about who was in the building? The man was innocent...a protestant, yes, but just a father raising his brood. I couldn't take the idea of killing like that. I'm not a killer. I built the bombs, even though I didn't place them. I was as guilty as the men who did. So, I got my education, and as soon as the opportunity arose, I came here. It's all in the past."

"Good, then leave it there," she told him.

"Bridie, I'm pouring my heart out."

She closed her eyes. She felt her entire body stiffen. "I know, Dermot, but if you think that I'll be doing the same, you're sadly mistaken. My past is just that, mine! Keep yours to yourself and I'll keep mine to myself."

"I wasn't expectin' anything from you. I was just trying to tell you about me...why I..." He shrugged, not sure what else to say.

They didn't speak again for a long time. Bridget wanted him to leave, and she thought if she remained silent, he'd realize it. Yet, he continued to sit in the chair, just staring at his can of beer. Then he said, "You don't have to be afraid of me, Bridie."

"Oh, will you please just shut up," she yelled at him. "I'm not afraid of you because you built some bombs."

"I didn't mean that."

"Well, what did you mean?" Bridget started to clean off the table, throwing the take-out containers in her garbage pail, slamming the forks in the sink.

"I mean that you don't have to be afraid to tell me anything…to think that there's anything that you have done that would make me think less of you."

"There's nothing to tell."

"Bridie…"

"Dermot, it's time for you to leave. We both have work in the morning. I've got to get to bed."

She didn't look back at him. She just continued to clean the utensils and put away the glasses she'd just washed. When she finished, she closed up the bag of garbage and carried it over to him.

"Here, throw this in the incinerator on your way to your apartment."

He didn't take the bag. Instead, he took her elbow and pulled her to him. "You love me, Bridie."

"Go home," she said, turning her face away from his.

"You do. You love me. And you'll learn that I'm safe to be with…to trust…to love."

She felt a knot in her throat. He kissed her cheek and then her neck. "And I love you. It's why I told you what I did…what I am…no more than a murderer…not even a soldier. But I've made peace with it…I've found peace again, Bridie. You need to…"

She pushed at him then. "Go home, Dermot. Leave me be. You know nothing about me."

"I know you never receive Holy Communion when we go to Mass on Sunday. I know you have a secret. But I also know who you are," he pressed his finger against her chest, "in here."

"Fine, then take that knowledge and leave with it."

"You can be so cold and hard," he told her. He reached over and took the bag of trash. "But I won't give up no matter how hard you are."

♦ ♦ ♦ ♦

"Can you hear my heart beating, Father?" Bridget asked, standing in the corner of the confessional, her arms wrapped around herself.

Bridget had decided to take the advice that Joseph Kramer gave her so long ago and see the priest at Saint Patrick's. Her argument on Tuesday with Dermot had sat heavy on her the rest of the week. She'd never tell Dermot about The Lie, The Secret, but it was true that she couldn't deny the need to tell the priest…any priest…just to get it over with.

She entered the church, covered her head with the black lace chapel veil she always carried in her purse, blessed herself from the font, and then slid into the last pew. The light on the confessional behind her was on, and she knew each side was occupied, with a woman waiting in line.

Bridget knelt and looked at the sanctuary, trying to focus on examining her conscience, but she was unable to. How different the sanctuary was since she moved to Astoria. Big changes…unsettling changes to some…had taken place in that time. The church had celebrated its hundredth anniversary in 1968. It was a beautiful church, with its images of the apostles in the elaborate plaster circles. Most of the church was the same. It was in the sanctuary that the changes were most obvious.

The old altar had been removed, and a new one replaced it, away from the wall, where the priests could look at the congregation. The side altars were gone now and new, less elaborate statues were visible. All the Stations of the Cross were changed. So much had changed in the world and in the Church in the years since Bridget had moved to Astoria. Sometimes it made her head spin at how changed everything was…politics, fashion, and even the way the priest celebrated Mass.

She wondered where she fit in among all these changes, for she certainly didn't feel as though she had changed much. Her hair was the same color, although she wore it differently, straighter. She was still the same size she was when she arrived…still had the brogue that gave away her nationality…and she was still worried about the fire escape outside her window. The Lie, The Secret was the same.

Bridget placed her face in her hands and tried to examine her conscience more seriously, but there was only the one Sin…the one Lie…that she could think of. Anything else she may have done seemed insignificant.

What do I say? Bless me, Father, for I have sinned…let's see…I missed Mass six times, I used God's name in vain three times. I took the paper at the newsstand when the attendant wasn't there and couldn't get change, so I left …but I went back the next day to pay him, so does that count, Father? I got pregnant with a married man and had an abortion—just once—and I took a candy bar from my office mate's desk when she was on vacation one time.

Maybe if she said it fast enough, hid it between the other minor sins, he wouldn't catch it. At any rate, if he did, she didn't have to worry about him yelling at her about missing Mass six times…not with the whopper she was laying on him.

Another woman in a chapel veil, who had just left the confessional, slipped in beside Bridget to begin to say her penance. Bridget leaned over and asked, "Is he mean?"

The woman looked startled at the interruption, then confused, and then finally she smiled. "I thought you were asking about my husband for a minute." She laughed quietly but Bridget didn't join in. The other woman sobered and shook her head. "Nah, he's a good one. He's young…understanding… a Second Vatican Council man. Don't worry."

Bridget glanced up and noticed that there was no one else in line.

Within a minute, another woman came out of the confessional, leaving the door open.

Bridget was disappointed. The woman hadn't been in there very long. That must have meant that she didn't have much to confess. Bridget had been hoping that maybe the person ahead of her would have a terrible confession that would make Bridget look like a saint. But then, what could possibly be more horrible than what she was going to tell him?

Bridget glanced at the heavy doors to the vestibule, considering that she could just walk out, forget the whole thing. Then her eyes fell on the dark walnut confessional. She stood on trembling legs and moved past the penance-saying woman. She grabbed the brass door handle, pulled it open wide, closed her eyes, and entered the dark, silent box.

She didn't kneel on the velvet cushioned kneeler. Instead she pushed her back into the corner, and wrapped her arms around herself. She was trembling. She wondered if this was what it felt like to be in a coffin…the dark, the silence.

The little door behind the screen slid open, and Bridget jumped. There was a pause…an anticipation.

"Can you hear my heart beating, Father?" was what she said.

There was a long silence, or at least to Bridget it seemed to be long, before a deep voice from the other side of the grate said, "I think so…it sounds like the heart of a frightened and troubled woman. Am I right?"

"Ye are that, Father," she whispered.

"Come on over and kneel down—take a load off your heart."

"It's not that simple, Father," she told him.

"It never is," he answered.

Bridget did what she was told and when it was over, when she had told him all of it, he gave her absolution…or rather, he explained to her that it wasn't him giving her absolution, but Jesus himself, for he was just standing in for the Lord, the One—the only One—who could forgive her once and for all.

He told her not to recite the Act of Contrition until after she'd heard him say the absolution in its entirety…he wanted her to hear every word, to believe every word.

He moved his head closer to the grate and spoke in Latin. In the dim light coming from his part of the confessional, Bridget saw him make the sign of the cross. He paused for a moment, and then asked, "Did you hear every word?"

"I did," she whispered, almost unable to speak. "Is that it, then, Father? Is it gone…I mean the…the…"

"The sin…all of the sins," he said for her, "yes, your sins are forgiven. You are free of them. Now say your Act of Contrition so that I can hear every word of it."

Bridget recited the prayer, and when she was finished she looked around her, at the wooden walls that surrounded her, and she thought that the confessional was indeed like a coffin. She walked into it dead…dead in her soul from all the pain and grief and agony of The Sin and The Lie, and how they had stolen away her faith in the loving and forgiving God she had grown up believing in, how they had stolen away her belief in herself...in her own likeness of God. Now she was about to leave that coffin alive...breathing again...believing again. For the first time in Bridget's life, she was grateful that she was a Catholic.

Yet, she realized that confession wasn't voodoo; it wasn't hocus-pocus-you're-free-to-go-and-sin-no-more-and-forget-you-ever-did. Maybe her soul was wiped clean again, but her mind couldn't accept the fact that having the priest make the sign of the cross and say his words of absolution would make what she'd done just disappear. The guilt started to creep up to her throat again.

"Can you forgive yourself now?" the priest asked very softly as though he knew...as though he could smell the bile that was choking her.

"I want to...I do, Father..."

He said, "Perhaps if you know what the words of absolution mean. I'll translate for you the best I can. What I said was 'May Almighty God have mercy on you, forgive you of your sins, and bring you to everlasting life...May the almighty and merciful Lord grant you pardon, absolution and remission of your sins. May Our Lord Jesus Christ absolve you, and I, by His authority, *do* absolve you from every bond of excommunication...as far as I am able and you are needful.' Do you hear and understand?"

When she didn't answer him, he placed his palm on the grate between them, his fingers splayed against the elaborate scroll work, "I have absolved you from your sins in the name of the Father, and of the Son, and of the Holy Ghost...dear girl, *know* that you are forgiven, and if God has forgiven you, you should and *must* forgive yourself. Do you understand now? Go and be happy. You *are* forgiven." Very softly and with a smile in his voice he added, "I promise."

6B

SOMMER

Germaine stood in the center of her living room looking uncomfortable and embarrassed.

"Oh, Granny, you look absolutely beautiful. That color on you is wonderful!"

Germaine smiled. "I'm an old woman…and an old woman can't look beautiful."

"If you're the old woman, then it's possible. You are beautiful. Do you know that you still have golden streaks that run through your gray hair? It makes you shine."

Germaine looked down at herself. The powder blue dress was stunning, if she said so herself. And the lace jacket over it of the same color made her look stylish. Even her shoes were new; not the old fashioned tie up shoes she wore every day, but bone colored pumps that had just a little stacked heel. She hadn't felt this nice in a long time.

Alice Carroll, Germaine's granddaughter, got down on one knee to fix Germaine's stocking, which had started to puddle around her ankle. "Here let me tighten this to your garter…like this…perfect. It was just a little too loose. That's all."

Germaine reached down and touched the woman's blond hair. Flaxen hair, really. Like Germaine's own mother's hair had been…and her precious daughter's.

The first time Alice came to Astoria, Germaine thought that her daughter—long dead as she was—was walking into the living room. It took her breath away when she saw Alice for the first time. Alice was the same age as Germaine's daughter had been when she died. For Germaine, for just a moment in time, it was as if her daughter were there with her, in the flesh and not in the dreams she had so often.

It was an awkward first meeting, because Germaine began to cry as she hadn't in many, many years. Alice didn't know what to do, how to comfort her. Luckily, Germaine had talked Eleanor and Audra into being in the apartment when the woman arrived. Eleanor took over immediately, inviting Alice farther into the room, offering her a drink, and passing a tray of hors d'oeuvres. While Eleanor fussed, Audra moved close to Germaine, handed her two tissues, and stroked her back. She leaned down and whispered, "Don't, Mrs. Sommer, please don't cry. This should be a happy time."

Germaine pulled herself together and held out her hand to her granddaughter. The woman placed her purse on a chair and moved over to Germaine quickly. She knelt in front of her, smiling gently. Her own eyes filled with tears. "I think I used to call you Granny? Isn't that right?"

Germaine nodded, and wiped at the tears that were pouring from her eyes and down her cheeks and chin.

"I'm so sorry, Granny. I'm so very sorry that we haven't written or called. It's just that my stepmother took over without missing a step, and we—Donald and I—knew that it upset our father whenever we asked about you...or our mother. We saw the hurt in our stepmother's eyes whenever you sent cards or gifts; hurt and maybe a little fear. She was afraid we'd stop loving her or something foolish like that. It was as if they wanted to erase our mother from our lives—and of course, that would mean you, too. But they weren't trying to be cruel. I can't believe that. They were both very loving to us. They seemed to think it was better for us...healthier emotionally...so that we wouldn't pine away for our mother."

"It was wrong," Germaine managed to say between sobs. "They were wrong."

"Yes, they were. I know that now. So does Donald. He actually would have come with me, but his wife had a baby last week. His third child, Granny—your third great-grandchild. He couldn't leave his wife just yet, but he'll be coming soon to see you. He's tall and handsome, and he's a wonderful father."

Germaine could not control the tears. They had been buried so long in her heart that now that they were let loose they wouldn't stop. She looked up and noticed that Eleanor and Audra were crying too, and she laughed at them and waved her hand. "Oh, now, one sobbing mess in this apartment is enough. You stop that, you two."

They all laughed then.

"We're going to leave. We're just on the other side of the hall, Mrs. Carroll. When you leave, would you just ring my bell? I like to help her get into bed."

"May I do it?" Alice Carroll asked. "May I do it tonight? I'll let you know when I leave, but is it all right if I stay and tuck her in?"

Audra immediately said, "Oh, you can't do that. We know how to do it…we have our own way of helping her to bed. You wouldn't know what to do. But thanks anyway. We take care of her."

The others all looked at her, surprised. Then Germaine said, "It's true. My darling Audra is the best tucker-inner that I've ever known." She had smiled up at Audra. How darling of her, how kind of her, to be a little jealous of Alice's attention.

"Well," Audra said, then, sighing. "Really, we don't have to do it tonight…right, Mom?" She looked at Eleanor who shook her head no, smiling. Audra looked back at Alice. "All right…you go ahead and do it this one time. We have her all the time to tuck in."

It had been a grand reunion. Once Eleanor and Audra left, Germaine and her granddaughter talked for hours. Alice seemed to not want to leave anything out…and she was so descriptive in her story telling that Germaine could almost see how she looked at every stage of her life and what happened to her from the time Germaine was forced to go to the plane that heartbreaking afternoon, until the minute Alice walked through the door of apartment 6B. Alice was married with a baby on the way, and when she found out that she was pregnant after trying for seven years, she was compelled to know her grandmother, and to hear about her own mother— what she was like, who she was as a person. Who better to tell her than her grandmother? And she promised that now that they had met, she would never let Germaine out of her life again, and her baby would know her great-grandmother.

"How did you find me?" Germaine wanted to know. Alice had already helped get her into her nightclothes and Germaine was sitting on the side of her bed, Alice beside her.

"I asked my stepmother. I told her how important it was to me, and that it wasn't a threat to her…I mean, at this point, she had to know that. Right? I've been a devoted daughter to her. And she went into a closet in the basement and pulled out a box. It had all sorts of cards and letters from you. The return address was on the envelopes. My husband did a little detective work, spoke to your superintendent's wife—a Mrs. Beirmann, I think?—and she told him you were still living here. I sent the letter to you that day. I had read every single letter and card my stepmother gave me before I wrote it. I felt as though I knew you."

There was another bright and tearful reunion when her grandson Donald and his eldest child, a boy named Ernest, came to meet her a month later. As promised by Alice, he was a tall and handsome man and obviously a good father. She loved the way he always included the boy in the conversation, and looked at him with such pride.

He took her out for lunch, and talked mostly about his wife and the two children at home. But it was clear to Germaine that the boy sitting at their table was her Grandson's pride and joy.

She understood why—he was sweet and polite, and everything she would want in a great-grandson.

She loved that he was named for his grandfather. Here was the proof that once upon a time, many years before, there had been a great love between two young German-Americans. There in the blue eyes and the blond hair of the little boy at their table was proof that there had existed— had lived and loved and who had been loved—a beautiful blond girl, who turned into a beautiful woman, who had been Germaine and Ernest's daughter.

The years since that time that Germaine reunited with her grandchildren had been rich. Only twelve years before, she was completely alone, with just a little dog to love and be loved by. Now Germaine had two families—her granddaughter and grandson and their families—and the Walshes, whom she loved as dearly. And she had to laugh that since the reunion, her sister called her more frequently, and her nephews had actually come to get her and drive her back to New Jersey for dinner several Sundays. Let it not be said that Gertzy didn't take care of her sister properly—she wouldn't want the long-lost grandchildren thinking that she and her children hadn't been caring for their grandmother all along.

"Where will Audra live after the wedding?" Alice asked, helping her grandmother to the rocking chair, being careful to pull the dress taut so it wouldn't wrinkle under Germaine.

"Connecticut," Germaine said sadly. "She'll commute from there to her secretarial job in New York. She's a Katharine Gibbs graduate, you know. And now she goes to college at night to finish her degree. She promised to come over to see me, but I don't know how she'll find the time. I'll miss her something fierce."

"I know, Granny. I know how much you love her. They've been good to you, haven't they?"

"I think sometimes they saved my life," Germaine admitted. "I wasn't much good before I started babysitting for that little urchin in 1960." Germaine took Alice's hand and said, "She filled a hole in my heart."

"I have some news for you, too," Alice said. "We're moving east…my husband's job is relocating to New York. At first we weren't certain we'd do it. He thought it might be best to look for a new job and we'd stay there. But the baby is only two, and we really don't have anything keeping us from moving. My parents are retired and living in California. It will be hard leaving Donald and his family, but he thinks it's a good idea for us to take this opportunity. The company will pay for all the relocation expenses. We're actually thinking of New Jersey or Long Island…but Connecticut was our other idea. In fact, coming here for the wedding this weekend was perfect for us. When I came here to get you dressed, Justin went to look at different neighborhoods with one of his co-workers. That's why we left the baby with Donald and his wife...so we could shop around for where we want to live." Alice took Germaine's hands in hers. "So, Granny, what do you think? Are you happy about my news?"

Germaine was too surprised to say anything. Her mind was a little foggy these days. It took time to comprehend what Alice was telling her. "I don't know what to think...no, that's not true...I think it's wonderful. I think it's grand. But you should realize that if you're doing it because of me, you shouldn't. I'm a very old woman now. I could die tomorrow...today for that matter...and it wouldn't be right if you moved here because of me."

Alice laughed, "No—not that it isn't the icing on the cake to know we'll be nearer to you—but that wasn't the main purpose for our decision. It's just a very nice coincidence. And we would never pressure you, but the house we want to buy—the kind that Justin is looking at—will be what they call a 'mother-daughter' house, with a separate section for you to live in when you're ready to leave Astoria. We want you to live with us...but only when you're ready."

"What if I'm never..." Germaine stopped. She didn't want to hurt her granddaughter, but all if this was much too sudden, too surprising. Yet, Audra was leaving...maybe it was time for her to leave, too. Looking at her watch, she asked, "What time are we supposed to leave for the wedding?"

And at that moment the doorbell rang. Alice answered the door. Eleanor walked in, dressed in a floor length aqua gown, her silvery hair done up, crystal beads around her throat. Brendan was close behind in a black tuxedo, and a cummerbund that matched Eleanor's dress. He was fussing at the shirt, pressing down the ruffles and mumbling, "Since when does a man wear a ruffled shirt? Why the hell do I have to wear a ruffled shirt?"

"Oh, be quiet!" Eleanor hissed. "It's the fashion."

They walked into the living room, and Eleanor said to Germaine "Wait until you see this." They turned and there stood the bride, all white lace and satin. Her long hair was up in curls that dangled down the back of her head, and a long veil—a mantilla she had called it when she described it to Germaine—flowed to the end of the long satin train.

Germaine sighed. "Oh, my dear...my dear..."

"Do you like it?" Audra asked. It wasn't spoken of then, but everyone knew that Germaine had insisted upon paying for the wedding dress, the veil, the shoes and the gloves, even the underclothes...everything...she wanted to clothe Audra from top to bottom on her wedding day.

"I like it very much. I like it very much indeed."

"Well, good," Brendan said brusquely, "because it's time to go to the church and get this kid married and let someone else support her."

Germaine knew that for all the gruffness, Brendan's heart was aching. His child was leaving and getting married. Germaine was impressed at how well he had been behaving the last six months. Not a drink...not one "drink with the men" as he used to call it.

It had helped that Audra had threatened that she'd move out and elope with her fiancé if Brendan even sniffed a drink before the wedding. That if he fell off the wagon, there would be no big wedding, and he would never walk her down the aisle. It worked. He had been coming home every night sober. Once again, Germaine was astounded at the complicated Walsh relationships...and perpetually confused by Brendan.

"We want you to ride in the limousine with me," Eleanor said. "Right behind the bride and her daddy."

Alice helped Germaine to her feet. "How wonderful," Alice said. "I'll drive myself to the church. This way, when you get tired at the reception, I can bring you back and tuck you in."

"Come, Mrs. Sommer," Audra said. "Come on with me."

When they entered the hallway, Audra's bridesmaids were standing there waiting for them in a sea of royal blue taffeta. Paige, the matron of honor, came to them and kissed Mrs. Sommer's cheek, then wiped off the lipstick she'd left there with her thumb. "You look gorgeous," she said to Germaine. "Just dazzling."

She stepped back and took the hand of a small girl of seven who was dressed exactly like the other attendants, but with a fuller skirt and flowers in her hair, and she carried a basket of flowers. Paige's daughter, little Joanie, was jumping up and down with excitement. She looked so much like Paige that it never stopped amazing Germaine. And she was bright...bright and full of life. Germaine reached out and touched the little girl's head. Joanie was yet another person for her to love. She felt like a great-grandmother to her, and Paige shared her with Germaine as she had shared her little sister with her.

She knew the other bridesmaids, too. The groom's sister, Rose, quiet, tall and dark haired, who nodded and smiled at Germaine sweetly. Another girl who worked with Audra. And there was Mercedes.

Mercedes hugged Germaine. Germaine said to her, "You look beautiful, Merry."

"And so do you, Mrs. Sommer. Isn't this wonderful? Now, we've made a pact, you and I...we're not going to cry at the wedding ceremony, right? No running mascara. You promised, because if you cry, then I'll lose it altogether."

Mercedes had really never left their lives—Audra's and Germaine's. After the incident in the alley, and the terrible argument the girls had had the next day, Germaine thought they would never be friends again...how could they after all that had been said? But she had been wrong. Mercedes realized that there had been some truth in Audra's bitter words that day— bigotry and prejudice had started to separate them. That was never what she wanted.

At first, Audra didn't want to have anything to do with Mercedes. She made new friends at school, tried to ignore Mercedes. But Mercedes pursued Audra, insisted on walking home with her, even if she had to walk a few steps behind Audra. Mercedes refused to allow any bitterness to remain inside Audra or herself. She fought for their friendship. Germaine had never seen anyone fight for a friendship the way Mercedes did.

Eventually Audra softened, and they established a friendship again...a different kind of friendship...one built more on understanding and acceptance of each other's cultures...and each other's faults. Eventually, they realized that they could have other friends, but still have each other, too. Germaine hoped that it was a friendship that would last forever, but she knew only too well that friendship was usually the first victim of change. And in life, everything was always changing.

Eamon Williams stood in his own doorway, leaning against the jamb, his white shirt sleeves rolled up to his elbows, smiling from ear to ear. He said nothing...just looked at the bride...he wanted to share the moment when she left for the church.

Bridget Riordan and Dermot Gallagher were sitting on the stairs that led to the roof. They had just come home from a long Saturday morning walk, but made sure they were back in time for this. "Ah, she's the loveliest bride I've ever seen," Bridget said, jumping up and kissing the bride. "Many happy years and God's blessing to you, dear girl. I can't believe you're gettin' married. I still think of you as the little girl who helped me with my trunk that first day we met."

They heard the bolt on Frances LaCorte's door release, and the door opened. She stepped out to see what the commotion was about. She hadn't known that the girl who lived next door was getting married. She was surprised to see Audra in a bridal gown, and the Walsh clan standing there in gowns and tuxedoes. Frances was dressed in a housecoat and slippers, her auburn hair disheveled. Her face was blotchy and bloated.

"I'm sorry, I didn't mean to intrude...I heard the noise and wondered," she began to say to Eleanor who just nodded and smiled. "She's getting married? I didn't know. She looks beautiful...your daughter...she's a beautiful bride."

"Thank you," Eleanor said looking over at Audra, then back at Frances.

Frances said, "I wish her luck. I wish her..." she shrugged as though not believing that it was possible, but saying it anyway, "happily ever after."

Eleanor reached out and touched Frances's arm. Eleanor didn't believe in it either, but a wedding day was a good day to pretend there was a possibility.

"Otis is here," Audra said when the elevator arrived and there was a flurry of activity from the bridal party, with giggles and instructions about which way Audra should stand, who was going to hold the train and the veil, and how there wasn't enough room for all of them. In the end, Brendan and two of the bridesmaids decided to walk down the six flights because the elevator was too crowded.

Alice Carroll followed them, giving a final wave to her grandmother.

And all too suddenly the hallway was very quiet.

Eamon continued to stand in his doorway. Frances looked over at him and smiled wanly, running her hand over her messy hair. Bridget and Dermot stood near Bridget's door.

The four remaining tenants on the sixth floor of Ashley Hall just stood silently in the aftermath of the noisy bridal party, lost in their own thoughts, their own memories.

Bridget was thinking of the day she moved into the building and met the tiny little girl, with one shoe unbuckled, who helped her up the lobby stairs with her trunk, promising that she was a good girl and wouldn't bother Bridget.

Eamon was remembering the October day he recited poetry with Paige and Eleanor in the elevator and gave Paige the book of poems.

Frances was recalling the blood on the floor from Joseph's nosebleed, and how the little girl had screamed for her father that someone was bleeding to death, and how they both came into the apartment to see if she—and Joseph when they realized he was the blood-soaked victim—were all right. Joseph joked that he forgot to duck and Frances was a better boxer. Little Audra had told them her father's boxer name was Kid Candle—one blow and he was out—and they all laughed. It was the day she fell in love with Joseph Kramer.

Dermot didn't really have a memory of the bride who'd left the sixth floor. Instead, he was thinking about how beautiful Bridget would look in the white gown and long veil when he took her to Saint Patrick's Church as his bride. His problem was persuading her to marry him.

6A

RIORDAN

"I can't take it anymore," Dermot Gallagher said when they entered her apartment. He slid his arm around Bridget's waist and pulled her against him. "I'm on fire with the need for you, woman."

"Now, that's enough of that." She pushed at him, but he wouldn't let her go.

"Two years, Bridget...that's long enough for you to decide if I'm on the up and up as you said that first day we met. You know I am. You know that the company wants me to go to Poughkeepsie, to the main office, and this job is too big for me to turn down. But I'll not go without ye. I'll stay here and be a pauper before I'll leave ye. Marry me, Bridget Riordan. We'll get a home in Poughkeepsie...in the country, where there's grass as green as Ireland's and hills and valleys and good schools for our children."

"Stop!" Bridget struggled, but this time Dermot wasn't letting her go.

"Is it the bullocks from way back when...the scum that hurt you all those years ago? Is that why you keep pushing me away?"

Bridget was stunned. She stopped struggling. How could he know? They'd never spoken of it. She never mentioned it in all their time together. Not even after going to confession.

Yet he knew. How? And how long had he known?

He pulled her close again. "I knew from the second week. I waited for you to tell me the story, and when you never did, I figured it wasn't my business. It's not, y'know. I couldn't care less about what happened then."

"How did you find out?" she managed to ask him.

"My sister wrote when I told them I'd met you and was courtin' you. She knew a girl from your parish, and how everyone suspected why you left school...why you left Ireland. No one knew for sure, but my sister wanted me to know before I got serious about you."

Bridget felt light headed. Her mother always said no one knew.

"Let it go. I said, and I'll say again a thousand times, I don't care a hoot about it. Ah, Bridie, you're the finest lass I've ever known. Smart, pretty, sexy, with a sense of humor that would keep me laughing the rest of me life. I need you. Marry me, girl."

"I'm not a girl, Dermot. I haven't been a girl for a long time."

"All the more reason for us to get this thing going before you're too old and you get fat and wrinkly."

She had to smile, but she was frightened. There was so much more to the story that he didn't know about...or at least she prayed that he didn't know about.

"Bridie, listen to me, I've never been in love before. And I know I have your heart. A man knows when a woman loves him. And a woman knows when a man loves her...and you know that I do. What more do either of us need? What else could possibly be more important?"

He planted a kiss on her forehead, her cheeks, and on her lips. "Bridie, we do things when we're young that we'd never do when we get older. I've done things that I cringe over—things you know about. I got out of it...it's behind me. Just like all of what you did is behind you. We're new people here in America. We're free to move on...to love...Christ help us and bless us, Bridie, we're free to be happy. Don't we have the right to be happy?"

Did she dare to believe him? She had been forgiven for The Sin and The Lie, but just as the priest had suspected, she had a harder time forgiving herself. "Be happy," the priest had said. It seemed so much easier in that confessional, but within days, the guilt came in the night to worry her again.

If Dermot ever knew, what would he think of her?

Now, in his arms, Dermot whispered in her ear, and pressed close to her, trapping her between the wall and himself, "I'm at peace with what I've done in my past. Be at peace, Bridie, with whatever it was in yours. Love me and come with me to this magical place called Poughkeepsie."

Did she dare? Oh, God almighty in His high heaven, could she dare to do it?

"Yes," Dermot whispered to her, "you can...dare to do it."

Bridget hadn't realized that she had spoken the words aloud. He smiled at her with the smile she'd come to love...crooked tooth and all. His eyes bore into hers, and she wanted to know that those eyes would look into hers for the rest of her life. The very night she bought him pizza and beer, she knew she could love him...and love him she did.

What did Joseph Kramer tell her that night? She couldn't remember exactly...she just remembered that he was wise and forgiving, and told her to forgive herself because it was such a waste not to. He was so alone then.

She decided that night that she never wanted to be as alone as dear Mr. Kramer was. For whatever he had done to his wife, he didn't deserve to be alone and dying with no love surrounding him.

She didn't deserve that either...no one did.

With Dermot, she'd never be alone again. With Dermot she could move on, maybe even forgive herself.

She put her arms around him and kissed him deeply. When her head fell back, she asked him, "What's so magical about this Poughkeepsie anyway?"

"You'll be there...married to me...what could be more magical than that?"

OTIS

"Is that the last of the boxes then?"

"Yes, but there's still the trunk…I brought it with me from Ireland and with me it will go to Poughkeepsie." Bridget brushed her hair from her eyes and scoured the tiny sink in her kitchenette. When she finished, she threw the wet paper towels in a paper bag and took it to the incinerator closet.

All that remained in the apartment was the trunk. She looked around, and her eyes settled on the window where the fire escape was. *Won't be worrying about that anymore.*

Dermot had laughed when he first saw all the coke bottles on the windowsill. "An Irish colleen's burglar alarm, then?" he had asked. "I'll put a better lock on the window for you."

"No need. Brendan Walsh has already put three on there for me. There's no way anyone could open that window. The bottles are added protection nonetheless. I couldn't sleep without them there."

The bottles were gone now, discarded that morning.

"Well, I guess you'll be leaving soon. I see the place is empty," Mrs. Beirmann said from the doorway. "I have the painters coming tomorrow. I'll have to keep a portion of your security, don't you know, because you painted the walls blue. Takes several coats to cover that color. I don't know why you people just can't leave the walls white. Everyone's got to paint the walls and the trim when they move in. What color is that trim? Beige?"

Bridget smiled. "Ivory, Mrs. Beirmann. I liked the ivory color against the blue walls. It's classy…elegant." Twelve years of Mrs. Beirmann was enough. Twelve years of Mrs. Beirmann was twelve years too many.

"Maybe, but it will cost you from your security."

Bridget locked the trunk just as Dermot came in. "Ready?" he asked, putting his arm around the shoulders of the wire-haired superintendent. He may have been the only tenant she ever had that she liked. His charm was wicked if it could even get to the Beirmann woman. And even the old man liked him. He'd show his shiny gums every time Dermot was around. It helped that Dermot gave him a fifth of the finest Scotch he could afford— every two to three months—and shared a jigger in the basement from time to time. He told Bridget it was for security reasons.

"Oh, we'll miss *you*, Mr. Gallagher, don't you know, even though it means renting two apartments on the same floor," Mrs. Beirmann said to him.

He pulled a box of chocolate candy from behind his back. "A little goin' away present for you, Missus," he said.

Bridget shook her head and sighed, but she smiled at him all the same. "Bugger," she mouthed to him, wanting to laugh.

"Well, isn't that nice," Mrs. Biermann said. "I guess we can forego keeping that security deposit after all, Miss Riordan. A little wedding present for the both of you."

Dermot kissed the old woman's temple. "Ah, you're the best, ye are. Well, come on, wife o'mine, let's get this trunk in the elevator and off we are to Poughkeepsie."

They carried the trunk between them, bid a final goodbye to the old woman, and got on the elevator.

"Otis" moved smoothly from the sixth floor. Bridget was suddenly overcome with emotion. She tried to hide it from Dermot, but he said, "Hey, now, what's this about? Tears? Is it Mrs. Beirmann you'll be missing?" He laughed at his own joke.

"Shut up," she said, taking a tissue from her jeans pocket and wiping at her eyes. "I don't know what's wrong with me. I guess it's because I was so low when I came here…so lost and homesick. I kind of fell in love with the building…with its name—Ashley Hall—and I think it knew that. I feel as though this building wrapped its arms around me and tucked me safely into it until I could find my way out into the world again."

He reached out and touched her shoulder gently. "It's not like you to wax poetic."

She shrugged. "I've lived in this building twelve years and I barely know a soul who lived in it with me. Yet, I feel like that was the best way for me to live. No one knew my skeletons, my burdens, so I didn't have to pretend for anyone. I didn't have to be anything I wasn't; I was anonymous. We all were, except maybe the Walshes, but no, they're anonymous, too. We knew their issues, yet we don't know *why* they have those issues. In Ireland we would have known why; or been able to guess. We'd have known who their parents were, their brothers and sisters, where they lived as children, and what made the family tick. Here we haven't a clue. But it makes us safe, that anonymity. It protects us."

"It's a lonely way to live," Dermot said. He had never liked living in the city.

"No, it wasn't lonely, not really, because even in that anonymity, we were there for one another. We were connected and could count on one another. We just knew that somehow. If something broke down or I was afraid of noises, I could call Brendan Walsh and he'd be with me in a blink of an eye. Eleanor Walsh, too. Look at how she cares for Mrs. Sommer. All of them...poor Mr. Kramer...Mr. Williams...Mrs. Sommer...the Allcocks when they were here. Just ring their bells, and they come for you. It's sort of a code among New York apartment dwellers...an unspoken agreement...I'm here if you need me, but don't ask me about my life and I won't ask you about yours. And once the crisis is over, we all go back into our lives again, no one ever mentioning that there ever was a crisis."

The elevator stopped and they each took a handle of the trunk. Two people walked up the small flight of lobby steps, barely looking at them, just a nod of the head and a quick smile. Bridget looked at Dermot and he rolled his eyes.

He whispered, "It's that unspoken code...don't speak to me if I don't speak to you...but I'll come save your life if you need me. Ah, yes...gotta love that New York City apartment building code."

She laughed in spite of the fact that he was making fun of her. Their U-Haul was parked at the curb in front of the courtyard. Together they lifted the trunk and put it in place in the crowded van. Bridget got into the cab of the truck and stared at the entryway with all its shining glass and wrought iron grids. She took a last look at the boxwood hedges against the wrought iron fence—the impatiens had just been planted along the bricks of the raised garden. A lump formed in her throat again and her eyes burned.

Dermot started the truck and they moved down the one-way street. Bridget opened her window and stuck her head out so that she could look back, to the top of the building, to the windows of the sixth floor, and then to the words that had spoken to her, called to her, on that hot summer day twelve years before: *Ashley Hall...guardian of secrets and broken hearts.*

BOOKS BY THIS AUTHOR

FICTION
Ashley Hall
Tears of the Willow
and watch for the upcoming release of
Holding Silk: In the Arms of Angels and Hummingbirds

NON-FICTION
Joshua's Ring
Colonial Inns and Taverns of Bucks County
The Delaware Canal: From Stone Coal Highway to Historic Landmark

ABOUT THE AUTHOR

In addition to writing novels and non-fiction histories, Marie Murphy Duess develops and conducts creative writing workshops, and gives presentations about local history based on her non-fiction titles. She also served as a photojournalist for a medical mission to refugee camps in Bosnia-Herzegovina for a humanitarian aid organization.

She is a member of the International Women's Writing Guild, Historical Novel Society, the Independent Book Publishers Association, and The Questers Organization. She is the Vice President of Duess Consulting Services, a communications and graphic arts company.

A native New Yorker, she now lives in beautiful Bucks County, Pennsylvania, with her husband, Ed.

For more information, visit her website at www.MarieDuess.com

BOOK DISCUSSION QUESTIONS

1. Was the general theme of the story clear? What do you believe was the overall message of *Ashley Hall*?

2. Did you feel that all the characters were equal in their importance, or was one more prominent than the others?

3. Was not having a clearly prominent character bothersome? Or did you enjoy getting to know each character equally and his or her story?

4. What scene resonated most with you personally in either a positive or negative way? Did you live through the 1960s? Did you experience the death of President Kennedy, the blackout in the northeast, the Viet Nam War, Woodstock? Was your reaction similar to the characters in *Ashley Hall*?

5. How important was the time period to the story? Would things have played out differently in a different time period?

6. The 1960s was a very turbulent and transforming decade, with many changes in clothing styles, moral attitudes, social behaviors, politics and civil rights. Do you think this book identified those changes?

7. What surprised you most about the book? Did you feel that the author was making political statements or presenting life the way it really was in the 1960s?

8. How do you think the characters were realistically portrayed?

9. We're introduced to *Ashley Hall* through Bridget Riordan. Were you able to "see" the building and the surrounding neighborhood through her eyes? Were you able to understand her draw to this particular building? Her emotion when leaving it?

10. What would you have done if you lived beside a family like the Walsh family? Would people react differently today than they did in the 1960s? Has much changed legally or socially in helping children like the girls in this family?

11. What role did Eleanor Walsh play at *Ashley Hall*?

12. How do you view Eleanor as a mother?

13. What disturbed you most about Brendan Walsh? Was there anything that you found redeeming about him? Where do you think his rage came from? Would you have liked Brendan if you were a resident of *Ashley Hall*?

14. How did the Walsh family impact the lives of the other residents on the sixth floor? Discuss where there might have been a positive influence on others as well as negative.

15. Was it easy or difficult to understand the relationship between Martha and Joseph Kramer? Did you understand his choices? Did you agree with Martha's choices?

16. In what way do you think Germaine's reaction to her granddaughter's letter would have been different if she didn't have a relationship with Audra Walsh?

17. Explain your feelings about the choices Eamon and John made throughout the book, and discuss how different relationships like theirs are today as opposed to then. Would John have made the decision he did if they lived in today's environment?

18. What do you think was the most pivotal change that took place during this time period? What are other substantial changes that would have made some of the characters' lives different today?

19. How did you view each of the characters? How did the characters change by the end of the book?

20. What do you think will happen next for these characters?

Want to discuss *Ashley Hall* with the author?
Visit her website at www.marieduess.com
or blog with her at blog.mariduess.com